The WORLD
ABOVE the SKY

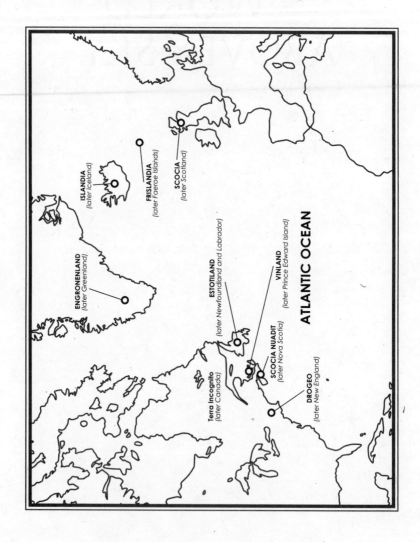

ISLANDIA
(later Iceland)

FRISLANDIA
(later Faeroe Islands)

SCOCIA
(later Scotland)

ENGRONENLAND
(later Greenland)

ESTOTILAND
(later Newfoundland and Labrador)

VINLAND
(later Prince Edward Island)

SCOCIA NUADIT
(later Nova Scotia)

Terra Incognito
(later Canada)

DROGEO
(later New England)

ATLANTIC OCEAN

NEW ARCADIA

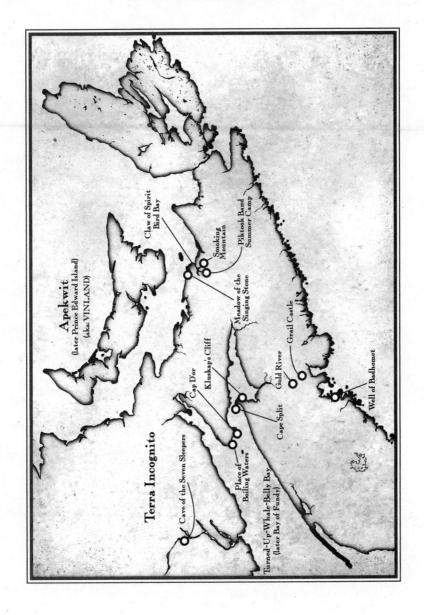

The WORLD ABOVE *the* SKY

KENT STETSON

McArthur & Company
Toronto

Published in Canada in 2010 by
McArthur & Company
322 King Street West, Suite 402
Toronto, Ontario
M5V 1J2
www.mcarthur-co.com

Library and Archives Canada Cataloguing in Publication

Stetson, Kent, 1948-
The world above the sky / Kent Stetson.

ISBN 978-1-55278-851-6

I. Title.

PS8587.T47128W67 2010   C813'.54   C2010-901112-0

The publisher would like to acknowledge the financial support of the Government
of Canada through the Canada Book Fund and the Canada Council for our
publishing activities. The publisher further wishes to acknowledge the financial
support of the Ontario Arts Council and the OMDC for our publishing program.

Design and composition by Tania Craan
Map design by Szol Design
Copy editing by Pamela Erlichman
Cover painting: *Boundless*, 1979, by Boris Smirnov-Radetsky /
Private Collection / The Bridgeman Art Library International

Printed in Canada by Webcom

10 9 8 7 6 5 4 3 2 1

To Helen (MacPherson) Stetson,
For her Highland fortitude, grace, and great good humour.

&

C. Paul Stetson, my brother,
For his insight, wisdom, and his great good heart.

In the time of the Two Made One
The People still walked free.
The rocks of the earth still sang,
And the soul of the world was the sea.

A canoe made of fire and stars
And light from the Great Spirit's eye,
Filled with portents and prayers for peace fell
From The World Above the Sky.

PART ONE

....

THE WORLD BELOW THE SEA

Autumn 1397–Summer 1398

CHAPTER ONE

Dusk became night. A lantern held low and tightly shuttered cut two androgynous silhouettes—one sleek and elongated, the other squat and rotund—into thickening mist. Eugainia St. Clair Delacroix and her nurse-companion, the Lady Morgase Burray of Kirkwall and Brodgar, boarded a round-bottomed curragh hidden beneath a willow overhang.

Eugainia scanned the surface of Edinburgh's great bay, the Firth of Forth. A pale light fought wisps of fog hanging low on the water, its beam intermittent, its distance difficult to determine. Eugainia set their course. Morgase took the single oar, pressed the blade against the bank, squared her shoulders and dug below the surface of the cold black bay.

Eugainia turned to speak. Morgase expected, as always, to feel the calm of her Lady's regard. She was surprised. Eugainia's gaze slipped past her, back toward shore, her eyes masked and non-committal. A jolt of pain shot down Morgase's arm. Her fingers locked tight on the oar, then relaxed. She glanced over her shoulder, set her sights on the ship.

The day's events hung between Eugainia and her companion like dank air in a windowless room. That afternoon, two years from the day she married him, Eugainia's demented old husband had finally managed both penetration and ejaculation with manual intervention by Morgase and court doctors. Morgase prayed the freshly planted seeds would flourish.

Eugainia extinguished the lantern and closed the little door.

At fifteen years of age, Eugainia had been wed to Morgase's half-brother, the already greatly aged Lord Ard whose ancestry curved back to Joseph of Arimathea and beyond. The same blood flowed in Eugainia's veins, concentrated through centuries of selective pairings to the point where she was considered more divine than human. If beauty, compassion and intelligence are marks of divinity, Morgase thought as she fell into the dig-pull-lift rhythm of the oar, the faith of those who adored Eugainia—that is to say, all who came to know her—was rightly placed.

Tugged by the turn of the tide, *Reclamation*, flagship of the great fleet New Arcadia, came about. She strained at her anchors mid-channel where the Firth of Forth opens out to the North Sea. The bulk of the fleet—twelve vessels in all—waited a night's sail north, cached in scattered bays around the outer Orkney Islands. The arrival of the galley *Reclamation* and their Lady would set the fleet sailing north, then west, then south and west again across the great Atlantic sea.

"I felt like a brood mare covered by a sway-backed old stallion," Eugainia confided to Morgase as they were handed aboard *Reclamation*. "I tried to love him. Perhaps I did. A little."

They dissolved into the heavy curtained darkness of the aft-castle where they shed wet cloaks.

"I'm surprised the effort didn't kill him, poor old lad," Morgase sighed as she sat, the tightness in her chest a recent and persistent nuisance. She loosened Eugainia's corona of tightly plaited braids.

"Perhaps it did." Eugainia winced at the memory of foul

breath from the toothless old mouth. "If so, a blessed mercy....Such gasping and wheezing. Then terrible moments of no breath at all."

"You did your duty, child. And there's an end to it."

"It was a loveless match from the beginning."

"Love is an unwelcome complication in these affairs. The poor old soul's only asset is his bloodline. He was a beauty in his youth, my brother. And a sweet child, by all accounts. What will happen to him now?"

"If I am pregnant, please God, he'll be sent to the monastery at Frislandia. One prays a peaceful end awaits him."

"If you're not?"

"I'll decide when I reach Vinland."

"My Lady...?" The voice outside the curtains was respectful and assured.

"Henry. Please. Come in."

Prince Henry Sinclair did as bidden. The oiled canvas curtain fell back into place behind him.

"Welcome aboard, My Lady. Morgase."

"Thank you, Henry." Eugainia sat on the cowhide coverlet, combing out her damp hair. "*Et félicitations.* Your plan worked to perfection. *Comme d'habitude!*"

Henry smiled and kissed the proffered hand. "*Merci, chère madame.*"

Fair, thin-skinned Lord Henry, Eugainia thought as she considered the refined angles of his profile. Henry was given to sentiment, quick to anger, slow to forgive. And loyal to a fault. This same Sinclair flush, with dirk and broadsword in hand, left little room for speculation. None for negotiation. On the field, Henry carried no shield; war was attack, not defence. Yet in court he was respected as a fair and forthright arbiter of the aggrieved.

Subjects came in troubled waves before him, seeking justice, revenge or favour. None left unanswered.

From her infancy onward Eugainia's smile disarmed her Lord Protector completely. Her regard was particularly soft and gentle tonight, reflecting their shared relief at the success of this most recent in a series of bolts to freedom.

"The simpler the better, I thought."

"Aye. Well conceived, Henry, my dear," Morgase added. Her familiarity with Prince Henry Sinclair, Baron of Rosslyn, Earl of Orkney and Liegeman to the Prince of Norway had a motherly quality to it, though there was no blood bond between them. Henry chose Morgase to nurse the infant goddess/queen the day Eugainia had come into his tending, the day her mother had been dishonoured then murdered and her father dismembered in the bloodied fields of lavender sweeping down the slopes at Albi in Provence. The last stronghold of the Cathars still stood, though the Cathari Heresy had been purged from the face of the earth some eighty years earlier. The few Templars who survived the same purge took and held Albi until their sword was broken. They fled in disarray to secluded corners of disease-ravaged Europe. The once-mighty band was reduced to a handful of exhausted stragglers.

Morgase shook out their wet cloaks. "Well conceived indeed. An odd, monkish figure with 'his' portly little companion slipping into the mist aroused no suspicion. Two black ghosts simply dissolved in the Firth of Forth fog."

"No doubt they'd expect the Lady of the Grail to escape on a white stallion, or some such," Eugainia smiled, "surrounded by aged knights and fatuous sycophants."

Morgase stood ready behind Eugainia, unravelling the tight braids. "No more of that, the Goddess and Her God be praised.

First, mind, your young God, your equal on earth must be found."

"And so He shall. I will find him, yes?"

"You will. I've seen him in a dream. Oh, My Lady! He is a braugh brown laddie. Well made and bonny. A god among men. He walks the earth with strength and humility."

Morgase's Celtic foresight, usually accurate and dependable, had lately tended toward flights of adolescent fantasy. Henry closed the discussion. "Well. The great adventure begins. A new world free of fear and artifice awaits us all."

"Well begun is half done, one hopes."

"Aye. Sleep well, My Lady. Morgase. "

Henry bowed and departed. The aft-castle curtains fell quietly into place.

Henry assumed the helm. The crew worked swiftly, spoken orders belayed. Sails fell from the cross trees with barely a whisper, then bellied out gently in the growing breeze. *Reclamation* weighed anchor in silence and, borne on the fall of the autumnal tide, slipped through thinning mist into the North Sea. She nosed quietly into her nor'ward course and dissolved into the night.

The fat-bellied vessel found a constant wind. The indigo sky crackled with stars. The helm lantern, trimmed close, cast pale light in a discrete arc as it swayed on its short tether.

Fleet commander Prince Henry Sinclair was widely considered a good man—loved, respected and, when circumstance demanded, feared. He presented the three strains of his ancestry in well-proportioned balance. Broad-shouldered, he enjoyed a robust constitution, *grâce à* his Highland Scots ancestry. His straight nose, scarred at the bridge, buttressed a lofty Highland Scot brow, the "Campbell brow," his mother, who would know, assured him. Long blond hair, tied back with a leather thong, confirmed Nordic descent, as did light blue eyes of moderate size generously spaced, set precisely in fine, strong bone. Long at the leg and waist, he showed the natural grace of the Parisien St. Clairs, with whom his clan's worldly fortunes were linked through blood and generations of cross-channel commerce. A finely worked silver-cross pattée, insignia of the disbanded Knights Templar, hung on a thin gold chain around his neck.

The small gold cross had become a touchstone for Henry, infused with memory of the anger and grief of Henry's father, William Sinclair—First Earl of Caithness, Third Earl of Orkney, Baron of Rosslyn and last true Knight of the Inner Temple. William had never admitted defeat, though defeat sat heavy upon him. Rome's second outrage against man and God, the Papal Inquisition, had succeeded beyond expectation. In league with the crowns of England, France and Spain—all deep in debt to the Temple Knights since the first great crusade—The Church at Rome achieved its goal: erase their liabilities and, when done, hunt down and eradicate the last vestiges of the Templar heresy.

The battered Templars went to ground. The church, mistaking absence for victory, relaxed its vigil. The great heresy thought dead and beyond resurrection resurfaced. At its core squalled the infant Eugainia St. Clair Delacroix. To the great joy of many, the Goddess and her earthborn mate, the unseen Man/God known only to the future, would rule together at last. To Eugainia's great misfortune, her ascendance churned the guts of those who would eradicate her and her followers. Henry and his straggling band were hounded to the outer edges of western Europe, to the shores of Portugal, then northern Scotland, and now from the outer Orkney Islands to the New World beyond.

Dawn defined the broadening arc of the western horizon.

Silence prevailed. *Reclamation* sailed past John o' Groats, rounded the headland at Skaill, where the remaining eleven vessels of the fleet waited. *Reclamation* slipped among them. Henry roused the captains and manoeuvred the ships, their crews quick and practised, into an arrowhead formation.

Each vessel was ordered to stand at anchor within easy hail of the next. Henry took stock of the fleet.

Along with *Reclamation*, two similar single-decked double-masted Venetian galleys—*Speranza* and *Constante*—defined a triangle, the tip of the arrow.

Antonio Zeno felt like a feral cat among domesticated pigeons. A small, dark, liquid man cloaked in wealth and power, he paced the foredeck of *Speranza*, off *Reclamation*'s port bow. Scion of the Venetian Zeno family, New Arcadia's financiers, Antonio knew each vessel's worth down to its last *denari*. Irony had twisted back upon itself, casting him as co-conspirator in the company of these ghost-sons of defeated Templars. Antonio stood unamused. He regarded their belief in the absolute equality of a fictive goddess more worthy of pity than scorn. The dark days of the goddess cults, with their blood-hungry priestesses and their castrated sycophant males, their open mouths pressed to the earth, their musky filaments sapping the virility of the Son of God's good realm had ended once and for all. Yet these fools had cast up another goddess queen.

Antonio glanced across the water at Henry and the girl he assumed to be Henry's Templar harlot. He recoiled when the beautiful young heretic's fat companion caught his eye. He'd disliked Morgase the instant they'd met. He knew he must hold his tongue until he achieved his mission. He needed Sinclair's skills as navigator. Sinclair needed the Zeno family's great wealth. The charts Antonio carried would lead Sinclair to his heart's desire—a perplexing well at the edge of the New World sea. And Antonio to the fabled River of Gold.

The Great Fleet New Arcadia's galleys, their prototypes developed and deployed victoriously by Carlo "the Lion," brother to Nicolo and Antonio in the great sea battles at Chioggia, had been re-fitted and double-hulled for the rigours of the northern seas. Winter conditions in the North Atlantic had been well known to Henry and his Norse cousins for centuries. Each galley, crewed by Scottish and Mediterranean sailors and skilled Norse warriors, was armed for combat. Though heavy and slow, Antonio assured Henry the well-armed vessels with their innovative rotating cannons mounted amidships would answer every contingency. The fabled monstrosities, both human and bestial, rumoured to inhabit the New World would prove no match for Antonio Zeno's ships nor his bred-in-the-bone Holy See cosmology. Every living thing knew its place in Antonio's narrow, vertical world. God sat in glory, in heaven, at the top. The lowest worm, blind and insensate, tunnelled the earth below. Mankind trod impermanently between. God gave man dominion over everything that walked, squawked, crawled on its belly, flew in the air or swam the sea. Man with his divinely ordained intelligence and divinely inspired machines was born to subdue the natural world.

The three full-bellied, oak-decked, single-masted caravels stood ready behind the galleys. The caravels sat low in the water, laden with food, tools and supplies. At the lateral edges of the fleet, abaft the caravels, sculled two sleek Viking ships of war and four broad-beamed open-decked Viking freighters—bows and sterns swept up to a point. Each bow's pinnacle held the gilded head of a bare-fanged dragon. Their oaken tongues lashed scarlet flame upon the morning air, calling forth the sun. Each vessel showed a dozen portals to starboard and to port. Oars were manned—two men per oar—by rotating shifts of forty-eight men, twenty-four to port, twenty-four to starboard. Girls and women supplied a continuous round of rough-grain breads, fat salt-meat and honeyed barley water. Elder women skilled in domestic and medical arts, along with mature artisans marked by age and toil, completed the one hundred fifty-person compliment of each Viking vessel. Boys manipulated hide shelters angled to protect the oarsmen from salt spume, which blistered already rough skin raw. Unattached young men stood by, ready to replace injured or exhausted oarsmen.

Nothing stood between man and God on the open sea but the hide and fur layered upon the their backs. Laminated keels footed a single square-shouldered mast, set with a broad sail of tightly woven wool. Lacking the shelter provided by the wooden decks of the galleys and caravels, the sail would be lowered in a full-blown torrent and snugged to the gunwales. Only the salt-lashed ironman tethered at the starboard-stern tiller remained exposed to fight the ocean's vindictive immortals, ancient Norse deities frequently confused these days with the three-personed god of the ubiquitous Christians. When old religions fail to answer, faith is quick to shift its shape. God the Father was simply the Norse God Woden redressed—lightly clad in desert garb, relieved of the grim wool and fur, the damp and cold, the *Sturm und Drang* of hard-scrabble northern winters. The irrepressible Son—the benevolent, recycled Fisher of Men—was a welcome relief from the thundering Gods of Ragnarok and Götterdämmerung. The youthful Christ, perennially at the peak of his powers, was a benign soul with a kind heart and a mind of steel. It was he, not horn-headed breast-plated Valkyrie, who beckoned the dead toward the new but familiar eternally shining world. The third and most elusive expression of the tri-person Godhead,

Christianity's preternatural shape-shifter, the Holy Ghost, became desperately popular, blunting as it did the unsettling, age-old uncertainties. Death, no matter its camouflage, troubles all with the same soul-stinging intensity. The Holy Ghost tore holes in the veil through which the shades of the blessed flock might pass. The doors to Valhalla, the exclusive purview of fallen heroes with its endless feasting and vigorous contests for delights of the flesh, were flung open. Asgard's majestic hall became a house of many mansions with room for all. God and His Son waited smiling at the refurbished gates of the more decorous Christian heaven, calm and welcoming, extending the balm of full bellies, sated desire and eternal, bliss-filled peace.

Under constant pressure from a stiffening southeast breeze, anchors were weighed. At Prince Henry's command, twelve hundred souls, with their Goddess at the helm, left the Old World forever. The Great Fleet New Arcadia vanished into the rising sun. Its golden light flared in Morgase's eyes.

She looked back, longing for one day more in Kirkwall. A promontory rose, obscuring her heart's desire, the village nestled in a safe harbour beyond the range of worn hills where she had been born. Eugainia laid a gentle hand on the small of her companion's back. Too soon for both women, the last of the Shetlands, the outer Skerries, Fetlar and Unst faded from view.

In the days and weeks and months that followed, the lumbering convoy with its overburdened fat-bellied vessels sailed a cautious route north to Kristiansand in southern Norway, where they took shelter—the first of many rest and provisioning layovers. They gained then left the archipelago Frislandia in their wake. They sailed north and west to Eslanda, where molten lava boiled at the edge of the frozen sea. Steaming vents sent plumes of vapour up from underground fires through churning waters high into the air where it froze and fell as snow on the upturned faces of Eugainia and her band of New World pilgrims. The fleet pushed westward past uninhabited Engronelanda's walls of glacier-capped rock. Tonnes of the ancient ice—hard as granite and as grey with age—slid slowly seaward. Massive slabs thundered down, split on basalt pinnacles honed keen as lances by grinding ice and pounding seas.

In the final weeks of New Arcadia's long passage, near the end of the eighth month, the warm surface stream flowing up from the south then curling east lost its stalling grip. The iceberg-laden current from the north shot them south and west, then due south.

In the ninth month, on June 21, 1398, they made landfall off Estotiland, lately known as the newe found lande, though it had been found and lost time and time again. Its inclination to disappear in fog then reappear in less cranky weather made it something of a chimera. This island of rock, relieved by bog and marsh, was a troublesome place. Its once-gentle tribes—the ochre-reddened Beothic—lost battle after battle, first to waves of savage Vikings, then to the merciless Thules. In the face of ceaseless assault the coastal Beothic had, according to the Mi'kmaq—their gentler cousins to the south and west—become surly, hard-bitten and cruel.

Sails hung loose. The fleet lay in crimson silhouette, immobilized, Henry supposed, by the sudden loss of the easterlies. The outsized sun, increased fourfold in the cool north Atlantic air, touched the northwest horizon.

Henry stood at *Reclamation*'s bow, Eugainia at his side, less than a mile from the newfound land's southeast shore. The weeks ashore scheduled to purge the vessels and sustain Eugainia had the opposite effect. The Lady of the Grail had begun to fail.

Her fair skin had roughened. Dark hollows marked her cheeks and shadows circled her eyes.

"Set me ashore. If only for an hour." Her voice was tight with impatience. "I'm sickened by this foul vessel."

Henry called across the short distance between *Reclamation* and *Speranza* to his kinsman, friend and strong right hand. At Henry's signal Sir Athol Gunn, a great-kilted, flame-haired hulk of a man, ordered a curragh lowered. His eight-man landing crew clambered down the side sticks, boarded the elongated tar-and-skin boat, the clatter of armour and arms sharp in the evening's calm. With four men to starboard and four to port, and Athol sculling at the stern, they made for shore where they'd seek a safe place—a sheltered grove, a defensible cave or grotto, perhaps—where Eugainia might rest and, if The Almighty so ordained, bear The Holy Child.

As one adores a wife, reveres a daughter, and shields his kin, Henry adored, revered and championed Eugainia St. Clair Delacroix. At the age of majority, Prince Henry, like all Sinclair males before him, had knelt—the Templar cross in his right hand, the sword of submission in his left—and spoken his clan's sacred pledge: Commit Thy Work to God. His was the devotion a true Knight of the Grail bore his Lady. He knew his duty: nurture and protect. She was, from birth, Henry Sinclair's chief reason for living.

Eugainia filled her lungs. She brightened at the thought of clean air, green and heavy with the scent of pine and fir. She could only guess at Henry's thoughts, so intense was his concentration on Athol Gunn's progress. The mutual regard she and Henry felt for each other was easy and comfortable as that of any loving father and daughter, though their bloodlines had diverged generations ago. Traces of the Royal and Holy Blood flowed in Henry's veins, diluted beyond privilege. No Sinclair male would perpetuate the ancient line.

Athol Gunn's landing party ran the curragh up the round-stone beach. These were formidable, robust men, these Highland Scot and Norse defenders of The Lady of the Grail. Each was selected for his prowess in battle and his demonstrated loyalty. Scarred and battered, each exceeded two metres in height, weighed more than sixteen stone. They climbed the cliff with an agility belied by their chain-mailed, breast-plated bulk. They disappeared into the salt-wind tangle of stunted conifers.

A slight breeze stirred. Yet nothing moved. Henry scanned the horizon. As far as the eye could see densely packed shoals of fish vast beyond comprehension rose to churn the dead-calm surface of the sea. It would take more than a stiff breeze to remobilize the Great Fleet New Arcadia; they were mired in fathoms of fish.

Henry and Eugainia stared, fascinated by the swirl of fins roiling the calm surface.

"Are these fish your first miracle in the New World?" Henry asked.

"God and Goddess sanctify us, no," Eugainia replied. "Fish were my progenitor's symbol, as you well know."

Henry dropped his glance, bowed slightly from the waist. His pale skin flushed.

"My Lady. I presume too much."

Eugainia softened her tone. "I'm moved by your faith, Henry. Each manifestation of God and Goddess on this earth builds upon the last. The Christ, Lord Pisces, was both the fisher and, as it turned out, the fish. Mine is a different time. When Christ was Lord the faith strained to grow; now we strive merely to survive. Compared to Christ's humble twelve, we're a vast army, but one weak and scattered. We've found our purpose but lost our way. The church serves the very merchants the Son of God and I would drive from the temple. No, Lord Henry. I'm akin to the fishes themselves, but also to something greater...the *milieu* in which they swim. I'm Aquarius, the bearer of life, at once the chalice and *l'eau de vie.* I'm sent to flood the world with Grace. The time of the solitary Christ nailed in sorrow to the Roman tree is passed: Aquarius is the time of the Two Made One. None will see the face of God Almighty without acknowledging the ascent of the Goddess and her God, with whom she shall reign upon the earth as his equal until the next great turn of the wheel. I cross the sea to meet my earthborn God who is, I know—I have seen it—awake and waiting. I pray a time of peace awaits us, He and I. It will be good to be together, gather strength in a secret place where mortal sorrows howl unheard beyond the highest range of hills."

Henry held his tongue. There was one husband for Eugainia, and he had been found. There would be none other than Lord Ard. Henry fixed his attention on the boiling surface of the sea.

Eugainia gripped the rail and quietly, very quietly, she moaned.

"God help me. Call Morg—"

"Morgase!" Prince Henry called. "Come. See to Eugainia!"

Morgase dozed in *Reclamation*'s aft-castle. Despite the weight of years, the volume of muscle and flesh, she rose swift and certain. She cast off the cowhide cover. She was at her Lady's side in an instant. She slipped an arm around Eugainia's waist, laid her square hand gently on the great, round belly.

Eugainia's chin fell to her chest. Her eyes fluttered and rolled. She threw back her head. A rattling gasp expanded her chest. Her breath, held too long, broke in a visceral wail.

In a luminous mist, Eugainia's soul departed her body. Her essence resolved in the clear air above *Reclamation,* formed a spectral likeness of the body of the young Goddess Queen, from which it had emerged. The vision—robed in blue, golden hair floating—hung above her mortal flesh as though lost, taking its bearings. Eugainia's airborne image wavered, elongated, traced the arc of a spear in flight, shot high above the fleet, shimmered, pulsed, then plunged in a bright bolt of scarlet flame below the fish-rippled surface of the sea.

Eugainia's body remained extremely vulnerable in her altered state. "A soul lightly tethered to its body drifts beyond the ends of the earth, forever irretrievable, if the golden cord tying soul to body snaps, or is cut," she once told Morgase and Henry. "When my soul departs you must protect my body with nothing less than your lives. Time simply dissolves when the rapture comes upon me. You must be patient and wait, firm in the belief that I will return. This world loses shape and rhythm, but somehow gains meaning. I—my soul—rises from my body. Then shoots up and away. In what seems an instant to you, I've gone to the ends of the earth and lived a dozen lives. I don't intend to be vague or mysterious. It's the only way I can describe these...travels that come upon me."

Eugainia stood firm. Her hands remained fixed on the rail. Morgase searched her face. The Lady of the Grail stared, in thrall to the infinite, her body rigid as death.

Eugainia's airborne spirit sensed no threat as it plunged below the surface of this pristine sea. Quite the opposite: the bright sea world into which her soul had plunged seethed with a jubilation of sound and motion. Seabirds fractured the crimson surface with a snap and swam like fish; thunder boomed from whales, thousands of leagues' distant—echoing and re-echoing from the far side of the world. Others of their kind answered nearby in high, thin song. Seal and walrus chattered and clacked. Shoals of silver herring, pursued by silver-bellied, black-backed mackerel—themselves pursued by their great, nimble tuna cousins—twisted and swooped. Curtains of liquid silk seemed to rustle in what Eugainia, her hearing distorted but still acute, imagined to be an undersea wind.

A luminous round-eyed creature materialized from the shimmer and hung suspended in the water before and above her.

It's a noisy place, the sea, the creature thought.

Intrigued, Eugainia drew near. No words flowed between Eugainia and the Selkie; words were unnecessary. Thought and feeling shot back and forth, fluid as the sea in which they hovered, face to face.

You are a seal but not a seal.

Yes. And I am woman but not a woman.

You are a Selkie, a Spirit Seal, a human woman in sealskin form.

I am. And you are a spirit dislodged from your human body. Which stands wide-eyed and still, gripping the rail of the vessel above.

I am. You've been following My Lord Henry's fleet these last nine months—

No. I've been leading.

I know your kind, but not your name.

Garathia.

Garathia. My human mother.

Yes. Just so.

Heaven's radiance, diffused by clear, cold saltwater, dappled the Spirit Seal's mottled head, and glistened in her eyes. A Selkie's gift to womankind is this: Spirit Seals accommodate another's soul, without displacing or jeopardizing her own. Garathia rolled to her back, exposing the cream yellow hair of her sleek belly. She opened herself to her daughter. Eugainia flowed inside her seal mother where she settled, separate but connected. The old womb-link was re-established. Eugainia felt safe for the first time in years.

With a lift of her chin and tilt of her head Garathia rose, describing an elegant arc. Through Garathia's eyes, Eugainia saw fish stretching in all directions filling three watery dimensions, league upon league. They slipped inside a vast shoal of brown-backed, white-bellied fish, their fat flanks mottled grey, each fish with a single fleshy "whisker," a barbel, dangling from its lower jaw.

Codfish, Eugainia thought. These are the fabled shoals of northern cod.

A particular delight when I'm in this form, Daughter. Splendid white flesh. Succulent, oily livers....Delicious.

Garathia seized a fat-bellied cod and, with a sharp twist of her head, eviscerated the roe-laden female. The writhing carcass drifted downward trailing curtains of blood and squandered roe. Garathia swallowed the liver whole. Eugainia rode the dizzying burst of energy.

On *Reclamation*, Morgase checked Eugainia's pulse. Strong and regular. The first time the rapture overtook Eugainia, she was twelve months old. Those unschooled in the ways of the Holy Blood diagnosed a kind of infantile catatonia. Morgase and Prince Henry gave thanks: this endlessly questing spirit was the sign they awaited—the mark of the Royal and Holy Blood.

Morgase taught Eugainia to remain alert on her "travels," to record and remember, to receive, not repel, the unknown. The ecstatic astonishment and the great, great distance were there, as always, when the rapture was upon her. The moment the rapture overtook her, she had suffered the first contraction of labour. Eugainia's pupils were dilated, her torso rigid with pain. Her body stood in stasis, awaiting her spirit's return from its journey in the World Below the Sea.

The swirling mass of cod above Garathia and Eugainia blocked surface light. Enough fish, thought disembodied Eugainia, to feed starving Europe until the end of time.

Garathia and Eugainia sped away. It seemed to Eugainia her mother flew rather than swam toward shore. Eugainia, thrilled, laughed.

What is more bird than bird itself?

A seal in flight, Garathia proposed.

And what, Mother, is the sea but the dreaming mind of the world?

Yes. Just so. Mountain and rock are the earth's bones. The soil is her flesh. Water her blood. Her churning gut is the earth's molten core. Rivers of flowing lava, my dear, forever consume, digest—renew the bone, flesh and blood of us all.

And the air above, still as it is today?

In the end, Garathia supposed, the human spirit, fluid though it may be, is more like breath than water. Wind or calm, cold or warm, it's always the same. The earth's breath unites the dreaming sea and the great dome of heaven—

Where the mysteries are revealed. Heaven and earth united. The human soul undivided—

The Two Made One.

Yes.

Exalting in the knowledge, Garathia sped upward, broke the surface, exhaled and, swift as thought at the top of her arc, filled her lungs with air. There was delight in the smack of her belly on the surface. When she dove and breached again, there was no need to flip, as she did, mid-air—aside from the joy of it. She revolved a full three hundred and sixty degrees before slicing the surface without raising a ripple. A diminishing trail of bubbles marked her descent. She resumed her course. Together in one sleek body mother and daughter sped toward shore.

Have you been to the centre of the earth, Mother?

I have.

And...?

It was hot...very hot.

What form did you take?

I went as myself. It was a mistake. Next time, I go as lightning.

Oh?

I'm determined to penetrate the sphere at the core. It pulls me to it with great force.

What is it made of, the earth's core? Eugainia asked.

Nothing I'd encountered before. Neither solid nor liquid. Inconceivably dense. It's polished to prophetic brilliance by this...swirling mass that surrounds it. Radiant heat, as much energy as matter, sears without burning. As does fire. In a dream. It's hot beyond imagination or description.

This core. It's in my dreams too. Why does it haunt us?

Patience, Child. It is only destiny. All will be revealed in the fullness of time.

Garathia rose toward the surface. Her slow, tightening spiral parted the curtain of fish. In the way of all seals, her head broke the surface muzzle first. Clear membranes protecting her eyes against the salt slid up and back. Her nostril slits, inverted commas pinched tight against the depths, flexed then opened. An outward rush of fishy breath rippled the surface. The inhalation was measured. Her sensitive nostrils assessed the air above the sea. Her little ears accustomed themselves to the shocking silence. Garathia slipped below the surface, sped to still shallower water where she braced a vertical stance, her hind flippers splayed, her body tense, her head a glistening sphere mirrored in the still surface.

With her mother's ears, Eugainia heard cries of battle. Through her mother's eyes, she watched a screaming bundle of human flesh clothed in fur tumble down the face of the cliff. The falling man struck out-cropped rocks with thud after bone-cracking thud. Puffins, terns and guillemots took wing, circled and dove, screaming their outrage, their hatchlings crushed by the tumbling body, or knocked to the exposed beach below—most crippled, some mortally wounded.

The man lay splayed, a heap of broken bone and failing flesh. His astonished lungs refused, despite desperate attempts to inhale, ever to inflate again.

Garathia and Eugainia inched closer. Garathia's belly scraped the round grey stones.

The dying man's face, arms and legs were scarlet, not with blood, but with red ochre.

A single word flashed through mother and daughter's shared consciousness: Skreling. One of the ferocious figures of the Old Norse sagas lay broken on the beach. No one knew the Skrelings' origins, though some suspected them to be hybrids born of the worst of the North Atlantic's rape-and-pillage cultures. The peaceful Beothic, native to the newfound land, feared the feral Skreling more than death itself. They had managed to contain the wretched mongrels to the south and eastern shores at great cost.

Black-backed gulls swooped, snatched bewildered chicks from the beach, flapped seaward, the naked hatchlings writhing in their beaks. The more seasoned gulls lit within pecking distance of the greater prize, the broken Skreling's eyes.

Eugainia's soul recoiled. Monstrous in repute and imagination, the dying man on the beach before her was human after all, vulnerable to fear and pain as any. The Skreling's last vision became Garathia's and, thereby, her daughter's. The man's raw terror whetted the gulls' appetites. Their macabre, flap-and-squawk dance astonished the Skreling. How was it he couldn't flap his arms and drive them away? His only defence became a lure: the cold, hard stare of the dying man, directed with all the force he could muster, served only to inflame their dark desire. Their heads cocked, soulless yellow eyes peering, the gulls shuffled nearer, advancing and retreating uncertain when—not where—to jab. Before the light faded from the poor man's eyes, the flesh feast began.

Mother. This cannot be.

What, child?

We came to build our New Arcadia on this grim rock?

This isn't the world you and the Holy Child seek, Eugainia. I'll direct your Lord Protector to Vinland, south and west across the great gulf, past Apekwit, the red isle of summer feasting, to the Smoking Mountain.

I can't bear another day on that stinking, grinding ship.

The passage will be swift. You'll find a gentle welcome among the people there, I promise.

Gunn's mass of red hair blazed in the setting sun. He pushed back his helmet, glanced down the cliff. The seal sculling near the shore caught but couldn't hold his attention. The battered corpse of his most recent victim disappeared amid the squawk and flap below.

Gunn towered, helmet, head and shoulders, above the tallest of his tall men. To the half-sized Skreling awaiting his next move, this was not a man like them, but a savage force of nature, an evil spirit. And a gift from the sea. To a man, they imagined Gunn's throat slit, his body dismembered, his bones burned, his liver fed to their dogs, its power theirs. Skreling technology had advanced over the centuries as the Scots and Viking assaults increased. The wealth of metal skin plied from an invader's body transformed their lives. Death made life easy. His chain mail they'd convert to cooking baskets. His breastplate would be hammered flat, fitted with hide rope to make a sledge their women would load with meat, then haul back to the winter camp. Shoulder and knee flaps and forged codpiece would be pounded and folded, pounded and folded again into spear tips and arrowheads.

Gunn had other plans for his body and its metal shell. He advanced inland, his broadsword a windmill in full gust. His six surviving men scrambled down the cliff face, trailed by Sir Athol, himself pursued by thirty infuriated red-ochred Skrelings.

At the water's edge Eugainia stared through her Selkie mother's eyes at the gull-ravaged corpse. A sharp sting of recognition jolted Eugainia. She felt rage, repulsion, but also great compassion. And fear. A soul untethered—hers—might, in misguided compassion, follow the panicked soul of the Skreling to certain darkness.

Aboard *Reclamation*, Henry and Morgase, one on either side of Eugainia's inert body, were torn between the danger faced by their friends onshore, and their Lady's sudden gasp of distress. One look into her eyes confirmed the worst: Eugainia was in mortal danger. This separation of spirit and body had gone on far too long.

Sir Athol held the gap between two granite rocks at the bottom of the cliff. A wedged boulder restricted passage to one stooping figure at a time. Skrelings poured through the narrow gap. One after the other they came. One after the other they died. The Skreling flood spilled over the boulder. Athol was ignored. The greater prize to Skreling eyes was his metal-skinned men, and the hide-and-pitch boat they dragged to the water's edge. Sir Athol unleashed an ungodly roar. Gunn's last outburst had preceded the death of eight of the Skreling brothers. Two dozen ochred faces turned up on the beach and stared. Sir Athol unbuckled the side-straps of his breastplate, which clanged to the stones on the beach. With one hand, he pulled his chain-mail vest and coarse wool undershirt over his head. He slid both down his sword arm to the blade itself. He whirled the sword in a great circle, slung mail and shirt off its tip toward the Skrelings. One advanced, then retreated, both attracted and repelled by the undershirt's bearish stench. Athol unwrapped his great kilt, wound it around his forearm. Naked but for his great boots he stood, fearless and alone, his barrel chest expanded, its red hair matted with the sweat of battle and unwashed months at sea. His calf and thigh muscles tensed, then relaxed. He circled his head left then right, loosening the muscles of his shoulders and neck. His testicles, with minds of their own, drew snug to his body, less likely targets of stone-flake knives and sharp Skreling teeth. He exhaled. He filled his lungs. The ancient Celtish cry of war rose from a rumble low in his belly and burst forth in deep-throated whoops, bellows and growls.

The Skrelings cocked their heads, like dogs listening to music, intrigued, but unable to make sense of the fantastic sounds.

"Stand where you are. I say, stand where you are, murderous little cutthroats," he ordered. "Touch one man or that boat and by God above, in the name of His Holy Daughter, whom I love and serve, I will carve you, I say, I will carve you into quarters and feed you to the sea wolves."

A cry of rage rose among the Skrelings. They flooded the beach. In the manner of naked Celts in the flush of battle, Sir Athol's manhood rose to full menace. Tree-trunk legs pumping, Sir Athol broke into a full, roaring run. His broadsword held aloft mimicked, in angle and intent, its fleshy prototype below.

The little red-ochred men had never seen a berserker Norse or Scot in the full throes of battle madness. They split to the left and the right. Sir Athol turned and made for the boat where his men, ankle-deep in round stones, scrambled for a foothold.

The Skrelings outflanked the Vikings and Celts and took to the water. Infuriated little bears on land, they became sleek otters and ravening sharks in the sea. Two of Athol's men disappeared below the water. It bloomed red with their blood. Sir Athol was about to suffer their cut-tendon, slit-throat fate.

Speeding through salt blood and water, Garathia flung herself with knee-wrenching fury against Sir Athol's submerged attacker. Gunn tumbled into the curragh, rose to his knees. His broadsword slipped from his grip, fell to rest on the stones below. He propped his axe on the gunwale, urged his men to the oars.

Eugainia felt Sir Athol Gunn's sudden panic. She followed his line of vision. A new sound rumbled in Garathia's ears. Orca! Garathia listened intently. Cod, like most fish, are sensitive to motion but deaf to sound. The killer whales know mammals' underwater hearing is acute. They're chatty creatures when hunting cod, Garathia warned. They hunt seal and walrus, the great ice bear and men in lethal silence.

The black-and-white sea wolves went suddenly, eerily, quiet. Garathia knew they smelled blood. She peered above the surface, sculled quietly. Three sets of slick, towering black fins—two old Orca bulls and a young cow—carved a steady course toward them. Three or four others, she couldn't be certain of the number, followed. Garathia slipped below the surface. Six, maybe seven in all. Coming fast. She turned and sped out to sea.

On *Reclamation*, Eugainia, caught between life and death— her death and the life of her child—moaned.

In the ocean, she and her Selkie mother knew hope lay in greater depths. A black shadow loomed above. Eugainia recoiled instinctively as Garathia veered. Both were relieved when oar blades cut the surface. Garathia cut a wake at the curragh's bow. Sir Athol missed the Selkie's leap but heard her splash. He caught the second leap and smiled. The seal flipped mid-air, landed with a full-belly-smack, drawing the Orca's attention to herself, away from the fragile craft.

Garathia and Eugainia angled off to the east. Two dorsal fins followed. The Orca cow held her line, slicing toward the curragh.

Sir Athol estimated the distance to *Reclamation*. Too far.

He looked back to the shore. Skrelings struggled through the bloodied water. Most made it; some did not. Four voracious juvenile Orcas, who had trailed the main pack, hurled their slick bulks up the slope, clamped jaws on the legs and torsos of terrified Skrelings who flailed for a foothold in the treacherous stones. The twisting whales slid down the slope, back into the sea, their human prey writhing in blood-and-sea-slicked jaws. The Skrelings' screams careened across the surface before being drowned in water reddened by their own blood, and the blood of the men they'd slaughtered. The Skrelings' anguish flooded Athol's blood. He pulled deep on his oar, roaring his fear, wringing strength from aching arms, terror tearing muscle roped into knots on his back.

The Orca cow rose, jaws open, the frail curragh within reach. Sir Athol raised his double-headed axe. He released his last jolt of power. The Orca sank, the axe embedded in her head, where snout slopes up to join the glistening skull.

The Orca bulls circled back, toward *Reclamation*.

Directly below the galley's port bow, Henry and Morgase witnessed the day's second miracle; Garathia rolled to her back, exposing her belly. For a moment she floated, motionless and vulnerable. Then, a shudder...

Still grasping the rail, Eugainia's spirit departed her mother's Selkie body, rose high above *Reclamation*. Her spectral image reformed then floated briefly, her blonde hair flowing away from her head as though awash in the sea. Her wavering sapphire garments shed light as glass sheds beaded water. Soft rain fell from a cloudless sky on the upturned faces of her people.

Eugainia's body shuddered. A sharp intake of breath. Her fixed stare softened.

"Thanks be to Almighty God," Prince Henry said. "You're back among us."

Gunn and his men clambered up *Constante*'s side-sticks. An Orca bull clamped its jaws on the bow of the abandoned curragh; a second seized the stern. With a single twist they ripped the craft in two. They dove and rose in a double arc over the wreckage, wolves pissing victory on the corpse of a rival.

Eugainia was seized by her second contraction. Her breath became rapid and shallow. Her heart began to race.

Morgase tightened her grip.

"Come, my dear. It's time to bring forth the Holy Child."

Morgase's attempt to lead Eugainia to the aft-castle failed utterly. Eugainia would not permit herself to be moved from the rail.

A seal shot through the surface not five metres distant. Its graceful arc ended in two rows of ivory teeth. The Orca cow, Sir Athol's axe protruding from her snout, rolled to her back, her squirming prey clamped in her jaws. Predator and prey slid from sight.

Eugainia slumped, unconscious, too soon to witness the flash of light rise from the bloodied surface and shoot high into the sky where it faded from sight. Garathia's spirit sped home to the stars.

Henry carried Eugainia to the aft-castle, set her gently on the bed. Morgase drew the curtains against the chill of a rising wind.

The mirrored sky blazed vermilion, then orange, then a deep lustrous gold. The sun flared crimson then slipped below the surface of the sea.

CHAPTER TWO

The wind in the gulf was kind enough at first. A slate-grey mass of cloud rolled in from the north masking the moon and stars. Henry could make no sense of the luminous haze rising through darkness from the surface of the sea. Mist became rain, resolved back to mist and then ceased. The wind remained light and held its quarter. The twelve ships of the fleet rode a moderate swell.

Dawn flushed the sky a sickly green. The unseen force behind rising wind seemed befuddled at first, then enraged. Winds driven directly down clashed with squalls hurled out of the north. Crosswinds erupted, confounding surface currents. Waves rose and broke mast-high from four points of the compass. The Viking ships with their gaping hulls were swept high into the air. Men at the portals flailed the wind with useless oars. The wave's crest and voyagers' hopes were blown to scudding foam.

The downward rush on the backside of the wave seemed endless. It seemed to Henry a great hole was torn in the bottom of the sea. A vast depression formed on the surface of the gulf. The longboats sank from sight as though they'd never existed. Seeds and sets, bolts of wool and canvas circled the walls of a deepening vortex. Lives fragile as froth dissolved in God's preposterous fury. The fat caravels—flightless ducks in a towering sinkhole—

spun down in the widening eddy. Men, women and children, cattle, sheep and goats whirled silently to deep and quiet graves. They would plant no crops, build no shelter, know no issue.

Henry's last sight of *Speranza* gave no reason to hope. She rolled beneath the surge, sank from view then bobbed inverted to the surface, her rudder ripped from its housing. There were no masts. No house, fore or aft. All that remained was the stripped-down hull and naked deck. *Speranza* foundered again, resurfaced and hove out of sight, her fate at the mercy of wind and tide.

Constante did not reappear. Her last tortuous rise and the torque of the twist as she fell split her open like an axed barrel. Nicolo's still-living flesh and bones, until that moment securely sealed in the vessel he helped his brother Carlo perfect, spilled from the ship with all her provisions. He joined the host of lost Arcadians, their arms and legs spread wide, as if in flight. They wafted wide-eyed and lifeless down to the bottom of the sea.

Reclamation was wrung like a rag. Her seams strained as she corkscrewed end for end up then down one mountain of water after the next. Seasoned cross-members, her bones, dug deep within seeking strength, found their pith still green and aching with life. Henry's pride rose with *Reclamation* to another crest where she hovered. Down the far side of the mountain she plunged in a sickening, elliptic arc to the belly of the following trough. She groaned up another, hove to her keel, then plunged to what Henry felt must be the very depths of hell. Joints strained. Caulking sprung free. Frigid jets of cold saltwater stung raw flesh. Livestock bleated and bawled. No human voice was raised in fear. Or in prayer.

Dim light from the one surviving lantern gave form to Henry's fears. Stowed supplies securely lashed had broken free.

Sacks of oats, flour, dried peas and barley had tumbled and split. Barrels rolled, collided, their contents burst from sprung hoops and split staves. Honey, vinegar, sweet water, and the gallons of precious olive oil amassed from lands bordering the great Mediterranean Sea sloshed forward and back. Buckets filled with gastric spew, and worse, slopped over crusted rims or spilled entirely, their contents mixed with the spilt provisions. *Reclamation* groaned, twisted, plunged, was raised again, fell, then settled. Henry braced for the next sickening rise.

It did not come. God's wrath had fallen upon them without warning: without decrease it ceased. There was no jubilant shout, no prayer of thanksgiving. Deliverance smelled of vomit and tasted of fear.

Henry assessed the carnage and slop, the foul mockery of soup sloshing back and forth hip-deep in the hull. Hell surely exists, he thought. And hell is likely very much like this. He looked forward. His heart softened. Heaven might be very like the vision sheltered in the secure if ill-formed grotto tucked in the upper reaches of the bow. Eugainia was lost in fretful sleep. Sir Athol Gunn, with all his great strength, secured the pallet on which she lay, held tight to the breast of her guardian. Morgase sang quietly, stroking her Lady's temple. Henry caught Morgase's eye: she couldn't reassure. Henry waded to his Lady through the thickening sludge.

"Instead of increasing in strength and frequency, her contractions weaken," Morgase told Henry. "If she isn't delivered of this child soon, the Sacred Cauldron of the Five Trees will putrefy," Morgase continued. "Both Our Lady and the Holy Child will die."

Athol Gunn footed a ladder and opened the hatch. Sunlight pierced the hold. Sweet air flooded in.

"Both fore- and aft-castles have sustained severe damage, but are in tact," he reported. "The aft-mast stands. The main mast has been snapped in two."

The news below decks was better than that from above. Amid the ruined provisions, rasped skin and broken bone, Henry saw that none of his Knights of the New Temple had perished. *Reclamation*'s entire company, including her most precious cargo were shaken but alive. Their strength had been tested, Henry thought. They had been judged and found worthy. The smithies, wheelwrights, ship's carpenters, glaziers, masons—all the unmarried, childless artisans chosen for their skill and, more importantly, their monklike loyalty to both Henry and Eugainia—had survived to build Her New Arcadia.

In her delirium, Eugainia walked a forest path, her skin indistinguishable from the scented air. She turned at the sound of the voice, a man's voice calling her name. No man stood behind her. Where her feet had fallen, moss expired and decayed. No birds sang. Leaves fell green to the ground where they shrivelled and died. Eugainia turned and ran. The ground fell from beneath her. She willed her shadow to rise. She tumbled end for end into a fiery pit from which, she knew, there was no hope of escape. A devil's child, scorched and twisted, caught her eye and beckoned.

"I'd rather die than follow you," she whispered.

Morgase bent close.

"Eugainia?"

Reclamation keeled to starboard as the tide fell and nested in the mud. Sunlight bounced from the surface of the slop, shot up at an angle, brightening the makeshift grotto in the peak of the bow. Eugainia woke to the feel of light on her face. Fresh air filled her nostrils.

"Take me from this stinking hole," she begged.

Morgase ordered her pallet carried toward the hatch.

Henry joined Sir Athol on the listing deck. The wide, pleasant bay in which the ship had come to ground was still. The morning sun sat well established halfway to the zenith. In the near distance, a plume of smoke rose from the highest elevation in a range of moderate hills. The smoke, curious though it was, rising as it did from the earth with no visible flame, didn't hold Henry's interest for long. Neither he nor his kinsman Sir Athol Gunn could fathom what drew near.

From the wide mouth of a bay a hundred canoes, each carrying two adults, many with several children, approached at speed. The flotilla swept around and past *Reclamation*. On board the ravaged ship, not a hand reached for sword or lance, axe or bow. Even burley Athol Gunn's arms hung loose. A feeling akin to joy tugged at the corners of his battered spirit. There was no need for alarm. The revellers in the sleek canoes laughed and chatted among themselves, shouting what Henry assumed to be good-natured jibes aimed at laggard and braggart alike.

Was this a dream? If so, it came as a welcome relief from the nightmare they'd survived. The travellers' smiles were friendly and open. Blue black hair glistened in the sun. White teeth flashed as they directed the briefest of smiles up to the dishevelled creatures lining the sides of the enormous, stinking apparition that had appeared overnight in the Bay of the Smoking Mountain, also known to The People, the Europeans would come to learn, as Claw of Spirit Bird Bay.

The travellers seemed to Henry to be drawn across the surface as if by a magnet, so inevitable was their motion, so silent their paddles in the calm waters of the bay. Their bark-and-hide canoes rode low, laden with sleeping robes of luxurious fur, tightly woven baskets, perfectly square birchbark boxes and intricately decorated clay pots, many open to the air, all empty. Their destination was a low stretch of land on the northwest horizon. From their great good cheer, Henry assumed the green and red shores in the near distance must be a pleasant place indeed.

Canoes continued to stream past *Reclamation*. The ship posed no apparent threat, roused only passing curiosity. Perhaps this was a longhouse experimenting with Whale form. Perhaps the reverse. Such things were well known to L'nuk, The People, in story and in legend. In the Six Worlds, nothing remained static. At any given moment, the spirit of one object might transfer itself into the being of another. Its journey or destination was no one's business but that of the questing entity. The great wooden creature towering above them with its personlike spirits who smelled like the dead would make its purpose known in time.

Morgase steadied Her Lady at the rail. Eugainia's battered spirit rose to the flood of joy streaming round the battered vessel.

A young man, his brown skin artfully tattooed in vivid reds, yellows and blues, paddled with even, powerful strokes. The woman behind him, lithe and strong, not young, not old, held her own, matching him stroke for stroke. Unlike the others, theirs was a wary curiosity. They glanced up frequently, their expressions neutral.

Mimkitawo'qu'sk found Eugainia. And she him. She pulled herself up to her full height, lifted her hand in greeting. Mimkitawo'qu'sk wavered in his dig, thrust and lift motion, not fully registering what stood above and before him. He fell one then two then three strokes out of rhythm.

Mimkitawo'qu'sk and Eugainia couldn't look away, one from the other. He saw an exhausted young woman, pale, worn, pregnant, her blonde hair a tangled mat, her fair skin ashen grey. He felt what the morning sun, low on the horizon behind Eugainia, wished him to feel. He felt a golden arc around her. It came not from the sun, but from within.

Eugainia felt rather than observed Mimkitawo'qu'sk. A wave

of uncertainty washed up the length of her body. She felt she was being held upright, not by Morgase, whose stout arm circled her waist, but by this strange young man's lustrous eyes. For the first time since fleeing Scotland, Eugainia felt safe.

Mimkitawo'qu'sk wrested his regard from Eugainia. He found his rhythm.

Keswalqw knelt behind Mimkitawo'qu'sk in the canoe's stern. Keswalqw's open face rested simply in kind repose. Her doeskin dress clothed a tight and supple body. Her black hair shone, shot through with blue and gold reflected from the sky. Keswalqw's glance slipped from Eugainia to Henry, where it lingered.

Henry inclined his head in a greeting. Keswalqw returned the nod, then looked away.

Athol Gunn made no sense to Keswalqw. Was this a bear or a man? She couldn't catch his individual scent, such was the stink from the vessel. Nor—with sun above and behind him—could she make "the meeting of the eyes" to assess his spirit. Perhaps his was bear clan. Perhaps he was a moose-clan man.

Keswalqw returned Morgase's smile. Morgase experienced a tremor of recognition. I'm in the presence of someone ancient, Morgase thought. More ancient even than me.

The canoe slipped away. In that briefest of moments, as the sleek craft slid silently past the battered galley, five persons' fates were sealed.

"I looked at her but saw a tree, a pine tree, in silhouette, on a hill, in a landscape I don't recall but long to know," Mimkitawo'qu'sk said quietly to Keswalqw.

"I saw a tall, slender larch in spring, tufted with rosy plumelets, in the full beauty of her youth," Keswalqw replied. "Though at present she is ragged and unwell."

A light southeasterly carried a call-and-response chant—the

call spoken, the response sung—back to the Arcadians. Soon the flotilla was indistinguishable from the low red shores across the strait into which the wide bay opened.

Reclamation groaned as she sank deeper in the mud. She settled in spreading silence.

A curragh was lowered at *Reclamation*'s port rail. When their Lady was secure, the oars manned, Morgase, Henry and Sir Athol set out for shore. Athol noticed a single canoe break from the distant fleet, swing northwest and make for shore. He caught Henry's attention. Henry nodded.

From the deck on the seaward side of the stranded vessel, a great roll of canvas, two corners secured to the rail by clamps, was thrown over the side. Men in waiting curraghs unrolled the tarpaulin over the surface, allowing it to sink as their distance from *Reclamation* increased. The canvas made a natural swimming pool.

Whoops of laughter distracted Morgase. She turned back to *Reclamation*. Stripped to their filthy skins, the men hurled their foul clothes and then themselves from the ship into their makeshift saltwater tub.

A crouched figure hidden in low scrub watched Mimkitawo'qu'sk step from the canoe into knee-deep water. Keswalqw stepped ashore with practised ease. Mimkitawo'qu'sk drew her attention to an oddity up the beach. Two barrels, lashed together with a length of rope were lifted from the sand by the rising tide.

Mimkitawo'qu'sk moved toward the barrels. Some sea creature, its breathing unsuccessfully muffled, didn't wish to be seen. Mimkitawo'qu'sk secured the canoe. He caught Keswalqw's warning glance. They climbed the low bank and slipped quietly into thick woods, where they watched as the creature, still soaked and dripping, picked his way from his hiding place, gingerly lifting and setting his unshod feet among jagged stones.

Hatless, shoeless, and without his cape, clad in black hose, and black velvet jacket shot through with threads of gold, Antonio Zeno felt naked. He poked at the contents of the canoe. Empty containers. Heavy fur robes. Nothing of interest to an empty belly on a hot day. He made his way along the rocky shore toward the beached curragh.

Mimkitawo'qu'sk and Keswalqw exchanged bemused glances, at once entertained and befuddled by his peculiar, tenderfooted, toe-stepping dance among the stones. Each knew what the other thought; this was not a man, but another shape-shifter, a creature perhaps human, perhaps not—likely, because of the black jacket, a crow or raven on a spirit quest. In the waking world, beaked creatures were selfish and unpredictable. No less so in the spirit world. They'd give this one a wide berth.

"Perhaps, Aunt," Mimkitawo'qu'sk said, as Antonio high-stepped it out of earshot, "it fell off the great wooden whale too."

Keswalqw looked back to *Reclamation*. Its back was no longer covered with basking seal persons experimenting with human form. They were all naked now, clearly in man form, leaping off the wooden whale into the sea. They'd climb back up the whale's side only to leap again, happy as otters. As if by prearranged signal, they climbed back aboard, covered themselves in their wet clothing. From the stump of a great tree that protruded from the whale's back, the seal or otter persons suspended the great blanket, presumably to dry in the breeze. It was a very human thing to do. Very unlike a seal or an otter.

"Why seals would assume such pale, unhealthy forms, then cover themselves in that hot clothing?" Keswalqw wondered.

"I wonder what brought them here, of all places?"

"What their spirit quest might be is their business, not ours," Keswalqw replied.

"Apparently they have lice. Several of the older bulls seem preoccupied with scratching themselves."

"Yes. I noticed."

"And the terrible stink..."

Keswalqw and Mimkitawo'qu'sk slipped into the brush. They cut a line directly southeast through thickening forest.

Antonio had no idea he'd been so closely observed. He was grateful the stone patch finally resolved into a long stretch of sandy beach. He abandoned his tiptoe terpsichore and made headway.

"Please," Eugainia pleaded as they penetrated the hushed forest. "If you love me, set me down."

Morgase's heavy dress was soaked with perspiration. Sweat beaded on Her Lady's cold, white brow.

"When your contractions should be getting stronger," Morgase told her, "they weaken. Goddess of spring in your maiden flesh I tell you this. Bring forth this child or you will die."

The circular meadow into which they stumbled was a silent, pleasant place edged by stripling birch.

"We need a silver fir or a seasoned oak." Morgase staggered forward. "A child born amid these weedy birches will be pliant and weak of will."

The clearing was dominated, dead centre, by an oblong stone. The rock, twice their height and shaped like a tongue, thrust up from the grass at an angle, its black surface polished by the dry heat of the sun.

"I beg you, Morgase. If you love me, let me sink into this strange soil—"

"Hush, child." Morgase reshouldered her burden. "Where there's no oak, a good rock serves a Royal and Holy Birth."

Eugainia removed a slender dagger from the folds of her mantle. "Take this knife and cut it from me."

"Put that away."

"God wills it."

"God may will what He will. I tell you it's too soon for that."

Morgase and Eugainia made slow progress to the stone.

"I beg you. If I don't lie down I will—"

"If you do lie down, you will perish."

Eugainia cried out for her protector. "Prince Henry!"

Henry, screened from "women's business" by custom and a certain squeamishness, and a stand of young pines, responded. "Morgase? Shall I—?"

"Stay back, Henry." Morgase forced Eugainia back to her feet. "This is no place for fainting men."

Eugainia slumped against the standing stone, her knees about to buckle, her back grateful for the support.

"Now. Squat, child. Just so. Place your hands on my knees. Good. Look at me. Eugainia! Pull power from the stone."

"Morgase, what will become of us in this strange place?"

Morgase recoiled as though struck.

"Morgase?"

"Niniane!"

"Niniane is back at Castle Rosslyn, in Edinburgh—"

"Send to the kitchens for honeyed barley water, girl." Morgase stumbled toward the unseen figure behind the rock. "Impudent girl! Niniane! Come here!"

"Morgase...?"

"Look! My Lady...the maidens of the hall, spindles whirring, turn linen threads for your first...your first...child....Help me. My heart...it bursts within..."

Morgase fell, her eyes fixed on the blazing sun. Eugainia strained forward, gripped Morgase by the wrist. The slight breeze abated. The great rock began to vibrate. Leaves trembled in gentle resonance. As lightning seared the core of a standing tree, divine authority burned a channel through Eugainia. A sharp intake of breath propelled Morgase to her feet. She pried Eugainia's fingers free. "Enough. Let go." Eugainia redoubled her grip. "Eugainia. Let go. I am well."

Eugainia's consciousness wavered. Her grip faltered. She fell back hard against the stone, knocking the breath from her chest. She watched as Morgase's face became a mask divided: one side fixed, immobilized by joy, the other rigid with fatigue and sorrow. She fell—this time, Eugainia feared, for good. Her Shepherd's full weight lay across Eugainia's thighs. Pinned to the earth by earth itself, she thought. Please, Morgase. Don't abandon me now. Eugainia was assaulted by a strong contraction, the strongest since the Selkie Garathia had restored her to the *Reclamation* on the fish-filled Newfoundland seas. "Lord Henry!" Eugainia called. "The Shepherd of the Grail has fallen!"

Eugainia struggled from under Morgase, fell to her back, her skin sallow, her matted hair a tangle of meadow grass and crushed flowers, her skirts in disarray. She found she couldn't raise her torso.

"Lord Henry. I need you!"

Henry fought a wave of nausea. A scarlet patch of blood seeped through Eugainia's underskirts. Blood in battle honed his rage; birthing-blood defeated him. No weapon had been forged that could defend him from this inconstant force of nature, this too-frequent killer of the women he loved. Equanimity returned the instant he took and held Eugainia's hand. This was a field of battle. Nothing more or less. He knelt behind His Lady, his thighs and torso curved to support her upper body. Eugainia's back sunk into her Lord Protector. Still within her reach, she caressed Morgase's brow.

"What ails her?" Henry asked.

"Take my hand. Pray with me." Eugainia's grip caused Henry's eyes to water.

Henry felt his breastbone vibrate. His shins, pressed to the ground, trembled. The resonance, he realized, came from the earth itself.

The great stone in the centre of the meadow pulsed then held a deep, resonant tone.

As if in answer, Eugainia vanished. Only a shimmer of light remained. The light intensified. Henry shaded his eyes. Morgase stirred, sat strong and refreshed and, to all outward appearances, completely healed. The stone fell silent. Eugainia stepped from the widening pulse of light, bent to Morgase. Morgase took her hand. Eugainia struggled to remain standing. Brusque and practical, as though her journey to the valley of the shadow had not occurred, Morgase led Eugainia back to the stone.

"Lord Henry. Fetch sprigs of willow to ease her pain. And yarrow for cleansing. Find lady's mantle. It will loosen the gate. Calophyllum will strengthen her heart and speed the pulse."

"Morgase, I'm not schooled in women's affairs."

"Ah. Of course. Why would you be? Then stay and tend Eugainia."

Before Henry could object further, Morgase took a southward bearing and moved to leave the meadow. She stumbled, recovered immediately. She looked back at Henry and Eugainia. She smirked. "Oh, ye of little faith. I tripped, for goodness' sake. I tripped. That's all. You look like two lost children, newly orphaned. Straighten up, for goodness' sake, the pair of you."

She turned. Had she taken another step, she would have

collided with the shoeless figure clad in black who sprouted from the earth, it seemed, in a fungal instant. She stared at him, her hatred for the Venetian merchant raw and completely unveiled. Nor did Antonio Zeno make any attempt to hide his contempt for Morgase.

The day they'd met in Edinburgh, their instant mutual dislike had alarmed Henry. He thought that problem solved when *Speranza* disappeared in the storm. But there stood Antonio, sudden as a mushroom, frayed but unbent, a devil he knew in this strange land.

"Papist viper!" Morgase spat. "No God I could love would let you live, let alone lead you to this sacred place."

"Morgase. Please," Henry whispered, "this is not the—"

"I thought I'd never see a living face again," Antonio said.

"Keep that man away from my Eugainia, Lord Henry, or I'll not be held responsible for my actions."

"You will indeed be held responsible for your actions, Morgase. You'll find the herbs Our Lady requires. Admiral Zeno will accompany you. I'll not have the Shepherd of the Grail wandering these wild woods alone. While you search, my place is with Our Lady."

Morgase stiffened. "Me? With him?"

"You wish me to accompany her where, exactly?" Antonio asked.

"To seek the medicines required by Eugainia."

"My very soul recoils—"

"The old witch's charms are undiminished, I see."

"You smug, hopped-up papist wee popinjay—"

"Enough! You will get along, the pair of you, for the sake of Our Lady. Look about you. Lost in a foreign wood. Reduced by eight in ten of our numbers. No seeds. No livestock. No provisions. Beset about by God knows what manner of men and creatures. If we are to survive, it will be because we learn to depend upon each other; you will co-operate or we will perish."

Eugainia shifted, easing the strain on her back and thighs. "Morgase. You poison this new well before we've drunk its waters. Put your ancient grievances aside. If not for your own sake, then for mine. Henry is correct. Do as he says."

"Antonio?" Henry asked. "*D'accord?*"

Antonio knew Henry for the leader he was, and recognized practical good sense when he heard it. If his desires in this New World were to be fulfilled, his one option was co-operation.

"For the sake of a moment's calm, if not eternal peace," Antonio said, "shoeless and hatless though I be, I will accompany her."

"Hold on, child." Morgase kissed Eugainia's forehead. "Hold on."

Morgase swept past Antonio.

"Come, viper. Close your gaping yaw and follow me. "

Henry sat when bidden beside Eugainia. She took his hand.

"I am the moon, Lord Henry, stopped in her orbit."

"How so, My Lady?"

"I wax and wane in the same instant," she said. "Comes a jolt of pain, and I wish it twice as strong. The urge to push fades. Another weak jolt. It dissipates. I slip further away. Then great pain without contraction. Look how I bleed. Lord Henry. You're as white as a sheet. Can you abide my agony of blood?"

"My heart is your agony, as though my own child suffered."

At the edge of their vision, a shadow figure stirred, then dissolved in absolute immobility. Henry scanned the dark wall of spruce.

"Don't worry, child. Though my senses reel, I'll not desert you."

"Good. Your presence gives great comfort. The Shepherd of the Grail will not survive this day."

"How do you know?"

"I've seen it."

"Forgive me, My Lady. Will you?"

"In moments of prayer and meditation, I feel the sacred past pulse through me: back past our Lord Muhammad, blest be his name; back to my brother, My Lord Christ and His beloved wife the Lady Magdalene. Back to the Royal House of David; beyond Solomon, to the ancient tribes, yet further back, to Hector and Osiris, back beyond our ancient Goddess kin, to the Ones Before Time. Back to the One True Mystery—God and Goddess incarnate; back to the Two Made One."

"This same blood spilled upon the Holy Rood by the Prince of Peace, lost to the sons of men? Not possible. No. It cannot be. In your veins runs the very blood of God. You are the last. You are the Sacred Vessel."

"I am the Holy Grail."

Eugainia laid her hands on her too-hard belly. "Why do you linger, little stranger? You're afraid. I cannot reassure. Prince Henry. A moment may soon come when I give you an order, an order you must obey."

She withdrew her dagger.

"No, Lord Henry. No! Do not object. If this child dies because I...because I failed...everything for which thousands of men and woman have suffered, bled and died perishes with us. Please." She offered the dagger, handle forward, to Henry. "If I die, God wills it. The child must live. I've nowhere else to turn."

The figure in the trees stepped forward. Keswalqw took his arm and pulled him back.

"Don't ask this of me," Henry said.

"I'm not asking. As you became father to me, when my earthly father's blood was spilled at Albi, so you'll be earthly father of this reluctant child."

"My Lady, please—"

"Whom do you serve?"

"The Kingdom of The Holy Grail."

"Just so. Swear."

"My Lady—"

"Swear!"

"If your soul departs…and your child lives, I swear…"

Henry's chin fell to his chest. Eugainia took his hand. She laid the dagger handle in his open palm. She closed his fist around it.

"Henry, whom do you serve?"

"Madam. I serve Thee."

"And…?"

"My Lady, I swear: the Royal and Holy Blood will reign again."

"It has been spoken."

"God wills it."

Eugainia lay back. She prepared her soul's ascent to her Heavenly Father.

Mimkitawo'qu'sk emerged from the forest. He smiled to reassure. Vine tattoos rose from either side of his navel, spiralling outward to circle his ribs. A red sunburst circled his heart. A tattooed serpent climbed his arm, draped itself across his shoulders. A soft hide *cache-sexe*, held in place with a braided thong, gave a contradictory sense of virility and vulnerability. His right hand clasped an artfully wrought spear. Its stone head glistened black as the rock against which Eugainia in her agony reclined.

Henry rose, dagger poised. His free hand found his sword hilt.

Mimkɨtawo'qu'sk offered sprigs of willow. Eugainia nodded. Mimkɨtawo'qu'sk set the willow on the ground. He slipped quietly back into the woods where Keswalqw waited, aware the drama unfolding before them had not reached its climax, knowing soon she would be required to play a major role.

"Lord Henry?" Eugainia turned, seeking the young man in the shadowed forest beyond the fringe of birch. "Is he man or God?"

"The young man from the canoe."

"Yes."

"Real enough."

Morgase thrashed into the clearing. She grasped uprooted plants, her face, skirts and mantle smeared with earth. She rounded on Antonio, who followed closely behind.

"Venetian viper! Clement's evil clings to you like stink from barbarous death. Stand back!"

"She takes me for some scarlet Prince of Rome. I'm a humble merchant, m'am—"

"You want my death—he wants my death! Evil. Evil! I have seen it!"

"The old witch is mad."

"You knew my weakened state and bewildered me, on purpose—"

"She dug the earth, chewed grass and bush, crawled about, sniffed the soil like a rooting sow, then fainted dead away."

"Yes, I fell."

"I tried to raise her up. She turned on me—"

"Liar! Viper!! Brute!!! You struck me to the ground—"

"You sunk your filthy teeth into my forearm!"

"I couldn't breathe. You stood by, amused by my agony. Amused! When I asked your help, you thundered reprimands, cursing me and all women to the lowest depths of your unchristian hell."

"I stand amazed—"

"You purposefully provoked this killing rage in me. Purposefully! We may worship but one God, you said. There are no other gods to worship, you said. One God made all the world? One God, one male God rules heaven and earth? My ancient Goddess? Her Druid priests? No longer living? Oh, My Lady....Can this be? How have I failed you? Why have you deserted me?"

Antonio Zeno believed Christ's blood had been spilled for him alone. He fingered the cross at his neck, finely wrought gold filigree—at its centre a single discreet ruby, red as his Redeemer's blood. Red as the blood of the heretic bleeding to death before him. Red as the fires of hell, which would claim her soul. God's plan was clear to Antonio: Eugainia's death would pay the balance. Order would be restored. Their lady dead, the resurgent Templar connivance would dissolve for good in complete disarray. The rational world of the virtuous Christ would once again prevail.

"Come, Morgase." Eugainia extended her hand. "Your ancient Goddess lies before you, here."

Antonio made the sign of the cross, sank to his knees, near Eugainia. "Intercede, Holy Father, on this poor child's behalf—"

Morgase strode to him. Antonio blocked the blow. Morgase twisted away.

Her speech began to slur. "Cruel boys grown to murderous men. Your astonishing tale tells that through woman all evil enters the world." She retreated to her Lady and the rock. "You torture us, burn us for witches. You slaughter our sons, rape our daughters, butcher our nurslings in your unholy wars." She glared at Antonio. "You drove the Goddess from the earth. You and your kind. Viper! Deny it if you dare."

"The King of Kings dispatched your pagan Gods to free the world of Goddess tyranny—"

"Who would you be, you runtish puffed-up little peddler, without the power of the pope at Rome?"

"Your pagan women's sacraments were obliterated by the one true God and his one true church, at the behest of His one true Son, Christ the Lord himself."

"Christ hacked and burned our sacred groves of oak? No. It was you. Christ broke our bodies with rack and wheel? No. It was you. With hammer and spike, Christ nailed us to the bloodied gates of your unholy Papist hell? No. It was you. Roman men. Catholic men. Men! You place your foot upon our necks. You throw us a crumb— Mary, the poor bewildered mother of Christ, condemned forever, poor unwitting creature, to wipe the snotty noses of your cutthroat Christian whelps."

Morgase stood before Eugainia. She squatted, cupped her Lady's face. "But we're still here; aren't we, My Lamb? We rose and still we rise through Phillip the Cruel and grim Pope Clement's smoke, up to the uncharred air where God and the Goddess make us whole again."

Morgase lost herself in Eugainia's tender glance. "Morgase?" Eugainia spoke gently, as to a child. "Morgase? Your face is fire. Your hands are ice. Morgase, my dear. Can you hear me?"

Morgase stood, her face half twisted in pain. "They've poisoned the well! Flaming balls of tar o'er sail our castle walls and set the court aflame. Listen! They batter the great doors. I hear the voice of the unborn child: 'Run, Mother of God,' it cries. 'Flee the dying world!'"

"And so we have, my dear...Lord Henry, tell her."

"Morgase. We fled Castle Rosslyn and Edinburgh months ago. Papal Rome is two thousand leagues behind us now."

Morgase turned away, entranced. "Look! It is Herself. The Goddess emerges from her last great standing oak, branches of silver fir and lady's yew in either hand. She speaks…"

Morgase turned, addressed Eugainia who, from that instant, did not recognize her lifelong companion. The Shepherd of the Grail, round and solid as the earth itself, was rendered insubstantial as air. Morgase's body rose from the earth, light as a thistledown. She spoke with the voice of the Selkie Garathia, not her own.

"Eugainia. Daughter. Successor. Go where water, rock and tree sprites lead you."

Eugainia strained to rise. "Mother?"

"Lord Henry," Morgase said in the voice not her own.

Henry fell to his knees.

"Lead my daughter to the Well of Baphomet. Let her drink from the sacred vessel. She will be restored. Then set her free."

"Set her free?"

"Let the Goddess reign refreshed in the forests and plains beyond the five inland seas."

Morgase's mortal remains slumped to the ground. Eugainia strained toward Her Shepherd's lifeless form. She kissed Morgase's forehead, closed her staring eyes. Despair fell upon the clearing like a shroud.

The tattooed young man re-emerged from the forest. "Mimkitawo'qu'sk." He indicated himself. "I am Mimkitawo'qu'sk."

Henry accepted the willow branches, which he proffered. "My Lady," Henry asked, "what am I to do with the willow?"

Keswalqw emerged and stood at Mimkitawo'qu'sk's side. "Keswalqw," she said. "My name is Keswalqw. I can help this woman."

"What are they saying?" Antonio asked.

Eugainia gestured the woman forward. "Kes…wal…?"

Keswalqw approached. "Kes— wal— qw."

"Kes-wall-qwah," Eugainia repeated carefully.

Keswalqw nodded.

"I am Eugainia. Good soul, have you come to help me?"

Keswalqw chewed then spat a fibrous plug of pulped twigs into her palm. Eugainia opened her mouth and received the poultice.

"Good, little sister. You're safe. You will live." Keswalqw stroked Eugainia's brow. "Mimkitawo'qu'sk. Take these men from this place."

"Yes, Aunt." Mimkitawo'qu'sk turned to Henry and Antonio. "Come, kin-friends. Come." He moved to the edge of the clearing, expecting them to follow. They did not. He beckoned. "Come. This is no place for us. Birthing blood will weaken us...we...us...men....Aunt? They don't answer."

"They don't speak our tongue, poor things."

Henry hesitated. Eugainia reassured him: "Henry this woman, Keswalqw, is sent to the Goddess by God Almighty Himself. I have no fear. Nor shall you."

Henry bent to remove Morgase's body.

"No. Leave her."

Mimkitawo'qu'sk led Henry from the clearing. Antonio followed.

Life, it is said, begins with a miracle and ends with a mystery. Eugainia cried in ecstasy. Geese in flight, the full moon sailing. She lay precisely positioned on the fulcrum of the finest of balances. The memory of her swift flight with her mother through salt sea waters cleansed her blood. Seas of thunder, she whispered, great with whales. Garathia in Selkie form rose to the surface of her consciousness and opened her nostrils: she exhaled the scented earth alive and seeded. Eugainia threw her head back, opened her eyes. The sky hung blue, an open question begging no answer. Eugainia foresaw her destiny. The names of the Two Made One be praised. The sigh became a groan. She would soon become a frightening mystery to herself, unrecognizable to those who loved her. She would survive the birth of this child. She would have another. She compressed these assurance into one ecstatic push. In the thrust of muscle and gush of blood, seventeen-year-old Eugainia St. Clair Delacroix came to know the joy of the miracle that heralds life's beginning and, in the same instant, the sorrow that masks the mystery of death.

Keswalqw said a magic word she knew. She unfolded a square of soft hide. She received the silent infant.

"Keswalqw?"

Keswalqw showed Eugainia her misshapen, stillborn child, its frail torso blackened, as though shot through with a searing bolt of light.

The green world vanished. The golden cord snapped. Eugainia fell into the shadow world of ash and dust. Descent seemed without dimension and eternal. The Royal and Holy Blood purged of its purple bruise by Keswalqw's potion, rushed scarlet through her veins. She rode new waves of ecstasy propelled by Keswalqw's infusion. Fear dissolved in shadow. Anguish became transparent as the air and upon the air floated away. Eugainia turned and rose to heights unimagined, pulled up through wheels of pulsing light where Morgase, waiting, hovered. She reached down for the crippled child. The broken boy swept up too fast for her to capture. Morgase sped in pursuit. Eugainia could not follow. She plunged into the God's good sleep, her sorrow too great to bear or comprehend.

Keswalqw cut and knotted the cord. She wrapped the little corpse in the soft skin. She held the bundle aloft.

"*Akaia*," she chanted quietly. "*Akaia*."

Mid-day sun flooded the meadow. The black stone's surface rippled with heat. Birds took up their song, their warble and trill rattling air heavy with the scent of sweetgrass, dense as mist with the resins of fir and pine.

CHAPTER THREE

Henry established camp on a terrace of land overlooking the estuary of the great bay's central river. As the full moon tide fell, *Reclamation* exposed her belly for repairs.

Ignorance was sweet relief to Eugainia as she drifted in and out of consciousness. Latin, French, the Highland Scots Gaelic of Clan Sinclair's household and the Old West Norse dialect well known to Henry, as liegeman to the crown of Norway—all these tongues were familiar to Eugainia from the first days of her youth. The language of The People made no sense to her whatsoever. She put her urge to understand aside. She felt as though the gentle voices and their tongue's whispered sibilance washed her clean.

Early one still evening, light northeasterlies carried faint drumming across the waters from the low red island. Laughter rose and fell. Evening stretched into night. The night was half gone when fresh bursts of drumming and high-pitched chant/song woke Sir Athol Gunn. Shortly after dawn, he petitioned Prince Henry.

"This red island should be explored."

"The festivities may be sacred, Athol." Henry knew his

cousin's fondness for dance and drink. "Let's determine the nature of the *fête* before inviting ourselves."

Mimkitawo'qu'sk was not a shy man when it came to communication. It was soon established through gesture and repetition that the massive exodus to the red isle was occasion for both celebration and hard work. Its shores were rich with shellfish, its uninhabited interior rich with small game. The People perennially celebrated the first of the summer's great collecting cycles on the island. When Mimkitawo'qu'sk came to understand Athol's request (the great man was ham-fisted when it came to mime or gesture), he signed he'd be happy to lead Sir Athol across the strait, so long as he manned his own canoe and stayed down wind.

Despite misgivings at what had passed between Eugainia and Mimkitawo'qu'sk at their first encounter, Henry had taken an immediate liking to the young warrior. Though standing alone, and in spite of himself, Henry laughed aloud when Mimkitawo'qu'sk in the sleek canoe swung back and paddled circles around Sir Athol Gunn. Sir Athol struggled to keep pace with Mimkitawo'qu'sk. Henry felt a rush of admiration when Mimkitawo'qu'sk sped ahead—all grace and power. He couldn't decipher the details of Mimkitawo'qu'sk's shouted good-natured challenge, though both he and Athol caught a whiff of mockery.

Athol dug deep. He closed the distance. With no apparent effort, Mimkitawo'qu'sk stepped up his rhythm, and sped away as though propelled by a great wind under full sail.

Eugainia advanced from strength to strength in Keswalqw's care. As the days passed, the rudiments of a common vocabulary grew. Simple, direct, subject on occasion to speculation, and some verbal misadventure, their communion became efficient and intense. The best way to tell, they agreed at this stage of their acquaintance, was to show, say and then show again.

From the top of the hill on which Eugainia and Keswalqw stood, a mated pair of golden eagles took to the air from a gnarled old starrigan pine. The People depended upon their feathered brothers and sisters to carry their prayers up to the Great Spirit. The Lady of the Grail felt the air around her tremble when Keswalqw offered gratitude for Eugainia's healing and petitioned the Great Spirit to maintain The People. Up spiralled the stately birds until, small black specks tracing lines of supplication up from the Earth World, they dissolved in the blue barrier that separates the Sky World from the World Above the Sky.

Keswalqw showed Eugainia the name of the three-pronged bay—the open claw of the spirit bird its inspiration—and evoked the peculiarities of the surrounding territories. Looking eastward, toward the open sea, the most arresting feature of this rolling landscape was the low, rounded old mountain from the side of which issued the thin band of black smoke Henry had first identified the day the *Reclamation* arrived.

Keswalqw pointed. "Those ridges running the length of the valley? We say a great serpent grinds through the earth, its back cutting furrows where it rises through the ground to breathe before plunging back below the surface. We call this big snake *Jipijka'maq*."

"*Jipijka'maq*," Eugainia ventured, the staccato rhythm of the word suiting the image Keswalqw created.

"*Jipijka'maq* lays bare the soft black rocks we burn to set the clay when we shape our pots."

The black rock—coal, Eugainia gathered—was periodically ignited by lightning. Streams of run-off water from higher elevations overflowed into the crevasses, making a quick end to the mountain's sooty fussing. All would be quiet until the next storm re-ignited the coal. Rain fell, water pooled, the earth dried; clouds gathered, lightning struck and the cycle began anew.

Between the extremes of the Smoking Mountain's smoke and steam cycle, sulphurous vapours escaped from crevasses in faint wisps. Yet the air was normally sweet and clean. Prevailing winds carried the unpleasant odours south and east over the wide peninsula where they were absorbed by the great primeval forests, ancient stands of oak, maple and soaring white pine. The forest hills were the mothers of the bay's three rivers, Keswalqw explained. Below the trees, thick mats of moss regulated water extirpated by root, branch and leaf. Excess flowed into collector pools. Overflowing pools drained in rivulets. Rivulets deepened into streams. Streams expanded into creeks. Crystal-clear, nutrient-rich water coursed down the flanks of the Smoking Mountain, and her sister hills, to Claw of Spirit Bird Bay in three broad river systems.

Nothing was as it seemed at first glance. Below them, and a little to the west, Keswalqw indicated the elevated Meadow of the Singing Stone, the great black obelisk barely visible at this distance. In her agony, the stone had seemed enormous to Eugainia, saturated as she was with its primeval power. From this height and distance it was simply an odd feature in a benign landscape. She struggled to remember its significance.

All things in this strange land were infused with what Keswalqw called *Kji-kinap*—which translated, as far as Eugainia could tell, as Power. She felt its force, as ancient and particular as any Eugainia sensed in northern Europe, the lands surrounding the Mediterranean Sea, or the vast arid territories her ancestor walked, as described in the New Testament, which Eugainia experienced firsthand when she and Morgase had travelled the way of the Cross some ten years past. Eugainia felt great *Kiji-kinap* in her current companion. Keswalqw's power was indistinguishable from the bays, mountains and rivers—the terrain into which she, the Great Mother of The People, had been born.

Secure in its circling nest of low mountains, aligned on a northeast axis, the great bay opened to the strait through a narrow gut. Wind, sun and the push and pull of the moon churned fresh water from the hills and salt gulf waters into the bay's life-sustaining broth. Its marshland fringe thronged with life. Aquatic mammals and waterfowl came and went at the bidding of the four distinct seasons that regulated the lives of The People.

They began their descent to The People's summer camp along well-trod paths. Keswalqw regarded the village tucked in the curve of the east bank below as an extension of the rivers and their creatures, all beings sentient as herself, possessed of their own *Kiji-kinap*, a tangle of life requiring care and tending, a sentient being deserving care and respect. The entire system was enriched, each species serving another in a generative web where land and sea, forest, river and sky functioned as one breathing, flowing entity. The estuary's waters, within an easy walk of the lodges, offered the richest fishing of the entire bay. Ocean fish fat with roe driven to spawn in fresh waters collected here in early spring en route from the open sea. Mammals designed by nature to harvest the fish followed, feasted and, in their turn, fed The People.

The river transformed The People's lives seasonally as it was itself transformed. Keswalqw and her tribe followed game inland to winter camps when the brutal northern winter rode south, its killing winds riling the sea, turning bays and their estuaries to cracked plains of ice. The slick, stone-hard highway of ice the rivers became carried hunters deep inland to take moose, caribou, beaver and bear. The women followed, butchered the carcasses, hauled meat and raw hides to the winter camp, their toboggans' wooden runners watered slick with ice.

In spring great depths of packed snow gave way to the warming rays of Grandfather Sun. The old man he'd become over winter was reborn, a virile young shaman/warrior and provider. Power pulsed from his rejuvenated loins. His implacable stare—all melting fire—transformed ice and snow into clear running water. Spring floods cleansed the winter hunting grounds. Snowmelt rushed in torrents through the summer camp, cleansing it of the previous summer's dross, scrubbing the earth clean for the season of plenty to come.

Her pleasure in the ordered beauty of the village lay undisguised on Keswalqw's face. Three sorts of structures were positioned with regard to space and privacy along the inside curve of the cove where tidal and fresh waters met. Cone-shaped wigwams rose from a circular base. Round-roofed domes and more familiar rectangular peaked-roof buildings formed a loose perimeter. Eugainia learned the wigwams, cone-shaped or dome-roofed, were primarily sleeping quarters sheltering three, often four, generations. The long rectangular edifices housed stores and sheltered communal activities.

Each wigwam was distinguished by particular bird, animal or landscape forms. Narrow bands and sharp points of white pigment made of powdered clamshell and seal fat drew the eye to subtle, often geometric highlights. Red ochre. Yellow sulphur. Blue mussel shell. Grey or black ash. The palette was at once subtle and intense. On the door flap of a particular wigwam in which Keswalqw took pride, a spot of white, intense in this clear day's morning sun, highlighted the black eye of a boldly painted loon.

"My totem," Keswalqw explained. "She lives in three worlds and carries her young upon her back."

Keswalqw unlaced the neck of a distended moose bladder. Eugainia recoiled at its contents—putrid fat with a foul fishy odour. The seal oil water-proofed the wigwam's skin and kept it supple. Keswalqw leaned into the skin wall and inhaled. She indicated Eugainia do the same. The seal oil once applied lost its repulsive pungence. The sun's rays and sea air transformed the foul odour into a pleasant aroma, not unlike the scent of forest moss or fallen leaves.

Keswalqw held a lustrous hank of her blue black hair under Eugainia's nose. It carried the same woodland aroma. The oil, she explained, in combination with the aromatic oils of conifers, prevented infestations of common head and body parasites. This held particular interest to the visitors. Keswalqw made a host of friends when she shared the seal fat. Head and body lice had flourished in the confines of the voyage. Clouds of the New World's blood-sucking black flies, which plagued the Europeans to swollen-eyed, puff-faced near madness, kept their distance.

The wigwam's interior glowed opalescent. For the first time since the birth of her poor misshapen child, the Living Chalice of the Holy Grail smiled. Eugainia recalled Garathia in her Selkie manifestation, the fullness of her sleek cream-coloured belly and the comfort she'd found within. In her delirium, Eugainia had yearned to be with her mother again, flying through the sea; in Keswalqw's wigwam, her entire body felt soothed, as though she floated up to the top of a pail of warm cream.

Keswalqw opened the smoke flap. A shaft of sunlight shot through, the convergent poles casting radiating shadows like spokes on a wheel on the fresh-cut, artfully laid spruce-and-fir-bough floor. The soft green needles, the lungs of all conifers, exhaled their fragrance in the mid-day heat as Eugainia moved. She pulled scented air deep into her lungs. Tree Power entered her blood.

Sleeping robes of lustrous beaver fur, carefully rolled and stowed for all but the coolest nights of summer, ringed the perimeter of the wigwam. Eugainia counted fifteen in all. A blackened circle of sunken stone in the centre located the wigwam's hearth. Nearby, a small pile of dry tinder sat ready to ignite a larger blaze. Elegant woven baskets hung from thongs lashed to the poles. Smaller pouches of softened hide, their drawstrings tied, dangled in a jumble from a single braided rope. Eugainia touched one. Keswalqw placed it in her hand. Inside, Eugainia found a clamshell, three blue feathers and a small polished stone.

Under a spread of elms and maples at the camp's perimeter, up the slight slope from the tidal shore, cooking pots scoured clean by sand and moss rested inverted on wooden stakes. Communal cooking hearths under smoke-cured hide awnings showed evidence of recurrent use. At a well-trodden area near the edge of the woods shaded by an old elm, scraping tools, chipping flints and circular stone knives, all carefully wrapped in leather, each bundle stored in oiled hide boxes, awaited the hands that would wield them. Hide pouches protecting smaller tools were secured with drawstrings fashioned from tree-root tendrils. The French word *atelier* came to Eugainia's mind. This *petit quartier* had the universal feel of a craft guild, a highly ordered workshop where invention eased the toil of daily life.

Long before Eugainia noticed any sound, Keswalqw hurried down the slope toward the riverbank. In what seemed the blink of an eye, life pulsed through the village. The People returned, emptied beached canoes of clay pots filled with shellfish. Fires were lit. Wigwams aired. Lobsters soon steamed in boiling pots of water, though much of the seafood—muscles, clams, whelks, oysters—was cracked open and eaten raw. Shells discarded in a pile to one side of the firepit would be reduced in intense heat later, their lime and calcium critical to the hardening of clay pots.

Mimkitawo'qu'sk pulled his canoe ashore. He stowed his gear in the wigwam he shared with Keswalqw as part of her extended clan, unaware of the sea green eyes resting upon him.

Late that afternoon, Mimkitawo'qu'sk built a substantial fire at the edge of a meadow on the terrace above Henry's camp. At the base of the blaze, a dozen smooth granite rocks absorbed intense heat. Keswalqw lashed a circular canopy of aspen saplings, the little trees still rooted, stripped of their leaves. A perfect dome formed, about three-quarters her height. In the centre she dug a shallow pit.

Athol Gunn emerged from the trees at the edge of the clearing carrying a small oak table. He nodded and smiled in their direction. Mimkitawo'qu'sk and Keswalqw nodded and smiled in return as he left.

Keswalqw's opinion of Sir Athol formed instantly and, as it turned out, accurately, on their first meeting. "This one, this Sir-atol, seems friendly enough."

"He likes to sing, and last night, Aunt, on Apekwit he danced with one hand on his hip like this, the other over his head, and hopped first on one foot and then the other, like this, all the while pointing his toe and kicking out from under his many-coloured dress as if pestered by dogs. He produced a musical instrument shaped like a goose with many necks. He tossed it over his shoulder, blew into one of its necks—the one with what appeared to be a small round beak—then pretended to strangle it. He strutted around as it squawked and shrieked. It was very funny. Then he played a mournful tune. We saw it seemed to have some religious significance, such was the flow of his tears. We attempted to listen with respectful silence. It was difficult, especially for the children. In time we felt what he intended the music to tell us: love and a certain sorrow. Then he played a merry tune and danced his dog-kicking dance. So we joined him. It was great fun. The children came to love him. Who is this white-as-a-ghost-person bear man?"

Sir Athol returned with two elaborately carved oak chairs. He sat, head back, arms akimbo, legs splayed, absorbing the sun.

"This bear man, this ochre-headed one...Sir-atol...he is all hair—ochre hair on his head, his face, and here, and here. He turned salmon-pink then fiery red in the sun. He wouldn't swim with us."

A light breeze ruffled the edges of Athol's kilt, then whiffled its way across the grass. Mimkitawo'qu'sk turned his head to the side, exhaling forcefully through pursed lips.

"Oouff! He stinks like a bear."

"He may be a bear. Spirit bears sometimes quest in human shape, come to us for our medicine—come for the wisdom of The People."

"For a bath too, I hope."

Athol rose and stretched. He made his way to the terrace path. He nodded and smiled. They nodded and smiled in return. He continued on his way.

"He's quite friendly. And just your type, Aunt."

"My type!"

"You like them large and friendly. Yes?"

"Yes. And clean, and hairless. Never mind. I'm beyond all that now."

"Oh? That's not what Wosoqotesk tells me."

"It's true. Wosoqotesk leaves my sleeping robes a happy man.

But lately I think; why such energy for such a little pleasure? They've been here before, these white-as-a-ghost bear Persons. These kin-friends. They came in the time of my mother's mother."

"This tale is new to me."

"This tale isn't for everyone, Nephew."

"Not everyone will be the chief of The People."

"Time will tell."

"Still. I wonder why they came."

"It was said their land across the sea lost its medicine. The earth turned so cold snow fell in summer. Terrible wars cracked the earth. Great sickness fell from the stars. It was a starving time. They came to us across the sea in these great canoes with wind-catching blankets—"

"Like the one on its side in Claw of Spirit Bird Bay today."

"Maybe. They came for our medicine. Then they built the great stone lodge along the river of the yellow stones, near the well by the sea."

"*E'e!* The great stone lodge of the blistering deaths. That's how it came to be. Why was I not told this tale before?"

"Am I telling you now? The spear you carry was found by your father's father, found in the great stone lodge."

"This? Found in that house of death?"

"The sickness they brought ended their lives. The few who survived, barely enough to man their great canoe, returned to the land across the sea. For many years The People were afraid, afraid of the great stone house of death. But one young man, your father's father, dared to enter. Among their whitened bones, he found your spear."

"Tooth of Wolverine."

"Yes. The spear still had good medicine then. Strong medicine. It flew through the air like a living creature. Flew of its own accord and never missed its target. Brought swift death to moose and bear and caribou; killed seal and walrus, whale and wolf and man. Killed quick, kind, clean. It helped The People. It helped the animals."

"That was then. Its medicine is weak now."

"Before they died they dug a great well on the island of the twelve trees, on the ocean shore of the great peninsula. It's said they buried strong medicine in their well in the World Below the Sea. That was a long time ago."

"What strong medicine did they bury in this great well?"

"They say it was the severed head of their Great Father's messenger."

"There's our tale from the Six Worlds—the Tale of the Speaking Stones."

"Yes, yes. Inside the severed head of the noble warrior there was good medicine. It's the same tale."

"It's our tale."

"No one owns tales, Nephew. Only the Creator. Maybe we taught them, long ago. Maybe they taught us, long ago. No matter. So long as we learn we live. I should say their tale is similar to our tale. Not exactly the same. Similar. They said they'd come back one day, come back with their Creator's girl-child, open the well and retrieve the Severed Head."

"And today is that day."

"I think perhaps. Yes."

"Then they are on some sort of spirit quest."

"I think so."

"And maybe they are not bears. Or whales. Or trees."

"I cannot say. I don't know."

"Is Eu-gain-ia their Creator's girl-child?"

"We shall wait and we shall see."

"The 'Enry Orkney, I see today for the first time he wears a white cloak with a red cross on it."

"I saw this too. What's special about today, I wondered. That same cross the woman who was my grandmother's mother marked on her breast in the time of summer feasting. Marked with red ochre in the feast time a long time ago, on Apekwit, before the sickness fell upon the strangers. Soon a child came to her, a child with sun-coloured hair. A child with eyes the colour of the sky. Its white-as-a-ghost-person's skin frightened her."

"White skin and sky-colour eyes, yes," Mimkitawo'qu'sk reflected. "Now and then such a child is born to The People."

"Yes."

"There's nothing to fear in the eyes of such children. Is there, Aunt?"

"There's something to fear in the eyes of all people, Mimkitawo'qu'sk. But more than that, in the eyes of all, there's much to honour. Much to love."

"That is truth."

Sir Athol reappeared with poles and a canopy, which he erected over the table.

"Are we to honour these white-as-ghosts-persons?"

"We will wait and see. We will wait and we will see."

"Look, Aunt. The 'Enry Orkney."

Prince Henry emerged from the head of the trail and bowed to Keswalqw and Mimkitawo'qu'sk. A crisp white tunic emblazoned with the scarlet four-pointed cross pattée of the Scots Knights Templar fell from shoulder to knee. At the table, he extracted three rolled parchments from cylindrical leather carrying cases. With Athol's help, he flattened the fragile documents on the table, securing the corners of each with four small stones.

"Tall and yellow-haired with his sky-colour eyes," observed Mimkitawo'qu'sk. "He's no bear person."

"No. He has the Power of a sea creature. Lithe and swift like the dolphin. His heart's strong."

"I like the Henry Orkney."

"You're Moosewood Person. Moosewood Persons have much to learn from Sea Creature Persons."

"And much to teach."

"We'll see."

Keswalqw extracted wet hides from bark buckets, draped them over the still living arced branches of the sweat-lodge roof.

Mimkɨtawo'qu'sk returned to tend the fire. The rocks quivered with heat.

Henry took a seat at the near end of the table. Athol sat opposite.

"The death of her child alters everything," Henry began.

"In what way?" Athol asked.

From the terrace trail, sounds of men straining with great weight caught their attention. Both men rose. Mimkɨtawo'qu'sk and Keswalqw turned from their work, intrigued by the apparition emerging from the forest: Eugainia, screened by muslin, reclined in an elaborate gilded litter carried by four burley men.

She directed her bearers to set her in full sunlight, a little distant from the canopied table. She drew back the airy curtain, secured it with a tasselled cord of braided red and yellow silk. Sunlight fell directly on her shoulder.

The crystal beadwork on the neck of her sea green overdress sparkled in the late-afternoon sun. The long tapered sleeves of the fine linen undergarment were beaded with the same fine crystals. Her elaborate headdress, sheer silk draped from a whalebone bow that arched up and out, almost to shoulder width, was secured with a linen chinstrap. Her hair, pulled back severely from her broad, high brow and temples, was completely concealed. Her features were set in a resigned repose.

"That woman—the Eu-gain-i-a. *E'e*! She is beautiful."

Eugainia adjusted her veil and returned her attention to her distraction, needlework alive with leaves of grass and brightly coloured birds.

"She has Great Mother Moon in her eyes, and Great Father Sun for hair. Like the 'Enry Orkney. Keswalqw, do you think she is 'Enry Orkney's daughter?"

"No. He acts like her slave, always placing himself lower than her."

"I think her people captured his village."

Eugainia lifted her gaze from her work. She stared off into the distance. "God have mercy!" she suddenly cried. "I can't bear this ridiculous headgear a second longer." She undid the strap and tossed the cumbersome thing aside.

Henry and Athol looked from one to the other. "The sooner the Grail Castle is restored and you installed, My Lady," Henry said, "the easier I will rest."

Eugainia's attention returned to her work, where it remained fixed.

Henry unrolled and then rotated the remaining parchment in his hands. "These fragments make no sense without the key. Summon the Little Admiral, will you Athol?"

"My Lord."

"And wear your tunic. It's time we declared ourselves."

"Aye, My Lord."

Athol disappeared down the trail.

Mimkitawo'qu'sk stirred white-hot coals, heaped them about the rocks. "I think she has not yet seen eighteen summers."

"Nor have you, Mimkitawo'qu'sk. Yet you become an old man. Alone, with no one to warm your sleeping robes or give The People sons and daughters. Before you become chief, you must take another wife."

He looked toward Eugainia. "Never have I seen such power or beauty. Her yellow hair circles her head in little braids, look. And see where stones like water shining in an arc around her neck catch the light of Grandfather Sun. Look at the way her neck rises from her shoulders. And her breasts, I think, are neither large nor small. Have you seen her naked, Aunt?"

"Yes. Her skin has a white and rose-coloured beauty. Remember, Nephew. She bore a misshaped child, a child without life or breath. If you are to become the great chief and the signs say you will, you must become a great father, loved by many children, as well as a great hunter. You must take a wife who will bear The People strong youngsters."

"Yes, yes. I know all that."

Eugainia raised her face, stared straight forward again, her attention forced backward in time by unhappy thought. Mimkitawo'qu'sk saw her sorrow, a sorrow he felt deep in his own grieving heart.

"Come, Mimkitawo'qu'sk," Keswalqw said. "Your time of mourning is past."

"She's burdened with grief. As am I, Aunt. As am I."

"A winter has come and gone since your Muini'skw died. Yet you you still weep, Nephew."

"*E'e*! For the beautiful Eu'gaini'a."

"Walk softly, Mimkitawo'qu'sk....It's dangerous to talk to unknown Spirit Persons. She may not be for you."

"In my sorrow I am one with the beautiful Eu'gaini'a," Mimkitawo'qu'sk persisted. "Perhaps she is for me."

Henry pulled the muslin curtain aside. "My Lady? Listen. A feathered throat welcomes the Goddess."

Ignored, Henry pressed on. "I've seen the little creature. It's like our own song sparrow, but with a white throat. Particular to this New World, I think. Listen. Dah...dah...da-dah! And look there! How sweet. Summer's mysteries live in every bush and flower. One can almost hear the sound of a new leaf unfurling."

"One does."

"Yes. Of course. Forgive me."

"There—listen....Not ten feet distant: a blade of grass twists up to drink the yellow sun. And there....Well. Happily, you and the others are spared this constant barrage of blood and blood-ied nature. Life endlessly reinventing and devouring itself."

"My Lady?"

"See that small conifer at the far edge of the clearing? A weasel has taken a meadow vole." She set her needlework aside. "War and death, disease and suffering. Monstrous deeds of self-ish women; the bloody crimes of surly men. Europe a rotted shell. My infant son born twisted, dead, unfinished. Morgase gone."

"And yet you live. The Royal and Holy Blood has found its Eden, Lady. As you strengthen, the sacred cauldron of the five trees will yearn to be filled again. Lord Ard will be brought from Frislandia. There will be another child. With you restored, the great work will begin. The time has come. Temple Knights have re-emerged to build a New Jerusalem. And in the breast of our dominion, the Royal and Holy Heart will beat secure. You and your children, My Lady, and theirs, will rule this New World until the next great turning of the wheel."

Mimkitawo'qu'sk was touched by the tenderness with which Henry addressed Eugainia. "See how kind he is, Keswalqw? Perhaps the 'Enry Orkney comes especially to show The People his great canoe with its wind-catching blankets. Comes to share, to give knowledge and receive our wisdom; we'll learn the other's tongue. He'll show me how to make a great canoe. I'll give him wisdom. You The People's medicine. This is good."

"Perhaps it's good. Perhaps not. Eu'gaini'a. Once she had strong medicine. Something weakens her."

Eugainia rose. "This will not do."

She refused Henry's hand, stepped from the litter to the ground.

"My Lady?"

"I can't lay about like some half-living thing." She approached the table. "What are these?"

"Maps. Fragments, really. Somewhere out there, encoded here, is the route to the Grail Castle, and the Well of Baphomet."

"The southwest quadrant is incomplete."

"Admiral Zeno has the critical fragment. The segment held by the Vatican these last hundred years bears the key and is of particular interest. First we'll find the Grail Castle, then the Well of Baphomet."

"No," Eugainia's tone was flat and cold. "First the Well of Baphomet and the Stone Grail."

"Circumstances have changed, My Lady."

"I yearn for her comfort."

"We have no idea where the Well of Baphomet and the Stone Grail are, Eugainia. Like as not it's a long and perilous journey. One thousand, one hundred and fifty souls taken in an instant. We've lost all but fifty of our numbers. I haven't enough men to properly protect you—"

"Protect me? From whom? These sweet people?"

"I can't guarantee your safety."

"Go ahead. Reconstruct the Grail Castle first. Then install my skeleton. That's what I'll be unless I am refreshed by the Stone Grail. And that soon."

"I thought to secure you, then fetch your Lord; by now he will have reached the Friars of—"

"The poor old fool."

"My Lady. He dotes on you."

"Mindlessly, as dotage dotes. *Reclamation* lies on her side in the mud of the bay. You say yourself we have no men to spare, no crew. Leave old Ard in Frislandia to fade among the friars."

"He is your husband."

"I will never submit myself to such humiliation again. I'd rather consign the Holy Blood to oblivion."

"All I ask is two months, My Lady. I'll have your husband here by summer's end."

"Husband!" Eugainia fixed Henry with a cold, hard stare. "How should I call that desiccated old *queue sur l'étagère* husband? He brought the Goddess a feeble, misshapen child. I'm saturated with the Holy Blood. I've no more need of poor old Ard."

Mimkitawo'qu'sk stepped from the sweat lodge into the sunlight. Eugainia watched the hide flap fall back into place.

"I need the Source," she said. "I need the Holy Grail."

Mimkitawo'qu'sk walked the short distance to the fire. Eugainia lingered on his strong tapered back, followed the glistening trail of sweat running down to powerful thighs and legs.

"The Well of Baphomet and the Stone Grail, Lord Henry. Then the Grail Castle. These are my priorities. And your orders."

Eugainia walked toward the terrace trial. Henry followed.

"My Lady—"

"Let me alone."

"We hoped you'd stay, and direct our council."

"You know my wishes."

Henry returned to his table. In the middle of the clearing, her green dress glittering, Eugainia raised her arms to the sun, arched her back, sighed and continued on her way. Mimkitawo'qu'sk stared after her.

"I was wrong. She is not like the larch after all," Mimkitawo'qu'sk said. "She has great Tree Power. Power of the great pine. I see that now."

"Yes. Pine and oak."

"From such Power, Tree Power, came Lnu'k—The People," Mimkitawo'qu'sk said. "*E'e!* She is beautiful."

Eugainia slipped into forest shadows, unaware that Keswalqw followed silently behind.

CHAPTER FOUR

It was some time before Sir Athol reappeared in the meadow, Templar tunic ablaze, three paces behind Antonio Zeno. Mimkitawo'qu'sk sat near the sweat-lodge entrance. Antonio's glance passed over him as though he were no more than a stick or a stone. Antonio wore moccasins Mimkitawo'qu'sk had made with his own hands, moosehide moccasins taken from his own feet, going barefoot until he'd had a chance to cure, tan, cut and stitch another pair for himself. Open-handedness was central to The People's nature. Goods circulated easily. The tribe's needs superseded one's own. In The People's cosmos, guests were honoured without question. Antonio Zeno's lack of grace was noted. What interested The People more was Henry's generosity. *Reclamation* was open to all, her contents judiciously shared.

Mimkitawo'qu'sk forced his attention back to his task, shredding broad, fragrant tobacco leaves into strips. He raised each dry leaf in a perfunctory manner, the ritual today lacking solemn purpose. The preparation of the *nespipagn* respectfully alerts the Creator that prayers will soon arise on its smoke. He stuffed the shredded *nespipagn* roughly into a small leather pouch.

Antonio approached the canopied table, settled in what had been Athol Gunn's chair. He shuffled the maps, awaiting the arrival of Prince Henry who had strategically retreated, seeking the advantage of last arrival to strengthen his hand in the negotiations to come.

Mimkitawo'qu'sk calmed himself, apologized to the *nespipagn*.

This is no way to prepare, he thought, struggling to defuse his annoyance. I'm sorry, Great Spirit. But that little man, that little dark Anto'nio...from the moment we met, he wanted to cut me in pieces. He wanted to feed my body to the wolves, then scatter the ashes of my bones to the Six Worlds. 'Enry Orkney, he wouldn't permit it. Did he not know this would be the end of Mimkitawo'qu'sk for all time? No man or woman, no creature of woods or meadow, no bird of the air or fish of the sea may return from the Ghost World if their bones are not preserved. I don't like this Anto'nio. He is *Jipijka'maq*, Horned Serpent Person. He bursts into the Earth World from the World Below the Earth, and leaves a trail of destruction and woe.

In one clean motion, Mimkitawo'qu'sk rose from his cross-legged position, rose straight up without bending his torso, without the use of his hands. Up he flowed, pivoting as he ascended and, without pause, vanished into the shadow of the trees.

Henry paused at the edge of the clearing. Antonio waited to be formally addressed for no reason other than to impress his authority. How uncertain of himself he must be, Henry thought as he approached the prim and priggish little figure. And how unlike his brother Nicolo Zeno, heaven rest him.

No explanation for the long delay was offered, none asked.

"Well, Lord Henry," Antonio began, certain his quick glance at Henry's tunic had been noted. "I see despite your great charade these past months the dogged Templars rise again."

"We never died."

"It comes as no surprise. Though I expected you'd wait until you'd rid yourself of your obligations to my family and were shed of me to don your heretical rags."

Henry held his peace.

Antonio extracted the Vatican-held quadrant of the Grail Map from its tooled leather case, roughly the same shape and size of those already displayed, openly and in good faith, before him. He lay the rolled fragment in his lap, folded his hands, rested them lightly on the table.

Antonio waited.

Henry waited.

Then...

"Before we begin, Admiral Zeno, let me remind you: I require *Reclamation* immediately after her repairs are—"

"You take a high tone, Lord Henry. I remind you: the ship is mine. Before you dash away on your zealot's quest, you'd do well to remember what prizes you may unearth in this new land are already owned. All is claimed in the name of His Holiness Pope Boniface IX, this day, July 5, in the year of Our Lord one thousand three hundred and ninety-eight."

"This isn't Europe, Antonio. We're a long way from the crowned head upon which, given half a chance, you'd cock the feathered hat of your ambitions. No papal provenance is established here. Quite the opposite, in fact. Look about you. History tells us Templars walked these hills one hundred years ago, almost to the day. Far as the eye can see, and beyond. We were here first, my dear man. The future wears the Templar cross, not that of papal Rome."

"The 'future' will be plucked like an overripe plum when we decide the time is right." Antonio lifted the ragged map from his lap, secured it firmly under his arm. "Without my southwest quadrant, you are lost."

"That fragment was torn from Templar maps, wrenched

from our broken hands by Inquisitorial hounds of Rome not fifty years ago—"

"Maps first stolen by bloody Templar Knights from heathen Arabie."

Henry leaned back. He folded his hands in his lap. "Let me remind you, merchant, without my Templar maps your fragment leaves you deaf, blind and dumb. We had a deal. If you wish to reconsider—"

"I do not."

"Good. Then let's begin again. These three fragments spread before you—in all good faith—lead to the Gold River. The fragment you withhold bears the key to our destina—"

"Yes, yes. Your hole in the ground at the edge of the sea. We know what you seek. We also know where the true Grail lies— in His Holiness's vaults at Rome. Off you go. Waste your time. We don't care. Nor would we give a fig for the pile of rubble you intend to restore—your so-called Grail Castle. Nor the counterfeit paragon, the close-bred girl you call Goddess and intend to install as queen of your New Arcadia."

"*Radix malorum est cupiditas.* We have only to sit by and watch your fate unfold, Antonio. Your love of gold will be your undoing. In the meantime, will we or nil we, you and I have no alternative but to co-operate."

"There's always an alternative to co-operation."

"But none to servility," Henry replied.

Antonio's hands fell back to his lap, where he held them loosely joined, jewelled fingers interlaced. "We're reduced to one ship, which you may use when I'm finished. Then, with your business done, we return to France and go our separate ways, as agreed."

"You raise an interesting point. What prevents you from sailing back to Italy when *Reclamation* is repaired?"

Henry's question hung until he chose to answer it himself.

"Ah, yes. The paper admiral. You'll have a ship but no crew. We were aware of the wolves you attempted to conceal in our fold before we embarked. Most of our lambs and the greater number of your wolves lie drowned, may God forgive the sins that brought His tempest down upon all of us. Supposing you could seduce a bare-bones crew from amongst my men. You might even augment it by enslaving some of these good people—God and the Goddess know you've enslaved whole nations before. Even then...there remains one problem—you don't know the way home. As to the future? I put my faith in God, as always."

"You set sail from Edinburgh, of your own free will, encumbered with the weight and might of the One True Church at Rome. Men of honour acknowledge their debts."

Henry rose, walked to the edge of the high bank. The waters below teemed with the means to sustain life: seal and walrus littered coastal islands in the hundreds and thousands; forests ran with game; the sky flocked with swan, duck, partridge, quail and pheasant. He'd watched as flights of geese and pigeon darkened the sky. What could cause his New Arcadia—his kingdom of the Grail—to fail to flourish here?

A wayward breeze disturbed the strait's glassy calm. The sun, exalting in its own glory, sent light glancing off the rippling surface until the passing breeze abated and the mirror was restored. Henry drew great strength from long panoramas spilling from elevated landscapes, carrying the eye to a far horizon, lifting spirit and imagination up to the veiled glory of heaven itself. A sky this blue, its bold, improbable clouds arranged as in a child's drawing, never failed to deepen Henry's sense of gratitude and of wonder.

He returned to the table, his moment's doubt dissolved, the sting of the insult dispersed. He did not sit.

"Who dared sail west, past Frislandia, past Engronelanda, to savage Estotiland, then the new found land itself?" Henry asked Antonio. "No crowned king of Europe. Not your bloated pope at Rome. No Venetian scion imposing Rome's belligerent misery. It was my people. Northern fishers. Adventurers. Sailors drawn from hearth and home, bound for the greater glory of the Goddess and Her earthly God. When we've found what we seek, *Reclamation* will be at your service, as agreed, with free men of my choosing set to sail her where you will. Take her back to Venice and be damned. It makes no difference to me."

"Strand you here?"

"Was it not your original plan? When the time is ripe for my return, I'll simply build another ship." Henry resumed his seat. "Athol. Conduct the exchange."

"Yes, My Lord. Lay the fragments on the table, each of you. Then step back," Athol directed. "I'll hand them simultaneously."

The fragments were passed hand to hand, unrolled and laid flat. Rot had consumed both ink and hide: patches of mould obscured much of what remained. Where patterns should be clear, the mysteries deepened.

Henry scrutinized the Vatican quadrant.

"Ancient, beyond doubt. The mark of the library at Alexandria. It's a miracle it has survived."

Mimkitawo'qu'sk emerged from the spruce surround carrying two willow-ribbed birchbark pails from each of which he withdrew slings of woven roots, both thoroughly soaked and dripping water. He lay them close to the rocks shimmering with heat, took up a stout forked stick. He manipulated a hot stone into the centre of each hissing sling, hefted them to test their weight, secured rough handgrips padded with meadow grass against blistering the skin of his palms. He gingerly made for the sweat lodge, glancing at the table as he passed.

Henry rotated the fourth quadrant, first clockwise then, still baffled, a full one hundred and eighty degrees to the left.

"We were led to believe this fragment would render our predecessors' maps complete," Henry said, his suspicion aroused.

A certain sense of order began to emerge for Sir Athol, "No, no. It's here. Look."

He repositioned the fragments. "This is the northwest, I say, the northwest quadrant." Athol raised his hand from the map, pointed northeast to the red island across the strait. Mimkitawo'qu'sk emerged from the sweat lodge. He caught Sir Athol's gesture.

"And this, the northeast," Sir Athol continued, indicating the map. "Look. There's the red island, remarkable for its mastworthy pine. Note, I say, note, how elegantly its trees are represented on the map. Very like the real thing I might add."

Mimkitawo'qu'sk approached the table. The image spoke aloud to him immediately. "How is this drawing made?" he asked his uncomprehending visitors, to no reply. He held the opinion that if one spoke quietly, and slowly, all would be understood. He spoke slowly, softly and carefully. "It…looks…very… old." Blank faces stared back. He knew persistent repetition was the best teacher when dealing with the tribe's children, or those slow of wit, and saw no reason to apply other tactics here.

"We have a marking system as well. The Old Ones say persons from across the sea with hair as black as ours, not berry- or sun-coloured like yours, and brown with eyes the colour of oak bark—not sky-coloured—came from the far side of the sea. You came from the home of winter. They came from the place where summer lives. Came in ships made of reeds. The old tales, they tell their ruler's name was Pharo…"

Blank gazes showed they understood nothing of what he was saying. "The place where summer lives," he repeated, pointing south. "The place from where summer comes and sends winter back to the home of all cold." He pointed north. Nothing. He pointed south. Bafflement.

"Anyway," Mimkitawo'qu'sk persevered, "they brought picture signs that speak, like these, a long time gone by, back beyond the distant edge of story and of memory. See this picture mark here? It is like our picture mark for creek. And that island? These picture marks beside the drawing mean Apekwit."

"What's he saying?" Antonio asked.

"That word *Apekwit*...it's what they call the red island," Athol ventured. "I heard it mentioned frequently." He turned to Mimkitawo'qu'sk. "We had a grand weekend there, didn't we laddie! He's a great wee lad, this Mimk— Mimtic—"

"Mimkitawo'qu'sk," said Mimkitawo'qu'sk, laughing. "My name is Mimkitawo'qu'sk—how many times do I have to tell you?" he repeated, purposefully running the words together in one breath, smiling broadly.

"What's he saying?" Antonio repeated.

"That enormously long, half-whispered, extremely sibilant word appears to be his name. What a time we had! I say, what a time! Sang and danced the nights away. I introduced the bagpipes. They became great admirers of my skill, I say, great admirers, clearly much moved by the blessed pipe's music, all my stirring chants and mournful laments. Oh my. Aye. We walked delightful beaches—mile after mile of pinkish, golden sands, which they stroll for no apparent reason other than to chat among themselves, and walk off the excesses of the previous night, which are considerable and varied. There were dozens there. Not only the folk from around this bay, but their clans, and clan-friends who appeared to have come from great distances out of the northwest. They chat, laugh, take serious council, play at games of strength. Games of skill and courage. And they bathe! Daily! Some several times a day. Apparently for the pleasure of it! What madness. I can comprehend a bath after a long sea voyage. Or bloody great good battle. If absolutely, I say, if absolutely, necessary. They're forever hopping out of their leather clothes—scant though they be—and leaping into the salty sea. The men on one side of an outcropping; the women, secluded from prying eyes, on the other. I myself waded one day—not above my ankles, mind. The water on the red isle's northern shore is unnaturally warm. The beach slopes gently, stretching far offshore. The young lads dive from the sandstone rocks into shallow bays, three or four fathom, clear as crystal, swim like otters to the bottom and return to the surface, a lobster in either hand! Lobster, gentlemen, I say, lobster as big as cats and in great number. Bays and tidal rivers, rich beyond description, creep with all manner of crustacea. I gorged on clams, mussels, enormous oysters succulent and abundant. Near their main encampment luxuriant meadows abound, ripe with vine and berry. And, my! The vistas across the numerous bays and rivers. And the colours! Red-earth cliffs, blue sea and sky—the sky is vast—and the rolling landscape shows more shades of green then old Hibernia herself. Aye. The red island. It is a pretty place this Apekwit."

"Yes, A'thol! Apekwit." Mimkitawo'qu'sk pointed to the island, and then to the map. "Good for you. Means the-side-of-a-boat-when-you-see-it-a-long-way-off-and-it-is-low-in-the-water. We call it cradle-on-the-waves for short."

They looked at Mimkitawo'qu'sk, each blank as though they'd been struck on the back of the head with a stout plank.

"Apekwit," he repeated kindly, pointing again to the island.

"A-peg-weit?" Henry ventured.

"Yes. More or less," Mimkitawo'qu'sk replied. "No one lives there year-round. The winters are abysmal. No moose or caribou. No bear. We use A-pek-weit," he said, again with careful, exaggerated emphasis, "as a summer place of feasting and repose."

Henry smiled at Mimkitawo'qu'sk and nodded his thanks. "The sooner we master their gentle tongue, the better," he said.

Antonio was less willing to accommodate. "Pander at you peril, Sinclair. Let them come to us if they wish to know what we have to offer. Which is nothing less than ease full toil and life eternal."

Mimkitawo'qu'sk liked nothing about this man, in particular his high-pitched, tuneless, crudely whittled flute-stick voice. He returned to the fire.

Sir Athol cocked his head, first left, then to the right. "Rotate, I say, rotate your parchments. Like this. The segments integrate...just so."

Henry examined the edge of the Vatican quadrant closely. Had it been torn, the rip altered to mimic antique degradation?

"Antonio. I believe we're missing a fragment...here, the lower left."

"It's all I was given." Antonio drew his finger under two lines of elaborate script. "This seems familiar but makes no sense; it's neither Latin nor Persian, nor is it ancient Greek."

Henry studied the script. "Elements of all three, but something else. Something more ancient, perhaps. The illustration offers a clue. Steam or smoke rising from what appears to be a hollowed-out stump....It is at this point we are to base our explorations. So I was told."

"By whom?" Antonio enquired.

83

"The highest possible authority."

"Some senile *éminence grise* of your defunct temple directed you to establish your base camp at a stump? A burning stump?"

Mimkitawo'qu'sk re-approached. He studied the map. "The Place of Boiling Waters. Under the Cape which the setting sun turns to gold."

"Sorry. What?" Henry asked.

Mimkitawo'qu'sk glanced at the map, raised his arm, held it straight and steady.

"He points westward and slightly to the south," Athol noted. "What's there?"

Mimkitawo'qu'sk fluttered the fingers of his upturned hands rapidly, the hands rising and falling slightly to suggest liquid turbulence. "The Place of Boiling Waters." He repeated the gesture cycle.

"Something about a bird, perhaps? Or birds?" Henry speculated.

"Far across the waters from the cliffs of Kluscap," he said.

He searched their faces: nothing.

"Across from Kluscap's Cliffs."

"What?" Henry said.

"Come again?" said Athol.

"What's he pointing at?" Antonio wondered.

"I don't understand." Henry turned back to the maps.

Back at the fire, Mimkitawo'qu'sk dipped the slings in their buckets, spread them on the ground, rolled a second stone into each. He loped gingerly back to the sweat lodge, maintaining a gap between the steaming rocks and his naked calves. As he stooped to enter, laughter rushed up the trail behind him.

Keswalqw and Eugainia burst into the clearing at a full run, Keswalqw chased by Eugainia. It was Eugainia's hands

Mimkitawo'qu'sk first noticed. They were covered in black, sticky goo. Glistening sludge covered her from head to foot. Little natural skin colour remained, only two white circles where she'd squinted to save her eyes. They seemed to pop out of her head— the startled enthusiasm lending a bizarre infantile authority. Nothing of the sea green linen dress, or its crystal embellishments, remained visible. The curtain of tar it had become clung to Eugainia's every curve, concave, convex and otherwise.

"*E'e!*" exclaimed Mimkitawo'qu'sk, then laughed with delight.

"My Lady," Henry rubbed finger and thumb at the hem of her sleeve. "You're covered in pitch!"

"Below the Smoking Mountain, just there, is a hot, tranquil spring. A plume of tar rises through its waters, Henry—very like St. Katherine's healing well at Castle Rosslyn, where skin troubles vanish and a riotous stomach becomes sweet and refreshed." She massaged tar through her scalp, twisting matted hair into long black ropes. "Not that I drank the gruesome stuff." Her voluptuous red lips, where the tar had been licked away, amplified the wildly exaggerated eyes. "I floated among the little islands of tar, relieved for a time of my sorrows. I had the Goddess urge to cover myself entirely in it. And so I did. Watch this!"

She strode to the centre of the meadow.

"*Alors, mes amis. Un concours!* A little contest! *Tableau vivant.* Guess who I am!"

She angled her feet, the left foot at ninety degrees to her body, the right foot at ninety degrees to the left. She swivelled, aligning hips, shoulder and leading leg. She drew herself to her full height, lengthening upward through the spine. She raised her left arm. With her right hand, she removed an imaginary arrow from its quiver, threaded its notch and sighted along the invisible shaft.

"Well...come, gentlemen. Who am I?"

Silence. She looked toward Henry. Then Athol. Her eyes slid past Antonio, past Keswalqw and rested on Mimkitawo'qu'sk.

"I am Diana the huntress, bow drawn, arrow about to be loosed."

Eugainia knew the illusion depended upon artifice and impeccable detail. She drew the arrow back beyond her right shoulder, careful the imagined string would avoid her very real right breast when the string, were it real, was released. She paused, elongated, elegant, eternal; still as black marble.

Mimkitawo'qu'sk smiled.

A pulse of energy rose from Eugainia's feet to her torso. She let the imagined arrow, carefully set in the mind's eyes of her audience, fly. Her strategy worked. All eyes watched the invisible arrow soar, followed its imagined trajectory...all eyes but Mimkitawo'qu'sk's. Eugainia looked the young man straight in the eye, unobserved for one brief moment by Henry, Athol or Keswalqw. Mimkitawo'qu'sk held her gaze. Delight pulsed between them, hung in the air like perfume, and stirred their loins.

"Now who am I?" she said, walking among them, turning sharp angles first to the left, then the right, back then forward again, unwinding what appeared to be thread or twine from a spool. Again, nothing from the observers. She passed close to Sir Athol, whispered so that only he could hear.

"You are Ariadne unwinding the Golden Thread," Sir Athol proclaimed. "I say, Ariadne in the maze of the Minotaur, that foul product of bestial lust!"

"Excellent, Sir A!" Eugainia enthused with a conspiratorial wink. "Ariadne I am!"

She executed a perfect set of cartwheels, struck another pose, feet apart, knees bent and splayed. She crossed her eyes, opened them wide. She waggled her head. Her pink tongue darted through red lips, her white teeth startling in the black field of her face. Her arms jerked in unison through dual arcs from her waist, up over her head.

Her audience stared dumbfounded, their patience wearing thin.

"Perhaps Maha Durga is a touch arcane, considering the northern sensibility of my slack-jawed audience," she said aloud to no one in particular. "Maha Durga? The many-armed Hindu goddess of war. Invincible when armed with her various weapons." She surveyed the spectators. Still nothing. She walked to the centre of the clearing. "You disappoint me, Antonio. You of all people might have gotten Maha. Your family's been to the Indies, haven't they?"

Antonio nodded assent.

The sun fell below the tops of the spruce trees. Pyramid shadows gathered around Eugainia. She raised her left hand slowly until it came to rest near her downcast cheek, wrist straight, fingers curled in toward the palm. She raised the index finger heavenward. She crooked her right arm at the elbow. Her right hand lay, palm open, below her breasts, awaiting the birth of her heart. She dropped her eyes, her head angled modestly, her glance cast downward and to the left.

Eugainia stood silent and immobile. A moment of ancient artifice flicked though the meadow with the last of the afternoon light.

"And who am I now?" she murmured to the gathering dusk.

Keswalqw and Mimkitawo'qu'sk looked from the living statue radiating peace to her enraptured audience.

Sir Athol knelt. As did Henry.

"You are the Black Madonna." Henry lowered his eyes.

"I am indeed. You, my Good Lord Henry, protector and unprompted friend, win the final round!"

She attempted a handstand. The first attempt failed. The second? Perfect. Exactly vertical. She held it, the newfound strength in her inverted body apparent. The muscles in her upper arms began to twitch with strain. She struggled to remain vertically reversed, hand-walking a tight circle in the centre of the meadow. Her pitch-stiffened skirt, plastered to her legs, sagged and fell over her head. Embarrassed by her own impropriety if not her blackened undergarments, she aborted the trick, regained her feet. She giggled.

"Ha! You should see your faces. Henry, you are as red as rhubarb. And burly good Sir Athol, a brace of flies could circumnavigate your gaping yaw and exit dry and unharmed. And you, Antonio," she said with unfelt gravity. "Well...you smirk in an unkind way. I regret to inform you the Lady of the Grail hasn't lost her mind. Not completely. Not yet, at least."

Keswalqw and Mimkitawo'qu'sk returned, amused and unconcerned, to their tasks.

"How unlike your reactions compared to those of my new friends," Eugainia observed. "You shuffle and avoid my gaze. Keswalqw and Mimkitawo'qu'sk carry on, happy I'm resurrected."

Henry rallied. "I am delighted, My Lady. Your spirits do seem quite restored!"

"They are indeed." Eugainia ran to the centre of the meadow, she threw her head back, her arms shot straight out from her shoulders, she began to twirl. "For the first time in months, dear Lord Protector," she said, her rope hair springing snakelike from her tarred Medusa head. "Though covered in blackest pitch, I feel clean."

She staggered, righted herself. Henry stepped forward, then held his uncertain place.

"That's all very well, Eugainia, and I couldn't be more pleased. But I caution you. Restrain yourself, my dear. We can't have you injured or, worse still, addled beyond the council we require."

Eugainia fell to her knees. A wretched, histrionic look spread across her tar-smeared face. She raised her arms. She wavered. Henry rushed to her support. Too late. She fell, face forward, into the grass where she heightened Henry's anxiety by rolling and laughing in ecstasy.

Mimkitawo'qu'sk passed nearby, a rock hissing in its sling. "What's she doing now, Aunt?" he asked casually.

Keswalqw watched from the sweat-lodge entrance. "She's putting all the parts of herself back together. Now...? Tree person experimenting with dog person form. I wouldn't be surprised if at any moment she starts to bark."

"Oh," said Mimkitawo'qu'sk, and continued with his business, unfazed by what to the Europeans was extraordinary behaviour, but what to him and Keswalqw was a mild and unremarkable aspect of an ordinary spirit quest—a damaged spirit healing itself with spirit-leavening fun.

Eugainia sprung to her feet, grass and twigs and all manner of bracken stuck to her. She lunged at Prince Henry. He dodged her gooey embrace. She barked like a dog.

"Woof! Hah! Woof. Woof! Woof!"

"*E'e, ee*," said Mimkitawo'qu'sk. "Just as you predicted, Aunt."

Eugainia growled. She lunged at Antonio.

"The poor creature's barking mad," he said, backing away.

Keswalqw smiled. "I feared I'd given her too much. This is a good sign, you know, these antics of hers. Means the *gi'gwesuasgw* is working. Her spirit stirs, wishing to escape the hole in The World Below the Earth into which it tumbled, dragged into darkness by the spirit of her dead child."

"Eugainia," Henry said, his grimace out of balance with his words, "delighted as I am to see you animated and, ah, florally embellished—"

Eugainia, threw back her head, bayed like a hound. She launched another frontal assault. Henry held his ground—and Eugainia—at arm's-length, evading her gooey clench.

"Please, my dear," he said. "Collect yourself. "

"Must I?"

"You must. We need your advice."

"Yes, yes. All right," she relented.

Henry and Antonio resumed their places at the table. Sir Athol stood uneasy between them.

Eugania's attention wandered when Mimkitawo'qu'sk stooped, entered the sweat lodge with his third load of rocks.

"My Lady?"

"Ummm? Ah yes. Back to the business of Utopia." It's all so tedious and deeply false, she thought as she settled before the maps. "Now. Show me the location of the Well of Baphomet."

CHAPTER FIVE

Antonio broke off discussions, pleading lightness of head and an empty stomach. Henry agreed to a short recess. He and Athol descended to camp where a pot of venison stew awaited.

Evening light lingered in the clearing. Eugainia sat alone by the fire. She rolled the tarred linen sleeves of the once-prized gown up to her elbows. Rewarmed and less viscous, the tar soothed her skin. Her fingertips traced light circles on her cheekbones and brow.

Mimkitawo'qu'sk emerged from the sweat lodge. He watched Eugainia as she worked the tar first into the skin of one arm, then the other. He wished he was tar. He wished he were her fingertips. He wished he was the black curtain of tarred hair screening her face. He wished she'd look up.

"Bring the last rocks, Mimkitawo'qu'sk." Keswalqw adjusted the wet hides on the sweat-lodge dome. "By the time we smoke *nespipagn* and burn the *msigue'get*, the lodge will be hot enough."

"Come see their markings, Aunt."

Keswalqw joined Mimkitawo'qu'sk at the canopied table.

"Very like our picture words. But not exact. Perhaps older versions of the same things. Look...stream, cliff, village—picture words for ordinary things."

"They show where the land meets the sea in all directions. Even to the southeast of our peninsula, you see? And look at this…"

"Yes, yes. The island of the twelve standing oaks."

"And here, across the hills of two mountains, the great bay to the southwest—"

"Turned Up Whale Belly Bay."

Mimkitawo'qu'sk indicated the northwest quadrant. "This is The Place of Boiling Waters, beneath the Cape, at the head of Whale Belly Bay across from Kluscap's Cliffs."

He lifted a second map from the table, placed it beside the first.

"And there. Across the bay. The river of the yellow stones."

"*Sahkahwaychkik*, the Old Ones, said the last white-as-a-ghost-persons bore heavy sacks of the yellow stones upon their backs, even as they staggered and fell to their deaths from the blistering sickness."

"Such soft and useless things, those yellow stones."

"Children's trinkets," Keswalqw agreed. "I can't imagine their use for them."

"They look at these markings, Hen'ry Orkney and Sir Ath'ol and little dark Jipijka'maq, but their minds are clouded with ignorance. They know nothing."

"Poor unwitting creatures. It might be ill-mannered of us to interfere. Wait until they're ready, ready to receive the wisdom of The People."

"They are ready. Both Ath'ol and Hen'ry Orkney ask my opinion. Which I give, leaving them even more baffled. I wonder how long they'll stay."

"They show no signs of leaving."

"Is it possible for them to learn, do you think?"

"Yes, yes. Eugainia learns very quickly. I've mastered quite a few of their words."

"Am I to learn their grunting, fishbone-stuck-in-the-throat, rat-tat-tat tongue?"

"Yes, Nephew. Why would you not? You know the language of the earth and all her creatures. Why not these?"

Mimkitawo'qu'sk and Keswalqw failed to notice Antonio until he was upon them. He leaned in from the opposite side of the table, his fingers splayed atop the charts—a clear warning.

Mimkitawo'qu'sk smiled. "What do you say, Jipijka'maq. Should I learn your tongue? Would we have anything of interest to say to each other, you and I?"

Malice marked Antonio's unspoken response.

"Silent and watchful as a snake, aren't you?" Antonio stared dumbly. Mimkitawo'qu'sk walked away.

Eugainia leaned to the heat of the firepit, now a bowl of glowing embers. She massaged tar through her hair to the scalp. She was unaware of Mimkitawo'qu'sk until he rolled the last hot rock onto the steaming sling. Driblets of tar flared into flame among ashes when she turned and raised her face toward him.

"Why do the savages insist on speaking to me," Antonio asked Sir Athol who emerged from the trail carrying two shoulder-height torches, "when they know I don't understand a single word?"

"They know the territory hereabout as we know the palm of our hand. The more we know of their tongue, and vice versa, the better."

Athol drove the torches into the ground at either end of the table. He touched an ember to the frayed, tarred head of each. One easy breath...a flicker became a flame. Athol disappeared in the growing shadow of the evergreen surround, descended toward the main encampment to fetch Prince Henry.

Antonio was thrown into stark relief in the surging light of the torches. He angled his chair away from the table, the better to keep an eye on Mimkɨtawo'qu'sk and Keswalqw. He sat grim and silent, awaiting Henry and the conclusion of their discussion.

Mimkɨtawo'qu'sk loped past with the last of the hissing stones. "He *is* Jipijka'maq I think," he said when he reached the sweat lodge. "Look at him in this light. He's all circles and curves, sinuous and boneless as a serpent."

"Hush." Keswalqw held back the door flap. "We don't know for certain that Anto'nio doesn't understand."

"What if he does?"

Antonio felt a presence beside him. Eugainia stood at the table, drawing her fingers through her hair. Antonio drew the maps to him.

"Calm yourself, admiral. I'm not about to befoul artifacts sent to save my life."

Eugainia's attention moved across the parchment from east to west, where artfully executed hills and forest trailed off into blank space dominated by two words: *Terra Incognita.* Her attention remained fixed on the short phrase. She could not say what occupied her thoughts for one simple reason: her mind was blissfully and unusually silent. Try as she might, she could pull no meaning, only presentiment, from the chart fragments. Though she felt the words before her were freighted with meaning, something in the vastness of possibility suggested by the maps flooded her with peace. She sensed a lightening of spirit. These portents were good. Eugainia smelled freedom.

Antonio broke the silence.

"It seems this steambath is prepared for you."

"Oh?"

"These savages are like as not to cut your throat as you drowse," Antonio warned.

"You've no interest in these good people beyond what you can tear away and carry off, do you? Where you see savages, I see shining hair and skin like silk. They smell of earth and smoke, their hair scented by the forest and sea air. Our garments crawl with vermin. Our bodies stink. I see strong white teeth…not grey stumps and yellow pegs black with rot. We rarely see the age of forty. Their elders are fit, clear of eye and mind and easily thrice your age. I've seen them with their children, sir, some with as many as five generations of progeny in whom they delight. The love and respect children give their elders is as pure as any I have seen."

Keswalqw and Mimkɨtawo'qu'sk returned to the fire where they settled. Keswalqw added enough wood to revive a moderate flame. Mimkɨtawo'qu'sk kept a close eye on Antonio.

"Look at her," Mimkɨtawo'qu'sk said. "Such strength and beauty. I yearn to know what she's saying."

"She floated on the surface of the smoking pool," Keswalqw told him. "Like a leaf she turned this way and that, her yellow hair spread around her like rays of Grandfather Sun. She sang to the Ghost World. To her dead child. To her kin-friend, the old woman. She sang a sad and lonely song."

"Perhaps she sings a birth song to a new child's father. Perhaps she'll let me sing a new child to her. I wish to speak with her, Aunt. To know her. Eu-gain-i-a. But she looks at me with shaded eyes, as though I was a flame too bright."

"You flatter yourself, Mimkɨtawo'qu'sk. She avoids your eyes because you stare like a hungry child."

Antonio turned the amethyst ring on his index finger. "Renounce your heretical fantasy, madam. Say aloud 'I am merely flesh and bone. Human, not divine.' I can guarantee your safety wherever you choose to live for as long as God in heaven grants you breath."

"I'm exhausted by the endless wars waged in Our Holy

Names—King Solomon, Good King David, Lord Krishna, the blessed Lord Muhammad, Peace be upon him. I'm sickened by the blood spilled, first in the name of the Prince of Peace and now in mine. Nonetheless, I am here. I am alive. I am God's emissary on this earth. I do God's will. Not yours. Nor that of your bloated pope at Rome."

"Insult piled upon heresy, madam. Small matter. My cousin and the Holy Church suffer your presence, your life, because we require Sinclair's maps and his knowledge of the northern seas. You're merely an annoyance, the tattered Queen of defeated zealots who nip at the robes of our authority, and will not come to heel."

Unseen by Eugainia or Antonio, Mimkitawo'qu'sk left the circle of light and drifted back into shadow, prepared to intervene should he feel Eugainia endangered. He stood unseen not three metres from her side. He felt strength and assurance—no threat of danger—in her voice. He stepped back.

"If I so choose I'd give Lord Henry a sign and you'd be nothing more than wretched memory. We knew precisely what and who you were before we struck our devil-deal. You needed us. We needed you. Our time of mutual need will soon end."

Eugainia sat in Henry's chair.

"Here is my response to your...clement offer," Eugainia concluded. "I bear you no ill will, Admiral Zeno. Quite the opposite. I give you my love. Let kindness flood your heart, and forbearance grow in mine. Peace be with you."

What man, no matter the coldness of a fearful heart, refutes a pledge of fraternal or sororal love? Zeno's response formed but withered, unspoken. He rolled his map segment, bowed and left the clearing.

Mimkitawo'qu'sk reappeared from shadow. He sat opposite

Eugainia, in what had been Antonio's chair. He loosened the drawstrings of a small hip pouch, withdrew a willow-wood pipe, its shaft attached to an intricately carved stone bowl. He packed the assembled pipe with shredded *nespipagn*.

Henry followed Athol into the torch's dual circles of light. Keswalqw beckoned them toward the fire.

"Eu-gain-ia. Mimkitawo'qu'sk. You come too, please," Keswalqw said. "All, please come join."

Keswalqw opened a large clamshell. With delicate tongs carved from deer antler, she extracted a live ember packed in punk, touched it to the tobacco. Mimkitawo'qu'sk elevated the pipe, drew sharply, and exhaled. Smoke, thick and pungent, rose from the bowl. The twining vortex dissipated, a hopeful dream unmolested as it rose through the still night air. He passed the pipe to Keswalqw.

"As smoke rises, it calls down healing Power from the World Above the Sky," Keswalqw said. She inhaled deeply, exhaled slowly, watched the smoke ascend.

"What did she say?" Henry asked.

"An element of their religion," Eugainia speculated, recalling her walk up the Smoking Mountain with Keswalqw, and the spiralling flight of the spirit birds. "Smoke carries prayer to heaven. Or invites it down, I'm not sure. I still confuse their words for *up* and *down*. Ah...let me see. Oh yes. *Lame'g* is up and *gujm* is down."

"Why did she say *in* and *out*?" Mimkitawo'qu'sk wondered.

"She thinks she's saying *up* and *down*."

"She's very convincing, even when she's wrong."

"I smile and nod and pretend to know what's going on behind those sea- and sky-coloured eyes of her's. She's good with words, normally. Especially with the children."

"I smoked like a chimney on Apekwit," Athol told Eugainia as he received the pipe. "Became quite accustomed to it. Began to look for it. They finally hid it from me." He inhaled deeply before passing it on. "Can't say, I say, can't say why."

Eugainia examined the loonhead bowl. "It would be rude to refuse."

"Let me be first."

"No, Henry," Eugainia said. "It does no apparent harm. I'm next in line."

"Quite the opposite," Athol assured. "It baffles and then lifts the spirits."

Eugainia inhaled deeply, coughed, inhaled again. She held the smoke briefly, steadied herself, exhaled. "Very odd. A kind of euphoria." She inhaled again. "Very light. Pleasant."

Henry elevated the pipe, drew, savoured the smoke and exhaled. "Pungent. Very nice indeed." Another inhalation, then, "Very pleasant. I see no ill." He gestured his question to Keswalqw. "What is this?"

"*Nespipagn.*"

"*Nes-pi-pa-gen?*"

Keswalqw nodded.

Henry produced his wineskin, freed the spout, drank. In turn, Sir Athol directed the amber stream into his mouth, passed the wineskin on to Mimkitawo'qu'sk, who elevated it, aimed the stream with ease and drank. Then gagged.

Mimkitawo'qu'sk struggled to retain his composure. "It is horrible, Aunt. It tears my throat and burns my lungs."

"It has great significance to them. It would be rude to refuse."

Keswalqw took to the fiery liquid immediately. She gestured her question to Henry.

"Brandy wine."

"Bran-dy wine?"

"Yes. From my family's holdings in France....Ah...let's see. France. Across the water. Over the sea."

Keswalqw savoured the brandy. Henry withheld the pipe. The others watched amused, as Henry and Keswalqw passed tobacco and liquor back and forth, casual as old friends drifting off into the comfortable haze of what would soon become a familiar routine.

Sir Athol cleared his throat.

"Oh. I've been hogging it?"

"Aye, Henry. You have. Just a wee bit. Aye."

Henry pulled a deep draw and passed it on. He exhaled a slow stream of smoke, luxuriating in the rush of pleasure that heightened his senses without clouding thought.

Mimkitawo'qu'sk relieved Keswalqw of the wineskin, passed it along.

"Have I taken more than my share?"

"I think perhaps so, Aunt," Mimkitawo'qu'sk replied.

"At first my tongue was like an animal, caged in a burning trap," Keswalqw observed. "Then I swallowed. My mind became clear then twitched, like the skin shivers from fear or delight, not the cold. I feel light and clear."

Alcohol was well known to The People. Various brews from native fruits and berries enhanced their travels in the spirit world, and helped keep the bitter cold of winter at bay. But this. This brandy wine was something different.

Keswalqw passed the wineskin on with some reluctance. She opened a birchbark box from which she extracted several smaller boxes, double-wrapped in bark. She offered one to each, and took the last for herself. Neither Henry nor Eugainia made sense of the waxy mass inside. Athol knew the food from the red island. He dug in with gusto, scooping the contents with his index and middle fingers. "White fat, mixed with salt, nuts, seeds, dried strawberries and blueberries. Delicious."

"And honey. I taste honey. Delicious," Eugainia agreed. She turned to Mimkitawo'qu'sk. "What is it?"

"*T'iam mlageju'mi.*"

"This is very good." Henry smacked his lips. "Very tasty. A very high quality fat. But what is it?"

Mimkitawo'qu'sk turned to Keswalqw. "You see? I tell them something and they ask the very same question again."

"I find it better to tell *then* show."

"Ah! Good idea."

Mimkitawo'qu'sk set his *t'iam mlageju'mi* aside. "Watch me." He smiled at his expectant audience. "I'll…show…you…what… you're…eating."

Keswalqw seated herself cross-legged, indicated the others should do likewise. Eugainia and Henry, both naturally supple, slipped into position easily enough. Muscle-bound Sir Athol bent forward from the waist, kneeled, placed both hands on the ground, squatted, eased himself back onto his rump, manhandled his thick ankles into position under meaty calves. He shifted and grunted his way toward some semblance of comfort. Athol adjusted the folds of his great kilt too late to preserve his modesty or Keswalqw's composure. A long moment passed during which Keswalqw collected her thoughts.

"It's wonderful when the urge comes upon my nephew to show a tale. It's an urge we always encourage," she said when her thoughts and audience finally settled. "Mimkitawo'qu'sk is a great shower of The People's tales."

Mimkitawo'qu'sk gathered invisible objects around himself.

"What's he doing?" Athol wondered.

"I've no idea." Henry said.

Mimkitawo'qu'sk turned and scowled, as he might correct inattentive children. He squatted before them. "You have no idea what I'm saying, do you? I could tell you anything, you'd sit there and nod and smile like stupid, drunken animals."

"Watch closely," Keswalqw repeated. "And listen."

Eugainia smiled and nodded.

"What did they say?" Athol asked again.

"I don't know," Eugainia smiled.

"But you smile and nod as though you knew every word, I say, every word."

"How else am I to learn? By scowling and fidgeting?"

Mimkitawo'qu'sk raised a quiet, almost whispered chant.

"What was that?"

"Don't ask me, Athol." Henry's annoyance pulled at the edges of his tight, polite smile. "I don't know what he's saying anymore than you."

"Smile and nod, gentlemen. Smile and nod," said Eugainia.

Mimkitawo'qu'sk walked a small circle. A story circle. He began: "In the forest, where the high lake tumbles down into the salmon river lives our Brother the great *t'iam*."

Mimkitawo'qu'sk raised his arms, angled his elbows. He brought fisted hands to either temple. His fingers flashed open, splayed, rigid. He raised his shoulders and dropped his head. He pawed the ground with one foot. He rotated his head from side to side, slowly. He snorted. He scented the air, nose and upper lip quivering.

"Look," said Athol. "He's a large, horned...no, antlered, creature. Some kind of deer."

Mimkitawo'qu'sk's exhaled forcefully, raising a moan, the moan punctured by an unexpected grunt. His creature moved forward, at once awkward and graceful, with slow, high steps. He reverted seamlessly from the creature to himself, Mimkitawo'qu'sk the hunter. He collected his imaginary bow, slung a quiver of arrows over his shoulder, giving his audience the convincing impression of a spear. His attention shifted to the ground around at his feet.

Henry found himself completely engaged. "Let's see. He picks up his gear, and...something...some *things*...smaller than him...leap about in excitement."

"Children, perhaps?" Eugainia wondered.

Mimkitawo'qu'sk beat the overexcited figures into submission.

"God have mercy," Athol whispered. "The brute is beating his children."

Mimkitawo'qu'sk read Athol's alarm, reacted quickly. He opened his mouth and yelped like a chastised dog.

"They're dogs, Athol," Henry barked in confirmation.

Mimkitawo'qu'sk nodded and smiled. "Yes! You're no fool, Hen-ry Ork-nee. But your friend, Sir Ath-hol? Nice, but I think a little slow."

"What did he say?"

"Smile and nod, Athol," Eugainia advised. "Smile and nod."

Athol nodded and smiled.

"It is winter, and the snow is high," Mimkitawo'qu'sk continued. His creature ploughed through snow, grunting and snorting at the effort. "Our Brother *t'iam* soon tires and gives himself easily."

"It is a good winter," Keswalqw explained in an aside; her reassurance was met with smiling faces on nodding heads, eyes blank with incomprehension. "Not a starving time. There's lots of snow. The *t'iam* will soon get bogged down. Easy to kill."

"Keswalqw. They don't understand. Show, don't tell, remember?"

"Yes. Of course. Sorry, Nephew. Go on."

"I travel on the snow with my snowshoes and my dogs and I'm happy. I see that Brother t'iam knows we are hungry and will give himself to The People."

"What's he doing now?" Athol asked.

"I think...yes. He's tracking the big...antlered creature," Henry ventured. "No. The creature is stuck in the mud."

"I think it's winter. If he's stuck, he's stuck in the snow. Excuse me, Mimkitawo'qu'sk?" Eugainia said, gesturing cold, then falling snow. "Winter? Is it winter?"

Mimkitawo'qu'sk nodded and smiled. He wrapped his arms around himself, shivered. He blew hot breath into his cold hands. He mimed wind-blown snow. Long low sweeps of his body, his outstretched arms rising with each pass, indicated banks piling high among the trees. His large antlered creature became stuck once again.

"Hah! I thought so," Eugainia said. "The animal is bogged down, stuck in the snow."

"He is a most convincing comedien," Athol suggested.

Mimkitawo'qu'sk came to a wary stop. He revolved his antlered head and upper torso slowly. He scented the air. He moaned. He grunted. He quivered.

Eugainia agreed. "Most entrancing."

Athol elbowed Henry, lightly at first, then with some insistence. Henry's manners held where Athol's failed. Eugainia felt Sir Athol's glance, her attention on the handsome young hunter. Henry kept a scrupulous eye on the performer, not his ardent admirer whose cheeks he knew flushed a vibrant pink where tar had slid away in the rising heat of the fire.

"Brother t'iam smells us," Mimkitawo'qu'sk warned. "He says, 'You can't have me that easily. I'll run. If you're worthy of my life, you shall have it.' He breaks free of the deep snow. I set the dogs to run him down. They soon tire him. Once again, for the final time, Brother t'iam is caught and struggles to free himself. The dogs begin to tear his flesh. I drive them away for, like their cousin wolves, dogs kill slowly, cruelly, selfishly."

"They know no better," Keswalqw murmured.

"They tear still-living flesh from their prey's body, Aunt," Mimkitawo'qu'sk countered, his aversion of the young to death and its cruelties strong. "They snap and snarl, and in their fever—their blood fever—they turn on each other."

"They're only dogs."

"They dishonour the spirit of the creature they kill."

"Don't be so hard on them—"

"Who is telling this story, Aunt? You or I?"

"You."

"Thank you. I pull them apart, the fighting dogs, and drive my spear—my spear sharp as the tooth of the wolverine into the heart of Brother t'iam."

Mimkitawo'qu'sk raised the phantom spear over his head, one hand precisely placed above the other. He plunged it with all his force into the exhausted moose.

"Finally," said Athol, more invested than he knew, "I say, finally he killed the bloody thing."

"Shush, Athol," Henry whispered urgently. "He's not finished."

Mimkitawo'qu'sk threw back his head. "Akaia-aia-ah, akaia!" He extracted the spear, planted it in the snow beside the dying beast. "I bend low, close to Brother t'iam. I hear him speak. 'You shall give my body to The People,' he says. 'Eat my flesh. Honour my spirit. Treat my bones with respect, I will return to feed The People again.'"

Mimkitawo'qu'sk held out his hand to Henry. Henry, moved and, pleased he had followed the tale, stood to shake hands. "That was terrific. Well done, Mimktiki...Mimiko..."

Mimkitawo'qu'sk declined the handshake, indicated the pipe. "Oh. The pipe." Henry flushed. "You want the pipe." He returned red-faced to his place. "I thought he wanted to shake hands. A natural mistake, ah, Minktika— ah, Mitikimato...sorry. I, ah...sorry."

Henry sat.

Mimkitawo'qu'sk reclaimed the stage. "To thank him—my Brother *t'iam* for the gift of himself to The People—I light my pipe." He kneels. "I blow tobacco smoke into the nostrils of dying *t'iam.*"

"The smoke eases his passage," Keswalqw added quietly.

Mimkitawo'qu'sk strokes the invisible creature's snout.

"Because I show respect, and affection, and kindness, and because I promise to honour his bones, to keep them from the dogs and from fire, we know *t'iam* will come back and feed the people. In this way his life departs his body."

Mimkitawo'qu'sk and Keswalqw sat still. After a long moment of silence, Athol wondered aloud, "Now what?"

"It feels like prayer," Eugainia said quietly. "Yes. Keswalqw offers thanks, I think. They sit in silence and recall the creature's beauty and his spirit. Mimkitawo'qu'sk honours the life he has taken."

Keswalqw reached over and squeezed Eugainia's hand. Their understanding had grown far beyond what may be told by words, many of which were still beyond their grasp. A simple glance or touch conveyed the other's thoughts cleanly, with great depth of feeling, and near-perfect accuracy. When thoughts were given shape and volume, ideas crossed the baffled air between them with ease. In some way neither could articulate, their commune increased, rich with tone and feeling, their understanding expanded and accord hovered near.

"Yes, Eugainia," Keswalqw told her. "It is a prayer. In this way we honour the t'iam who makes the cheeks of our children round with fat."

Mimkitawo'qu'sk concluded the tale. "My Brother *t'iam*'s spirit will soon find another home. The rutting time is past. The season's young grow in the bellies of the females, waiting to house the wandering spirit of a fallen friend. When I know for certain *t'iam*'s spirit is gone, I cut him open and feed his entrails to the dogs."

Mimkitawo'qu'sk watched the dogs devour the guts. In his regard there rested a tinge of sorrow. He walked from the dogs who, in his mind's eye, snarled and tore at each other as they gorged, distending sagging bellies. He sat to one side, away from his audience, knowing the images he generated would flow to Henry, Keswalqw and Athol. Only Eugainia returned the thought, expanded, alive with the pain and glory Mimkitawo'qu'sk felt deep in his heart.

"To live we master our fear of death," he said at last. "We feed on death, grateful for the life we've taken. Death feeds us and death feeds upon us. In the end, death overtakes all."

"You are young, Nephew. When you reach the uncertainties of middle life, as I have, you'll learn there is nothing to fear. In the end life and death are one creature."

Keswalqw took the stage. "The women come and butcher the carcass. Back at camp, we strip the hide of fat and flesh, strip and joint his bones…"

"Bones!" Athol Gunn interjected. "Look! She's jointing bones…many a time I have done, I say, I have done the same things, as a lad at mother's wee ancestral croft when we'd flee the hurly-burly at Rosslyn for the quiet of the hills."

"We crack his bones," Keswalqw continued, "and grind them down."

"Smashing open the bones, yes?" said Athol.

"Yes, I think so," said Henry.

Keswalqw defined first a tall tree, then a segment of the trunk. She indicated the trunk and how it was hollowed out with glowing coals and embers.

"She burns the core out of the trunk," Athol offered. "To make a pot, I'll wager."

Mimkitawo'qu'sk's birchbark-and-pitch bucket became useful; Keswalqw filled the imaginary tree-trunk pot with imaginary water from the very real pail. She took up Mimkitawo'qu'sk's woven hot-rock slings, their use now familiar to the visitors.

"In a burned-out tree trunk filled with water," she says, "I drop hot, hot stones."

"We see this among the poorest of the poor when we visit your outer islands, Henry," Athol recalled. "A hollowed tree trunk—even a skin bag filled with water—serves in the absence of an iron or copper pot. The heat of the rocks boils the water and—"

"Look!" Eugainia followed Keswalqw intently. "In go the cracked bones."

Keswalqw's upward roiling motion made the process clear "Up to the top floats *mu'mi.*"

Eugainia indicated her birchbark container, extracted the last morsel with her index finger. "*Mu'mi...mu'mi...*marrow! The marrow melts, flows from the cracked bones and floats to the top." She slipped the last of the sweetened fat into her mouth. "*Mu'mi?*" she repeated.

"Yes," Keswalqw confirmed. "*Tia'mu'mi.*"

"This is the large creature's marrow." Henry observed. "Only one creature I know of could produce the marrow in such quantities."

"Moose! I thought in this New World it would be some giant exotic beast. But it's just a plain old moose! This means there are moose in the New Arcadia!"

Eugainia jumped to her feet, dropped her chin to her chest. She slowly raised her face which, streaked with tar and altered by the joy of invention, was quite transformed. She inflated her lungs. The sound that emerged was unmistakable. Part grunt, part snort, the call rose sharply, a trumpeted announcement that curled into a whine, fell into a deep-throated "humph." She repeated the call. Keswalqw laughed and clapped her hands.

Mimkitawo'qu'sk offered a broad-faced grin. "*Tia'm*, Eugainia! Exactly! You give us the cow. And here, I give you the bull."

Mimkitawo'qu'sk pawed the ground. He snorted. He swayed his head side to side, uttered the bull's harrumphing grunt, then a distressed bleat, then piteous rising and falling moans punctuated by sharp, nasal barks. The call terminated in a series of sloshing, guttural sounds, as though the moose's large wattle had filled with water, slopped back and forth, its ebb and flow reverberating in the ruminants lungs and many stomachs.

"We're eating moose marrow, mixed with herbs, nuts and honey, Lord Henry." Eugainia prized the last pine nut from the corner of her box. She repeated the cry of the female moose in estrus.

Mimkitawo'qu'sk responded with the snorting harrumph of the inflamed bull.

"Those were moose mating calls," Athol ventured quietly.

"Indeed they were," Henry replied, his enthusiasm diminishing. Sir Athol shared Henry's growing unease.

"We make a food very similar to this, Keswalqw, but in the stomach of a sheep." He persisted despite Keswalqw's blank stare. "Instead of nuts we use oats and barley, turnips and such. And, I must admit, a lower quality fat which—"

"This is hardly haggis, Sir Athol," Eugainia interrupted. She turned her attention back to the young hunter. "Mimkitawo'qu'sk," she mimed, "this is delicious!"

Mimkitawo'qu'sk smiled. Eugainia smiled in return. Mimkitawo'qu'sk left the story circle. He indicated the map fragment at the torchlit table, pointed to the symbol in question, mimed boiling water.

Athol missed the point. "What's he saying?"

Henry mistook his meaning, licked his fingers. "The place is named moose marrow? Ah, *t'ia'mu'mi̓?*"

Mimkitawo'qu'sk was encouraged. "No, Henry Orknee. Not quite." He repeated the gesture.

Eugainia copied the motion. "Water…? Boiling water…?"

Mimkitawo'qu'sk, excited, said, "*E'e!* I think she's got it, Keswalqw."

He turned Eugainia to the southwest and pointed. He indicated a distant location.

"*Eteg etligmiet samqwan.*"

"Think geography, not cuisine," Eugainia said aloud, more to herself than to Henry or Athol. "It's not just water boiling. I think it's 'where the water boils.'"

Eugainia indicated the precise spot on the map. "*Eteg etligmiet samqwan?*" she repeated distinctly.

"*E'e,*" Mimkitawo'qu'sk beamed his positive response. "*Eteg etligmiet samqwan.*"

Athol reflected on Mimkitawo'qu'sk's story. "What was all that business about the dogs and hunting? It seems a long way around to get to floating fat and boiling water."

"This man has killed a flock of birds with one stone," Eugainia explained. "He's taken us on a splendid hunt, given the name and direction to the place from which we can begin to explore. And he gave us the history of this wonderful food."

Henry offered Mimkitawo'qu'sk his hand. "I honour you, Mimkt...Mim-kitti..."

"Mim...k't...a...whoa...qwusk." She spoke softly, as to a lover. "Equal emphasis on the first and fourth syllables. His name is Mimkitawo'qu'sk."

Henry inclined his head in an abbreviated bow. "Thank you," he said. Then spoke the young man's name, at last, with ease. "Mimkitawo'qu'sk."

Mimkitawo'qu'sk nodded, pleased.

"May you walk with the Great Spirit at your side."

Mimkitawo'qu'sk shook Lord Henry's hand.

Keswalqw uncovered the ember from its punk clamshell bed. The gentle urging of her breath sparked a slender rope of sweetgrass, the hair of mother earth. Its transformation to air and smoke helped The People remember through whose world they walk. She held the sacred smoke to Mimkitawo'qu'sk. He closed his eyes. With open palms rotated upward he pulled the sweet, pungent smudge toward his face, then over and behind his head. He inhaled deeply. He completed three cleansing cycles, each strengthening his spirit.

Keswalqw stood before Eugainia. She honoured the ritual with dignity and gratitude, as did Henry and then Athol in their turn.

Keswalqw loosened an eagle feather from the thong around her neck. She circled the sweat lodge, wafting sweetgrass smoke over the hide-draped apex of the dome. The feather furled the rising smoke, urged it on its journey up through gathered darkness to the stars. Keswalqw indicated Eugainia should enter the sweat lodge.

Mimkitawo'qu'sk took his aunt aside. "What are you doing, Keswalqw?"

"Preparing to enter the sweat lodge. What does it look like?"

"The men first, Keswalqw, in our way. Not you women. You must go back to the village. I'll fetch you when we're finished."

"Who is the greatest warrior of the people?"

"I am."

"And who is the greatest shower of The People's stories."

"I am, Aunt."

"And who will become chief?"

"I will."

"And when will this happen?"

"When you, who sits in the centre of the circle, you who sits at the doorway to the spirit world, when you, who rules but does not lead, when you, keeper of the sacred Tales of the Six Worlds, when you, Great Mother of the Clan, keeper of the flame of L'nuk, The People, when you tell the grand council that I, in your opinion, am ready to be chief. Only then will it happen."

"You have kept us from the grandmother stones and their healing power long enough."

Eugainia slipped into the sweat lodge, the wineskin in her free hand. Keswalqw tucked a soft rolled package under her arm. She stooped to enter.

Inside, at Keswalqw's bidding, Eugainia removed her shoes. Keswalqw stowed the package wrapped in pliant sealskin, tied with braided spruce-root tendrils safely out of harm's way. Eugainia peeled the tarred garments from her body. With a stout stick, Keswalqw lifted the ruined linen gown from the fir-bough floor where it had fallen. She lifted the flap and called out to Mimkitawo'qu'sk. He carried her shed, tarry skinlike dress across the meadow to the fire. It flared into flame instantly, sending a thick plume of black smoke—a prayer he thought of thanksgiving and renewal—skyward.

Keswalqw emptied the contents of the birch pail directly onto the rocks. The seal-oil stone lamp, with its sweet-hay wick, disappeared in the sudden haze of steam. Heat, dense with weight and substance, struck Eugainia. She felt sweat bead on her forearm. Soon rivulets of tar dripped from her fingers to the boughs below. She inhaled deeply, held her breath, then exhaled with force. She drew her shoulders to her ears, then let them drop. A sigh arose from her belly. She felt safe and at peace.

Keswalqw took a long draught of brandy, handed the skin to Eugainia.

The torches guttered in the rising landward breeze. Henry reexamined the torn parchment, certain now the ragged tear across the bottom of the map was both strategic and recent.

"Sir Athol?"

"My Lord?"

"I think the little admiral withholds a fragment for some dark purpose of his own."

"The section of the map indicating the Grail Castle ruins, and the sacred well."

"Quite so. Take the good admiral for a little stroll tomorrow, will you Athol?"

"I will. And if I find he holds the chart and won't surrender it?"

"Slit his throat. The map to the Well of Baphomet must never return to Rome."

"Aye. God wills it."

Henry rolled the charts. "It has been spoken."

As he left the meadow, Sir Athol scraped the last of Mimkitawo'qu'sk moose butter from its container. He tossed the container on the fire. It flared into bright blue then red flame, then vanished. Unnoticed by Athol, but witnessed by Henry,

Mimkitawo'qu'sk grimaced at the waste of a perfectly good box. Sir Athol waved his thanks to Mimkitawo'qu'sk, nodded and smiled, then disappeared down the trail.

"Mimkitawo'qu'sk?"

Mimkitawo'qu'sk joined Henry at the table. Henry indicated the surrounding landscape. He pointed to the village below. "What is the name of this place? This place. Here. Where we are now."

"Ah. Piktuk."

"Pictou?"

"Pictook...tookh," Mimkitawo'qu'sk corrected, exaggerating the asperated *h*. "Tookh. Pic-tookh. It means fart."

Henry remained blank.

"Because of the smell of the winds which sometimes emerge from the Smoking Mountain," Mimkitawo'qu'sk explained.

Still nothing.

Mimkitawo'qu'sk considered for a moment. He brightened, made a fart noise. "Pictook." He repeated the tongue-flapping, lip-fluttering, spit-spattering sound.

"Ah." Henry laughed, repeated the noise. "Piktuk means fart. Ha! Very good. And appropriate, by times, no doubt when wind and mountain act in tandem."

Mimkitawo'qu'sk showed relief his message had not been misinterpreted but rightly understood.

Henry considered, then spoke and gestured his next question. He clarified his query with the aid of the map.

"'Pictook' to 'The Place of Boiling Waters'?"

"Less than two days."

"I'm sorry. I don't understand."

Mimkitawo'qu'sk indicated the sun, its rise and fall.

"Sunrise, yes, to sunset," Henry said.

Mimkitawo'qu'sk repeated the gesture, interrupting the second arc halfway along its course.

"Less than two days. So close."

Laughter erupted from the sweat lodge. Eugainia poked her head past the hide door.

"I'm not certain, but I think Keswalqw just told—I mean showed, me—a very naughty story." She tossed the wineskin to Henry. "We need more brandy wine." She disappeared inside.

Mimkitawo'qu'sk approached the lodge. "What's so funny, Aunt?"

Keswalqw pulled back the flap. "I just showed Eugainia the story of your poor fumbling father's first night with my sister."

"Shame on you, Keswalqw."

"What?"

"That story isn't as funny as the time you mistook your second husband for a bear. Remember? You were on the side of the small hill by the river—"

"Achhh!" Keswalqw snapped the flap shut.

Mimkitawo'qu'sk offered Henry his broad, open smile. "Thank you. 'Enry Orkney," he said, "for bringing this beautiful woman to walk among The People."

Henry smiled and nodded, not comprehending in the least words that would have alarmed him profoundly. He returned to the table, collected his charts and, torch in hand, walked toward the path.

Mimkitawo'qu'sk paused near the entrance to the sweat lodge, listening for a moment to soft murmurs of friendship from within.

Inside, Keswalqw moved behind Eugainia, squared her shoulders. From an open bladder, she scooped a daub of seal oil that she worked through Eugainia's matted hair. She ran a whale baleen comb through the tangled mass. Slick masses of tar and seal fat rolled onto the back of the comb.

Mimkitawo'qu'sk withdrew an alder wood flute, carved with the image of a bird in flight, from his sash. He moistened his lips. He rested the flute below his lower lip. He exhaled.

Keswalqw cleansed her hands clean of seal oil and tar. Eugainia washed the tar residue, sweat and seal oil from her hands, face and body with the porous swatches of soft rabbit hide Keswalqw offered. When done, Keswalqw retrieved the seal-skin package. She handed it to Eugainia. Porcupine quills and copper beads rattled delicately as the butter-soft doeskin dress revealed its hand-stitched beauty.

Outside, Mimkitawo'qu'sk sat cross-legged at a respectable distance and raised his flute to his lips. He invoked rustling grass, the sound of waves breaking on shore, flights of geese and the song of the white-throated sparrow.

CHAPTER SIX

Reclamation, recaulked and tight as a drum, righted herself in the rising tide. All attention was focused on the ship when Mimkitawo'qu'sk and Eugainia slipped away.

Mimkitawo'qu'sk determined pace and direction from the stern. His silent strokes dug deep below the light chop. Eugainia's paddle, drawn cleanly back, pulled hidden life to the surface. Jelly fish—the benign moon-fleshed variety, and the blood red sub-species trailing venomous stings—swirled up, inverted. The gelatinous pulsing masses struggled with mindless irritation to right themselves in the canoe's lengthening wake.

In the centre of the broad strait, the tide hovered, momentarily motionless, then fell away in two directions. Eugainia felt the craft pulled in a lateral tug of war. Sudden images of her recent encounters with good and evil in the waters off the new found land threw her concentration. For an instant, doubt obscured desire. The unfaltering push from the rear of the canoe refocused her intent.

The tide ebbed swiftly. Apekwit's east point and north cape were soon awash in late summer krill, shellfish spat, and swirling clouds of milt and roe.

Apekwit was regarded by The People as feminine in topography. Longer than wide, a family group could walk the island tip to tip in three days. At her narrowest point, on a well-trod path, a hunter could cross from the north to the south shore in a morning; at its widest, less than a day.

Apekwit's gulf coast, curved like a crescent moon, opened to the northeast. The north shore had the ragged look of an unravelled sleeve. Eroded by storm seas in high summer, ground by blocks of ice driven ashore by winter gales, the north shore was defined by discrete stretches of pale, salmon-hued dunes. Vistas to the east and west were defined by out-cropping sandstone that sheltered oyster bays and shellfish coves.

Human profiles—outlined in sandstone cliffs—recalled the faces of The People's ancients. Long, curved stretches of untrodden sand linked profile to profile. From season to season the profiles altered; one strong face replaced the next, one ancestor rested, another came alive. Not all the features carved by wind and sea were human. Creatures of the Six Worlds appeared on the horizon in silhouette according to the Great Spirit's pleasure: last year's high-cheeked chief might become this season's walrus, beaver or wolverine.

The south shore defined the strait side of the island; it was more protected, and a short journey from Pictook and the continent. Unlike the fine pink sands of the north-shore beaches, ebb tide exposed expansive flats of dense red grit, interrupted by much lower banks of red clay. Rarely more than twice the height of a man, the south-shore banks showed deep strata of bedrock and top soil, tufted with topmost layers of green. The grass was made more vivid by the red earth below and, on clear days, the luminous surround of water and the intense blue sky.

This island is as green as Eire, Eugainia thought as they drew near. Greener. Gentler. In all aspects a landscape carved by the Goddess, not her God. Apekwit had reached the peak of her summer beauty. So many shades of colour, all playing one off the other in the diffuse light of an overcast sky. The soil...rust red in places. Blood red in others. Cinibar here, vermilion there. Brilliant greens. Sombre greens. Greens so deeply hued they're almost black; yes...the black of the spruce against the yellow green of the larch. Silver birch. Oak and pine. Dazzling and subtle, all at once. My, my. We were in a pleasant mood the day We created Apekwit.

Eugainia regarded a grass-covered mound on the approaching shore as a natural element of the landscape. Had she recognized it for what it was—not a natural hill but a camouflaged mound of debris—she might have thought the less of it. Mounds of shells and burnt pottery, the detritus of plenty, lay heaped by generation upon generation of The People.

Invariably, a freshwater stream or small tidal river meandered from land to sea through red sand flats. These waters drained forest meadows, marshes and brackish *barachois*. The falling tide exposed rock pools, some ankle deep and several strides across. Eugainia could see the bottom clearly. Great round moon snails (and their tiny periwinkle cousins), hatchling cod and crab, lobster and shrimp miniatures—all foraged amid olive-drab bladder kelp and limpid greens of the filigree moss. There was no shortage of diatoms and algae. Their minuscule bodies, too small for the naked eye, clouded patches of water where the land-wash nutrients blended with the salt of the sea. Phosphorescent saltwater plankton, which pulsed and flashed vivid bluish green light when agitated this time of year had yet to bloom. Perhaps, Mimkitawo'qu'sk speculated, the sea green miracle of light awaits the arrival of she who will be my wife.

The canoe occasionally scraped bottom as they navigated the shallows. The abundance of life sustained by these waters was no longer matched by a surfeit of fauna on land. Only the wiliest of small game remained. Though her great primal stands of pine, hemlock and maple stood largely unmolested, generations of The People had hunted Apekwit's big game to extinction. No bear, moose or deer remained.

Apekwit had reverted to her natural solemnity. Having stripped the island of late-fruiting nuts and berries in the last of their summer visits, The People had recently abandoned her to the rigours of the winter to come. High summer days and short, cool nights had begun to reset her balance. One could almost hear the island breathe relief at the absence of the ravenous humans.

Apekwit in September was sweet to the eye, ear and nose, and as peaceful as any place on earth. Snow and ice were far from the minds of the young man and woman from opposite ends of the earth. Or so it suddenly seemed to them, finding themselves to be incomprehensible to each other as if they represented unmatched species.

Eugainia and Mimkitawo'qu'sk's clean escape from hawk-eyed Keswalqw and vigilant Lord Henry was at first a great relief. Now they stood on the shore, looking anywhere but at each other. Mimkitawo'qu'sk was alarmed when he glimpsed the longing in her blue green eyes, clear as crystal, which Eugainia attempted to hide by concentrating on long vistas or small tasks close at hand—looking anywhere but at the shining pupils of polished obsidian that pulled her, fixed and wanting, to him.

They moved apart.

It had been Mimkitawo'qu'sk's intent to arrive at night, not sunset. They would become as one on a starlit beach. The notion had come to him in a dream. He would stand behind her on this beach, known to generations of The People as *gwitn elsipugtug*: Canoe Great Cove. It was here the most joyous, most carefree days and nights of Mimkitawo'qu'sk's youth were spent. To him, and hundreds of children like him, *gwitn elsipugtug* represented the freedom of youth joyfully expressed amidst adults at their ease in the plenty of summer.

He would stand, he had dreamed, behind the beautiful Eugainia under the full moon. They would raise their eyes and stare together deep into the studded dome of the sky. They would become dizzy at the wheeling immensity above them. Both would waver. He would steady them with discreet hands on her waist, feel the rise and fall of her breath, allow his breathing to synchronize. They'd turn to each other. He'd touch her naked shoulder. She would lay her head upon his. They wouldn't kiss. Not yet. They'd lean together, lips barely touching. For the first time he would bathe in the full scent of her inner beauty. Her lips would part. As would his.

With infinite tenderness, with great care and affection they would come to know each other...slowly, at first. Then, with all the strength of their young bodies, unable to distinguish passion from duty, love from lust, day from night, heaven from earth, woman from man, they would become one.

Mimkitawo'qu'sk had known great love. Like Eugainia, Mimkitawo'qu'sk had been raised for two great purposes: to lead the people and swell the numbers of his community. Love was a vague, abstract notion to Eugainia, best locked way from the attention of a high-born vessel of the Holy Blood. Courtiers and balladeers made much of love's overpowering mysteries and the fate of the heart in story and song. It had little relevance. Duty was destiny: until in the heat of an early summer's day, in the shadow of a great singing stone in an unknown world, duty and destiny died. From an early age Morgase diverted Eugainia's attention from such questions. Eugainia would conceive a holy child; Morgase would devote her life to the child's safe delivery and nurture. Morgase loved Eugainia. Eugainia would love the child. As would Morgase. As would God. That was all she knew and all she needed to know about love.

Mimkitawo'qu'sk glanced at the horizon. Then up to the zenith. The sky grew more heavily overcast. The tide, it seemed, had forgotten to rise. To all appearances, there would be no full moon, no stars, tonight. He'd been too eager to satisfy his selfish needs to correctly read the dream the Creator sent him.

Time, stymied, left the would-be lovers standing dumb and silent on the edge of a dream. They became wary of each other. Dream time and reality rarely synchronize. Time, they would come to learn, had different meanings for each of them. Mimkitawo'qu'sk's senses were aligned with the movements of the seasons and the creatures whose lives, including his own, cycled through the Great Wheel, at the centre of which revolved all the Powers of the Six Worlds. Eugainia lived in constant tension, the Christian pull of right and wrong. Good and evil. Damnation and redemption. God and the devil. The plague- and war-wearied Christian's unhappy existence—life a long, dark night of the soul's hell on earth—was made bearable by the hope of the bright, eternal days of heaven.

Mimkitawo'qu'sk stared at his foot, then the trail left in the wet sand by a delinquent moon snail, lugging its ponderous abode in pursuit of the falling tide. The sun fell perceptually toward the long arc of the horizon, etched to perfection by the edge of the indigo sea. It flared below slate clouds, flooding the narrow band of clear sky. A stiff landward breeze chilled the air. Eugainia felt the need of a light covering. Instead, she stood where she was, although a light moleskin robe was within easy reach. She folded her arms close across her breasts, and pondered the red shore. Mimkitawo'qu'sk turned abruptly, walked to the margin of the forest—its green conifers crested gold in the sudden burst of light. He set to work, constructed a bivouac on deep sand piled by wind and water amid a spacious stand of young pines.

Eugainia took her time unloading the canoe, making several trips across the damp red sand when one or two trips would do. Mimkitawo'qu'sk mumbled as she approached, made a vague, unfathomable gesture, then disappeared into the forest. Eugainia sat in the shelter of the bivouac on the hide-and-fir-bough floor, protected from sand stirred by the rising breeze. She pulled her knees to her chest, wondering...what in the name of all things holy has come over him. And what's come over me? I stood there dumb as a ruminating moose!

She felt disconnected from herself and, to greater alarm, the cosmos she had travelled so widely, with such ease, throughout her charmed young life. Memories of her last physical intimacies began to plague her. From the moment it had entered her body until the birth of the dead child she'd felt poisoned by Lord Ard's seed. Could that grim coupling have been love? Or anything like it? If so, what was this? Unless she misread the situation entirely, seeds would be sown tonight, and soon.

I'm sick and dizzy and elated all at once, she thought. Fear and yearning, all mixed together 'til I can't tell one from the other. Can this misery be the love of which the troubadours sing with such passion?

She tried to conjure an image of her and Mimkitawo'qu'sk coupled. All that arose was the memory of frail, boney old Ard, impotent upon top of her, her desire to rid herself of his aged flesh and fowl breath paramount. Yet she had gone willingly to the old man's feeble bed, time and fruitless time again, consumed by her sense of duty, the divine directive from which she dare not deviate.

All had changed so quickly. She sat on a strange island across the ocean, alone and cold. The Rosslyn Court, transported these thousands of miles to serve her, had all but disappeared. Morgase was dead. Henry grew increasingly ill at ease, his debt to Antonio distracting him from his and his Lady's all-consuming purpose. Eugainia had begun to despise the weight imposed by Henry and his burden. She fled Pictook before her tongue, which could be sharp and unkind, betrayed her and she began to hate herself.

The freedom for which she had yearned was finally hers. Why was she suddenly so driven to bind herself to someone else, to commit everything to this young man with whom she shared no culture, no spiritual tradition, not even language? She who had soared with the holy dove to the pinnacle of her people's spiritual yearning? The consequences of this union, she feared, would be yet another burden, this one everlasting. No one knew better, or more greatly feared, the implications of the word *eternity* than she. This was no ordinary man, this Mimkitawo'qu'sk. Had the Goddess found her God?

With one last wash of the red cliffs, the sun slipped into the sea. The land began to cool instantly. Eugainia unrolled a beaver robe and drifted into a shallow, restive sleep.

On a dream-time moonlit beach, not this one on which she slept on this island called Apekwit, but a granite cove on a distant coast to the north, Mimkitawo'qu'sk threw flat, hard stones into the grey rolling sea. Though distant in the dream, his voice was near. She dreamed his thoughts, as clear to her and as present as though he stood not beside but, somehow, inside her. The farther

I throw this stone, she heard his dream-voice say, this perfect round stone which I choose with the greatest possible care, the farther I throw it, the more Eugainia will admire me.

Why does he throw those stupid stones? she wondered. Why won't he come talk to me?

Swift as thought, without moving a muscle, she was behind him. Not high in the realm of illusory dream time. Not on the shore of some distant land. Not asleep in a dream. Here. On Apekwit. In a dream awake and standing.

This island. This beach. This island. Him. Standing before me. You.

When he turned, Mimkitawo'qu'sk's quick regard was a question.

He stepped inside her.

Eugainia didn't find it at all odd when he bent down then straightened through her torso, as though she were a column of smoke without substance in which he had taken habitation. Her body didn't resist the intrusion. Rather, she felt herself expand to absorb him. He bent, her with him this time, to choose another stone, a flat, round smooth stone the size of his palm. He turned back to sea, stepped away and outside her, prepared to throw the stone.

Eugainia felt bereft. She cried out in her sleep, terrified. I will be alone forever. She woke. The sky had cleared. Night had fallen. A small fire burned nearby, sputtering sparks high into the air where they faded, like children lost in the stars. Mimkitawo'qu'sk, very real, stood distant at the tip of an outcrop in rising water.

Under the full moon, the Sturgeon Moon of late summer, Apekwit gave her heat to the night. The offshore breeze fell light and steady, cooled the whispering pines. A nightbird sang. Mimkitawo'qu'sk's voice flowed through Eugainia's thoughts, in a tongue she recognized, a tongue she knew no mortal man or woman, none but she and Mimkitawo'qu'sk would ever speak.

 If I throw this stone out past the fifth wave, his thought resonated inside her, you will touch my arm. I'll turn, lift your chin…

He yearned to turn to her and lift her chin but knew it was too soon. He struggled, held his gaze to the horizon.

Don't turn to her now, fool. The beauty of the light of the moon on her hair will cause your eyes to weep. I'll strike the moon by accident. It will fall from the sky in a shower of stars and crush my bursting heart.

He leaned, inclined laterally, and cast the stone. The lustrous hank of black hair, normally braided with tight precision, fell loose around his shoulders. Black bolts of tattooed lightning glistened on the oiled skin of his flanks. As he tested the weight of the second stone, the tattooed serpent form, sinuous on his forearm, seemed to climb as the muscles below the skin flexed and stretched. River and stream tattoos, blue and green, flowed up his belly where they merged with clouds afloat on his upper chest, flowed over his shoulders and fell, etched as rain on his back.

A densely packed flock of shorebirds, preparing for long days and nights of migration, swept low, close to the surface. Wheeling swiftly as one, they obliterated the reflected moon. Nearby, the cry of an unseen loon….Beyond that, the barking of a solitary seal.

His powerful calves, tight thighs and buttocks flexed then contracted as Mimkitawo'qu'sk launched a second stone. He straightened to watch its progress. The stone skipped the surface in declining intervals until it slipped below the surface leaving barely a ripple.

Eugainia stepped out of the beaded doeskin dress Keswalqw

had made for her. Her hair fell and fanned loose at her waist. She walked naked down the beach toward Mimkitawo'qu'sk.

Mimkitawo'qu'sk turned to her, still some ten or twelve paces distant. His urge to stride up the beach and possess her faded at the sight of her moonlit beauty. Was he worthy of her sweet red mouth? Would she offer the tender breasts for which he yearned, curtained now beneath the honey-coloured hair curling down past her slender waist? Would the long tapered legs part in ecstasy for him? Would his child swell the flat belly and narrow waist until they rivalled in girth then exceeded the full circle of her broad hips? Would she invite him to drink from the salt ocean of her dreams until his thirst was quenched, if only for the moment, then let him drink again when thirst returned insatiate?

Could she love him as he loved her, Mimkitawo'qu'sk wondered?

Fragments of an ancient Irish air rose in Eugainia's memory. She refashioned the lyric, as a cobbler at her last transforms skin and hide. In my dream I make a pair of shoes for you, Mimkitawo'qu'sk. Made from the skin of a loon. You, my love, are the seabird who soars where I may follow. In my dream, I made for you a pair of gloves...made from the skin of a fish. For you are the whale fish and I am the sea, which you alone may enter.

He turned away. He cast a third stone.

In my sleep, the plover and the curlew spoke your name. Now I am awake. Your strong right arm throws perfect stones far into the sea. I'll touch this strong arm of yours. You'll turn, touch my face, I'll look into you bright black eyes. You'll hold me close. Your hand will cup my breast. You hand caress my belly. My thigh...

She touched his shoulder. Mimkitawo'qu'sk looked deep into her moon-washed eyes. They did not waver. Mimkitawo'qu'sk felt himself swell, then rise.

"I'll make for you a purse, my love," she said aloud, "of morning dew and whispers."

Mimkitawo'qu'sk bent to choose the final stone. "If this stone goes past that round red rock—I've never thrown a stone so far—I'll turn and greet you. I will shout! I'll see the white moon in your grass- and sky-coloured eyes. I will kiss your high white brow. I'll press my mouth to your rowanberry lips. I will show you the north and south, the east and west of my heart, my heart that beats for you. We will join our bodies and our spirits. We will make a spirit quest. You'll give me your Power. I'll give you my Power. As one, we'll walk the Six Worlds of L'nuk."

The People.

He gathered his strength. He launched the stone. The spinning sandstone disk skipped the surface in long intervals, losing no power or wavering in direction. The stone gained momentum as it passed the red rock outcrop, sped across the water below the wheeling birds, flashed beyond the last ripple of the moon, fell from sight beyond their range of vision.

Mimkitawo'qu'sk turned, amazed, to Eugainia. "Never have I thrown a stone so far! I believe it's still going! Ha!" He cupped her face and gently kissed her lips. Before she could respond, Mimkitawo'qu'sk threw back his head. "*E'e,*" he cried. "*E'e!*"

He splashed through the shallows, then dove beneath the surface of the black water. Eugainia followed. The late-summer miracle of light and water had finally bloomed. She dove into the spiralling trail of phosphors in Mimkitawo'qu'sk's wake. As though waiting for the lovers to ignite them, in their billions, the late-blooming phosphorescent plankton, radiant pinpricks of light, shimmered blue and green, streamed from their fingertips, their hair and their eyebrows as the lovers sped beneath the surface. Trails of light shot like falling stars past Eugainia's unblinking eyes, swirled in eddies around her breasts. The white length of her shone, awash in luminescent brilliance. She rose to the surface and floated on her back. Or did she? Was that great field of light the stars? Or was she still underwater, face down, eyes open, absorbing a million points of phosphorescent light? Stars. Yes. Black sky and water. Yes and yes. And the moon. Yes. She was on her back. She was floating.

Mimkitawo'qu'sk, sleek as an otter, slipped from view. Eugainia felt the delicate ripple of a current along her back. Or were his fingertips trailing down her spine?

Still fully submerged he urged her legs apart. Eugainia did not resist. Light coursed from Mimkitawo'qu'sk's hair as his head broke the surface. Eugainia opened herself to him.

Mimkitawo'qu'sk buried his face in the salt sea of eternity.

PART TWO

....

THE WORLD BELOW THE EARTH

Autumn/Winter 1398, 1399

CHAPTER SEVEN

Two hours by canoe and a short portage across a narrow isthmus brought Henry and Athol to the headwaters of Turned Up Whale Belly Bay, named for the belly-up sexual displays of fin-back bulls, roused to flopping turbidity in their behemothic battles for mates. Sheer rock faces buttressed the windswept promontory on which the Sinclair kinsmen stood. The soaring wedge of rock and tumbled glacial shale offered unobstructed water vistas to three points of the compass, divided the northern extreme of Turned Up Whale Belly Bay into two dynamic basins, one due east, the other spreading westward. Tidal rivers snaked far inland through salt marshes to the arable heart of the peninsula. Twice daily out-rushes of heavily silted water drained the basins and their rivers: masses of incoming sea water, forced up the narrowing funnel the great bay formed, raced inland with what seemed to the visitor's eyes unnatural speed and power. The tidal outrace was equally astonishing, not only for its power, but what the fallen tide revealed. The disagreeable image of expansive flats of hip-deep mud laid bare, then drowned by the in-rushing sea twelve hours later, suited Henry's grim frame of mind.

Across the turbulent basin to the east, a second towering cliff appeared cloven as if by a blow from a mighty axe. Some nine leagues distant, so-named Cape Split mirrored in height and latitude their current point of observation. Farther west, hills ablaze with autumn's ambivalent exuberance marked the horizon. Beyond the rippled line of gold and scarlet foliage, crisp in the slanting sun, sprawled the New World.

Henry paced the cliff, dangerously close to the edge. An unfamiliar passion gripped him and would not let go. His thoughts were knotted with worry; his conscience a tangle of contradictions. The day Eugainia and Mimkitawo'qu'sk disappeared, his first thought was of the map to the Well of Baphomet. He'd found a clamshell and dried flowers in its place. He had no doubt as to Eugainia's intentions. Nor the source of the knot of anger in his heart.

She'll unearth the Grail without us, heal herself. She'll disappear, taking the Sacred Vessel with her. What died with my father will stay dead forever. All my work on his behalf, on my own, will come to nothing. Our tattered order will lose what little heart remains; without Her, the Temple Knights will never reassemble. Why would they?

"The Place of Boiling Waters," he murmured aloud, mesmerized by the roiling foam below. He stepped closer to the edge. He wavered.

Sir Athol lay a firm hand on his cousin's shoulder. "Steady there, laddie."

Henry stepped back. "'Laddie' indeed! It's been awhile since anyone called me 'laddie,' laddie."

"Aye. Take no offence, Henry. It popped out. I say, it just popped out!"

"No doubt an echo from our boyhood cliff-hopping days."

"No doubt."

"The People named this place well. These waters do indeed

boil with contrary currents. I've never seen such extremes of ebb and flow."

"Magnificent. I say—"

"Yes, yes. Magnificent. I heard."

"It bears repeating. Magnificent!" Athol persisted, exulting in the crisp blue and white beauty of the sky. "And singular. We've measured fifty feet vertical rise and fall between low and high tide."

"Extraordinary." Henry's concern was his former ship, not the turbid waters, no matter their extraordinary rise and fall. *Reclamation* rested at anchor below the cliff. In an informal ceremony after the noon meal, some three hours earlier, the ship had reverted to her owner. Antonio had what he came for. The terms of agreement struck in Venice two years past came due. Antonio would return. Henry and his chosen few would stay.

Any seagoing excursions would await the construction of a new ship. There was little possibility of that, Henry knew, before spring. Though the loss of her cut like a knife, Henry knew he had no further need of *Reclamation*. Sooner than intended, Henry the grudging navigator had become, by force of circumstance, Henry the land-based explorer.

Antonio Zeno's crew—Arcadian volunteers disheartened and eager for a chance to reunite with their families—and several young men of the Pictook band seduced by the promise of adventure, had sailed *Reclamation* around the great peninsula the preceding day. The capricious winds of the open ocean, then Turned Up Whale Belly Bay's contrary currents, set the final tests of the ship's seaworthiness. Masters and crew, green as they were, rose to the challenge: *Reclamation*'s very presence in these difficult waters, where she awaited the falling tide and her return to Venice, affirmed their mastery. On the turn of the tide, not half an hour hence, Henry's fate, along with those of Sir Athol, Eugainia and the few men who remained loyal to Henry's vision, would be sealed.

The alternate heat and frost of mid-October bred conflicting desires in The People, and in Henry's men. In this, Athol was typical: he required a nap. He succumbed to a full-belly urge to snooze in a nearby rock-and-spruce bower flooded with afternoon sun, perfumed with sweetgrass, intruded upon by dolorous flies and the last fat bee, its progress random, its haunches two bright pantaloons stuffed with yellow pollen, its striped abdomen—loaded with nectar—drooping like an old man's drawers. The buzzing lummox was determined to return to the hive, fully loaded, one last time, despite a trajectory skewed by an intermittent acquaintance with the horizontal, impossible aerodynamics, and the onset of late-season senility.

It was a season of plenty. For anxious man and senile bee alike, the compulsion to conserve won over the desire to lounge. Hips, busts, waistlines swelled as the harvest peaked. The People, Athol reflected, strained to absorb the last of the wavering light, along with every root, briar and berry.

Henry's men took direction from The People, embracing their gather-cure-and-stow zeal. Their methods, they discovered, were not so different from those of Rosslyn and the Scots country people surrounding the great castle fort. Dried fruits and berries; sun- and wind-dried fish and the flesh of lesser animals; smoked haunches of venison, moose and bear; great vats boiled then cooled, meat from the butchered creatures sealed and stowed in congealed masses of their own fat, awaiting the liquefying fires of winter. The most efficient storage vessels were The People themselves: the cheeks of the children, in Keswalqw's happy words, grew round with fat.

Henry sat cross-legged on the cliff edge. His attention shifted from the loss of *Reclamation* to Eugainia. Keswalqw had impressed the dimensions of the continent upon him. As he scanned the westward horizon, his anxiety flowed from the turbulent waters of the bay to vast incomprehensible territory marked on his charts as "*Terra Incognito*." Mimkitawo'qu'sk and Eugainia disappeared in a land mass vast beyond comprehension.

Inland oceans—Keswalqw could find no better word for bodies of water too large to be contained by the word *lake*—lay in the interior of a contiguous land mass. Fresh water. Not salt. Five in all, she told him. Oceans in all but tide and salinity framed by wide horizons, their waters folding beneath the northern wind, rolling into waves of size and power to challenge those of the open sea.

On August tenth, to honour his patron saint's feast day, Henry named the river draining these ocean/lakes, and the gulf into which it flowed. They'd bear the name and title of a monk grilled for apostasy to eternal perfection some one thousand six hundred years ago. The unfortunate St. Lawrence would become associated with the great river of The People for centuries to come. The mighty St. Lawrence, fed by her five central inland seas, opened paths to lesser rivers, rivers draining numberless lakes leading to still more rivers and lakes—an intricate network of waterways and trade routes ranging north past the treeline, west to the mountains and south to southern seas.

Keswalqw described another broad, fresh river The People's western cousins called *Misi-ziibi*. The Mississippi (Sir Athol's best approximation) flowed south, draining fertile inland planes and forests beyond the five ocean lakes, feeding fresh water to another great gulf far to the south where summer was perpetual and winter dared not come. Farther west, beyond the *Misi-ziibi*, a great treeless meadow, a seemingly endless grassland plain Henry's Norman cousins would call a *praierie*, stretched to impassable mountains. Beyond the mountains themselves (here Keswalqw's topographical information remained speculative) a second salt sea was said to spread westward to the far distant horizon.

Though it may have seemed wild and majestic to the conquer-then-subdue European eye, it became clear to Henry from Keswalqw's description that much of this New World was as carefully managed as any feudal lord's ancestral estate. Henry's New Acadia was not new at all. Nor were its people simple or in any way unsophisticated. Vast numbers inhabited this ancient world, gathered in all manner of tribes representing widely varied, ancient and honourable traditions. The People were engaged in all manner of practice, holding worldviews as ancient, varied and complex as those of the warring fiefdoms and city-states of Europe and Arabia.

Henry had much to learn and was an apt, attentive student. Long conversations with Keswalqw expanded his and Sir Athol's vocabulary. Their survival depended upon information; The People were as generous with knowledge as they were with clothing and food. A deep desire to know brought The People close to Athol and Henry's hearts and illuminated their imaginations. Need spurred dedication: conversation, increasingly fluid and intense, brought the foreseeable future into sharp focus.

Keswalqw spoke of great cities a little to the west, then due south where a temperate climate allowed close relatives of The People to farm vast tracts of land. They led settled lives in great cities supporting thousands upon thousands of peace-loving, law-abiding citizens, whose systems of government surpassed in sophistication and human intent many practised in a Europe rendered dissolute by centuries of plague and plunder.

Most northern tribes, they learned, remained seasonally nomadic. Coastal tribes, like Keswalqw's, harvested seal, walrus, cod, halibut, small offshore whales—and, in particular, the giant sturgeon favoured by The People and their far distant trading partners for its succulent smoked flesh and abundant, fat-laden roe. The People were careful stewards, sharing their abundance when their near neighbour's plenty failed. Though his acquaintance with The People was recent, Henry felt he knew the Piktook Mi'kmaq as he had known no others. Perhaps it was Keswalqw's reverent stewardship that touched his prudent Scottish heart.

The People, like Henry, were widely travelled traders and adventurers. In times of excess—much more frequent than times of want—a trading excursion would take the hardiest men (often, as at present, a party led by the chief...hence clan mother Keswalqw's temporary, elevated status of tribal elder and leader) from their villages for several years. The trading missions led them halfway across the continent or deep into the great coastal plains and forests to the south.

Keswalqw knew of the customs and laws of distant peoples first hand. Willful and adventurous in her youth, she'd accompanied her young husband on long voyages of trade and discovery, to the shock of tribal elders and certain clan mothers. Her cache of antelope hides and buffalo robes confirmed oft-told tales of wealth and prairie abundance...and the great trade expeditions required to bring such treasures from such great distances this far east.

The People of the Buffalo, she told Henry as she displayed three large hides dense with rough brown hair, managed the grasslands with controlled prairie fire. The plains were burned annually, the grass lands refreshed, new territory cleared of trees. Antelope and the ungulate bison populations expanded continuously with the prairie People's careful tending. Seas of thundering buffalo swept across the prairies, shaking the earth and filling the bellies of man and wolf alike.

Woodland hunters in the boreal forests of the north, Keswalqw explained, managed a careful balance beneficial to their own populations, and the populations of bear, wolverine, lynx and caribou on which they depended for survival. Farther north still lived the Ice Hunters. Henry, as it turned out, had more information than Keswalqw (much of it secondhand, all exaggerated) on the lives of these eaters of raw meat. He shared his tales of the great white ice bear with adults and children whose minds spun with wonder at the power and beauty of the ferocious white-as-a-ghost-person predator.

"I would give much," Keswalqw admitted one day, "to possess the pelt of such a creature. White and warm. So much Power, such *Kji-knap* against winter."

"One day I'll take you there, aboard *Reclamation*," Henry replied, fully aware the possibility of such an adventure aboard the ship he had come to love as one loves a person faded as the moment of Antonio's departure loomed.

That day is now upon me, Henry thought. God and Goddess help us. Scant hope of help, now she's gone. My Kingdom of the Grail is a ship with no rudder, running nose first before a gale of wind in a hard, contrary tide.

Henry watched unmoved as the last of the round coracles were loaded aboard *Reclamation*. He was happy to be shed of the unwieldy "soup bowls," as Keswalqw called them, which his men soon abandoned in favour of the canoe. In Henry's mind, the sleek vessels perfectly symbolized the power and efficiency of The People. The key to the visitor's very survival in this water-veined land, it became apparent, would be the lightweight, ash-ribbed, craft. The hide- or bark-skinned canoe's speed and efficiency, load-bearing capabilities, portability over rough terrain—and sheer elegance when seated on the water—erased any question as to its superiority.

Sir Athol returned still drowsy from his bee-buzzed bower. He sat nearby, silent, unable to judge his kinsman's mood.

Henry had no wish to be scrutinized. He turned his attention to the southern horizon. "Who could have imagined such a thing?" The question was directed not toward Athol, but inward to his own aggrieved heart.

Henry's darkening mood unsettled his cousin. The early attempt at filial chumminess had captured but failed to hold Henry's attention. Silence wasn't an option. At the best of times silence was a vacuum Athol abhorred more than thoughts of death itself. The notion of eternal peace distressed him. An opinion withheld when demanded by his vociferous father earned the young Athol Gunn, and his siblings, a swift backhand to the side of the head. Paradise to Sir Athol Gunn was a rollicking place filled with too many children and a great deal of noise. In the Gunn household, an opinion once proffered, in a house were all are prone to speak at once, was thought to benefit from immediate restatement. "Many children, I say, many children, from an indefinite number of wives. That's the ticket!" Athol's recently widowed heart yearned for the wide-hipped women and fantastic erotic adventures in tales he'd heard told and retold of exotic sultanates in wild Arabie. Hope faded as time passed. This New Arcadia seemed much subdued in comparison.

Since their boyhood days together, Athol was always bigger, and the stronger if not the more agile of the two. As time passed and power shifted, he learned to hold his peace, to place himself below his lord and cousin, not because he thought himself in any way inferior. Athol admired Henry's selfless capacity to lead, to serve and protect. Despite his cousin's skill at hiding his emotions, and his own respectful reluctance to pry, he knew how deeply Eugainia's flight had injured Henry. With the impending departure of *Reclamation*, Athol found himself at a loss and had no words of encouragement or comfort. Like Henry, Athol recognized that faith and action, harnessed in a pure heart, beckoned the sacred and sheltered grace. Both men agreed with St. Paul who, in his letter to the Hebrews, conceived faith to be "the substance of things hoped for, the evidence of things not seen." Their faith would be tested today.

Faith required patience, and submission; Templar practice permitted both to bend, without compunction, a deferential knee to mysteries fluttering beyond the grasp of their understanding. They desired a better country, a heavenly county here on earth where Goddess and God, acknowledged as equals in the eyes of all men and all women, would walk freely and together so the world might see, follow with grace their example, despise the duplicitous lesson of the Garden, and learn to love each other, man and woman, woman and woman, man and man as equals in the eyes of God once again.

The proper course and the time to act would become evident, Athol counselled Henry after Eugainia had fled. He took the council to heart himself today. There was nothing to do but wait. Their Lady Goddess would return, Athol believed, for she loved them and knew it her duty to show the way.

One warm night aboard *Reclamation*, beyond the halfway mark of their trans-Atlantic voyage, Athol stood his watch on deck. Eugainia rose from troubled sleep and stood quiet beside him, at once distant and near. Despite a growing pallor, and the appearance of dark circles around her eyes, Eugainia emanated grace, as light shines from the purest of oils aflame on a silken wick. He felt it. He saw it. She gave him peace. He venerated Eugainia for what he most admired but lacked in himself: vision. Her great capacity for love elevated her, he knew, above the common. He wondered how it felt to be indentured to the divine, in Henry's case and, in Eugainia's, to be the embodiment of divinity itself. He waited quietly for her to speak, or return to her bed in *Reclamation*'s aft-castle. He was not in the least surprised when she picked up the thread of his musings and put words to his unuttered thoughts. Since childhood, Eugainia's mind roamed freely through those of the people she loved. Nothing, she had discovered, is as private or jealously guarded as thought. She learned to withdraw at the first sign of discomfort. In Athol's often scrambled thoughts, Eugainia's cool council provided welcome relief.

"God and Goddess learn to love alone."

"My Lady?"

"Agape lifts us to the realm of the scared. The sheer power required to love with such unrequited intensity terrifies women and men."

"I'm afraid I'm lost."

"Agape," she confided, "is the greatest love of all: the divine love of God and Goddess for humankind, which humanity acknowledges, in Our names, and repays with acts of simple charity. Agape is manifest in brotherly, sisterly love, the love of one person for another with no thought for the self. Agape demands complete submission, not woman to man or man to woman but each to the other, the self to the self. In Our names. In the presence of the Sacred. In this way, human kind and the Divine become one—a state, I hasten to tell you, I'm inclined to resist in my fleshy desire-driven presence among you. I struggle with a human's pride which seems embedded in the very bones of my body."

"Aye. As do I. A proud and willful creature....A willful villain am I."

"Hush, Athol. I've known your heart since my childhood. It's a great strong thing of beauty, proud and free."

"Freely assigned. I'm a man of duty above all."

"Aye," she admitted. "We're all bound together in this mortal coil. There are times the Sinclair blood makes me so willful I fear I will snap."

"You were always a head-strong, energetic child."

"My heart is tethered by a golden cord to both heaven and earth. I sometimes look at my body—strong and young and well formed though it be—and think my quicksilver soul has hitched a ride on a slow-witted donkey."

"The world ambles along, lass. You are inclined to sprint."

"Who on earth is more constrained by duty and expectation than me? These wretched clothes, this fleshy cell—anything which limits my freedom drives me to near madness. I wonder at the wisdom of this current incarnation. How long I'll last. Still, I'm not alone. Divine avatars all suffer their fated moment. Buddha. Lakshmi. Krishna. The Kumajri Devi. Muhammad, Peace be upon him. The Christ. Now me. Pouring the immensity of the divine into these frail human vessels? Well. It no longer serves to ask why we walk the earth infrequently. Too much is expected of us. Too little permitted. It's just too bloody damned difficult."

Athol shifted uncomfortably.

"Henry winces when my language inclines toward the vulgar. He prefers it when I speak as though I'd just stepped out of the Bible!"

"I suppose it's what the folks want," offered Sir Athol. "We like our God manly, and our Goddess gracious and demure."

"Yes, well...one can't always get what one wants. It's extremely perilous, too, being confined—the ancient wine we are—in these brittle little bottles when we're sent down to earth," she continued. "We forget and push beyond the poor thing's capabilities. We're always in danger of extinguishing our most exquisite creation—scorching the delicate human brain with too pure a celestial flame. Human consciousness continues to astonish us, nevertheless. Eclipsing the flesh and bone limitations the mortal body imposes—poor, doomed donkey that it is. The Creator had no idea the pain inflicted when mankind was made aware of the body's impermanence. The Creator told us it would bring you closer, that you'd become more godlike, less obscene. We'd flow through you, praying your peevish souls might come, like ours, to know a well-considered peace. You'd learn to love as we love you. You'd long to be free of the flesh, to become spirit once again and return to us fulfilled and refreshed. Instead, your fear of death makes you cruel. We erred. I know why now. To have the great river dammed in this..." she indicated her rib cage, specifically, her heart, "...well, one has the sensation of sinking to the stagnant depths of a weed-choked pond."

From first waking consciousness, Eugainia knew instinctively that God and Goddess guide mankind not from some far distant realm, but from within. She learned to free herself from the mire, she told Athol, and to re-enter the garden by slowing the rhythm of her own beating heart.

"Prayer emerges from silence. Silence beckons prayer. The divine cycle revolves."

"Ach, lass. They say silence is golden. Silence makes my arse itch and my blood boil."

Eugainia stared at her friend as though he'd emerged from a crack in the deck below their feet.

"I beg your pardon..." he blithered, ashamed. He flushed an even deeper red, which hardly seemed possible—the big round face always glowed with such rude good health. Eugainia laughed aloud. "You should see the look on your face. As if you farted at a party. Relax, old friend. I came for conversation, not to preach. Though lately I hardly know the difference."

"The horse leaves the stable the instant I remember I forgot, I say, the instant I forgot to remember to bolt the door," Athol said gratefully, relief forestalling further shame. "Or words, I say, words to that effect."

"It will comfort you to know we're all subject to folly. No one truth shapes and re-revises every mote and twitch of the living cosmos: nothing, small or large, is set in stone. Chaos rules. Order emerges, brief and impermanent. Revision is endless; certainty breeds contradiction; peace depends upon war; night exists not to counter the day alone, but to reveal the stars, which mimic the workings of the waking mind. We all move homeward. We—God's benevolent avatars—are no different from you in this. We're omnipresent, yes. Yes, we are indeed eternal. We're on the earth, yes, and absent from it. We existed before the universe, which we made, which we will destroy to rebuild when our understanding of what we have wrought, and where we have failed, is revealed to us in our time amongst you."

"In the darkest days following the first inquisition, she confessed, the Goddess, exhausted by humankind's vindictive outrage against heaven and earth, slept a deep long sleep. While she slept, plague piled thousands of distraught souls on misery's overburdened cart. The Goddess woke. Mary, the Mother of Christ, the girlish untouched virgin appeared reimagined. The

Great Mother emerged. Disease retreated. Abundance re-emerged in a land purged of pestilence; a time of peace, a woman's time, prevailed."

Eugainia gathered her cloak close about her.

"Then a second bout of vengeful rage erupted. This time, women were targeted by the Roman inquisition in numbers rivalling men. The truth rose to heaven on the agonized prayers of innocent girls and matrons; women may live as figureheads, embodiments of the divine, but never rule. Poor exhausted Mother Mary fought awhile then slept. Now I emerge. Here I stand, trembling alone before...well, before Myself. I can't do what must be done alone. Nor could she. I seek my companion God. Two are doubly equipped to counter divine indifference and human cruelty. "

Sir Athol lifted his gaze from the black of the midnight sea. "I'm guilty, guilty as any. What am I to make of this evil, this madness in myself? The men. The women. The children I've slaughtered in..."

"In Our name. When you speak to me you converse with God. Which is not to say you may not speak to God directly, yourself. I'm merely more efficient. There's no queue. What is it you struggle to say?"

"Surely evil wasn't invented on purpose? I mean to say, when you created us, you didn't, I say, surely you didn't—"

"Purposefully create evil? No, no. There was no need. Evil existed at the primal pulse. As did good. Evil is irrational. Dark and sudden as an unloved child. At each advance of the human heart, evil draws back its cloak. More of itself is revealed. Humans' natural desire for good fails, sometimes utterly. Evil poisons the weakened soil. Darkness descends. Time becomes undone. We returned to earth to rend the shadows."

"I'll see this? In my lifetime?"

"Yes, Athol. Oh my yes. Together, He and I, when I find him, will drink from the Stone Grail. And be refreshed."

"This God will walk the earth with You, m'am, in human form?"

"Yes, yes. I shall find Him. Or he Me. We'll rest and be refreshed. Then rule together for a while. Till one of us needs sleep."

"I will actually see God on earth, walking beside—I say, walking beside the Goddess, beside you, My Lady."

"You will." Eugainia smiled and took his hand. "You have an important role, Athol. What it is I cannot say. I'm not being mysterious. I simply don't know. I do see you present at a crucial moment, holding a book, reading words that change the world forever. It shall be, Athol my friend. It is written. Up there. Clearly. In the stars..."

The constellation Aquarius dominated the glittering dome.

"That which awaits..." Eugainia raised her arm. "Begins." She passed her open hand across the star-field.

In the black of the night Aquaria, The Water Bearer, Eugainia's celestial sign and symbol, emerged as though a child had drawn lines linking each defining star. Eugainia opened her palm. High above, Aquaria tipped her star-stone vessel. Stars poured forth, cascading down like water. Shafts of light shot earth ward, pierced the atmosphere, flashed to the horizon where they pulsed and died.

Eugainia swept her arms through three hundred and sixty degrees of horizon. A jagged corona of wavering light—translucent layers of red, violet and green—rose like flame halfway to the zenith where it hung, pulsed, shimmered, crackled with a dry, unearthly sound.

Sir Athol gasped at the beauty of the illusion. His attention was focused heavenward when Eugainia suffered a sharp stab of pain to the stomach. I'm poisoned by the old man's spawn, she thought. Either I or it shall die. The spasm passed. Eugainia continued as though neither the miracle nor sudden agony had just occurred.

"What, Sir Athol, do you think when you hear the word *love*?"

Athol brought his attention back to *Reclamation*, a fragile craft on the endless sea. "Ah...love?"

"Yes. Love. I've had my say. What do you make of it?"

"Love, My Lady," Athol answered with no hesitation, "is simple kindness. I dare say love is simple kindness."

"Yes," she said. "Then let me ask this...of whom do you think when I say the word?"

"I think of my wife, God be with her."

"God is with her." Eugainia placed a hand on her belly. "Not your children?"

"No. A child's love is simple and direct. No thought required. Endless worry, I'd say. But no doubt. One returns a child's affection automatically, with the ease with which it is offered."

"Different from the adult's love for the other....Which I sense will be entirely familiar and mysterious as a magnet."

"Aye. A love of one's own—a wife or, I suppose, a husband— is hard-won and not to be taken for granted. Yes. I say a love of one's own, my Lady, is a complex thing. A treasure when lost, a trial when upon you. My Lady. If I may be so bold. Your husband?"

"Lord Ard? No, no. Mistaken signs. False visions. An error made by Morgase, compounded by Lord Henry. Then sanctioned by an overweening sense of duty, gut instinct ignored, by me."

"And this child you carry?"

"Never a king, alas. A servant, I think. If it survives. If not, an unhappy memory. Sired in despair, nurtured by regret." She lightly covered Sir Athol's hand with hers. She kept her greatest fear to herself. The child was poisoning her. She prayed she'd see the New World shore. "In my heart of hearts I feel the time for regrets has past. God awaits Goddess. I tell you Athol Gunn, I can barely breathe when I think of it! Please God he'll be young and virile. Morgase said he would. And in good health. Thank you for listening, good Sir Athol."

"My great pleasure, m'am."

"Goodnight, my friend."

Sir Athol bowed low. "Good night, My Lady."

Eugainia paused at the aft-castle curtains. She passed her hand across the sky. The Aurora Borealis collapsed to the horizon, flickered once and was gone. Aquarius, her vessel upright and, Athol presumed, refilled, stood waiting still and silent in the black of the northern sky.

Athol fixed his attention on the polar star. He adjusted *Reclamation*'s course. She sailed west by southwest, inching closer wave by furrowed wave to the promise of the New World.

From that night forward, the Lady of Grail occupied Sir Athol Gunn's waking thoughts and frequently visited his dreams, where they spoke of these and many things.

CHAPTER EIGHT

On Kluscap's Cliffs across Turned Up Whale Belly Bay, Henry and Athol awaited the turn of the tide.

"Where better, I thought, to start afresh. We're an ocean away from the stench of Rome."

"I'm surprised you're letting him go."

"What choice have I? Zeno fulfilled his side of the bargain. One sniff of our dilemma, Athol, our *raison d'être* gone...well, aside from the danger, the gloating would've been intolerable."

"Aye. He has what he needs. We have no further use of him."

"We've no need of France or England, or Scotland, come to that. We need Eugainia. Our venture is pointless without her." Henry turned his back on *Reclamation*. "Let the little merchant go, and be damned."

A slight rise afforded a clear view to the west. Henry stooped to pull a shaft of grass. "The world of women and men advances toward the common good, I once told Eugainia. I felt her words as I heard them. 'Yes, the world flourishes for a time in peace and harmony then collapses in upon itself,' she said. 'Dreams of equality and fraternity in an ordered earthly garden flourish. But only for a time. Evil fails where good prevails. It's a cycle older than Adam.' She was six years old at the time. How does she know such things?"

"She's divine," Athol replied. "She has benefited from your stewardship. She has had a thorough education. She's well travelled. Well read. She's inquisitive. She's fit as a she-bear. She's well equipped to thrive in any circumstance."

Well equipped by me to betray me, Henry thought. A man born to rule must have a kingdom. Eugainia's provocation, and the baffling enormity of the stage upon which his response would unfold, threatened to undo Henry. The mortal union of Goddess and God should have prompted a great feast of celebration. The intolerable and inevitable fused, rumbled through his imagination shooting bolts of light and rolling tonnes of thunder.

"What made her think it's Mimkitawo'qu'sk?"

"Who but the Goddess can know her God?"

Henry drew his cloak tight against a sudden gust of chill October wind. Athol might be right.

"Lord help us. This promontory will be no fit place for man or beast come winter."

"We'll need a clear view down the bay," Athol offered. "I say we build a simple stone sentry post here."

"Good. Then set up shop near the ruins."

"Aye. Get about the business at hand, not brood on what might or might not be. That's the answer, laddie."

Henry smiled in spite of himself. Athol felt the air between them warm a degree or two.

"If what we're told of winter here is true, we'll need everything The People have to offer. What's the final count?"

"After extracting Zeno's crew?" Athol consulted a tightly rolled parchment. "One blacksmith stayed behind. The seven master carpenters. One joiner. Three stonemasons. Four journeymen glaziers. No apprentices. Henry, I fear—"

"Yes. I know your feelings on the matter. Barely enough to restore the castle. If they wouldn't stay of their own free will, I've no use for them."

Athol changed his tack. "The young adventurers, those young lads of Keswalqw's soon got the hang of *Reclamation*. One quick turn around the southwest peninsula, a round trip to and from the mouth of Turned Up Whale Belly Bay here, *et voilà*! Skilled sailors every one. Mind, they're natural mariners, these Pictook folk. Those great seagoing canoes of theirs. And the way they take a whale! I have no doubt....Along with our own good lads they'll see, I say, they'll see the little admiral home."

"We'll see about that. In any event, we're well rid of him."

"Aye. We are that. Eugainia will come to her senses and return, Henry. You'll see. The Grail Castle will be restored. Our Lady will be installed. Come spring, your family will join us."

"And the great work will begin." Henry glanced down at *Reclamation*. "I see the bowsprit's clean."

"Aye. Our Lady's likeness has been removed. As directed."

"A gaping hole of indifference where once Our Lady showed the way."

Shouts from the beach, then an angry man's cries, rattled up the rocks. The wails of a woman's grief ricocheted across the water and rose, magnified by an updraft of wind.

Antonio, bound and gagged, trussed and poled like a hog for slaughter was lowered from the rail of the *Reclamation* into a waiting canoe.

"It appears we're not quite rid of the little admiral yet," Henry observed.

Two crying children, a boy and a girl, were handed down from the ship to their parents' arms. Soon after, three of the young warriors who'd answered Antonio's call to adventure, were manhandled, bound and gagged, into a hastily lowered coracle. The seriousness of their crime precluded the use of a canoe: a coracle, a "soup bowl" so-called by The People would bear their shame to shore.

Keswalqw and her clanswomen waited on the beach. The Piktook men materialized at the edge of the woods, as if from air. They stood shoulder to shoulder, a discreet wall of force. The women formed two parallel lines. Each woman brandished a rod stout as her thumb, the length of her arm. They waited in silence.

One by one the young men were manhandled from the coracle onto the sand. Keswalqw stripped the disgraced young warriors of their ill-fitting mariner's clothes. With a shove to the back and a well-aimed moccasin, she booted the naked traitors forward into the mouth of the gauntlet, one at a time in quick succession. The women raised their rods and set upon the young men. No mercy was expected. None was shown. They stumbled from one well-aimed cut to the next, unable to right themselves before the next blows, which came in pairs, fell hard upon them. They bore their welts with failing arrogance, heads and backs fully exposed, their genitals protected by cupped hands, the backs of which were soon split and bloody. Keswalqw waited at the end of the alley of shame, her unhappy task to land the final blows. The outcasts emerged trembling, bruised purple, bleeding, bowed and broken. Their past lay naked and bloodied upon them; the present—the promise of The People to nurture and protect them—lay desolate, as far beyond comfort as the cloudless sky to which they raised eyes awash in dreadful comprehension. The past was dead. The present lost. The future beckoned no more.

Keswalqw threw back her head and howled. A wail arose from the women. Grief pitched eerily high broke the young men's hearts.

From the throat of every man, woman and child rose a tribal howl—a collective cry of shame. A single resonant collective tone emerged, quavered, hung in the air as though uttered by one voice.

The young men joined the cry, the final commune between them and their clan. Henry's heart went cold. The earth itself seemed to turn its stony back, sullen and flayed, on the disgraced young men. They would no longer walk in peace upon the good earth; nor would they, without the love and comfort of The People, wish to exist upon it, supposing each could find the strength and means to live alone. Death, when it found them, would carry a double disgrace. The insatiable giant *Chenoo*, cannibal spirit/man, an outcast Ghost Person, stalked these wild woods hungry for love and the taste of human flesh. His glare would transfix the castaway young men. His bite would transform them—those he did not smother and devour outright—into one of his kind. Better dead, it was agreed, than to become one such as him.

The young men walked, bloodied and naked, each in his own direction, to a shared fate he must endure alone. Their complicity with Antonio Zeno, merchant-adventurer, zealot, despoiler and thief would lead them to a quiet place in the forest where they would lay down and, through sheer force of will, empty themselves of their *Kji-kinap*, their Power. They would return their still vigorous, untried spirits to the World Above the Sky. The flesh of their strong young bodies would nurture the Earth World. As time, scavengers and the eternal turning of the seasons wrought final transformation, the residue of their shamed flesh—none would raise their remains to the safety of the trees— would sink unmourned into the World Below the Earth until all that remained was their unloved bones.

Keswalqw glanced up to the promontory where Athol and

Henry watched. She stripped Antonio of his clothing. A slip-knotted noose, at the end of a stout, braided moosehide rope, tightened around his neck. Keswalqw led the Venetian noble, calf to the slaughter, to the foot of the cliffside path and up the promontory.

Henry and Athol moved to the edge of the forest plateau where the path opened before them. Ancient shadow pillars stood in judgment, their twisted roots protruding from mats of bracken fern and moss. The canopies of frost-killed ash and oak cast soft golden light on The People's dark purpose.

Angry taunts and cries preceded Keswalqw and her prisoner. She emerged briefly as the path curved up and over a granite outcrop. She reappeared in the high meadow, the rope slung over her shoulder.

Antonio stumbled into view. Keswalqw dragged him forward. Alternately taught and slack, his tether trailed on the ground, snapped to singing tension when he faltered. Village children landed running blows on the naked merchant's buttocks with the women's stout ash switches.

Antonio stumbled to an unbalanced halt. The hide rope marked the flesh of his neck. Keswalqw aimed a blow to the back of his legs. Antonio fell to his knees in front of Henry. Keswalqw grabbed a scruff of hair and flung him face forward. The arch of her moccasined foot, pressed tight to the base of his skull pinned him, right cheek to the ground, mouth splayed open, grit in his teeth, the earth raw and pungent on his tongue.

Antonio squirmed. Keswalqw shifted her weight. Antonio winced, alert as a snared ferret, his attention fixed on the back of his neck, awaiting the fatal snap.

Keswalqw lifted her foot, jerked the bight end of the rope taut. Antonio's head snapped up. His mouth lolled open. His eyes rolled with fear. The abducted children stood silent nearby, their aggrieved parents distraught but calm. Keswalqw coiled the rope, taking time to form loop after perfect loop.

At Keswalqw's signal, Plawej, the bright, shy boy who had become a favourite of Henry's, and Eugainia's forthright little friend, Mn'tmu'k, nicknamed Oyster Girl for her love of the bivalves, stepped forward. They stood beside Keswalqw, quiet and shy. Keswalqw spoke slowly, distinctly, in carefully considered English. "Listen closely, 'Enry Orkney. I'll speak in what I have come to know of your tongue, and hope you will hear what little you have come to know of mine."

Henry nodded.

"This serpent stole our..." She indicated the children, a word Henry knew was in their shared vocabulary. "How do you say in your language...?"

"Keswalqw, you know the word for child—"

"Yes." She held his eye. "I know the word for children."

"Let me assure you," Henry countered. "We stand with you here in shared pain and sorrow, and acknowledge the gravity of the offence."

"Mn'tmu'k, not six winters," she continued, "and her brother, Plawej, not yet five, stolen from these good people who love them more than life itself...wrapped so tight in beaver robes they could hardly breathe. Their mouths were gagged." She inserted a finger under Antonio's gag. "Like this." She wrenched it. He yelped. "Their little hands bound." She gripped the leather thong binding Antonio's hands together behind his back and yanked, splaying his shoulder blades upward and out to the side. "Like this." Antonio inhaled sharply. Keswalqw released the pressure. Antonio groaned.

"Our children, Henry Orkney. He wished to steal the sacred

gifts of the Creator. Our children! He plundered our burial ground. He stole the bones of our Old Ones. And their spirit gifts. Loaded them on your ship, with his bags of yellow stones. I want to kill this serpent man, your An'to'ni'o. I want to feed his flesh to the dogs. I want to spit upon his ghost, and scatter the ashes of his bones to the four winds. But he is not one of The People. He is yours. And you are my friend."

"May we remove the gag?"

"I will not touch him. Unless to slit his throat."

"May Sir Athol?"

Keswalqw nodded her assent. Athol removed the gag.

"Answer the charge, Antonio."

"I only thought to show The Holy Father...the bones and trinkets, for the Vatican Museum."

"Bones? Trinkets?" Keswalqw squatted, raised Antonio's chin. She caught and held his eye. She fumbled with the strings of a doehide pouch. She withdrew a black disc, thick on one side, tapering on the other to a thin, slicing edge.

This was no ordinary palm-knife used to gut carcasses or scrap hair from hides. Nor was its purpose personal or domestic. Its purpose was ceremonial. The blade's extreme edge assured swift and merciful dispatch. Keen, shining, a black night of obsidian, the blade had come to Keswalqw from the mountains on the far side of the continent, traded through many hands before it found hers. "To this hand," she had told Henry when she first revealed the blade weeks ago, "it came to my hand, for which the Great Spirit made it. My sharp-toothed master of life and death."

"The children would be instructed," Antonio snarled. "Civilized. She should thank me, not threaten my life. The young savages' souls would have been sav—"

Keswalqw twisted the rope tight and held it tight. Antonio's face flushed scarlet. His features soon bloated beyond recognition. He slumped to the right. The People had come to know the white word savage, and its connotations, especially ugly when uttered by Antonio, whose eyes fluttered rapidly, then closed.

Keswalqw released the pressure. After a long moment of dreadful silence, Keswalqw landed a well-aimed kick to Antonio's ribs. His eyes snapped open. He gasped, then exhaled in a hiss of resentment. "—Their heathen souls would have been saved."

Henry stooped, untied the thong binding Antonio's wrists. "What am I to do with you?"

"What would your Lady do?" Antonio demanded, rising to his knees, massaging first his wrists, then his throat.

"If you showed contrition, and made reparation, My Lady would set you free. But it is not her you have aggrieved. Keswalqw?"

"What is this contrition?"

"He will say that he feels sorrow for what he has done."

"And reparation?"

"Because he stole from you, he will return what he took, and he will give you anything you choose of his possessions."

"He will give his iron blades, and his blankets."

"Antonio?"

"Yes."

"All his blades."

"Yes."

"All his blankets."

"Yes, yes. All—"

"What else?" Keswalqw demanded.

"He will swear that he will never assault The People in this disgraceful way again."

"I'll hear his words of sorrow. His contrition. For what he has done to our children. His reparation? I'll take his blades. I'll take his blankets." The edge of the blade lay lightly on Antonio's throat. "And I will take his sacks of the yellow stones."

Antonio moved to speak. He averted his eyes. Slight pressure from the blade silenced him.

"Where is this contrition?"

He stared up at her, his mouth slack, his eyes blank.

"I'm sorry."

"I look in your serpent eyes. I see that you have none of this contrition. I see greed and selfishness. I see that you are not sorry. You are *Jipijka'maq*, Horned Serpent Person. You burst from the World Below the Earth. Burst into the Earth World and leave your trail of destruction and of woe."

"I...am...sorry."

"I don't believe you."

"I am sorry I desecrated the graves of your ancestors. I am sorry I lured the little sav— the children aboard my ship. I will give you my blankets, I will give you my swords and daggers. Please. I beg you. You have no use for the gold....The soft yellow stones..."

"You may keep the yellow stones. I'll take your bright red blood instead!"

Her blade, deft and certain, grazed the merchant's skin. A thin trickle of blood, deftly drawn, trailed down to Antonio's collarbone.

Keswalqw held the blade below the cut. Blood pooled on its upper plane. She slanted the blade toward the ground. Antonio's eyes widened. Drop by scarlet drop Zeno blood, Christian blood, vanished into gravel leaving neither trace nor stain. She brought the blade back to his throat. All that he was would soon follow the blood, sink into this foreign soil and disappear, lost, unmourned, despised.

"No, no!" Antonio cried. "Take what you will, but spare my life."

Keswalqw spit on her blade, drew it through Antonio's hair to clean it. She twisted the bloodied hank of hair into a knot, sliced it from his head, tossed it to Henry. He caught the warning glance that crossed the short space between them. Keswalqw tucked the blade back into its pouch. Her back straight, her face showing no emotion whatsoever, Keswalqw turned and strode down the path, followed by the children, their aggrieved parents and members of the clan.

Henry offered Antonio his hand.

"You are brought low, Antonio."

Antonio rose to his feet unaided, though unsteady. Fear's aftermath twisted his guts.

"I am alive."

"And in debt."

Henry offered Antonio the hank of his hair. "A trinket for the Holy Father."

Antonio accepted the grim indenture. The hair hung lifeless in his hands. "I acknowledge that I am in your debt."

"And?" Henry pressed him.

"I owe you my life."

Antonio's thin, sinewy body, more that of an underfed adolescent than a man in his prime, trembled. A cold gust of wind amplified his shame.

"Your obligation will be forgiven provided you swear you will forget our Templar maps, make no copies, and tell no tales."

"It's easy to promise the world to a dead man. But I won't. I'll tell the tale of an errant knight and his apostate mistress to whom and when I choose."

Henry removed his cloak. He held it out to Antonio. Antonio could make no sense of the gesture. Misgiving dissolved when he remembered his chilled and naked state. He reached for the cloak. "They'd already gutted *Reclamation*," he said as he swung it over his shoulders. "Stripped it all but bare. Over half our arms were stolen. Most of our blankets. Clothing. Personal property. Gone. We're barely provisioned. Now they'll have it all."

"There's no end of fish in the sea. Or rain water this time of year on the cold grey Atlantic. You have your gold. What more do you need?"

"You did nothing to stop them. You encouraged them from the beginning. Gave them free run of a vessel you didn't own when my back was turned. In exchange for what? They were payment, the trinkets and the children." Antonio straightened his spine. "This bitter land will bring your lives and this damned heresy of yours to an end once and for all."

He turned and strode away.

Henry called to him.

"Antonio!"

Antonio stopped, stood silent, his back to Prince Henry Sinclair and Sir Athol Gunn.

"My cloak," Henry directed.

"What of it?"

"Fold it nicely, will you?"

Antonio turned to face Henry, whose gaze remained soft and benign.

"What?" Antonio demanded.

"Fold it nicely and leave it on the beach."

Antonio searched Henry's face for traces of contempt or mockery. He found neither.

"You asked what My Lady would do. She would give her cloak

and never ask its return. I'm not so generous. In her stead, I wish you well."

Antonio wrapped the cloak close against the freshening breeze. "I'd return the sentiment, but in truth I feel only scorn and pity. None but brute beast and savage will survive the coming cold, if what we're told is true. You're welcome to this bewitched, uncivil place. I leave it all to you. And be damned."

Antonio gained the path and disappeared.

"You should have let Keswalqw slit his throat for sport."

"A ship, no matter how sturdy, loaded with that much gold? Scantly provisioned? The North Atlantic in her full autumnal tumult is my revenge on Antonio Zeno."

Henry walked to the edge of the cliff. Alone and naked, Antonio struggled to steer the ungainly coracle, over which he had no mastery, toward his ship. Henry's mood was briefly eased by the pitiful ineptness of the man.

Antonio was handed naked aboard *Reclamation*. Henry felt a great weight descend, the same choking grief he suffered the day Eugainia and Mimkitawo'qu'sk fled, leaving sorrow to thicken, then harden into anger in his heart.

"I've a stone in my chest and a head full of wasps," Henry said.

"You've...what?" Athol asked.

"I don't know what I'd do if she appeared before us now; fall on my knees, my own sword, or fall upon him and do her harm."

"You'd fling your sword aside and fall upon your knees. You'd ask her forgiveness for thinking such things. We are Clan Sinclair, Henry. We've always known our purpose. Our lives are not our own, I say, our lives are not our own. And if you've forgotten that, you'd do better to throw yourself on Antonio's mercy and beg him to take you to Rome, where you can fall upon your sword or worse...your knees before the very devil himself. You're useless here, worse than useless, unless you set your foot upon the proper path."

Henry stood chastened. As he struggled to formulate a response, ship's orders bounced up the cliff from rock face to rock face.

Her sails puffed full, her anchors weighed, *Reclamation* swung nose-first to the south, settled to the sou'east. In the outrush of the falling tide, the galley sped down Turned Up Whale Belly Bay.

The stone in Henry's heart turned to water. In his head, blessed silence.

"Feel that breeze, kinsman," he said. "What lends the day this sudden pleasant air?"

"The stink of greed is purged."

"*Au revoir, Reclamation.* Or I should say *Adieu.*"

Keswalqw emerged from the forest, a bulky leather bundle under either arm.

"I will tell you the truth, Henry Orkney," she said gravely, setting her burdens on the ground. "All the signs tell that the coming winter will be a starving time. Little snow. Great cold. Great hunger."

"Yes. Winter. Cold. I understand."

"No. More than winter. More than cold. There will be great cold. The beaver's house will be hard as stone: we'll not break his roof and capture him. There'll be little snow; the game will flee with ease, will not offer themselves to The People. Our round cheeks will vanish; the sharp bones of anguish will appear. Nonetheless, you are here. We will not abandon you. I have gifts for you, gifts from The People."

Keswalqw unfolded and then spread two luxuriant beaver

robes at their feet, guard hairs glistening in the sun. Thick under-fur resisted the wind's attempts to ruffle it. Keswalqw placed the first robe on Henry's shoulders, the second on Sir Athol's.

"Thank you, Keswalqw."

"Thank you."

"Thank The People."

Henry produced his wineskin. "Then here's to The People."

Keswalqw produced her pipe and clamshell. The punk-packed ember released the sacred smoke. She sent a prayer up to the Great Spirit with the first exhalation. Henry presumed she offered her thanks for the safe return of the children, or her gratitude that Antonio no longer walked among them. Henry exhaled the same prayer then, with the upward spiral of rising smoke, asked forgiveness for consigning good men to the care of the Venetian viper. Would their souls be rewarded, as Henry had promised, should the north sea devour them? He prayed it would be so.

Keswalqw sensed his apprehension. "Kluscap rides the backs of the whales."

"I beg your pardon?" said Henry.

"Seabirds are his messengers."

"I don't—"

"Kluscap will send lesser spirits to oversee the journey."

"Kluscap. The Creator?" Sir Athol ventured.

"No, no. Kisúlkw is the Creator. Kluscap is more like your Jesus, maybe. But with a sense of humour. Kluscap likes a joke. He makes what you call...miracles, but only with the Great Spirit's help. Like your Eugainia and your Christ."

"Miracles?"

"Kluscap created men's bones from the heart of the ash tree, his flesh from the mud of Turned Up Whale Belly Bay. Not long

after, Kluscap opened man's mouth and the names of all the animals came out. He gave the names of all the animals to The
People. And told The People the animals' stories. Like that cliff,
there, across the water. Before Kluscap's time the beavers were
huge, powerful beasts. They had built a great dam, eh? Anchored
it here, and across the water, at what you call Cape Split. Made a
huge pond. One day, by speaking a word he knew and waving
his stick, Kluscap became a giant beaver, bigger than the others,
broke the dam and let the fierce Turned Up Whale Belly Bay tides
rush in and out, as they have done ever since."

"Is this story true?" Athol chided.

Keswalqw looked Athol Gunn dead in the eye. "It's a story
we tell to our children. Of course it's true."

Athol grinned. "Really, Keswalqw. A beaver that big?"

"Tell me again your story of that man born of a virgin and
nailed to a tree. The same man, wasn't it, who turned air into
fish and water into brandy wine?"

Athol contemplated the miraculous.

"Has anyone seen them?" Henry asked.

Keswalqw answered in time. "They left Apekwit."

"Where would he have taken her?"

"A place he knows."

"They'll be in no great hurry to see either of you," Athol
interjected. "Eugainia has tasted freedom and won't take well to
prison, no matter how splendidly we restore it."

"She needs time to heal and strengthen. Mimkitawo'qu'sk
won't abandon her."

"What if there is a starving time?"

"Two may live easier than many. We'll have two less mouths
to feed. Mimkitawo'qu'sk knows the way of the starving time.
He will provide."

"And I'm to stand here and wait."

"What would you have me do? They'll come back when they are ready. We will wait and we will see."

Athol spread his beaver robe upon the ground. Henry did likewise. Keswalqw joined Athol. Henry and Keswalqw drank and smoked. They sat cross-legged, all three, united in comfort shared by those of a common age, possessing amongst them decades of accumulated wisdom, happy in each other's company, letting brandy and tobacco gently alter their senses, ease their apprehension, reshape their views of what would soon become their common world.

"Why did you let Antonio go, Keswalqw?" Henry asked. "Had he touched a hair on my children's head I would have cut his throat without a second thought."

"And had his spirit wandering your village forever? We have our own Horned Serpent Persons, our own Jipijka'maqs. We don't need yours as well."

Time dissolved as the sun moved west. Leagues down the bay *Reclamation* vanished where Turned Up Whale Belly Bay flowed into the southern reaches of the North Atlantic Sea.

CHAPTER NINE

Eugainia felt everything she knew, or thought she knew, fall away. In these wild days, lessons old as humankind and the earth upon which she trod were learned anew by the young Goddess. Perched on the crown of a high bald hill—the night cold, their robes warm, the stars a vivid, brittle blue—she knew she'd met her match in Mimkɨtawo'qu'sk. She couldn't have been happier.

In the same way, Mimkɨtawo'qu'sk felt reborn. He spoke the names of things—names he'd always known—as if for the first time. Great was her hunger to know his world: great his joy in revelation. Greater still was the joy he found in the flesh of the apple-breasted Goddess, her honey-coloured hair curling down to snowy hips.

Five moons had come and gone since they left Apekwit. Eugainia and Mimkɨtawo'qu'sk brought each other great comfort: they were no longer extraordinary or peculiar in their singularity. They'd travelled into the heart of the lands Henry's maps showed as uncharted, travelling the great river that emptied into the western shore of Turned Up Whale Belly Bay, skirting the foaming rapids at its mouth that flowed in opposite directions with every turn of the tide. Days and weeks and months slid past as the wide river narrowed. A day or two of travel. A week of hunting. Rest. Sleep. Love. Exploration for the sake of exploration itself. Repetitious tasks that would stupify their divine manifestations, feeding and sheltering their robust young bodies, travelling unsparing territory with only flesh and bone feet to transport them, their bodies' tiresome need to sleep, their rest often fraught with visions, some frightening, some beautiful, all intriguing, these became joyful acts of discovery. All this is deepest solitude. Mimkitawo'qu'sk purposefully avoided encounters with other Mi'kmaq clans and their Abenaki cousins. It was, as Keswalqw said, their time to be together and alone.

When in repose, or lulled by the rhythm of a long march, Mimkitawo'qu'sk and Eugainia slipped easily into silent communion. Images and unspoken lines of narrative flowed between them. Each showed the other realms mystic and divine through which they'd wandered separate and alone, free from their flesh, in God and Goddess form; realms ancient, realms vast and varied, realms forged in conflagration, realms born in agony and glory at the beginning and end and rebirth of time.

Mimkitawo'qu'sk rose to his feet, boneless as smoke. He stood behind Eugainia, his hand on her shoulder. She inclined toward it.

"Since we last saw Piktook, and Apekwit, the red island Cradled on the Waves where we became one," Mimkitawo'qu'sk began, "Grandmother Moon has come and gone many times—"

"Let me see...the Blueberry Moon; the Blackberry Moon; the Deer Paws the Earth Moon; the Dry Grass Moon. Yes?"

"Yes."

"And this is...?"

Mimkitawo'qu'sk slipped his chilled fingers below the neckline of her robe, where they absorbed the heat of her body, heat trapped in the long guard hairs and thick underfur of rabbit and wolverine.

"Tonight, in the presence of the Snow Moon, I'll show you the Six Worlds of Lnu'k, The People."

Eugainia eased back against him. Her head lay soft on his belly.

"This," he gestured, "is the Earth World. Below us, the World Below the Earth. Over our heads, the World Above the Earth, also called the Sky World. Above that—?"

"The World Above the Sky."

"Yes." He pointed down to the shore where blue white snow melted in the blue black breakers of the sea.

"There, beyond the water's edge, the World Below the Sea." He filled his lungs with cold, dry air, held his breath a long moment. He exhaled lightly through pursed lips. His breath hung in a cloud of moon blue vapour.

"And everywhere," he said to the lucent plume, hanging motionless in the tranquil night, "the Ghost World."

He squatted, then knelt. He wrapped his arms around Eugainia from behind. She slipped his hands through the side-slits of her robe. She covered his hands with hers and laid them on the thin layer of fat which softened the hard layers of muscle on her warm belly.

"Everything in the Six Worlds is a Person, and Persons live forever," Mimkitawo'qu'sk continued. "In the Earth World, the days of warmth and sunshine, the days and weeks and months, all these things which your people call time are Persons. The days of rest and plenty—what you call summer—these are Persons. As are the dark days of cold and hunger; winter is a Person. Rocks and stones are Persons. Plenty is a Person. Hunger is a Person. Life is a Person. And so is death.

Rocks and stones are the living bones of the Earth World. But beware. A rock may be a sleeping Person. Perhaps a wind Person grew tired, became a mountain to rest and to sleep. Perhaps a tired and hungry bear Person—a hungry angry bear Person— lay down, became a rock to rest and to sleep. Treat all rock and stone Persons with great respect The People tell us. One might awaken—might awaken and devour you if you disturb it, or act with disrespect.

Jipijka'maq, Horned Serpent Persons, tunnel through rock and stone in the World Below the Earth. Horned Serpent Persons have great Power. They carve great ruts in the earth. Sometimes they burst through into the Earth World. They leave mountains and valleys in their wake. Sometimes Jipijka'maq *is* a mountain, *becomes* a mountain when he's tired and needs to sleep; jagged plates of horn rise from his back, thrust out of the earth, rise into the Sky World and slice the clouds.

All is as one in the Six Worlds. A bird flies through the World Above the Earth, then plunges into the World Below the Sea where it swims like a fish. Seal Persons leave the sea and bear their young upon the ice or on the rock beside the shore."

"In our Outer Hebrides, seals take the shape of a woman or a man. They live among us, sire and bear offspring. They're happy for a time, walking the Earth World with women and men. Soon the Sea World calls them home. They return to the sea. My mother was one of these for a time. Her name is Garathia."

"Seal Persons follow our canoes, swim with us when we bathe in the ocean, come near us on the rocks and watch, their big eyes wet with longing."

"Seals remember."

"Yes."

"We're lost seal children."

"When we saw your people leaping off *Reclamation*, we said, 'Ha! Seal persons on a spirit quest.' Then we smelled you. No, we thought. They're bear Persons in seal Person form. You were quite confusing."

Eugainia relived her struggle back from death when air and sunlight flooded the stinking hold, the day *Reclamation*'s hatch was flung open. She shuddered at the memory.

Mimkitawo'qu'sk buried his nose in her hair, inhaled deeply. "You smell just right now, beloved. E'eee!" he whispered softly. "This is the scent of my wife."

"I know something of seals and their life in the World Below the Sea," Eugainia said quietly, her head awash in curtains of fish, her heart full of Garathia. "Nothing was as I thought it would be."

"Nothing is as it seems. Persons go on spirit quests to the World Below the Sea to dream and to imagine. The World Below the Sea holds all knowledge, remembers all things."

"Persons witness miracles in the World Below the Sea."

"And the greatest miracle of all?"

"The fish is in the sea and the sea is in the fish."

"We are in the Six Worlds and the Six Worlds are in us."

"We are in our people and our people are in us."

Mimkitawo'qu'sk spread his arms wide, a newborn visitor raising his eyes from the well-known earth to the oft-seen sky as though for the first time. "Persons move swift as thought in the World Above the Earth. Thunder lives in enormous bird-shaped Persons. They beat their wings and crack the sky. Thunders rumble through the air and cause the earth to tremble."

"Thunder Persons. Wind Persons. Enormous bird Persons. Their great wings flap and cause the winds to blow. Yes?"

"Yes. The wind is a Person. So is the cool place where the sun sets, and the warm place also where the sun rises. Where the birds go in winter, the place from which they return when winter days are done—all these are Persons.

"And the stars?"

"Stars are silent hunters who move through the Sky World day and night. Star Persons guide L'nuk, record our stories, remind us who we are. Great Power lives in the World Above the Sky. Grandfather Sun and Grandmother Moon, the ancestors of Lnu'k, The People, have the greatest Power. His heat feeds The People; her light makes us dream."

"For this we thank them."

"For this we give thanks. The last of the Six Worlds is the Ghost World. There live those who came and went before. A man or woman, boy or girl, a tree or an animal, any living thing—and in the Six Worlds all things live—may become a Ghost Person. But only once. Some, we say, some strong and brave Persons, some Persons with great Power have gone there—gone there in the living flesh, gone and returned from the Ghost World where they see the ones who've gone before."

"The ones they love."

Memories of loss and bereavement drew them close against the chill. Sorrow, a sudden halo of pale mist, circled the high hill.

"Mimkitawo'qu'sk, I ask this question of all I meet. What do you say when you speak about love?"

"The Creator's greatest gift is love."

"And what do you make of death?"

"There is no death in the Six Worlds. Not as you know it. We say life is death and death is life. And to live is to love. We say love unites life and death, as thunder unifies earth and sky. When it's silent, has thunder died? We say no. It merely rests in the ground and gathers strength. In this same way, we think love can't die. The People learn to love all creatures, all Persons in each of the Six Worlds."

An odd shimmer pulled Eugainia's gaze to the shale at her feet. A line of pale light seemed, though still, to meander among the ragged stones. A seam of ice in rock, perhaps, reflecting the moon? Perhaps a length of leather thong, sheathed in frost? Or a white man's rope of hemp or jute sheathed in frost? No, not rope. Not here. None of the visitors had ventured this far, either from Piktook or Turned Up Whale Belly Bay. Some sort of lucent tube? She bent close. She passed her hand between the moon and the trail of light in the shale. The curious object disappeared. She removed her hand. The delicate coil glowed again.

Eugainia touched Mimkitawo'qu'sk's sleeve, indicated the little mystery at her feet. He raised the shed skin of a small snake. It hung crisp and transparent in the pale light. "Ha! You can see....She became too big for her house. Slithered out her own mouth. A young snake, Tutji'j Jipijka'maq, racing toward adulthood lived here for a time. She sheds her skin with every turn of the moon until she becomes full-grown."

Eugainia peered at the shed skin's spectral head, the grotesque mouth de-fanged, agape, its angry scowl a vacant threat backlit by the moon.

"How perfect!" she said, holding the snakeskin gingerly, its fragility essential to its beauty. The form of the eyes remained, the ghostly pupils raised, every counterfeit scale the full length of it in tact, its existence a memory clearly etched yet insubstantial as the light moon that defined it.

"She came to the top of this hill, in the last days of the Grandfather Sun's warmth, to renew herself. Crawled out her mouth then slithered down to a den in a small cave for the winter, knotted in a bundle of her kind, safe below the killing frost..."

"Silent in a dreamless sleep."

"Silent, yes. But dreaming. Everything dreams in the Six Worlds. A Person of great Power, Tutji'j Jipijka'maq, this tiny Serpent Person. Size is no advantage in the Six Worlds. A beetle is a powerful Person. An ant is a powerful Person. All living Persons in the Six Worlds, including the earth and its bones of rock—water in all its forms, air restless or at rest, the heat and light of fire—all have Power; all have *Kji-kinap*."

"Wandering the earth in our mortal frames we gather *Kji-kinap* and refresh ourselves," Eugainia said. "Is this not so?"

"These are the words of The People. In the Six Worlds, *Kji-kinap* is the essence. *Kji-kinap* knows itself, thinks of itself and remembers. *Kji-kinap*, with its great strength, its force which can't be resisted, made or taken away, is everywhere. *Kji-kinap* comes and goes as it pleases. It is everywhere and forever. Everything we see and know, everything we do and feel; everything comes from *Kji-kinap*. *Kji-kinap* moves Persons. *Kji-kinap* moves through Persons. *Kji-kinap* changes Persons and gives them life. *Kji-kinap* knows the way of things. *Kji-kinap* is the way of things. *Kji-kinap* is a Person's fire and you, My Wife, by the light of Grandmother Moon, you do burn bright! Yet even the loveliest fur-clad Goddess is no higher or lower than the shed skin of the child of a snake. Both have Power. Woman or snake, so long as she receives *Kji-kinap*, and uses it wisely, each becomes a greater Person."

"Keswalqw has great *Kji-kinap*."

"She does. Hers is the *Kji-kinap* that opens a channel between the Earth and Sky Worlds. Your friend Athol Gunn has great *Kji-kinap*, though he doesn't know it yet."

"So does poor Lord Henry, though his Power is blocked. My mother the Selkie Garathia has great Power. In the way Keswalqw brings the Earth World up to heaven, and heaven down to the earth, Garathia brings the waters up to heaven, and the heavens down to the sea." Eugainia lay her hand on Mimkitawo'qu'sk's chest. "Does it frighten you?"

"What?"

"This mortal body."

"No."

"It frightens me. When I see the flesh of other creatures wither and rot."

"This is the way of things. The moon Person wanes. The star Person falls from the World Above the Sky in a burst of fire. Even the stone Person is worn away. The river Person rises to the sun, its bed dry and empty for a time. The air becomes wind, the wind a shadow. The shadow becomes a cloud. The cloud becomes rain. The rain falls and the river runs again. *Kji-kinap* accumulates and is spent, accumulates again so long as Persons move through and live in the Six Worlds. There is nothing to fear where all is one."

Mimkitawo'qu'sk moved a little distance away. He felt Eugainia's presence behind him. When he turned, he saw the full moon in her eyes, as on the night they gave their mortal bodies to each other on Apekwit. "We walk the Six Worlds together," he said. "We gather *Kji-kinap*. When we're strong enough, a child with great Power, great *Kji-kinap*, will walk among The People and your people."

"Just so. A child will be born, will grow wise in the ways of The People and my people and guide them while we rest."

They stood in silence, the bright stars pulsing, the moon white on the snow. The Sky World washed the Earth World clean.

Mimkitawo'qu'sk spoke quietly. "Before you came, before I remembered who I was, I said: I'll gather Power and go to the

Ghost World. I'll visit Muini'skw my wife, my beloved wife, my human soul, my Muini'skw who went too soon to the Ghost World and left me here to grieve and weep alone."

"How did she die?"

"She followed our child. My great love and Keswalqw's tree-Person potions were no match for the pull of the Ghost World."

"We'll go there, Mimkitawo'qu'sk. We'll go to the Ghost World. Together. When you see Muini'skw, your beloved wife and your little child, your heart will heal and water will no longer flow from your eyes."

"Or your eyes," he said, unashamed that she should see his mortal's tears. "When you see Morgase, your kin-friend healed and laughing, your spirit will mend and time will have no meaning."

"When I watch Morgase, healed and laughing, tend my broken baby boy."

"Who himself will be healed. If we go we may not come back, such is the beauty and Power of the Ghost World."

"We'll gather strength. Wrap our grief in Power. A man or woman who has seen the Ghost World and returns brings great strength, becomes beloved of The People—a clan mother, a shaman or a chief."

Mimkitawo'qu'sk began their descent of the hill. Eugainia followed. She realized the young God had a scent about him, at once familiar and obscure. She relived the day she lost Lord Ard's misshapen child, in the Meadow of the Singing Stone, across Spirit Bird Bay from Pictook's Smoking Mountain. It seemed centuries ago. Yet only eight moons past, Keswalqw's child-birthing medicine, made from the bark of seven trees, hurled Eugainia into a swirl of celestial fire, raised her higher into realms exquisite and more familiar than her epiphanous journeys had ever done. Instead of snapping back to reality, as she normally did when the golden cord that bound her soul and body was stretched beyond its limit, she wafted back to earth on a beguiling scent she could not identify.

In her cream white wigwam, Keswalqw had assembled a group of children, boys and girls below the age of six. When asked why this white-as-a-ghost-person woman appeared on the great wooden whale with its wind-catching blanket, Keswalqw answered: "She came to us to learn and teach and be our friend." Satisfied, the children sat quietly in a circle around the sleeping Eugainia, awaiting her return from her spirit quest. When Eugainia woke, the image of her twisted child flickered once and then vanished. The children rustled like poplar leaves. She turned from one sweet face to the other, her heart awash in their open smiles, their black-haired, tan-skinned, brown-eyed beauty. Joy filled her heart. She inhaled, deep as at the first breath, as though fresh from the womb herself. She thought at first the scent her lungs devoured rose from her fir-bough bed. Her second breath revealed the truth: the children of The People smelled of smoke and fire, of woodland scents and pure ocean air. They smelled of earth and wind and moss and meadow. They smelled of light and joy. They were life, and the breath of life. They were heaven and they were the earth. Like blades of grass in the meadow, they were not born into the world but from it. They were made of stars and stardust. And light from the Great Spirit's eye.

On this night, descending this hillside path in the cold light of the moon, Eugainia noticed that the same scent, the earth and sky scent of The People's children, rose from Mimkitawo'qu'sk and trailed him as he walked.

Eugainia, nibbled pink these last five moons, addled and elevated by love, realized until Mimkitawo'qu'sk she lived but was only half alive. He taught her to follow the ways of the animal Powers. She was no longer the pampered Lady of the Grail. Eugainia the huntress learned the habits of the creatures that sustained her. She learned their speech. She came to know their thoughts and feelings. She felt the outrage of their mortal flesh. She shared their fear when she killed.

"Our brother and sister animals," Mimkitawo'qu'sk mused as they walked, "speak with tongues, yes, but also with the very flesh of their bodies. The joy you feel? Their great hunger? Their fear of injury? Their fear of death....This is animal knowledge common to all. We were born, as were you, they say. So that you may live, they say, we must die. The People say it is the meat speaking."

"The *meat* speaking?" Eugainia recoiled at the brutal phrase. Yet she knew exactly what he meant. Once she heard the flesh of a moose speak its outrage when she plunged Mimkitawo'qu'sk's spear, Tooth of Wolverine, into its exhausted heart. Resigned to its fate, she heard the moose meat say, "Honour the bones of my body, and the skin of my unborn calf, and I will come and feed and clothe you again."

Unborn calf? Eugainia felt herself crack open, like an egg.

She heard the meat speak caution as she sliced through the wall of the uterus, extracted and butchered the calf, whose heart still beat, whose hide she stretched on a frame of ash, soaked in saltwater and stretched again, then tanned with the brains and liver of a seabird—the tender hide she wore beneath her winter robe, soft on her breasts, kind to her nipples, soft as the finest silken camisole. She felt the meat speak when she reclined after eating, sated and drowsy. At her sexual awakening, and subsequently—hers was the flesh of a starved animal, a creature willing to sacrifice itself completely, to devour and be devoured—the meat of her body and the marrow of her bones sang love. "*Akaia-aia-ah*," her flesh and bones had whispered. "*Akaia-ia*!"

In the still of the night, as they moved down the path under crackling stars, Mimkitawo'qu'sk's mind was clear and sharp—a gift of the night, he mused, a gift from the light of the moon on the snow, from the rounded mounds bending the branches of black spruce. *Kji-kinap* grows quickly through L'nuk, he thought, when the blood is roused on a cold night's march. A man thinks that he might walk, but walks that he might think. Ha!

Eugainia was surprised when they continued down past the small moosehide wigwam they'd built that afternoon, where heated rocks and rolled beaver robes waited their return. She was tired. Her body, poor weary donkey, needed rest.

Mimkitawo'qu'sk turned and smiled. "We've borne The People's yearning long enough. It's time to ride their spirits for a while."

"Where are you taking me?"

"Tonight we enter the Cave of the Seven Seekers."

"What? The Seven Sleepers of Ephesus? Have we come so far?"

"No, no, dear one. The Cave of the Seven Seekers of The People. Tonight we become bears and serpents."

CHAPTER TEN

A cleft in the rock face the height of the man and as wide as his shoulders offered Mimkitawo'qu'sk entrance to the World Below the Earth. He stepped inside without considering Eugainia. There was no need. Though still some distance behind, when he entered the darkened cave he knew he'd find her waiting.

Mimkitawo'qu'sk passed his hand over the tip of Tooth of Wolverine. Warm light filled the cavern. It cast no shadow. Eugainia eyes adjusted quickly. Lying in their great bulk before her, seven sleeping bears, arranged heads inward in a well-spaced circle, snored gently.

"Who are they?"

"In the time of my grandmother's mother, seven of The People went on a spirit quest, seeking to know why so many of the first white-as-ghost-persons—the ones who came many years before you and Henry—died such swift and painful deaths."

"The poor beleaguered Templars on their first flight to the New World. The beginning of their time of plague and woe."

"Keswalqw tells they dug the great well by the sea."

"They came to hide the Holy Grail."

"Then built the Stone House of Death where my grandfather's father found Tooth of Wolverine. The white-as-a-ghost-persons' skin erupted in black sores. Those few People who came to know them—slept in their scratchy beds, wore their stiff clothes—became ill and died with them. The People left their camps and started over, far away. But still the questions lingered. Why had these kind and good red-cross men come among them? Surely not to suffer such terrible deaths. A council was called. It was decided to send two clan mothers and five brave young warriors on a spirit quest to find the answers. They set out. After a time, lost and starving, the seven seekers found this cave and fell asleep."

"They've been asleep for a hundred years, these gigantic bear Persons?"

"Two lifetime winters. The seven seekers woke as Spirit bears. They had no need of water. No need of meat or nuts, honey, grass or berry. Of *tagawan*, the young salmon when it first returns from the sea. They lay here, not awake or sleeping. Somewhere in-between. Dreaming dreams of strength and courage. Bear dreams."

"They all dream the same dreams?"

"In their sleep, bear totem People travel great distances to the bears. All seek the answer he or she requires."

"The bears dream for them."

"Yes. For all the bear totem People. Medicine dreams. Answer their questions. Where to hunt. Where to fish. How to deal with cranky wives or husbands. Willful children. Envious neighbours. All things of life." He propped Tooth of Wolverine against the cave wall. "In this same way, dolphins dream medicine dreams for dolphin totem People. Trees dream for tree totem People. As moose and trees dream together for moose/wood Persons like me, Persons with blended totems."

Mimkitawo'qu'sk stood before a brown mass of rumbling fur. A grunt preceded a throaty rumble. "This great she-bear calls me," he said.

Mimkitawo'qu'sk wavered, turned from mist to vapour. Eugainia clapped her hands with delight when the she-bear inhaled. Feet first, he disappeared up the great bear's nostrils. Eugainia chose another, a great rumbling male. Her feet, then legs and torso became insubstantial. She found herself inside the snoring bear, standing face to face with Sir Athol Gunn who stood wide-eyed, fast asleep, paralyzed with fear. She placed her hand on his shoulder. Instantly, she was swept up into the churning sea of Sir Athol's dream:

A dying man, bloodied by battle, reaches toward a boy. The boy is Athol. Six or seven years old. The man near death is Athol's father, still caged in his bloodied armour, his torso bruised, his organs ruptured. He clasps Athol's hand. The light fades from the battered man's eyes. Young Athol lowers his dead father's visor.

In dream time, Athol leaps to a place unknown to him. Eugainia follows. Athol is a boy watching another boy. This boy is Kulu, not yet six, a tender boy, still full of magic, a handsome son of The People.

Eugainia hears Athol say, "No. I'm too young..."

A young woman, one of The People, Kulu's mother, says, "No. He's still too young to hunt."

In separate wisps of colour that twine like smoke into one, Eugainia and Sir Athol rise from the fur of the he-bear and float near the zenith of the cave. Keswalqw and Mimkitawo'qu'sk emerge from the nearby she-bear's nostrils. They ascend to the ceiling and hover near Eugainia and Sir Athol.

From deep in the earth, a tremor.

Sir Athol's shade wavers. Eugainia's shadow trembles. Keswalqw's dream shape whispers…"Jipijka'maq!"

Mimkitawo'qu'sk doubles his size, puffs up, like a cobra. He hisses. The tremor subsides. "Still distant," Athol hears Mimkitawo'qu'sk murmur as he resumes his familiar shape. "But coming this way." Sir Athol dreams the childhood dream of the boy again. He sees a face, painted ochre, a wide, black, eye-width stripe drawn from forehead to chin. Eagle and raven feathers radiate through three hundred and sixty degrees, fixed at the back of the dreadful head in a knot of greased-back, blue black hair.

The warrior/hunter towers above the little boy Kulu. "Why do you stare without mercy, Father?" Athol asks him. Keswalqw's voice calms him, "This man is not your father, Athol." She extends her hand. "The boy is not you but like you." Athol, reassured, holds it tightly. "This is Kulu's stepfather. He has no fondness for the boy." Keswalqw leads Athol, a boy himself now, deeper into the cave. "He is a jealous man," the mothering Keswalqw says. "A spiteful man and he dislikes you because he fears I care more for you than him."

"Wife," says the feathered menace, "it is time the boy learned something of the forest. I'll take him with me today. I'll take him hunting."

"No!" Eugainia re-enters the dream, clasping Sir Athol the man's arm tightly, holding him back. "Kulu is far too young!"

Mimkitawo'qu'sk touches Eugainia's arm. "Let him go where he must."

Kulu, the son of The People, or is it Athol the boy of the Highlands, follows the befeathered Stepfather, meek as a lamb. The mother weeps, for she is powerless before Kulu's cruel stepfather and knows his jealous heart.

The Stepfather knows of a cave deep in the forest, on the side of a rock-strewn hill, a cave that leads to the depths of the earth. It is this cave, this bear cave. The Cave of the Seven Seekers before the time of the bears. The Jealous Stepfather leads his stepson to its open mouth. "Go inside," he tells the boy, "and hunt for rabbit tracks."

Kulu hangs back. "It's dark in there. I'm afraid."

"It's dark and he's afraid," Sir Athol, the grown man dreaming, tells Keswalqw.

"Afraid!" scoffs the man. "A fine hunter you'll make." He pushes the dream boy Kulu into the cave. "Stay in there until I tell you to come out." He thrusts a pole under a huge boulder. It tumbles, covers the mouth of the cave.

Athol assaults the boulder. "Kulu will soon die of starvation," he cries. Even Athol the great hairy bear of a man is too small to move it. Even in a spirit quest. Even in a dream.

"I'll not return home at once," the cruel Stepfather says as Athol and Keswalqw watch powerless from a distance. "I'll go to the beach and collect a bag of Kluscap's purple stones to take to her as a peace offering. I'll make her think I was looking for the boy. I'll let time pass, time enough for Kulu to starve and die. She'll be angry. She'll be sad. She'll blame me. But only for a while. I'll win her back. She'll have my child and forget her snivelling boy. No one will ever know what had happened."

"No one?" Mimkɨtawo'qu'sk appears before Sir Athol. "There is one who knows already. I am Kluscap the Great Chief. I am Kluscap taller than the tallest pine tree. I am Kluscap whose arms encircle the world....I am Kluscap. I know. Come, Sir Athol." Mimkɨtawo'qu'sk touches Athol's arm and takes him on a journey. "Look. I, the Mighty Kluscap, appear from behind his cliff called Blom-i'-don. I am well aware of what the wicked Stepfather has done and I am angry."

The Mighty Kluscap, Mimkɨtawo'qu'sk in his Kluscap form,

watches as the cruel Stepfather picks the finest purple stones from the beach. He cracks them open with his stone axe, for they are hollow as goose eggs after Clever Fox—who once learned to puncture them and suck them dry—has finished feasting. Inside the egg-rock, purple crystals glint in the sun.

"In time she will love me as she loved the boy," the cruel Stepfather, a weak and selfish man, says. "The child we will have, my child, will be a real child. My boy-child. Strong like his father, not the weakling boy who hates to hunt, tells tales and sings the woman songs."

Mimkitawo'qu'sk, in the guise of the mighty Kluscap, grown taller than the tallest mountain, strikes the red stone cliff of Blom-i'-don with Tooth of Wolverine, his mighty spear. Athol watches in dream-awe. The great cape splits. Earth and stones tumble down, down, down to the beach, burying the wicked Stepfather, killing him instantly.

Led by Mimkitawo'qu'sk, who is once again himself, not Kluscap, Sir Athol flies back to the cave from their journey to Blom-i'don. In the darkness, Kulu sits and weeps out his loneliness and fear. Keswalqw walks from shadow, takes Sir Athol by the hand. "He has only seen six summers, after all, and wants his mother."

Suddenly, an almighty voice!

"Kulu!" almighty Mimkitawo'qu'sk calls to the boy. "Come this way."

In his dream, Athol sees two eyes glowing in the depths of the cave. He is afraid for the boy. He is afraid for himself.

"Come, Kulu," the Great Chief Mimkitawo'qu'sk, calls. "You have nothing to fear."

Athol watches Kulu walk toward the glowing eyes. Kulu trembles. Great burly Sir Athol, man of war and destiny, trembles, his fear no less than the boy's, be they both awake or dreaming. Flat as a leaf, Keswalqw appears on the wall of the cave. As though drawn in ash and ochre, outlined in black, her body red, rendered in two dimensions, she ripples over the rough surface. She speaks: "Look. My dear Athol," she reassures, "Kulu is afraid no longer."

The glowing eyes in the dark of the cave grow bigger and brighter. At last Sir Athol sees they belong to an old porcupine.

"Don't cry anymore, my son," says Porcupine. "I'm here to help."

The leafy Keswalqw slips from the wall. She stands fully formed at Athol's side, his sword-arm side. Joy spreads across his ruddy face. "I'm no longer afraid," Athol tells Eugainia, who has come to stand behind them. "I have this woman, Keswalqw, a woman of The People who walks beside me now." They watch Porcupine waddle from the darkness to the crack of light at the cave entrance. Porcupine tries to push away the stone, but the stone is too heavy. Porcupine puts his lips to the crack of light and shouts to the forest outside, "Friends of Kluscap! Sons and daughters of Great Chief Mimkitawo'qu'sk. Come around, all of you!" Woodland animal and bird Persons hear him and come—Wolf, Raccoon, Caribou, Turtle, Opossum, Rabbit, and Squirrel, and birds of all kinds from the Great Chuckling Turkey to the little Hummingdird. "A child has been left here to die," calls old Porcupine from inside the cave. "I am old, and not strong enough to move the rock. Help me or he is lost."

The animals call back. "We will try." Bold Raccoon, who is known to act before he thinks, marches up and tries to wrap his arms around the stone, but they are much too short. "If only I had arms like Brother Bear, I would lift and hurl this rock past Grandfather Sun," Raccoon laments. "Come, Fox. You are swift and clever. You'll find a way to move the rock." Fox, who is known by times to think too much, bites and scratches at the boulder, but this only makes his paws and lips bleed. "Blood. Bright red fox blood. Too precious to leave on a rock that will not move," he complains. "Call Caribou." Caribou, vain and fleet, steps up and thrusts her long antlers into the crack, tries to pry loose the stone. Her antler breaks. She stamps in rage. "Who will mate with a one-antlered caribou? They'll think the Creator gives a warning. No calves that jump, and butt and suck for me. I'll have to wait until next spring, until my antler grows back, before I am beautiful again," she moans as she walks away, shaking her lopsided head.

In the end, all give up. It's no use. They can't move the stone.

"*Kwah-ee,*" a new voice speaks.

"Who comes?" they ask.

They turn and see she-bear Mooinskw. Who is more steadfast and dependable than she? Mooinskw comes quietly out of the woods. The small animals hide. Fox tells Mooinskw what has happened: a child has been imprisoned by a selfish man, left to stave and die. Mooinskw's great bear heart is moved to pity. She wraps her strong arms around the boulder and heaves with all her great strength. With a rumble and a crash, the stone rolls over, tumbling end for end down the steep slope of the hill, cutting a path through the forest. "Sorry trees," Mooinskw says as the trees crack and splinter and call out in their pain. Mooinskw turns back to the mouth of the cave. Out come Kulu and Porcupine, followed by Sir Athol and Keswalqw, their faces radiant with joy.

"From now on, Kulu," Mooinskw, her great paws on Kulu's slender shoulders, says, "You are a bear person. The cruel man is wrong. I see into your heart. Strong and brave is your totem." Kulu runs off into the forest, chatting and laughing with the other animals, for he is a magic boy now and knows their tongues. Kulu will grow into a great shaman, a good man, and heal The People of many ills.

The she-bear turns to Sir Athol. She places her great paws lightly on the big man's broad shoulders. "I am Mooinskw, your totem animal and your mother while on earth. From now on, white-as-a-ghost-person from across the great sea," she says, "your totem gives strength and courage, to you and to those you love who love you. Go. Walk among The People. Gather *Kji-kinap* for the great task that awaits you." Mooinskw ambles into the cave, takes her place among the Seven Sleepers. Soon her gentle, rumbling snores are indistinguishable from the others.

It isn't the snores of the bears that cause the rock walls to vibrate, then rattle. What evil force disturbs the World Below the Earth? Rock splinters fly past the dreamers and the dreamed. The cave wall splits open with the sound of seven thunders. Great and terrible is the bone-plated head of Jipijka'maq, Horned Serpent Person. His eyes are like Cannibal Ghost Person's—flaming pinwheels spurting blood. His pupils are black rectangles, his forked tongue flicks sparks and ropes of flame lick his hard-as-bone serpent lips. Jipijka'maq opens his gigantic mouth. Eugainia cries out in anger and in fear. Caught between the serpent's terrible teeth is Prince Henry Sinclair, Earl of the Orkney Isles, Liegeman to the King of Norway, Baron of Rosslyn, Protector of Scotland, Protector of the Holy Grail. His right side is pierced by a fang, below the lowest rib. Arched unnaturally backward, in terrible agony, repelled at the stench of Jipijka'maq's awful breath, the air he gasps to breathe, Henry calls to Eugainia. "Eugainia. Come back to us. We need you!" His face fixed in horror, his chest heaving, Henry Sinclair's last breath is about to be wrung from him. Eugainia steps forward. She raises her arms. Light streams from the tips of Eugainia's fingers.

Jipijka'maq squints in the blinding light. He drops Henry. He shakes his great head, scales rattling. Jipijka'maq hisses radiant, flesh-melting fire. The fiery gust breaks and flows around Eugainia. She wavers. She weakens.

"Mimkitawo'qu'sk," she calls out in distress. "Help me."

Mimkitawo'qu'sk brandishes Tooth of Wolverine. "No," he bellows, "you shall not have her."

Gentle as a lynx retrieving her wayward kitten, Jipijka'maq bends, plucks Henry from the floor of the cave. Jipijka'maq's stone-plated scales, each the size of a swordsman's shield, rattle to life. Horned Serpent Person speeds away down the cave, its prize, Prince Henry Sinclair, limp as a rag doll, dangling from its jaws. Above the rattle and clamour, Henry's cries for help trail to nothing as the monster's endless length speeds past them, down into the depths of the cave. Mimkitawo'qu'sk, swift as lightning, secures his grip on the spear shaft. He plants Tooth of Wolverine deep into Jipijka'maq's lashing tail. Eugainia grabs Mimkitawo'qu'sk's extended arm. With her free hand, she takes a firm hold of Sir Athol Gunn's tunic. All three, twisting like kites in a Thunder-bird wind, disappear down the tunnel.

Keswalqw stands before the she-bear. She raises her arms, throws back her head.

"*Akaia-aia-ah*," she chants. "*Akaia-ia!*"

The dream time ends.

In Keswalqw's lodge, the thin breath of sleeping people, living people, not spirit bears, hung in a perceptible layer, frozen mist in the burning cold. The starving time was upon them. Sir Athol, not awake, not asleep, his skin wet with perspiration despite the bitter cold, gasped. He cast his sleeping robe aside. He sat, naked, confounded, with no idea who or where he is. He came fully awake when Jipijka'maq rose from two glowing embers in the wigwam's central firepit. Sir Athol lashed out at the hunger-induced vision. "Henry!" he cried.

No answer came from the dark. Henry's sleeping robe was turned back. His fir-bough bed vacated.

Athol woke Keswalqw. "Keswalqw. Henry is gone. Come."

"No. Would you have three die seeking one? Henry will find his way."

"We can't leave him wandering the woods in this cold."

"Nor can we find him in the dark. Henry will find his way. If he's not back by dawn, we will seek him."

The hunger song of a pack of wolves echoed in the night.

"Dawn may be too late."

"It might. It might not. There's nothing to do but wait." Keswalqw urged Athol back beneath the sleeping robes. "I heard you speak in your sleep. What were you dreaming?"

"I thought I was a boy. The Son of The People. A cruel step-father. Me the son. Then the dream was not about me. It was about Henry. It seemed so real..."

Keswalqw offered what spare comfort she could. "Your hunger has found a voice and now it's speaking."

"But the bear. She was for me. She loved me. She became my mother."

"Your totem. Your bear-clan totem."

"Yes. Then this monstrous snake. Now Henry's gone. It's as though the dream became real, but only when I woke."

"Shh, my love. Rest. The morning soon will come. In the light of Grandfather Sun, we'll see what we must do."

The scent arising from warm fir boughs calmed him. Sir Athol folded himself back into Keswalqw's embrace. He set his lips to her breast. He held the nipple lightly, not exerting the slightest pressure, not daring, in a starving time, to suck, lest there be blood. For a time, Keswalqw and Sir Athol lay awake in each other's arms. When they slept, briefly, feverishly, they dreamed of flesh and blood.

In the little moosehide wigwam on a far-distant hill, the little moosehide wigwam warmed by stones heated to perfection before they climbed the hill to speak to the moon, Mimkitawo'qu'sk and Eugainia, tired from their journey through Sir Athol's bear-man dream, prepared to sleep.

In this place untouched by the starving time, three weeks' travel from the winter camp of The People, their life was full and rich. They knew The People suffered. They also knew they could not interfere. It was the way of The People to endure the starving time, to let nature take its course. They knew what was expected of them. It was their time to be together, to gather the strength to fight the great battle they knew would come, a battle greater than that being waged against cold and hunger. Mimkitawo'qu'sk and Eugainia would lead a fight for the very survival of The People. They could not go home to The People until their spirit journey was complete. Victory would demand all the Power they could gather from their walk through the Six Worlds.

Eugainia settled beneath the weight and warmth of the furs. Mimkitawo'qu'sk opened the smoke flap at the apex of wigwam, not to release smoke, for they had no need of fire, but to open the night to the moon and stars. Mimkitawo'qu'sk shed his garments, raised his arms to the revolving night. Eugainia marvelled at the moon-washed beauty of her young Man/God, starlight shooting through his moon black hair. Mimkitawo'qu'sk, despite the bite of the cold, paused, gazed down at the Woman/Goddess he loved. He knew what awaited...his skin quivered, yes, in response to the cold, but also in mounting desire. Eugainia threw back the robes.

"Hurry, Mimkitawo'qu'sk. We'll freeze!"

Still he lingered. The long line of her waist, the tight plane of her stomach, her breasts, at once generous and discrete, the strong and supple legs, the honey-coloured patch tightly curled, the warmth of her gaze, the cold of the night, the love in his heart, the tender joy he knew lay before him...

Mimkitawo'qu'sk was seized by an unreasonable fear that it was all an illusion forged by the moon. He scrambled beneath the robe, pressed his naked body to her's. Real enough. Almost more than even a strong young Man/God could bear.

"You are beautiful, Eugainia. Beautiful in the cold fire of Grandmother Moon. I give myself, my *Kji-kinap*, to you."

"The night we loved on Apekwit," Eugainia responded after a moment's thought, "I became Lnu'k, a Person, one of The People. Since then, I have walked with you and gathered Power. Mimkitawo'qu'sk. Tonight...here on this far distant hill...tonight I give myself, my *Kji-kinap*, to you."

His hand drifted over ribs which, when he first knew her, were covered with a thin layer of soft yielding fat. Now her torso was laced tight with muscle and sinew. Her flesh was hard and warm, polished marble, not weak, pampered flesh.

His fingers trailed the natural curve of her waist, rose with the rise of her hip, descended to the gates of the Cauldron of the Five Trees. He furled and unfurled her tight, honey-coloured curls. He traced the swollen curves of her outer lips, his pause a question, asking permission to enter.

"Yes, beloved. Enter, and be welcome."

Mimkitawo'qu'sk watched Eugainia's eyes close then open softly. Her lips parted. The sweet breath of her sigh washed his brow and temple. He hovered above her. "You are Eugainia, White Goddess from across the Sea no more," he whispered. "You are Eugainia—Woman Who Fell in Love with the Moon."

"And you, my God on earth, formed of sand and stone, air and water, fire and ice," she said as she rose to meet and enfold him. "You are my Mimkitawo'qu'sk. Thank you for showing me the Six Worlds of The People. "

"It was my great pleasure."

"From this night forward, beloved," she said as her hips rose to meet his gentle downward pressure, "we weep and grieve alone no more."

CHAPTER ELEVEN

Henry woke with a start to the howl of a wolf. This was no dream wolf. A feverish rose and purple radiance thinned the indigo night. He'd slept standing. How long, he didn't know. He raised an arm, a ghost of a thing against the wisp of a crescent moon. A thin layer of ice, a second skin, caught and held the slow, uncertain dawn. The matted guard hairs of his beaver robe and ragged chain mail glistened.

I'm clothed, he marvelled, in a sheath of light.

Beneath the begrimed robe, Henry's flesh quivered. He remembered stumbling through these young maples in the last light of a baffling day. The bitter cold had lifted briefly as the sun set. The wind lost its equilibrium. Pelting rain angled off the horizontal when the wind dropped and fell straight down. The temperature plummeted in the upper atmosphere then swept down from the World Above the Earth. Rain, cold beyond freezing, yet liquid while in motion, became ice on contact. After the rain, more bitter cold. Dry air was a sabre lacerating his nostrils. Water pooling at the corners of his eyes froze.

The once-patrician brow protruded, an apocalyptic ridge of bone. Tendons and ligaments lay stark on desiccated muscle. His malnourished, parchment yellow skin was cold as marble. Blood vessels roped up his torso in high relief. Blood pulsed erratic at his throat before disappearing below his jaw on its ascent to further chill his brain. Nostril blood, blackened by the cold, caked his frosted moustache. His blue eyes were ringed, dark with privation and despair.

In a lifetime as a leader of men, Henry had lured more than one dying mind back from paradise. Could he do the same for himself? He'd seen cold men die in deliriums of heat, pulling frozen clothes from convulsed bodies, mistaking death's intimacy for the warmth of a loved one's touch. He'd heard their bright rambles, these doomed men, their flashes of counterfeit logic stirring the deaths of a congealing mind.

Henry forced his mind to this: in the darkest hour of a snowless night in the coldest days of the starving time, he was lost and alone in a grove of young maples, their trunks frozen stone. How he'd come there, he could not imagine. He released his grip on the trunk to which he'd clung the long night through, grim with instinctual purpose. He forced one foot forward. Then the other. What seemed progress to Henry would rouse the deepest sympathy of an observer: two months shy of forty years of age, his was the slow, ponderous gate of an enfeebled old man.

What better place to relieve The People of the burden of his care, he'd reasoned as he rose from his sleeping robes and wandered out into the night. How better to atone for his great failure? Where better to offer his soul to God?

The dying night gave no answer. Nor was there solace in the growing dawn.

How have I come to this frigid, savage place? The stars. Yes. I followed the stars westward. Across the great northern sea. In the great dome of heaven, the ancient gods are near. God guides me. No. God did guide me. No more. God brought me here, then deserted me. Can it be? All these years of struggle? I lived to die alone. A wasted life? No. The ancients tell that every age proclaims its God. God's emissaries, patterned there in the stars. Human longing written in the heavens. Horus, Krishna, Vishnu, Muhammad—Peace be upon him. Peace be upon me. Aye. God obliged me to usher out this bloodied, plague-ridden arc of the wheel. To usher in the new. Our Lord the Christ appeared at the sign of the fish. His time has all but passed. In my soul Aquaria, Eugainia, the true Madonna sings the sweeter song. At last, the Goddess star is once again risen. All fear shall dwindle. Cruelty diffuse. Anger born of ignorance shall be overwhelmed by patience and love. Or so I thought. 'Til some cruel viper laid her egg in me. Was it yesterday? Last week? An ancient man of Keswalqw's clan told his sons and daughters his time to die had come. Great peace descends upon the dying grieved by loving kin, I think. Anguish chills the failing hearts of those who journey alone. The old warrior had seen one hundred and forty winters. The starving family struggled to rise from their torpor. They wept through the night, grieved together with their father, grandfather, father-in-law. Great uncle to Keswalqw. Newfound kin-friend to Athol Gunn and to me. The old man's breath was shallow but regular. His heart beats irregular but strong. He said, I know from the sound of your voices and in my own heart that I need suffer the burden of being L'nuk no more. Though I breathe and my blood still flows, I am dead now. Please, take me out so that I might end my walk upon the earth in open air. Let the snow-coloured Person from the place of ice and frost lead my willing spirit to the Ghost World. He slipped into the quiet sleep of the winter dead. His sons carried his frozen body back inside the communal hut. Wrapped in his finest robes, they lay him far from the heat of the fire, secure against decay and predation.

They say when the starving time ends, the old man will be raised to the upper branches of a funeral tree. After two summers the bundle of bones, all that will remain—the flesh withered away by wind and sun—will be taken to the burial mound and interred with his hunting kit and spirit gifts. He will be mourned with proper feasting. I wish I could be there to honour him. Who will honour me?

Three big-eyed children, all skin and bones, were taken next. The death of the old man unsettled Henry: the death of the children cracked his gallant heart. He confronted Keswalqw:

"Surely something could have been done to save them. Two dogs remain uneaten. Why were the children not fed?"

"The bitch is fat with pups," Keswalqw replied. "We do not eat the future. "

Henry was not satisfied. "Then leave the bitch and kill the dog."

"Destroy half of the last mated pair?" Keswalqw's patience thinned. "No. We need both to run the deer."

"There are no deer."

"There will be deer."

Henry said no more.

"Our stores are empty, Henry. The ground is bare. There is no snow. The earth is hard as your iron axes. The water like a stone. Moose and deer hear every snapping twig, the crush of each dry leaf. Even if we could get near enough to plant a spear, none in our feebleness, not us, not the dogs, could chase a wounded animal down. Don't be downhearted, Henry. Or waste your strength on anger. You say you wish to know our ways, that you can better respect them. Hear this: it's time for the creatures of stream, sky and forest to multiply, our time to decrease. This is the way of the starving time."

"A sad, miserable waste."

"It may not be your way. It's how it must be for The People."

"We spend much time at home laying up stores against these starving times—"

"And how much blood to defend your cache against your friends and neighbours, not to mention your enemies? And how much blood is shed to gather in food that is not yours? You see? I listen to your tales too."

"I never doubted for a second that I had less than your full attention."

"No. I don't suppose you did." Keswalqw's smile was little more than a tug at the corners of once-full, now ruined lips. "Nor is there need for sorrow. Those unable to live, the old and tired among us, the child born weak or unfinished, the man killed in battle, the women dead in childbirth...all go to prepare a place for us who stay to walk the Earth World without them for a time. Those who wish walk to the Ghost World, to which we all one day must travel...let them go. Give thanks they show the way and make the Ghost World pleasant for us."

"I watched the children die and felt such anger."

"Spirit children have a task. They leave the Ghost World in time of need and lead the animals to us. Simple and sweet are their childish natures; trusting and generous the creatures who follow them. Put your anger aside. A starving time is not a time of waste. A shift in balance, for certain. A change of spirit, yes. A time of pain and sorrow yes. But not waste."

Henry held his silence. Keswalqw caught and held Henry's ambivalent eye.

"You have no wish to follow the old man to the Ghost World, do you?"

"No."

"Good. Then stay. Take heart, Henry. The snows will come. The cold will end. The sun will warm our bones. Our cheeks will be round with fat once again. Men and women will join together when their bellies are full. The children will come back, my friend. They always do. We will survive. We always do."

Henry walked along a frozen stream in the early days of the starving time. He happened upon a young woman in the forest at the edge of its stone-hard waters. Her head was cloaked. Her face in silhouette. He was about to call her by name. Eugainia! No. A young woman of The People. She had not seen sixteen summers. Her newborn child, still wet from her mother's womb, cord bitten and knotted, steam rising from its infant body, lay naked on an untanned hide nearby. No matter the time of year of its birth, an infant born to The People must be cleansed quickly by complete submersion in moving water lest evil spirits catch its scent and stalk it. Beside its mother at the edge of the frozen stream the baby's miniature arms and legs pumped the frigid air with infant fury. The mother raised a rock the size of her child and brought it down with all her force on the glassy surface of the stream. One blow fractured the thick ice. Clear water flowed swiftly. She watched, momentarily mesmerized, as fragments of ice swirled, caught the jagged edges of the hole. The rock slipped from her grasp, fell from view below the surface. She raised her naked child to the Creator, asked a blessing and then plunged the infant through shards of ice into frigid water. She held the child below the surface for what seemed an eternity to Henry but was, in fact, only ten short beats of his racing heart. He was on the verge of interfering when Keswalqw stepped from shadowed spruce and grasped his arm.

"You have no place here, Henry Orkney. This is woman's business. Go back to the men. Watch and wait with them."

"But the child..." he protested.

"Cold is not our enemy. We walk with the cold and we gather Power. Cold walks with us and it gathers Power from L'nuk. In this way winter and The People become a single Person. The child will decide to live and walk the Earth World with us or, before three nights have passed, will travel to the Ghost World. Either way, The People become stronger. Only the strongest survive the winter cleansing. Only those who wish to walk with the cold will survive the cold. You see how we embrace it, teach our bodies to live with it, to use what the Great Spirit provides. 'Walk quickly in the frost and snow,' He tells us. 'Walk slowly in the heat of summer. Walk with joy amid the bounty I provide, with your head raised up when your belly is full. Walk softly, with patience and humility when provisions fail until I restore the balance.'"

If he could cross the short distance to the next set of trees, Henry reasoned, those beyond the perimeter of the woods where the rising sun would warm him, he'd survive. To his fevered mind, light, no matter how faint or febrile meant heat. He attempted another step, his breathing rapid and shallow. He fell to his knees. He stared, unable at first to make sense of the glistening surface. Ice. Frozen water. A pool. In width the height of the fallen man, in depth no more than the length of his arm, wrist to elbow. The frozen pond mirrored the fading stars. He strained to lift his head. His chin broke contact with his chest, where it had found brief relief. He forced his eyes to the horizon. His clouded mind rose from his body. His heart stopped beating.

No...not now. Too soon. I've yet to make my peace with God.

An involuntary gasp from lungs near collapse, then a sharp inhalation, reunited Henry's body and soul. He forced his gaze up to the zenith still dark above the fringed horizon. His chin fell back to his chest. He addressed the image of the helmeted, thin-faced man reflected in the ice below. The Great Architect, with square and compass, sets our destiny. Among the stars, God writes it. All sacred texts lay open on our Templar pulpits. Bible. Qur'an. Talmud. In each the same great mystery is laid bare. But now the Temple's razed. All books but one are burned. Temple Knights, in their ones and their thousands, hanged by the neck until near death. Cut down...death's blessings unreasonably withheld. Their private agony becomes the rabble's ecstasy. Strapped down naked, angled upright to the mob's best advantage, private pain made spectacle. My Brother's shame repellent and instructive washes the leering mob, evoking not their pity but their lust. A poor soul's eyes held open, forced to watch his living bowels drawn and draped about him. His privy parts held high for all to see, dripping blood. His mutilated corpse hacked in quarters, or pulled apart by horses. The Temple Knight's final resting place a shameful lime-slaked grave.

The struggle to raise his head from the sickening images alive in the ice mirror below forced tears to Henry's lashes, their fanned shafts already flared thick with shards of ice. On ape-knuckle hands—his wrist rigid with cold, his knees insensible—he straightened his elbows, raised his torso, but only slightly. The stars in the ice snapped into focus. Were they on the ice? In it? No. The stars swam in the air between his chilled pupils and the surface of the ice itself.

Look how the stars speed across the surface of the ice. The entire history of the heavens and our place below...displayed for my benefit. Praise be to God! God wills it. As one star sets westward, another is born, low in the east. Morning star. Guiding light. Goddess star. Our own eternal Venus. You led the sun through Cancer in the days of the stone-circle queens and kings. You led the sun to Aries the Ram heralding the Shepherd dynasties of the Hittites...then Horus, and Ramses, King of all Egyptian kings. In his turn, Christ followed you through Pisces. Now, morning star, in the flood of this frozen dawn light the path for My Lady. Aquaria. Bearer of the sacred water. Chalice divine. Eugainia. The Living Holy Grail.

A single cry became the cry of many: a distant pack of wolves called to their leader. The alpha wolf replied. He was close. He'd found meat. The howl that chilled the soul of man from the dawn of time warmed Henry. He took comfort from the thought that other living hearts, though feral and predacious, beat nearby.

God help me. I'm as mad as the Christ in the desert. No garden or grove existed more terrible than Gethsemane, Henry believed as a child. He knew better now. Lord, is it necessary that I be torn apart?

God and the wolf kept silence. Henry considered fang and jaw.

If it is to be done, let it be done cleanly. And soon.

A light snap, much closer. A twig beneath a paw? A breath. Not his. Not distant.

Poor pickings here, you ravening bastards.

An act of grim will, perhaps his last, forced rigid fingers to close around the handle of his knife. My flesh. My bones. My blood. My God....You will it. How will it be? Fangs tear living flesh. Jaws crack my bones for their marrow. I wait. Frozen and alone.

A white wolf materialized before him, its fur lustrous, its frost-blunted ears upright.

"Alone?" a deeply pitched voice corrected. "What makes you think you're alone?"

"Am I not?" Henry mumbled to the loping shadow, moving with studied disinterest through trees at the edge of his perception. "Prove to me you're more than frost or shadow. Come. Try me, wolf."

"In my own good time. The great wheel turns, and marks our passage from age to age, season to season...from life to little life."

"Look, wolf. Behind you. Where there's light there's life."

The White Wolf cocked its head, first to one side, then the other.

"Look at what?"

"Behind you. Look."

The White Wolf turned.

"I see nothing"

"There. Among the fading stars. Low on the horizon, Orion—the ancient Lord Osiris, Hunter King of Winter. And at his heel the faithful star-dog Sirius. Dog and jackal. Jackal, dog and wolf. Wolf and man. God made us."

The White Wolf stared through Henry. "I'm no man's dog or jackal."

"No. I don't suppose you are. Come closer. Let me look my death directly in the eye."

The White Wolf's breath, mixed with Henry's, hung in the air, the finest of veils between them.

"How strange."

"What?" the wolf asked.

"As my body chills my mind glows more alert."

"It is the way of the freezing death. Do you feel pain?"

"No. Sudden heat. Intense. Pleasant."

"Good. You'll feel ecstasy as you're devoured. God's final kindness."

Henry studied the pink albino snout. The wolf scented the

air, his tongue moistening his nose. Fine hairs spiked with ice twitched. "You will be a light meal. There's not much left but ropy muscle and bone. Shrunken heart. Empty head."

"Flesh of your flesh."

"The two shall become one."

Henry raised his eyes from its snout to the eyes of the great predator. He made no sense of what he saw. Opaque pupils clouded white rendered death unfathomable. Henry's heart raced with sympathy.

"You're blind," he said.

"I am." The White Wolf stood unmoved before him. "I was born blind and have remained so."

"How did you survive?"

"When I was a whelp, I kept my nose to my sire's flank and ran full tilt behind him. Now I keep my snout to my alpha bitch and run with her. I never miss so much as a single stride. If I do I'm lost."

"You run blind through the woods without injury?"

"Woods. Rocky barrens. Meadow. Marsh. The edge of the sea. I run like the wind that I am. Never trip. Never fall. Never falter. Rivers are difficult. And tidal flats. If I lose scent, I'm likely to wander. Like all my kind, and likely yours, my sense of smell declines in this cold."

"Yet you found me."

"I have a nose for uncertainty."

"Ah."

"I smell another creature's doubt and the next thing I know, my belly's full to bursting."

"Frailty. The prey's curse."

"The predator's prerogative. Another gift from the Creator."

"How is another's doubt to your advantage?"

"The unschooled calf errs. Its mother becomes confused by her desire to protect her child and her own life. She wavers. In that instant both are ours for the taking."

"As am I."

"We shall see."

"You're not alone."

"No. I called. They answered. "

"They'll filter through these trees like smoke or mist."

"Yes. They await my order." The wolf sat back on its haunches. "As I await yours."

"I'm not in the world of the Christ Lord Jesus now, am I?"

"I know nothing of that. You called me. I'm here. That's all."

"I called on God. Not you."

"As you wish."

"Moments ago I longed for death. I'm no longer certain."

"I can help you. What is it you wish?"

"Nothing."

"All men enter the world with a question."

"Few leave with an answer."

"Not the answer they sought. Yet all leave."

"None wiser. I've lost my faith in God."

"God stands before you."

"You...?"

"I offer life and death. The choice is yours."

The White Wolf licked a paw and then washed its face, his last meal's blood licked clean.

"This woman you call upon," he said, "this Eugainia."

"I nurtured her in France. Then Scotland, always watchful, ready to run, fleeing her enemies, often only days and hours beyond the grasp of a closing fist. Raised her as I would my own child, mindful that I nourished the very Daughter of God."

"She's not the daughter of God. She is God Herself."

"You are God," Henry taunted. "You just said as much—"

"One manifestation in the long line of those made flesh. As are you, no?"

"I am God's servant, and protector of the Goddess here on earth."

"As you wish. I've seen her."

"Alive?"

"Never more so."

"Where is she?"

"Safe."

"Thank God. And the thief who stole her?"

"The thief is no thief. He is her equal in every way. Teaches her the Ways of The People. The Ways of the Animal Powers. The Two have become One."

"How dare he presume to be her equal."

"Is God a single thing to you? A man or woman, a human cast in your pale image wearing your frail, naked form?"

"Eugainia is the daughter of God made manifest on earth, that she may teach us."

"Simple man. Let the scales fall from your eyes. Each and every one of us is God made manifest on earth that we may help and teach each other."

"Why can't I heal the sick? Alleviate the suffering of the poor? The downtrodden? I can't transform air and earth into loaves and fishes. Can he, this seducer thief who killed my dreams of a New Arcadia?"

"They are more than the cup that holds the blood, these two. They are both the cup and the blood itself."

"Her blood is exhausted and diseased and needs to be refreshed."

The White Wolf rose and walked a pace or two to the westward. "Your Sky Goddess walks with Mimkitawo'qu'sk, the God of the Earth who was made with her and for her. He will guide her to this cup you seek. What you'll witness, Henry Sinclair, if you have eyes to see, is nothing less than the marriage of heaven and earth. I know your heart. You're jealous of the Goddess and wish in your fear to control her. To cage her. You'll cheat death, you think, though none but one has so done before. When the last trumpet sounds, it will be you who'll rise from the dead and march through heaven, leading the Goddess, chained to you by her gratitude with links forged from your self-sacrifice. Your wife and children will follow Eugainia, not walking at your side, or hers, but two steps behind.

"We long to be safe in a garden. A sacred bower. God's home on earth."

"You'll live on in an earthly paradise forever, you think, your vain flesh incorruptible. The Goddess, whom you own, will bend her will to yours, indulge your delusion, restore the garden you despoil with your shameless indifference. Indolent man. This will not happen. I will not permit it. I live in your bones, which my pack will crack at my behest. I'd happily be shed of you. But I made you. I am constant. Unwavering. I'm the blood in your veins, which my pack will lap from the frozen earth. I am their God and your God. I am—"

"I know who you are! By the twisted logic and the dead pale eyes. You are the devil himself, sent to this frozen Gethsemane to taunt and test me—"

"Fool! You revel in this celestial parade of man-shaped gods. Divine intruders rise and fall, victims of your inability to comprehend anything of greater consequence than your next meal, your next war, the next warm body sent to comfort you, or submit their flesh to your desire in the night. You fear and despise the Goddess. You sent her to the wilderness to die. Now she flourishes. It is you who will die....You. Lost, adrift and alone."

"I'm not alone. And you're not God. Nor the devil! You're nothing more than cold-brain delusion, wolf. Some corner of my fevered brain conjured you. With one blast of my icy breath, I'll hurl you howling into oblivion. You'll no longer exist."

"You're not a man. No Temple Knight. You're nothing more than a self-styled saint who's failed to protect the daughter of god. My daughter. The child I sent you." The wolf licked Henry's cheek. The abrasive tongue raised welts. "Foolish man. You're meat. Sustenance. And I grow hungry."

"My bones. What of my bones?"

"Rasped clean. Cracked for their marrow. Gnawed by my subservient males until I drive them from your carcass."

"Keswalqw tells me I can't come back without my bones."

"You can't. You won't. God wills it."

Twigs snapped. The White Wolf turned toward the sound.

"My wolves," he murmured, "will soon be upon you."

Dry leaves, crisp and brittle, whispered adieu. Henry's vision wavered.

"Look, man. My pack. See how they filter through the trees like mist and smoke. Just as you predicted."

Henry loosed his knife from his belt.

"I'll not die alone in this savage place. Jackal, dog or wolf....One of you will serve me in eternity!"

The White Wolf leaned in, scented the corners of Henry's mouth. "I think not." With tender mercy, the White Wolf's tongue wet Henry's arid lips. The pink tongue flicked, soft as a lover's, in and out. The frosted muzzle grazed Henry's throat. The wolf's tongue traced the path of the artery pounding its last tattoo.

"Come," he heard the wolf say. "Give yourself to me. God wills it!"

Henry closed his eyes. He offered his throat.

"Aye. God wills it," Henry repeated. "Eugainia. Forgive me!"

Fangs indented Henry's thin yellow skin. Blood began to seep. The sun broke free of the horizon, washed the ice mirror's surface a deep blood red. Henry's world dissolved in a swirl of red and black.

A sound, hard and familiar. The twang of tight-drawn gut released. The hiss of an arrow sprung from the arc of a bow.

Henry opened his eyes. An arrowhead, shaft and feather passed through the torso of the White Wolf. Henry's tormenter dissolved in a cloud of bloody frost.

Henry searched the shadows. Two slender figures stood stretched against the sky.

Athol Gunn knelt. He removed his mitts. He raised Henry's stone-cold head. He passed gentle heat from his hands to Henry's eyes. Henry made no sense of the thin female face before him. "Blessed Crone," he whispered. "You're here for me. Take me home. Yes. There. Place me at Orion's feet, lower than his wolf-dog, faithful Sirius. For I am worthy of no more. God...wills...it."

Keswalqw pried the knife from Henry's hand. "No, Henry Orkney. Your spirit quest will not end today." She extracted and drank deeply from the bladder warmed by her skin. She forced Henry's lips apart. Honey water flowed from her mouth into his. Henry supped gratefully.

Gunn spoke his relief. "There you go, Henry. That's the way—I say, that's the way, my laddie."

"Athol Gunn. You're my cousin, and brother to my wife, the Lady Igidia."

"I am. Come back, I say, come back with us to the village."

"No!" Henry cried. "I took too much. The starving time!"

"The starving time is past," Keswalqw assured him. "The dogs chased three deer onto a frozen lake."

Henry clung to Keswalqw. "Hard hooves on harder ice. Legs splayed. They fell time and again. Didn't they? At last they could only stand and await their end, poor things. You took them easily. Torn flesh. Cracked bones. Blood spilled. All blood is God's blood. Wolves and men. We drink it."

"Yes. We do. There is plenty for all."

"Is the great hall prepared for feasting, Sir Athol?" he asked.

"My Lord?"

"Does my wife Igidia await me?"

"She will, Henry. Soon enough. Now put one foot before you. I say, put one foot before the other. Good, Henry. Good. Now, another step..."

"Are my daughters with her?"

"Where you left them. Sheltered in the outer Orkney Isles. Where else would they be?"

"Not here?"

"No."

Sunlight flooded the maple grove. Henry raised his grateful face to the sky. Beneath his feet Henry felt the frozen earth begin its spring surrender.

"Ah, yes. I remember now. Yes. Where we left them."

A sudden jubilation of sound filled the air. Migrating geese in a perfect chevron high above angled to the north.

On the Earth World below, Henry's weight rested on the shoulders of his friends.

"This is a strange, bewitching land," he said.

"Aye, laddie," Athol replied. "It is that."

PART THREE

....

THE SKY WORLD

Spring, 1399

CHAPTER TWELVE

Eugainia arched backward, exposing her chest and throat to the warming rays of the sun. She worked sheaths of low-back muscle with the heels of her palms. She straightened, bent forward, let her arms hang loose. Her hair screened her face and brushed the crusted snow. Mimkitawo'qu'sk'd found himself utterly unable to read her mood these days. He'd been rebuffed repeatedly by she whose heart and mind had become as available to him as his own. He stepped behind her. His fisted knuckles dug into knots on either side of her spine. He rolled the pressure downward, dissolving tension from her shoulder blades, then down rib by rib to her lower sacrum.

Eugainia sighed with pleasure, Mimkitawo'qu'sk with relief. Perhaps her foul mood was lifting at last.

"After autumn, spring's my favourite time of year," he ventured.

Eugainia did not reply.

"Except for summer, which is wonderful," he continued. "I like summer too much."

"Very much," Eugainia corrected.

"Very much. And there's something about a good, snowy winter..."

He waited. Again, nothing.

"But spring! *E'ee*! Grandfather Sun stirs in his sleep." Mimkitawo'qu'sk allowed his hands to rest on Eugainia's hips. "He wakes. His gaze grows strong." His hands slipped down her outer thighs. "He concentrates his Power." He pressed against her. "The frozen world concedes." She did not step away. "The earth becomes soft and warm. Receptive. Yielding. But—" he hastened to add when he felt her stiffen, "—not submissive. Grandmother Moon wakes the seeds, urges roots to grow."

Eugainia gently, but firmly, pushed him away. "I'm feeling very cranky and altogether ungoddesslike this morning."

"Oh?"

"I need something."

"What?"

"I don't know. Something human. I don't know what."

Mimkitawo'qu'sk embraced her again. She remained inert, incapable it seemed of either flight or concession.

"I know what it is," he whispered in her ear.

"No, not that."

"Are you certain?"

Eugainia untangled his fingers, laced low on her belly.

"Men. You're all the same. You think the solution to every problem lies at the tip of your guign. The entire world revolves around that tiny unblinking eye."

"You speak from much personal experience?" He slipped his hands into the hip-slits of her buckskin dress.

His fingers slid down. Her resolve wavered.

"No," he whispered. "No *guign* here."

"Get away from me..." Her annoyance was edged with amusement. She pressed back against him.

"Your mouth says stop, but your body says *e'eee...*!"

Eugainia fled. More or less. Running on snowshoes remained all but impossible. She huffed and puffed with frustration, aware the ungainly lift and fall of her big round feet over banks of soggy snow rendered her vulnerable and, even worse, ridiculous.

Mimkitawo'qu'sk pursued at a leisurely pace. He soon held his willing captive again. "Are you sure? Most times my *guign* is right!"

"Mimkitawo'qu'sk, I'm confused," she muttered, irritated by the pleasure of practised fingers bedevilling her ribs.

"Yes. I can tell."

"I thought I was, but I'm not in the mood."

"There's always later. We await your command."

Mimkitawo'qu'sk sped off, the essence of efficiency, to a plateau of bare rock angled out into the heart of the swollen stream. He executed a cartwheel, the wood-rimed snowshoes ringing on the rock surface, their silly clop-clop sound at odds with his elegant athleticism. He executed a second perfect cartwheel in a tight little clop-clop loop. Eugainia laughed aloud in spite of herself. He spun another. Then another...clop-clop spin. Clop-clop spin. Clop-clop spin....Seven complete revolutions brought him full circle.

Clop-clop stop.

He landed upright, four-square, still as a tree, nose to nose with his cranky, unable-to-conceal-her-love lover. He leaned forward. She pulled back. He caught the front of her robe, gently pulled her near. He kissed her. She opened briefly, then turned away.

"I really am sorry. I'm just not in the mood. And certainly not in the middle of the woods with these ridiculous things on my feet." She stomped her way back among the trees. "I'll never get used to these ruddy snow...boot...shoe...things. Anyway. It wouldn't kill us to wait a day or two. We've had enough to last most mortals four lifetimes."

"We aren't most mortals."

"No," Eugainia replied. "We're barely human at all when we make love. It frightens me."

A faint, distant airborne gabble disturbed the morning calm. The lovers stood silent in the spruce thicket. Eugainia could hear Mimkitawo'qu'sk's breathing quicken. Then her own. Then her beating heart. Then his. The silence was dense and moist. Eugainia could hear the snow melt. A great exultation, much nearer the ground, rattled the air. Three low-flying chevrons of black-necked, brown-bodied geese burst into view close above the trees.

"*Sulumgw!*" Mimkitawo'qu'sk cried in delight, the geese so near their white cheek pads flashed.

"Geese!" Eugainia echoed.

"Ha! If the sound of migrating *sulumgw* dosen't raise your spirits, nothing will."

Seasoned geese and ganders egged the young on. Dig deep, they seemed to say, down to the last of your reserves. Stay the course. The young responded with a joyful noise, happy their maiden migration back to their hatchling home was all but complete.

Mimkitawo'qu'sk followed the flying Vs with his heart and his stomach. "Home with their lifelong mates. Thus, and so the great wheel turns."

"The Two will become One."

"The two shall become many. Up to fourteen goslings in a nest, in a good year."

"Will this be a good year, do you think, for the geese and goslings?" she asked.

"It might be a too good year, I think. Already it's been a very good year. For me, at least. For you?"

Mimkitawo'qu'sk placed her hands, one on top of the other, on his chest. "I miss The People very much," he said. He searched her face. Nothing would have pleased Mimkitawo'qu'sk more than to hear his feelings echoed by the one he adored above all others. Echoed and expanded in his own language, spoken well or ill, it didn't matter. Eugainia kept her silence. He returned her arms to her sides.

"Maybe you need your people," he said.

Eugainia responded after a time. "I'm sorry, Mimkitawo'qu'sk. I truly am. Lately—well, last night, actually. When we made love, I felt a greater presence. An uninvited stranger at the feast. It was disconcerting."

"When we join I feel *e'ee*! I'm the Great Spirit Himself."

"I dread facing Henry."

"Stay near Keswalqw. She has my interests, therefore your interests at heart. Fat!"

"What?"

"Is it fat you need?"

"No. No more fat."

"Not fat. Then you need lean meat."

"No."

"Duck?"

"I swear if I eat another duck I'll start to lay eggs and quack."

"Seal?"

"No. Too gamey. Too salty. Too greasy."

"Walrus. I could take a walrus calf. It's the season."

"No. Nothing infant or childlike."

"Turkey? You love turkey."

"No."

"You couldn't get enough turkey this winter."

"It was winter. I was tired. Turkey helps me sleep."

"Spring tonic. She-bear. You need the liver of a she-bear."

Nausea bloomed carnivorous in Eugainia's gut. She suppressed a wave of revulsion.

"Fish?"

"Salmon! Yes. Salmon is exactly what I need!"

"For salmon, beloved, you'll need patience. But you're right. Little in life is sweeter than the first *taqawan* of spring. Except, perhaps, *sismo'qon*."

"What's *sismo'qon*?"

"*Sismo'qon* is patience rewarded with mawiulta'suaqan."

"*Ahsismo'qon* rewarded with *mawiulta'suaqan*. Sweetness rewarded with—don't tell me! *Ummawiulta'suaqan*. Happiness?"

"Happiness is more *mawiulta'sit*. Today you'll experience *mawiulta'suaqan*—pure joy, orally administered."

Eugainia tensed.

"Relax. I speak, uh, what is your English word? Metaphorically. Follow me."

The deer-cut trail crossed the feeder stream, then opened into a grove of sugar maples. Square birchbark buckets affixed to the trunks of the largest trees brimmed with clear liquid. Fresh v-shaped gashes in the bark directed the sap onto short twigs angled down into the drip pails, themselves cut and folded at the corners, their stitched joints seamed with pine resin to prevent leakage. Each bucket's rim was reinforced with a thin strip of wood, stitched to the rim with spruce-root fibre. The sturdy rim was secured to the tree trunk with strands of basswood bark and thicker spruce-root tendrils. The system was simple and elegant. From a distance it appeared the bucks grew natually from the side of the tree.

A pyramid of round stones protruded from the snow at the edge of the clearing. A second blunted pyramid, with rocks missing from its apex, sat nearby. In the centre of the maple grove, the remnants of what must have been a sizable blaze smoked.

"Did you do all this?"

"The People come here every *sismo'qonapu tepgunset* and have done so forever. Most of what you see was stashed last spring. I merely refreshed everything. The buckets needed a touch of pitch here and there. I gathered new rocks. To replace those split by the frost. Burned a new boiling trunk."

"When?"

"These last few afternoons. While you slept. Last night I fired the stones."

"*Sismo'qonapu tepgunset* means…?"

"Maple moon."

Eugainia dipped her finger in the sap, which overflowed from the nearest pail. "It has no particular taste."

"Not yet, it doesn't."

"Is it medicinal?" she asked.

"What it will become is, yes. Medicine for the spirit and the body. *Sismo'qon* takes The People by the hand and leads us from the wigwams of winter to the tepees of summer. It carries the same joyful spirit as those wild geese, and the first chirping frogs the, ah…"

"Spring peepers."

"Yes. The spring peepers in the ponds when the ice breaks free. When you taste what we'll prepare, you'll find the sky becomes more blue. The sun shines more brightly. We'll laugh more easily. And more often—and not through our noses, but up from our bellies, through our throats and out our mouths. When the laughter's finished, we'll find it easy to smile again.

And talk. Winter's sorrows and secrets will fly north with the geese. We'll discover what's troubling you. You'll tell me and put my heart at ease. Then we'll feel the urge to sleep. If the Great Spirit is kind, we'll wake and our life together will begin again. We'll dream a new dream." He took her hands. "I long to see your sea- and sky-coloured, ah, your blue green eyes grow big with delight and your snow white face turn pink and rosy again."

Eugainia managed a vague smile. "What can it be, this miracle food?"

"Wait and see. If it's not exactly what you need, it will certainly entertain us until what you do need comes along."

The air around the firepit in the centre of the clearing quivered with flameless heat. A fire-hollowed stump awaited the hot stones and cold maple sap. Mimkitawo'qu'sk retrieved two wooden shoulder yokes stowed in the lower branches of a big-bellied spruce. He fitted himself and Eugainia for their work. When filled, they hung the large collector pails from short thongs attached to the extreme ends of the yokes. They emptied the heavy pails into the boiling stump, then returned to the trees.

They soon found a common work rhythm, moving like dancers through the trees. The opening figure of their maple sugar ballet was light and enthusiastic. Carefree. Filled with anticipation. Mid-dance, the full weight of the task fell on yoked shoulders.

Eugainia reconciled the swinging pail's arcs with her own considered movement. Hips slightly angled and knees softly set quickly established a counter rhythm. Her task, she found, was made easier when she also adjusted her attitude. In submission to the joy of work, she found harmony of thought and action. The power of simple repetition dissolved time and gave rise to contemplation. Accommodation reaps greater rewards than grim, determined slogging. This thought alone lightened Eugainia's load: she knew she could bear what was to come.

Mimkitawo'qu'sk brushed away the layers of the ash and ember. He loaded the stones, vibrating with heat, on the hissing slings. The alchemy began in a frenzy of bubbles and steam. The sap quickly reduced to a fraction of its volume. At afternoon's end, a golden mass of a sticky, resinous substance coated the round stones and pooled in the spaces between.

Mimkitawo'qu'sk poured two palm-sized patches of the warm syrup on the snow. It congealed instantly. He rolled the near patch onto a short smooth stick. He gave it to Eugainia. Sunlight danced inside amber mass. Eugainia nipped tentatively. Sugar's fire set her blood pounding and her mind spinning. She licked the sticky mass from her lips and teeth with an eager tongue. She rode an upward rush of spirit. Her sighs of pleasure rippled across the clearing. She cocked her ear to the unfamiliar sounds. She peered at Mimkitawo'qu'sk. He raised an eyebrow. The mewling sounds of pleasure, she gathered from his smile, were hers. Laughter erupted between them in short, startled bursts.

Mimkitawo'qu'sk nipped congealed syrup from the shared stick. A long thread coiled on his chin. Eugainia stared.

"What?" he said.

She pulled him to her, licked his chin clean. He smiled. She pressed her mouth to his, licked his front teeth clean. She licked the maple-sweetened interiors of his upper and lower lips. Then scoured his tongue with hers.

Mimkitawo'qu'sk responded, delicately at first, then with intent.

Eugainia rolled the second dollop. "What is this?" she asked.

"We call it *sismo'qonapu*."

"Maple, ah, nectar?"

"Umm. I guess. Maple nectar is close. Do you remember the first food I gave you?"

"The moose butter. When you showed us the hunt and inter-
preted Henry's maps. The day I feared I'd fall in love with you.
You gave us little birchbark-wrapped packets of moose butter,
bone marrow, nuts and honey."

"It was sweetened with this. With *sismo'qonapu*."

"It tastes of leaves and wood and smoke. Roots and the earth.
You make those little blocks of the sugar we carried from Claw
of Spirit Bird Bay from this too, yes?"

"What's life, my dear," Mimkitawo'qu'sk asked, "without a
little sweetness?"

"Barely bearable. Thank you, Mimkitawo'qu'sk. You are a god
and a saint."

"You're welcome. I'm happy you enjoyed it too much."

She moved to speak. He put a quick finger to her lips.

"I'm joking."

"I'm not. I love you, Mimkitawo'qu'sk. I love you too much."

"I love you too much too!"

"'Too much too.' Sounds like Mi'kmaq word."

Mimkitawo'qu'sk tried it on. Giving the phrase a sibilant
spin. "Too'much'too. Too'much'too. Too'much'too. I declare it
a new word. Means 'my heart is happy when my cranky wife
finally smiles.'"

The walk back to camp was pleasant and companionable.
The day's tensions set with the red late-winter sun. A bright fire
soon replaced its heat. The lovers lay beneath their robes, faces
dappled gold and scarlet in the flicker of the maplewood flame.
Eugainia's sugar-induced ecstasy subsided. She admitted an urge
to sleep.

"It's good we sleep a good deep sleep if we can,"
Mimkitawo'qu'sk agreed. "Tonight when the Great Bear wakes,
I'll show you another mystery. We'll hunt beneath the stars and
feast like proper Gods."

"God. Goddess. I begin to despise these words. All these years I was told I was the Goddess. I no longer believe such a thing to be true. I've strayed from my purpose, Mimkitawo'qu'sk. I fear I've lost my way."

"Why?"

"They'll take all this away."

"Who?"

"People. Your people. My people. People."

"Not if we love them they won't. We're born to serve The People's need to worship something greater than themselves. We see more. Risk more. Bear more. We dream dreams. See visions. They need us. "

"They say they love us. It isn't love. It's fear. They learn they can't kill death. But they can kill the god who they think controls it. I tell you, Mimkitawo'qu'sk. They'll aim their fear and anger and frustration at us like a weapon when the fantasy fails. I sometimes think we're worshiped because we're clever and beautiful. And young. That our innocence makes us dispensable. We don't age. Our beauty becomes an affront."

"Your people ask you to show how they may live together kindly, in peace and harmony, as did your ancestor the Christ. My People ask me to interpret the ways of the animal powers, that they might survive, at one, with all Power of the Six Worlds. As the Creator guides me, so I do. Together you and I will show the way of all Power, human and animal, the *Kji-kinap* of sea and sky, rock and tree. No, no, dear one. Who we are isn't what we might wish for ourselves, or what others wish for themselves through us. Who we are is what we do with what we're given. Our only responsibility is to strengthen ourselves and share our gifts. That's all. Simple."

"To whom much is given, much is expected."

"Exactly." Mimkitawo'qu'sk cupped her face. "Why did you say you feared you'd love me?"

"What?"

"In the maple grove. When you spoke of the day I showed you the moose-hunt dance. You said you feared you'd love me."

"How could I give an uncertain heart?"

"I don't understand."

"I'd always been told whom to love. Which is everyone and no one. And how to love. With my head, not my heart. I had no idea what physical love could be. Its Power. But I sensed it. I loved you immediately. Not to perpetuate the Holy Blood. I wanted you. Body and soul. It frightened me. You frightened me. I didn't know who you were."

"Why should that matter?"

"Because from the moment I laid eyes on you, for the first time in my life, I thought I knew who I was."

"This is not good?"

"No."

"Why?"

"When I finally arrived at the feast, I wasn't whom I expected."

Mimkitawo'qu'sk withdrew a shining object from a chamois sack.

"This will show you who you are. And a new way to be."

He handed Eugainia a copper bracelet, wide as her thumb was long, its curved edges rolled neatly upward to protect her skin. "Copper clears the mind and eases the heart," Mimkitawo'qu'sk told her. "It ferrets out impurities. Makes us clean. I made it for you." He reconsidered. "For us, really."

"It's beautiful, Mimkitawo'qu'sk."

"It's beauty comes from you. From my 'Lady Wife,' as your people would say."

"I prefer your new name for me. It has more truth to it. More beauty."

"It tells our story, this bracelet. See here? On the outside? I etched two white whales streaming through turbulent waters."

"You and I."

"Travelling the great river..."

"Which Henry misguidedly named for poor St. Lawrence."

"We prefer Way to the Setting Sun."

"So do I."

"Who is this Lawrence?"

"Morgase said Henry spoiled me with too much education. All those grim-faced friars. All those useless facts."

"How can facts be useless? Unless they purposefully mislead. Can there be too much knowledge? No. Tell me the story of St. Lawrence and the grim-faced friars."

"St. Lawrence. A Christian martyr strapped by the Romans to the iron cooktop of an outdoor stove."

"*E'ee*! What was his sin?"

"He stole the Holy Grail and sent it to his parents in Spain."

"So they cooked him."

"They did."

"Then ate him."

"No."

"Thank goodness. I'm still confounded by this Christian business of drinking human blood."

Eugainia set further discussion of transubstantiation aside for the moment. "Lawrence was so eager to be helpful, to speed his passage to the waiting arms of God, he cried out 'I am already roasted on one side and, if thou wouldst have me well cooked, it is time to turn me on the other.' God help us. We venerate this misery."

"And the grim-faced friars?"

"Beat their perverted versions of God's simple mysteries into innocent foundlings. Ah… poor homeless little waifs and beggars in towns and villages. What a race of savages we've become." She turned the bracelet in her hands. "But this great river! Regardless who we've named it for. This Gateway to the Setting Sun. I long to see it one day."

"In the meantime, you have it here," he indicated the bracelet, "in miniature."

"Look! Bounding dolphins cleave the way. Our children?"

"Maybe. And here. See? Behind each, a walrus head pokes up through the foam."

"Who are they?"

"I don't know."

Eugainia considered a moment. A smile played at the corners of her lips. "Henry and Keswalqw."

"Ha!" Mimkitawo'qu'sk liked the notion. "Such fearsome tusks! Yet they seem to smile."

"Yes."

"They do smile, happy they'll spend their lives near you."

"And you."

"With us."

"Yes."

"Look inside," he urged.

"A beautiful tree, tall and elegant."

"When we first saw you, Keswalqw said she'd transformed herself into a tree Person. She's gathering tree Power. Already she has the standing power of an old white pine. Mother earth supports her. Strong and solid like mountain oak she reaches up to the Sky World. Yet she remains lithe and wan as a willow. I thought, no, not an oak or a pine, but a larch in spring bloom, tufted with rosy plumelets. So inside I graved this tree."

"My totem. Can there be such a thing as a tree clan?"

"I have two totems. Moose/Wood clan. You'll likely have a blended totem too. So it is with those who become great leaders of The People. You will be Pine Tree/Snow Goose Woman perhaps. Perhaps Pine Tree/Otter Woman. Who knows? No one until the Great Spirit shows you."

Mimkitawo'qu'sk slipped the bracelet on Eugainia's wrist.

"It's beautiful," she replied at length. "Thank you, Mimktawo'qu'sk."

"You're pleased?"

"I am. I was secluded. Pampered. Brood mare of the Holy Blood. Desired by all. Known by none. Feared and adored. A prisoner of the blood that runs in my veins. It will be our ruination, as it ruined my ancestor."

"The ancestor, nailed to the tree and pierced with a spear. Killed for his love of the people."

"Just so."

"Your enemies are my enemies now. No harm will come to you."

"The Christ, blessed be His name, wished three simple things for humanity: feed each other, he said; heal each other; let common decency prevail. Ten simple words."

"Powerful words."

"In My Reign on earth—"

"Your reign?"

"Forgive me. Our reign. No living person, priest or pope or king may proclaim who shall live forever or who shall not. Nor will any man or woman sanction or confound the redemption of another's sin."

"We'll go to your people, across the sea. Our *Kji-kinap* will be a light in their darkness. We'll heal them."

"We'd be more than the light in their darkness, I fear, my darling. When they see the Goddess has found her God, that

Her God is not of them—*E'ee*, beloved! We'll be the flame and the torch. Consumed by our own fire. They will burn me for a witch. They'll crucify then dismember you. They'll feed your flesh to the dogs, then burn your bones."

Mimkitawo'qu'sk, no stranger to human evil, took her hand. "I begin to understand what you fled. Even our worst enemies won't burn our bones. They are an ocean away, these monsters who would harm you."

"I came. They'll come. They will find me."

"Moon Woman. Look at me. This will never happen. This is why you journeyed to Lnu'k, The People."

"I swear, Mimkitawo'qu'sk, on the Royal and Holy Blood in my veins, the Ancient and Honourable blood in yours. I did not wish this. Nor did I foresee it..."

"What you can't foresee need not happen."

"What if it does?"

"We'll fight."

"I'm weary with strife. There comes a time in the great cycle of heaven and earth when the Goddess needs humankind, not to worship, but to resurrect her. I came to find a safe place where I might sleep awhile. Gather Power."

Mimkitawo'qu'sk drew her near. "These last six moons, I'd have sworn you were wide awake."

"Awake, but only half alive. You have no idea of the power of the seventh world. My world. The world of Europe's kings and their pope at Rome. Nor can I conjure for you the magnitude of the evil that stalks us."

"Tell me."

"Many years in the past, three times the number of moons a man may live, our people—Henry's people—fled across the sea to this New World—"

"This Ancient World," Mimkitawo'qu'sk corrected. "Yes."

"They came with a precious object; a bowl carved of star-stone, stone so ancient it no longer spoke. They built the Great Stone House of Death and dug a well at the edge of the sea. The Holy Grail and a sacred spear were hidden in this ancient world of yours, the world of L'nuk, The People, one hundred years ago by French Knights of the inner Temple."

"By the ancestors of Henry Orkney."

"Our ancestors placed the star-stone grail inside a brazen head called Baphomet, a ferocious hollow bust of bronze with sapphire eyes and hair of burnished copper. One half its face is agony. One looks and sees the deaths of all the martyrs. The other side is the great prophet Moses, facing God in his fury. "

"It sounds a wondrous thing, this head of Baphomet."

"Baphomet's is a face that even we as God and Goddess will shudder to behold. It contains strong medicine. It contains the Holy Grail."

"There was strong medicine in the ruins of Great Stone House of Death."

"The Grail Castle, yes. They believed we'd know to the end of the Christ time. When he was Lord alone. All humankind would be re-imagined. The God and Goddess time would come: The time of the Two Made One. And so it has. Now at last the Stone Grail has awakened. It feels that I'm near, Mimkitawo'qu'sk. It feels your presence too. It pulls power from the stars, the stars from which it fell. It calls to us from the Well of Baphomet in the World Below the Sea."

"I feel nothing, nor do I hear the voice of your speaking stone. Perhaps we're not the ones..."

"The spear you carry, Tooth of Wolverine, was found by the father of your father's father in the Grail Castle, was it not?"

Mimkitawo'qu'sk rolled to his back, reached for Wolverine which stood, as always, close to hand. The spearhead's black facets, polished by time to lustrous brilliance, reflected embers rising from the sudden slump of the fire. "It was. The tales tell that grandfather's father prized it for its beauty. Its weight. Balance. You say this spear, found by my grandfather's father, belongs to your people?"

"It did. It belongs to us now. You and I."

"Wolverine, fine as it is, is just a spear, like any other."

"Its head was split from the same star-stone as the Holy Grail. The Spear of Destiny—Tooth of Wolverine—pierced the side of the Christ in his ecstasy and agony upon the Roman cross. The Grail collected the Holy Blood pouring from his wound. When the Grail is filled and charged with the Power, the *Kji-kinap* of Wolverine, this spear will fly from your hands as if by its own will. It will pierce the heart of those who would harm you or the Goddess."

"Whatever medicine it had is gone."

"I tell you: its medicine will be restored."

Mimkitawo'qu'sk pondered the razor-edged stone. "A shooting star has great power in the Six Worlds. A man or woman who finds one becomes a great Shaman. Cures The People of many ills."

Eugainia threw back the beaver robe. She sat upright, cross-legged, her back straight, her upper body tense, her tone urgent.

"Only certain people can bear to gaze upon the Holy Grail, such is its power. Only those whose veins contain the Royal and Holy Blood may even dare to touch it. The Stone Grail pulls me in its silence, Mimkitawo'qu'sk, to the Well of Baphomet in the World Below the Sea. It calls and will not be resisted. The Grail and the Spear of Destiny united will infuse our blood with unimaginable power. The trumpets shall sound. The dead shall awake. The wounds of all mankind, living and dead, will be healed. God and Goddess will live again as one. Humankind shall be redeemed."

Eugainia extracted the pilfered quadrant of the Templar map from the pouch at her waist. "This map shows the Stone Grail's hiding place. Look. The Well of Baphomet."

"At the edge of the ocean. Yes. The Island of the Twelve Standing Trees."

"You know it?"

"Of course."

"Will you guide me—?"

"No."

Mimkitawo'qu'sk snatched the map. He rose, a coiled spring released. He impaled Eugainia's great hope, the map to the Well of Baphomet, on the black glinting tip of Wolverine.

"I will not help you find this stone."

He held the map over the flames.

"Mimktaw—"

The parchment flared, swirled up in a gust of flame. Mimkitawo'qu'sk's voice was flat, cryptic as the mask his face had become.

"You'll find this stone. You will find this stone and leave me."

"Mimkitawo'qu'sk, no—"

"You will leave me."

She reached for his hand. He pulled away.

"None shall have me if I don't find this stone," Eugainia persisted. "We must drink its power or I will die."

"You will not die, Woman Who Fell in Love with the Moon. Look at your eyes, shining like stars. Feel the strength in your arms. The strong heart beating in your breast. The power in your thighs and belly. When we are joined, when we are one, I call out to you. You answer in a high, sweet song. Such is the power of your pleasure. No, beloved. No. I have seen it. You will not die."

Mimkɨtawo'qu'sk laid a finger on her lips.

"Hush. While I live, you will not die."

Mimkɨtawo'qu'sk crouched just beyond the fringe of the bivouac overhang, urging new flame from the glowing mass of embers. Fire burst with a snap from a cache of pine oil trapped in a rock-hard knot. Flame outlined his broad shoulders. Sparks glinted crimson, then flickered, their ascent reflected in his long mane of blue black hair.

Eugania complied with her lover's call for silence, thinking it wise to bide her time. Certainty, its cuffs frayed, its hem spattered, was a dishevelled robe she no longer wore with ease. She knew all would change. Soon they would return to The People. And to her people. When they did, their lives would never be the same.

Mimkɨtawo'qu'sk felt her anxiety. "Never mind, Pine Tree Woman. Woods Woman. Woman Who Walks with Mimkɨtawo'qu'sk. Woman Who Fell in Love with the Moon. Now we rest, far from all, in the safety and comfort of this night. We'll sleep. Gather Power. Before Grandfather Sun wakes, we'll rise and harvest the sky."

Eugainia had never been held so close in her life. Or so tightly. Mimkɨtawo'qu'sk's need for comfort alarmed her. Her distance troubled him. If their bodies had melted into one governed by a single will, their Power that of a single beating heart, Mimkɨtawo'qu'sk would have rested easier.

Eugainia drifted to sleep, her last image that of a round-bellied coracle cast from its moorings, adrift in a gathering mist on the falling tide. A great ship strained at her anchors at the mouth of an unknown harbour, ready to transport Eugainia, and Henry's hopes for a New Arcadia, to an unknown destiny.

CHAPTER THIRTEEN

✧ ✧ ✧

In the dark of the sweat lodge, in the steady light of the seal-oil wick, Sir Athol Gunn radiated well-being. Not so Prince Henry Sinclair. Though no longer ghost-person pale, Henry retained the universal look of the thin man wanting. Perspiration beaded and ran, tracing thin lines down gaunt cheeks and sunken temples.

"It's said to be next to godliness, Athol. But like everything, this newfound devotion of yours to cleanliness can be taken to extreme."

"Keswalqw likes me clean from stem to stern, stem to—"

"Yes, yes. I take your meaning," Henry interrupted.

"A good scrub wouldn't go amiss on that much-neglected frame of yours, cousin," Athol advised.

"I appreciate Keswalqw's diligence in many things, including the improvement of your personal hygiene, but as you know, Sir William had a word about excess—"

"Och, I remember," Athol interrupted. "'Ye must learn the difference, lads, between scratching your ass and tearing the skin off.'"

"Always a man for a telling turn of phrase, my father—"

"Aye. That he was. "

"The phrase more telling of the man than the moral he wished to impress."

"He wasn't known as Old Itchy Arse for nothing."

"Yes, well that's all well and good." Henry bristled. "But your mother had her own reasons for disliking my father."

"Aye."

"He was a hard man drunk but a worse one sober."

"She never did forgive him for 'pawning her off—' her words, 'pawning her off on that all-brawn, no-brain pack of miscreant villains called Gunn.'"

"Mind you. They never did get on, even as children, your mother and my father."

"Rare to see a brother and sister so naturally opposed."

"One couldn't open his or her mouth without the other jumping in fist-first."

"They were a hard crew, the folk of our parents' generation."

"Men and women alike."

"Aye. That they were."

"Say what you will. We wouldn't be where we are today but for the strength of the women left alone to fend for themselves. Two great crusades. Families torn apart. Plague piled upon pestilence. War upon crippling war. The Holy Roman terror. Twice."

"A hundred years, yes, and more. Generations of dark."

"Your grandmother. Mine. Morgase and her kind. Hundreds of women whose names we'll never know. Running estates. Scraping bare existence from overplanted soil. Unnatural weather. Crops frozen in the field in August month. Scrawny children and a few half-mad old men the only labour. They held Rosslyn together these past hundred years, these womenfolk of ours."

"All this while managing the guilds to levels of prosperity never known before. Or since."

"The dark time behind us would have set the pattern for the future had it not been for the tenacity of our mothers."

"Aye. True enough."

The walls of the sweat lodge stirred. The roof-hides lifted, sighed slightly, settled back as the breeze passed and then lifted again. Little heat was lost, though both men felt the slight inrush of fresh air. Henry steadied himself against what his memory mistook to be a blast of winter cold. The last of the ice in my soul, he thought. Melting, finally.

"I'd be dead if not for Keswalqw."

"That you would. The strength of her! Steady-handed. Fair. Firm. I stand amazed, I say I stand amazed anyone survived the winter."

"Plenty and hardship shared by all in equal measure."

"Speaking of which, I'll be happier when we get some meat back on your bones, Henry Sinclair. You take too little nourishment."

"I know, I know. I try to eat. Everything tastes like sawdust or ash."

"Keswalqw says she's done what she can. The rest is up to you."

Henry gazed down at his chest and thighs. In the low light, he imagined the return of a ruddy glow. It was a trick of the light playing off blood lured by the heat to the surface of his body. Not so much as a pick of fat remained. Vein and tendon still roped beneath parchment skin. His sex, thin-veined and limp, lay like the dead upon desiccated testes compressed between sarcophagi thighs. A few fine wisps of hair, all that remained of luxuriance destroyed by want, caught the flickering light. Such terrible desolation in so short a time, he thought. His heart, muscle of rock it had always been, fell prey to erratic rhythms. Whether these alarming, intermittent failures of consciousness were linked he could not say. He resisted the enfeebling notion that Mimkitawo'qu'sk stole his spirit when

Eugainia broke his heart. I'll be back in the jaws of Jipijka'maq if I indulge these thoughts, he told himself.

"Athol, what progress with the castle?" he asked.

"The keep is strong. Our Lady's chamber's all but secure. We're months away from restoring either of the great halls. And as for the chambers of Our Lady's court—the rooms for your lady wife, the upper servants when they arrive, those of Eugainia's protector and the Shepherd of the Grail, well all the other suites and anterooms, really. Working with such reduced forces, I can hardly say—"

"But her bed and antechambers are secure?"

"Aye."

"Defensible and impenetrable?"

"Secure. Yes."

"Secure is not the same as impenetrable." Henry flicked perspiration from brow to hot stone. "The chapel?"

"The walls are sound. The slates are cut. So roof tile can soon be laid. The carpenters will have the roof beams in place today. Tomorrow at the latest we'll be boarded in."

"The glazing?"

"Poor Will has worked a little miracle. There's a great cache of proper sand not far down the coast to the east. He's managed good clear glass. Formulated a convincing red."

"There's no end of red and yellow ochre hereabout."

"Aye. There'll be no blue, of course."

"No. For lack of cobalt. So. It sounds to me we're far enough along with the Grail Castle to return our attention to the second most pressing matter."

"The boats. Aye."

Athol laced the sweat-stones with the last quarter-pail of water. Sufficient heat remained to produce a useful cloud of steam. Silence fell as the hiss subsided.

Henry wiped sweat from his eyes. "I'm concerned about deck nails," he said after a time.

"Excellent progress on that front. There's no end of coal hereabout. A mountain of it, so to speak. We've rendered a grand pile of charcoal. All this hardwood hereabout. Aeowald salvaged every scrap of metal from the ruins—I say, every superfluous hinge, every bolt and cotter. The barrel hoops, the pots, pikes and such we snatched from *Reclamation* before Zeno set sail are all reforged. There'll be a respectable quantity of nails."

"We were wise to settle on two longboats rather than 'one caravel."

"Aye. We've never enough iron—I say, never enough to forge the quantity of the two-pronged clasp nails a caravel hull requires. No. We're better off overlapping longboat hull-planks, I say, overlapping and using deck nails like rivets, pounding both ends flat once they're through the planks, in the Old Norse fashion."

"Good. And there's no end of tar for caulking."

"No. Mind, we lack the long wiry hair of our good Scottish cattle to mix with it."

"Bear fur mixed with the tar will do the same job better. When do you return to the castle?"

"I thought tomorrow."

"Good. Send what carpenters you can spare. I want both ships seaworthy first week July month. That'll give us half May and all of June to float the hulls and let their timbers swell."

"And Our Lady?"

"If I don't find Eugainia by early July we say farewell to her and New Arcadia for the foreseeable future."

Henry pushed the hide flap aside, doused himself with the bucket of cold sea water set outside for that purpose. He dried his frame with wadded moss. The scent of woodland root and fibre rose to his nostrils. He inhaled deeply, grateful his sense of smell was returning. When dressed, he regarded his headquarters across the high meadow. His field tent, with its view of his jerry-rigged shipyard on the beach below, seemed strange to him, foreign, inadequate, and in some way he couldn't determine, faintly ridiculous. Stripes and pendants. Box-cut fringe. Ropes and tassels. Frivolity, and the excess of another time and place. Hide and bark were normal now. Hide and bark had sheltered him through the starving time. Hide and bark had saved his life when wool and linen and canvas failed.

Henry paused at the meadow's edge. Claw of Spirit Bird Bay's estuary and beaches were long since free of ice. Late-spring snow clung in ragged patches to the upper flanks of the Smoking Mountain. Henry cast his glance to the northeast. Only Apekwit seemed reluctant to let go her mantle of snow. The Red Island rose from what he mistook on first glance to be banks of white fog, then low-lying cloud. Ice, he was told, was known to cling to her shores well into April.

Henry surveyed the work in the shipyard below. He'd directed two deep trenches be dug in the sand where the keels of the two ships, each carved from the trunk of a single massive oak, rested. Each keel was salt-cured twice daily with the rise and fall of the tides. After six weeks, Henry caused rock, sand and brush dams to be erected on the seaward end of each trench to hold back the sea. The keels soon dryed, exposed to sun and wind. When the last of the nails were forged, the overlapping hull planks would be laid. Once caulked, the hull would receive its oaken ribs, fanned out at present on the beach one either side of the trenches like the sand-flayed ribs of a storm-felled gull. By the end of the coming week, the dams would be breached, the sea let in, the riveted timbers would soon swell into tight, seaworthy hulls.

Henry settled in the field tent. Athol tied back the flap, stooped to enter and sat opposite. Spread before them were three sets of plans; one for each of the longboats, the third a thick sheaf containing detailed restoration renderings of the Grail Castle. Henry removed the top pages of the castle drawings, those detailing the refurbished chapel and His Lady's chambers. These he kept within reach, slipping them below the plans for the ships. He rolled the remaining castle drawings, the bulk of the plans, and slid them into their leather carrying case. He handed the case to Athol.

"Her chambers and the chapel are a fair start. Put these somewhere safe. We've no need of them this voyage."

"Aye, sire," Athol responded, slipping automatically into formal address, a courtesy marking the boundary between their personal and professional association. "We'll return soon enough with a full compliment of builders."

"Aye. If we find her, she'll not run off again."

"We can never take her back to Scotland."

"No."

"Presuming she still, I say—"

"What are your thoughts regarding the masts?"

"None better than the white pines of Apekwit, sir. Soon as the ice is cleared, we'll make the trip across. Mind there's no rush. We've six weeks away from footing the masts."

"And the decking?"

"The local mountain oak, I think. There's great lengths of it to be had for the central beam. Good stout timbers for the cross beams."

"A good solid oak deck gives lateral stability."

"Aye. Tight as they are, there's great flexibility in the hulls of these vessels. Nothing like a longboat to dampen the bow-to-stern twist and turn of a heavy sea."

"Then oak it is."

"I was amazed to find the stands of our English Oak. Groves at least a hundred years old."

"Groves, Sir Athol?"

"Yes, Lord Henry. At the mouth of the Castle River. On the western shore of Turned Up Whale Belly Bay—"

"Yes, yes. I know that grove. There's another?"

"On the seaward side of the great peninsula. A small island of well established oak, in appearance at least a hundred years—"

"You saw this island when?"

"On my first expedition. Last fall…"

Henry's tone was flat, his gaze steady. "Last fall."

"It didn't signify as important at the time. I thought it random chance—"

"Random chance? These oaks are not native here. This oak is quite a different species. Hand me what we've mapped of the southeast."

Athol unrolled and laid the new chart beside its ancient counterpart. Henry scanned both.

"Note the location of the English oaks on the first; the basin isle in Whale Belly Bay." Henry withdrew his rule, square and protractor from their leather pouch. "Draw a line to the Grail Castle. Measure carefully. Nine times nine. If I repeat a line of the exact length eastward." Henry's line ran off the edge of the southwest quadrant, ending exactly at the centre of the remapped segment. "Does it or does it not end precisely on the ocean side, at the heart of your second island of oak?"

"It does. Precisely."

"The plantings on both isles, Athol, appear at least one hundred years old because they are one hundred years old. Precisely one hundred years old. They were planted by Templars. In the year of Our Lord twelve hundred and ninety-eight."

"I'm sorry, Henry. An unforgivable oversight."

"Had this information not come forth, we could have set sail prematurely."

"At least we're certain to find the Well of Baphomet and recover the Stone Grail—"

Henry's ruddy skin flushed a deeper red. "At least?" The veins on the backs of his hands pulsed visibly. "What has 'at least' to do with our presence here? At least, sir, is the viper in the Garden of...in the Garden..."

"Henry?"

His breathing, suddenly erratic, fell shallow and weak, barely unsettling the surrounding air. Athol rose, alert, ready to catch his cousin should he fall. The spasm passed.

Henry lay his forearms on the table. He interlaced his fingers, their knuckles white. "If Eugainia is still out there, lost—or worse—will it be enough that men may say 'at least' she lived? 'At least' has brought us to our knees. 'At least' destroyed our Order, man by fragile man. 'At least' is the coward's call to infamy. 'At least' is an untilled meadow where Arcadia might have been. Eugainia is the Goddess made human upon this earth. We have sworn to protect Her with our faith, our honour, our lives. We cannot be worthy by offering less than our very best, all the time; to ourselves, to each other, and to our Lady God."

"It's my fault, sire."

"Fault has no currency here."

Athol knelt. He offered Henry his sword.

"Come, Athol. That will solve nothing. Stand up, man."

Athol stood. He sheathed his sword.

"Sit, man. Sit."

Athol resumed his place as directed.

"Ours is a sacred purpose, Athol. Take nothing for granted.

Be vigilant in the presence of the familiar, particularly on unfamiliar ground. Years of persecution taught us this: leave signs that are discreet or none at all. A pile of stone invites speculation. But a grove of trees? Nothing serves as a landmark quite so well as long-lived English oak. Signposts, Athol, as clear as any on a well-marked country road. Now there is hope."

"Hope, sire?"

Henry lifted the square and compass, laid them back on the table, arranged carefully, their alignment denoting in distance and direction the Island of the Twelve Standing Oaks, and the Well of Baphomet. He folded his bony hands, the pads of his thumbs attempting to press hope from uncertainty.

"If she lives, Mimkitawo'qu'sk is sure to guide her to the Well of Baphomet. The rivers have cleared. The snow recedes daily. The travelling couldn't be better. I know where the well is. They'll soon be on the move. And I'll be waiting."

"What if they've come and gone already?"

"Fetch Keswalqw for me, will you."

Athol bowed, left. Henry retested his calculations, secure the sacred knowledge set geometrically by hands such as his a century ago would lead him to both the Stone Grail and, in consequence, the Living Holy Grail Herself.

Keswalqw's shadow fell on the side of the tent. She listened quietly before calling his name.

"Henry. You wish to see me?"

"Keswalqw." He set the maps aside. "Yes, please."

"I'll come in?"

"No, no. I'll come out. I find I'm happier outside than in these days," Henry said as he emerged.

Keswalqw's smile was warm and reassuring. "You make progress, Henry. I think colour comes back to your cheeks. Now, for some light in those sky-coloured eyes…"

"I think it's not food or medicine I need."

"It's 'Your Lady.' When you first came I thought, he is Eugainia's father."

"She would be less pliant if she were my child, I assure you."

"Rarely in the lifetime of a person does one such as Eugainia appear. She has beauty, and grace. She is wise as Sa'qwe'ji'jk, the Oldest of our Old Ones."

"It is thus with those of the Royal and Holy Blood."

"What will you do if Eugainia is not found before the coming cold?"

"Lord in Heaven, Keswalqw. That horror is barely behind us. Winter is eight months away."

"Even so, it will come. Your men already speak with dread of another winter here. The People are fearful, too. The signs portend another starving time."

"We'll not tax your kindness further, Keswalqw. When found, Eugainia will be installed in the Grail Castle. I'll leave Sir Athol and a dozen well-armed men to stand guard until autumn when I'll return with stores to last the winter and a complete household to serve her needs. Among them, my wife and daughters, if they still live, God keep them."

"And if you don't find her?"

"We sail for Edinburgh."

"If you don't find her, you will leave. If you do find her, you'll leave. You'll leave regardless."

"Yes. And return next spring."

"She is not dead."

"Where is she?"

"With Mimkitawo'qu'sk."

"Is she well?"

"I'm told they thrive."

"You know where they are?"

"Yes, Henry. I know where they are."

"Well?"

"I don't like the look in your eyes. I don't like the sounds in your voice. You will do them harm."

"It is my sworn and sacred duty, Keswalqw, to secure her, and reunite her with her husband."

"The tired old man who covered her once and sired a broken child?"

"The same. Lord Ard—"

"Mimkitawo'qu'sk is her husband now."

"Eugainia's life is not her own to lead as she sees fit. Never was. She will say goodbye to Mimkitawo'qu'sk, and await the arrival of her chosen Lord."

"Chosen by whom?"

"The highest possible authority."

"The highest possible authority," Keswalqw repeated. "Who might that be?"

"I am not permitted to say."

Keswalqw sat cross-legged on a patch of dry ground. She sought and found a sprouting blade in a dry tuft of last summer's grass. She tugged carefully. The pale green lance slipped easily from its sheath. She severed the tender tip from its shaft and, with practised precision, sectioned it between her incisors. She motioned Henry to sit beside her.

"From what I can tell," she began when he'd settled, "it seems you are the highest possible authority."

Henry offered no reply.

She spit the pulped blade with a delicate purse of her lips and a barely audible out-rush of breath. "Perhaps you think our Mimkitawo'qu'sk is not good enough for your Eugainia." Henry's silence confirmed her suspicion. "Mimkitawo'qu'sk came to us, with power," she continued. "Great power in his little lungs and heart. We broke the ice the day he was born, broke the ice in the stream for the newborn's cleansing. Mimkitawo'qu'sk did not cry out. His flesh didn't so much as tremble. His eyes didn't close: even below the ice-filled water they shone calm with wisdom. His childhood days were filled with gentle wonders. He hunted like a man, so brave was his heart. Hunted like a skillful man, before he saw ten winters. He wept with the sick, the weak, the dying. He gave them his strength. His Power. His beauty and his kindness healed The People. Now he heals Eugainia. Let them be, Henry Orkney. It's their time to be one."

"Time is not their friend, Keswalqw," Henry replied. "Nor is it yours. I look out across this quiet strait and find I've come to dread the eastern horizon. They pursued Eugainia to the very edges of Europe. Portugal. Scotland. The outer Islands of the Hebrides. And now, I fear, beyond. I've come to fear the future as much as I abhor the past. They hanged our brothers and sisters—anyone even suspected of protecting Our Lady—by their thumbs. Suspended great weights. Stone by stone. Arms torn from shoulders. Legs pulled from hips. Most lived in the hope some mercy would be shown, prepared to live deprived of their teeth, their tongues, their eyes. Their limbs. Men lost their manhood. Women living breasts. Feet were bolted close to charcoal fires, held long past scream and plea, past promise to reveal. Skin blackened by flame curled away from flesh; their body fat ignited, burned before their eyes. Living bone became ash. All because of Eugainia and her ancient kin; all because the Royal and Holy Blood, the Blood they dare call heresy, runs in Her veins. I devoted my life to Eugainia's well-being, Keswalqw. And now you, dear friend, may soon be in terrible danger from these same monsters who would destroy her."

The low cliff at the northwest edge of the meadow offered an expansive view of the great gulf. It was toward the west Keswalqw turned when she rose and walked to the cliff edge. "The west is the place of old age and the end of things," she said as Henry rose to join her. "Also the source of wisdom and of knowing. From the west we draw comfort, for we shall know its secrets." She pointed north, beyond Apekwit. "What you call the north we call the home of Winter. Cold is the great purifier. Winter tests and strengthens us. Makes us who we are." She turned southward. "The south is warmth and plenty, yes. The south is also cruelty and death. Partway up the great river, beyond the southern borders of our Abenaki cousins, live The People of the Longhouse, the terrifying Iroquois. We're no strangers to the darkness at work in the depths of the human heart, Henry Orkney. They've seen to that. Our Huron friends fear Longhouse People more than a starving time. When their numbers fail the Longhouse People march up from the south, cross the great river, sometimes come to kill us in search of wives and slaves. They make examples of rebellious men and women whose love of family and children, of tribe and elders is so strong they will fight until the Ghost World beckons. And those strong ones whose wounds weaken but do not kill...? They strip living patches of skin the size of your palm from their prisoners' bodies. Piece by piece. They work up from wrist to shoulder, ankle to knee, thigh to hip. Belly, chest, back. They let the raw patch clot before they take the next. Enough to agonize but not to kill. They're marched through the forest. The spruce and pine needles that gave them medicine and made their bed now pierce and torture them. Three days pass before what was a man or woman, now a mass of blood and pain, falls and rises no more." Keswalqw took Henry's arm. "Revere the north, my friend. Regard the west with wonder. Fear the south. Where summer and evil live. But never fear the east. Grandfather Sun is an unending source of hope. Grandfather Sun is life. Let your heart seek his council. He will warm you. He will melt the last of the ice in your heart."

"I've no heart at all without My Lady."

"Then look to Grandmother Moon. I say this to you, Henry Orkney. When you look east, lift your eyes above the grey sea. Open your angry heart. Do this or an angry death awaits you."

"A living death infests me now. I beg you. Tell me where Eugainia hides."

Keswalqw watched the progress of the shipbuilders on the beach below. "If you stay, we are in danger. If you go, you are in danger."

"Keswalqw. Please. Take me to the Well of Baphomet."

"What?"

"The Island of the Twelve Standing Oaks on the ocean coast of the great peninsula."

"Ah. Yes. Your ancestor's well by the edge of the sea." Keswalqw indicated a column of grey smoke rising from the foundry adjacent to the ship keels. "I see you reshape your iron door-swingers and barrel-belts. All your iron objects."

"Yes. Into nails."

"The knives you gave us make long tasks short."

"It gives me pleasure to see The People profit from our technology."

"Arrow and spearheads made of this iron would make us stronger."

"May I speak to our farriers on your behalf?"

"Please. Do. And I'll speak with the Great Spirit on your's. I'll make a spirit quest. Then I'll know if I will or will not tell you where to find Mimkitawo'qu'sk and Eugainia."

CHAPTER FOURTEEN

Eugainia woke in the dark of the night. A single goose, white as the driven snow, fat with eggs, big as a Thunder Bird but silent, had flown through her dreams. Her wings seemed to envelope the sky. Beneath her pure white belly, a flock of her more common black-necked, white-cheeked, brown-bellied cousins flew in perfect formation. The snow goose wheeled away from the common flock, back to her home of winter, cold, ice, frost and snow. Is she my animal totem? Eugainia wondered as she watched the snow goose disappear. She reached for her lover. The space beside her was warm but empty. She sat up. Mimkɨtawo'qu'sk, cross-legged at the edge of the firepit, sifted ash in search of live coals.

"Where is the moon?" Eugainia asked.

"Still asleep, beloved. About to appear above the horizon. And there, look the Great Bear has already raised her head above the trees. Her cub will soon follow."

"We slept for hours."

"We did. Yes. We slept a good long sleep. May I have your fire shell?"

She handed him the punk-filled quahog. He inserted glowing remnants of hard pine knots that hadn't burst or burned as they slept.

"We'll build a new fire?"

"Not unless you're cold."

"No, no. I'm fine."

Eugainia reached through the back wall of the bivouac, scooped a handful of snow and washed her face. She rose, stretched. In the black of the night, in the crisp clear air, she felt she could pluck a star from the sky without fully extending her arm.

"Where will we sleep tonight, after our mysterious adventure?"

"I don't know. Take the robes. We should leave before we're fully awake."

"Oh?"

"It's better to hunt on the edge of a dream, The People say."

"Why?"

"The hunted and the hunter find each other more easily."

"What do we hunt tonight?"

"We won't hunt exactly. We pluck our food from the sky." Mimkɨtawo'qu'sk chuckled at Eugainia's confusion. "Wait and see, my love. Wait and see."

Eugainia slung the rolled robes, one over each shoulder. Mimkɨtawo'qu'sk hefted a stout club and a torch. They made their way to the stream. Where it widened, their canoe waited, tethered lightly to an overhang of willow. Mimkɨtawo'qu'sk gathered and coiled the braided thong. They slipped silently from the shore. Mid-stream, Eugainia reached for her oar.

"You won't need that, my love," Mimkɨtawo'qu'sk told her. "Tonight we drift into the middle of the harvest."

"I thought you said we'd pluck food from the sky."

"Patience, Moon Woman, is a virtue. Is that correct?"

"Correct."

The lovers boarded and then lay on the bottom of the canoe, their legs entwined at the centre, heads low in the bow and stern.

The stream widened. Its flow increased in speed as volume accumulated. The night sky emerged from the tunnel overhang of willow and alder. The crescent moon—old now, and feeble—broke free of the horizon. The stars crackled, vibrant and intense, their light eclipsing that of the dying moon.

Eugainia sensed they'd drifted into the open water of an estuary. One feeder steam after another funnelled late-spring snowmelt into the swollen out-rush of fresh water. The canoe wheeled freely, a compass needle subject to no magnetic imperative, circling first one way, pausing, flowing parallel to the shore awhile, then circling back in counter-rotation, dependent entirely on the spiralling currents of convergent streams. Eugainia couldn't identify the murmurs drifting across the estuary, nor the black shapes afloat on blacker water, barely discernable in the rippling light of the stars.

Mimkitawo'qu'sk slipped noiselessly to the centre of the canoe, where he knelt. He handed her the pine torch, its fire end shaved, sticky withresin. Dry tinder-grass held to the ember flickered to life at the slight urging of his breath. Smoke curled. Embers sparked, then leapt into flame. Eugainia angled the head of the torch to receive the fire. The resin flared immediately.

"Hold it high, high as you can."

Eugainia held the flame high above her head. Patches of white flashed in its light. Iridescent pricks of light shot back from eyes wide with curiosity. Then fear.

Mimkitawo'qu'sk, surefooted master of the round-bottomed canoe, stood. Eugainia reached instinctively to steady him, her free hand inadvertently clipped by the paddle he raised to shoulder height. He aligned it with the second paddle, extended both fully above his head. He slapped the blades together. Their sharp report startled Eugainia.

It terrified the geese.

Panic erupted. Webbed feet, stretched wide, ruptured the surface. Wings jolted into flight failed to grip the air. Migration-weary bodies confused by the unnatural sun sank in the drag of water on their bellies. Long black necks stretched and coiled, stretched and coiled again, pumping power into breast muscles and cries of alarm from beaks splayed open in fear.

The flock found their wings and rose blind in disarray. With no sun high in the dome to guide them, and the stars dimmed by the sudden flare, the geese—slaves to aerial order—formed a vortex. Wings tempered steel-hard by weeks of migratory flight battered one another: cries of distress became protests of anger and pain. Birds orbiting the outer fringes fought toward the centre, knocking kind and kin from the air. At the centre of the maelstrom shone Eugainia's torch, first a brand of alarm, now a beacon offering the hope of order. The panicked throng all but smothered the light. Eugainia and Mimkitawo'qu'sk felt wingtips brush their clothes, their hair, their faces. Quick as a cat among fledglings, his blood running hot, his mind calm and cool, Mimkitawo'qu'sk batted geese from the air. Dozens fell back to the water, injured or exhausted. Those tumbling into the canoe he throttled. The rest, battered and disoriented, floated downstream, their ultimate destination the open sea. Night predators or the natural passage of time, the great healer of all wounds, would determine their fate.

The gunwales soon rested a mere hand's breadth above the water. At first Eugainia had been enthralled by the spectacle. Her blood rose. The huntress was engaged, until the twitching mass of beak and feather accumulating at her feet drove her thoughts inward to the secret hope she carried. The same hope beat in their blood, urging the geese from the safety of the mating grounds in the southern bayous and estuaries to their nesting grounds high in the Arctic. Eugainia felt sudden nausea. She doused the torch. Darkness more profound than any she could remember enveloped the canoe. She required no light, only sound, to know what befell the airborne geese. Some dropped like stones to the surface of the water. One collided with the port gunwale. Another struck the upswept bow. One set of wings, then another, then a third rushed past. Many flew blind, full speed, her ears told her, into trees. Cries of distress decreased as others found the polar star and flew off unharmed into the night. They'd sweep low over meadow and forest until ocean breakers called, then plummet helter-skelter, safe to the surface of the sea.

Mimkitawo'qu'sk's eyes adjusted quickly to the dark.

"You dropped the torch."

"No. I doused it on purpose."

"How are we to find and dispatch the injured birds?"

"The canoe is half-full already—"

"It's wrong to leave these injured birds—"

"How many geese do we need?"

"I meant to fill it. As a gift to The People."

"We can't go to The People. Not yet."

"Why?"

"If the Holy Blood it is not refreshed, the child I carry, our child Mimkitawo'qu'sk, will be born as weak and twisted as the last."

"Our child, Woman with the Moon?"

"Yes."

Mimkitawo'qu'sk placed a hand on Eugainia's belly. "When?"

"I don't know. Autumn."

Mimkitawo'qu'sk removed his clothes.

"Mimkɨtawo'qu'sk. Put on your robe."

"Come. Stand beside me."

"You'll catch your death. Our child will be without an earthly father."

"We must bare ourselves to the stars to show we're strong and worthy. Then give thanks to the four winds. And ask the protection of the Great Bear."

Mimkɨtawo'qu'sk helped Eugainia to her feet. They drew each other near.

"See that star, the brightest..." Mimkɨtawo'qu'sk pointed north and west of the zenith, "...and the three stars clustered near it? That's the canoe of the three hunters; they try to kill Great Bear. Just there," he pointed. "Nearby. But the north star won't permit them to kill Great Bear, nor her cub, Little Bear. Just there."

"Bear Power." Eugainia felt encouraged. "Power from the Earth World written in the World Above the Sky."

"Yes. Star Power, Woman with the Moon."

"We'll ask Grandmother Moon to give us medicine to keep evil from our child," she whispered.

"Grandfather Sun will help me keep the evil priests from you. Come Woman with the Moon. Stand naked before the Great Spirit with your husband."

Eugainia raised her arms. Her robes slipped from her shoulders and fell to the bottom of the canoe, a warm heap of fur in the silence of the still, warm geese.

Mimkɨtawo'qu'sk raised his arms. The canoe, caught in a gentle eddy, began a measured, slow revolve.

"Hear us, Great Spirit. Hear us, Spirit Persons of the Six Worlds."

"We ask your blessings."

"Hear, Creator, the Spirit Call of the White Goddess, My Wife, and Mother of My Child—my Woman Who Fell in Love with the Moon."

"We ask your blessings."

"Hear the Spirit Call of Mimkitawo'qu'sk, Father, Healer, Warrior God of The People, I Who would be their Chief."

"I, the Bearer of the Royal and Holy Blood, the Lady of the Grail, the White Goddess and the Black Madonna ask your blessings. The Spirit of our Unborn Child, the Holy Child, the Two Made One," Eugainia said, "ask your blessings."

"We seek the blessings of the east, source of light and wisdom, that Eugainia's people may see the beauty of L'nuk, The People, and love us. That L'nuk, The People, may see the beauty in her people, that we might love them. That all people in all the worlds known and unknown to us may see the beauty in each other, that we may see the beauty of the world itself, and be kind."

The canoe revolved a quarter-turn. The Great Chief of the Six Worlds and Moon Woman, His Lady Wife, appeared to stand on water rippling with stars. "We seek the blessings of the south," Eugainia, Goddess of the old and uncertain world, continued, "source of heat and plenty, that the children of all may grow fat in the warmth and love of their people."

Mimkitawo'qu'sk faced the fading moon. "We seek the blessings of the west, home of the aged and of memory, home of the wind that reminds us that we are born of the earth and to the earth we return...we open our ears and our hearts to the west, to its whisperings and its raging."

"We seek the blessings of the north, oh Creator, home of darkness, home of the cold, home of winter, home of ice and frost and snow," Eugainia prayed. "Cleanse our minds, our hearts and our bodies. Strengthen us, with the north wind's purifying cold."

Mimkitawo'qu'sk offered the final supplication.

"Oh Great Spirit. Make us joyful in the light of the east, glad in the heat of the south, brave in the winds of the west. Keep us strong and free in the purging cold of the north. Hold our hearts and minds in Your hand at the centre of the Great Circling Heaven, the Great Circle of Heaven fashioned and set in motion by You."

"We ask these blessings in our Holy names, Goddess and God made incarnate by You, the Creator." Eugainia placed Mimkitawo'qu'sk's hand on her belly. "And in the name of our Child, Mijua'ji'j, the Two Made One."

Mimkitawo'qu'sk knelt, guiding Eugainia down to her knees before him. The canoe, caught in the gyre of two converging currents, turned end for end repeatedly without advance.

"You know me now as God, man and husband. Soon as the father of our child. Always as servant, protector, provider. "

"I do."

"And you know I love you."

"I do."

For the second time in as many days, Mimkitawo'qu'sk waited for words that did not come; no declaration of love crossed Eugainia's lips. It is my time, he thought to himself, to watch and wait.

"Mimkitawo'qu'sk. Please. I beg you. For the sake of your wife and the love she bears you, for the well-being of your child. Our child. Take me to the Well of Baphomet."

Mimkitawo'qu'sk and Eugainia lay back in a warm nest of fur and feather. The canoe rocked as they settled, then found its equilibrium. Amidst their flightless cargo of death and plenty, transformed by the little life that lay between and before them— Mimkitawo'qu'sk and Eugainia abandoned themselves to a more careful kind of love. The canoe broke the gyre and regained its rudderless course. Their passion traced a long slow spiral on the quiet surface of the estuary, pulled by spring run-off, pushed by the falling tide toward the extreme ebb and floe of Turned Up Whale Belly Bay.

CHAPTER FIFTEEN

To the uninitiated, the grove of English oaks betrayed no apparent meaning. The twelve great trees arranged in four equilateral triangles were precisely set to the corresponding points of the cross pattée of the Scottish Knights Templar. The set-square planting paid geometric homage both to the Holy Trinity and the twelve disciples of the Christ.

A slight depression where the apexes of the four inverted triangles converged confirmed Eugainia's calculations. She seized Tooth of Wolverine. Sacred though it was to her Christian mythology, iconic though it had become to The People, she hoisted it above her head—the Spear of Destiny, Tooth of Wolverine, hefted it in her hands undignified as a common crowbar—then drove the gleaming star-stone head into the earth, sparking surface stones and loosening rock-hard soil. All the while, she held one thought and one thought only: save our child.

Eugainia's grim determination irritated Mimkitawo'qu'sk. He sat cross-legged, banished to the bare, leafless shade of the nearest centurion oak. He fixed his attention on the shadow patterns thrown upon and about him by the spreading branches above. Weak though he was this time of year, Grandfather Sun remained the Earth World's greatest hope; life responded with inexorable vigour to the great warm jewel in the World Above the Sky. In the awakening earth below Mimkitawo'qu'sk, roots pumped sap through trunk and branch to pulsing twigs. Buds strained, engorged beyond constraint, pressed to unfold without resistance in the growing heat. Meadow grass, roots newly freed from the frosted earth, competed with early blooming bulbs for what little heat the earth offered.

Small hairs on the back of Mimkitawo'qu'sk's neck rose again, and trembled. He slapped the back of his neck, irritated, he supposed, by some small creature hungry for his blood. He examined his unblemished palm in vain for traces of victory.

"I feel something crawling down the back of my neck," he said.

Eugainia lifted the hair from the nape of his neck with the tip of the spear.

"There's nothing crawling down the back of your neck."

"I know. But something creeps nonetheless."

Eugainia returned to her work.

Unseen by either Eugainia or Mimkitawo'qu'sk, Henry—chain-mailed, steel-helmeted, visor up—emerged from an oceanside thicket of stunted spruce. The cross pattée of his undertunic had been dulled from bright crimson to a dry-blood red by the rusted rings of the mail. He assessed distance. Too far to make a rush. He slipped back into shadow.

"You dig the earth like a denning fox," Mimkitawo'qu'sk said.

"Mimkitawo'qu'sk, if you're not going to help, please do not interfere."

"You waste my time and your energy."

"If you don't want to be here, then go."

"I won't leave you in the presence of this evil."

"Then stay."

"Go. Stay. You want me here and gone at the same time."

"I'm doing what I need to do. You do what you please."

Mimkitawo'qu'sk grasped the shaft of Wolverine.

"I'm not going to fight you for it." Eugainia released the spear to his control. She sat beneath the oak.

"Very wise. You would not win."

Eugainia gathered her hair, damp with sweat, and began to plait a braid. We will see about that, she thought.

Mimkitawo'qu'sk inverted the spear and drove it into the ground. "You treat me as though I don't matter."

Eugainia retrieved the spear.

Correctly judging them too absorbed in their personal discord to notice him, Henry moved quickly from the scrub spruce to the outermost oak. Its stout trunk concealed him completely. He strained to hear conversation fragmented by the rise and fall of the freshening breeze.

"Mimkitawo'qu'sk. I…"

"You are not more sorry I am…"

"Hear me…my life before I'll…"

"…you seek is evil."

"Within the evil is good."

"Within evil only more evil. Any child knows…"

"…end my life…before I…another monstrous child."

Waving grasses stilled. Henry's breath ran shallow. The breeze died, revealing every word.

"What do you know of the evil of the world?" Eugainia demanded. "You who live in paradise."

"Paradise! Are you blind, deaf and dumb Woman with the Moon? Do The People not starve when the snows desert them? When illness, sorrow and grief infest their hearts, do they not sicken, grieve and die? You haven't seen the cruelty borne by The

People. Or born of them. Nor have you seen our women and children slaughtered by our enemies, or those we slaughter in return, their spirits wailing, lost, seeking entry to the Ghost World, yearning to be with those who went before. You think our world's pure and yours isn't? You do us harm, with this 'them not us,' this 'you not me' of yours."

"The stone that does not speak will bring true power to L'nuk."

"I have said and again I say: we have the Power of the Six Worlds."

"I dig and dream for you, Mimkitawo'qu'sk."

"We don't need your dead, mute bowl, or this star-stone spear."

"I need their Power. My child needs their Power."

"Your child?"

Henry feared Eugainia might suffer harm, though it was she, not Mimkitawo'qu'sk, who controlled the spear.

"I meant our—"

"Our spirits mingled to make this child. Now you claim it as your own? Perhaps you think, 'I'll take my child with me, away from this brown man, back across the sea.'"

"I don't know where the Holy Blood will lead me."

"I know. My wife will stay with The People. My child will stay with The People."

"You would force me to stay against my will?"

"I would. I will."

"And how will you do that?"

"Do not provoke me, Eugainia."

"I'm Eugainia again, am I?"

"You're no longer Woman Who Fell in Love with the Moon. Not in your spirit."

"Then who am I?"

"You are Eugainia; Woman Who Steals My Child. Woman whose people will give my bones to the red-robed priests to be burned. I know what you think I am. I know who you think I am. Maybe I am the god you seek to be your eternal celestial partner. Maybe I am not. I know this: I'm a man of eighteen winters, Eugainia. Already I have lost one wife. Already I have lost one child. My tribe awaits my council. The Great Spirit wishes me to hear His voice. Kluscap, his servant, waits for me to breathe the secrets of the earth, her ways and her creatures into The People's ears. You said you were sent to me by heaven. That you came from heaven. That you, like me, are the Great Spirit's emisary made manifest on earth. But in your heart I am not your equal."

"You are in every way my equal."

"You wish to steal my child, and run away. You wish to kill my soul. No! Do not object. Hear me. I will speak of this one time and one time only: if you steal my child, I will call all the Powers of the Six Worlds. I will make a great canoe. I will follow you wherever you go. I will find you. I will bring you and our child home."

"Would you leave The People to starve and die if you could prevent it?"

"Look around you. Where are your people?"

"In terrible darkness. I am their salvation."

"Your people killed their one God. Like Windego, Cannibal Ghost Person, your people drink his blood. Like Windego, Cannibal Ghost Person, they devour his flesh. Like Windego, Cannibal Ghost Person, the poor Christ though long dead still cannot satisfy your people's thirst or gluttony. Still they eat his flesh. Still they drink his blood. You say you're like him. That I'm like him. That you and I are this Christ reborn. Maybe we are.

Maybe we're not. Either way, I make you this promise: no one, not your people, not mine, will devour your flesh. Or eat the flesh of our child. Or eat mine. They will not drink my blood. Or your blood. Or the blood of our child. This land is vast, beyond what even I can know or imagine. You know my people, Moon Woman. Because you know me, they will love and cherish you. Protect you. We will not be torn apart. Or devoured. Or burned. Our child will walk between us. Together we'll travel the Six Worlds forever."

Eugainia took and held his hand in hers. "I thought the greatest love to be the selfless love one feels for all humankind," she said at last. "I was wrong. If we come to love only one other person in our lifetime, Mimkitawo'qu'sk, our journey upon this sorrowful earth has worth. I stand here and listen to you speak. I see the look in your eyes. I hear the words of your heart. I know this: For me, that person is not our unborn child. Not this child, nor the next child or any child that follows. The person I came to earth to know, the man I came to love is you. To walk side by side with someone of your grace and beauty Mimkitawo'qu'sk? The Creator's greatest gift to the goddess is her god. Still I fear for the child, Mimkitawo'qu'sk. I fear without the Grail not only the child will die but I will die with it. You alone in a world without me. Me alone in the world without you..."

"Stop this talk. We will not die—"

"Beloved, I heard you. Now you hear me. I tell you, I will know no peace until I hold the Grail. She is below us. Here. She waits to heal me and strengthen you. When our blood, your blood and mine are blended, in Her, and anointed with the Spear of Destiny, with Wolverine, I will be well. Our child will be well. We will be well. I beg you, Husband. You whom I love more than life itself. Help me retrieve the Holy Grail."

"If I help you, you will stay?"

"If you help me, I'll run wild and free with you forever. I swear it on our love."

Mimkitawo'qu'sk rested his hand at the nape of Eugainia's neck, as though cradling the head of an infant. "Swear on the life of our unborn child."

She held his glance. "I swear on the life of our unborn child."

"Do not doubt the *Kji-kinap* of the Six Worlds," he told her. "Because of *Kji-kinap*, I exist. Because of *Kji-kinap* all that exists, is."

"This is the World of Sa'qwe'ji'jk, the Oldest of the Old," she replied. "My ancestors, your ancients; they're all here, around above and below us."

"Yes. In your sky-coloured eyes, I see them all."

Mimkitawo'qu'sk held Eugainia in his arms.

"Come, my wife. Let's put aside strife and feed our yearning. Let's fill this evil place with love."

Delicately, insistent as spring—tendrils of forgiveness sprouted from the ragged ends of discord. Eugainia curled toward him. He responded. Limbs entwined. Lips swollen in argument, now full with desire, met. The world disappeared. In their hearts, there were only three persons on the ocean side of the Island of the Twelve Standing Oaks: two wrapped in love sheltered the unborn third.

The unseen fourth, Henry Sinclair, moved across the clearing with practised stealth. He froze when the lovers parted. He exhaled silently when they lay on their sides on a dry swath of last-year's meadow hay. Eugainia curled her leg across Mimkitawo'qu'sk's pelvis. He arched, rolled to his back. Eugainia raised her robe and straddled him. He freed himself. She guided him home.

"Ah. There you are," she murmured. "There you are..."

Eugainia arched back. Her sweat-dampened hair swung low in a cool wet arc. Her knees, her shins, the tops of her feet pressed into the earth. She lifted her hips, held still for a heartbeat. She settled her full weight upon him. The Goddess of Sea and Sky drove her desire down, through the body of her Earth and Sky World lover, into the rock and soil below. Mimkitawo'qu'sk reached up beneath her robe, hands to her breasts. His shoulders, neck, the back of his head pushed down and back. His heals dug into the soil. Strung taught and fully drawn, he pressed upward, his body a bow. The young God of the Sky, of the Earth and all its Creatures, yearned to launch an arc of light heavenward, to illuminate the sky with the fire of ten thousand suns, to remake the bond between him and the Sky Goddess that had all but come undone in waves of anger and of fear. Eugainia closed herself around him. Their blood—distinct though echoed in inflamed flesh—pulsed as if pumped from one heart. Each watched, in the eyes of the other, the last of the torn tendrils entwine.

"Stop, beloved," Mimkitawo'qu'sk spoke urgently, gently. "Hold still. Still as can be. Oh please. Yes. There. Just so. Hold me like this for eternity."

The lovers held their final pulse at bay, trembling, alive, suspended. Deep down the well, inside the brazen Head of Baphomet, the Stone Grail pulsed once, then rested.

The spreading branches and budding twigs of the oak above formed a lattice work of light and shadow. To distract his body Mimkitawo'qu'sk filled his mind with the scent of the crushed hay, the weave of the branches, the patches of blue, the glint of the sun, the face of Eugainia, her nipples light beneath his thumbs, her eyes closed, her head thrown back, turned to the left. Eugainia cast her memory to Lord Ard's fetid bed. The image repelled her. She raised her hips. Mimkitawo'qu'sk followed, pressing higher than she expected. She righted herself, let her weight fall. He lifted her again. She opened her eyes, knowing his were also wide with surprise. Fire danced between them. She imagined their child riding waves of their passion in the warm salt sea of her belly.

Mimkitawo'qu'sk's gaze shifted, his face a sudden mask of outraged disbelief.

Henry seized Eugainia by her shoulders, jerked her up and away.

Mimkitawo'qu'sk covered himself, rolled to his side. His seed spilled to wither on dry and sterile ground. He grunted, bewildered and ashamed. The force of Mimkitawo'qu'sk's humiliation, and the outrage pulsing deep in Eugainia's belly, herself appalled by the profanity visited upon them, merged in fractured anguish. Their shame burned with a terrible heat. Inexpressible, their fury took the form of a white-hot bolt of light and shot down the well. Inside the hollow brazen head of Baphomet, the Holy Grail was shattered by the fire of Henry's great betrayal and the aggrieved lover's shame.

In the silence that followed, the thoughts of each drove inward. None imagined the magnitude of the destruction below. Inside the Head of Baphomet, wrapped in coarse linen where all God's grace and beauty waited unmolested for one hundred years, nothing remained but tattered cloth, and the rubble and dust of the Christ's most precious relic.

In a moment of anger predicted by Keswalqw, Henry had breached his sacred trust. His behaviour sickened him. He had disgraced the past. He knew the damage was irreparable. Henry Sinclair had found his Lady. His victory was hollow. His misguided passion had once and for all hanged, gutted and quartered his hopes for a New Arcadia.

Still in Henry's frozen grip, Eugainia folded her hands on her belly. Yes. Life. Still there. Drowning in a sea of shame.

How Mimkitawo'qu'sk rose from his belly to standing, Tooth of Wolverine light in his hands, he could not tell. What he knew was this: he would give his life for those of his wife and child. If further provoked, he would take the life that had shamed and dishonoured them both.

"Your hands, 'Enry Orkney. Remove them from my wife."

Henry drew his broadsword.

"This woman belongs to another, Mimkitawo'qu'sk."

"I belong to no one but myself." Eugainia struggled to free herself. "Take your hands from my body."

"No, madam. I will not."

"Madam?" Eugainia rounded on Henry. She spit in his face. He wiped His Lady's spittle from his cheek and the bridge of his nose. He dropped the visor of his helmet.

Eugainia moved to Mimkitawo'qu'sk's side.

"Step aside, Eugainia. God wills it."

"God wills no such thing."

Mimkitawo'qu'sk advanced, spear held low, his two-handed grip readying him to thrust, not throw.

"The Ghost World calls to you, Henry Orkney."

Mimkitawo'qu'sk circled, his jabs deflected by Henry's sword. Neither man could find advantage. Mimkitawo'qu'sk stepped back, spun to the right. He forced every ounce of strength into his upper arms and shoulders. He aimed the flat of the spear head at Henry's right temple. Tooth of Wolverine connected with all the force Mimkitawo'qu'sk's eighteen years could muster.

Henry felt he'd been struck by lightning. Thunder shook the steel helmet, then rumbled down his spine to the pit of his stomach. He suppressed the urge to vomit. He lashed out. He swung his broadsword blindly, caught the shaft of Wolverine within a hair's breadth of Mimkɨtawo'qu'sk's leading hand. The Spear of Destiny was halved with a splintering crack.

Mimkɨtawo'qu'sk stood easy, his arms outstretched, a section of the halved spear in either hand, his naked chest vulnerable. Inviting. Henry raised his weapon two-handed above his head, his intention to bring it down with full force and split Mimkɨtawo'qu'sk's skull.

Henry stepped forward.

Mimkɨtawo'qu'sk stood his ground.

Henry lunged, brought his sword down with all his might.

Mimkɨtawo'qu'sk fell like a stone and rolled out of range.

Henry regained his balance. Mimkɨtawo'qu'sk crouched. Henry levelled his sword, spun to the left, a roar emerging as he gained momentum, powering the horizontal blow he hoped would strike the young warrior's head from his body.

Mimkɨtawo'qu'sk dove. He planted the Spear of Destiny in Henry's side.

Henry stood stupefied. He shifted his sword to his left hand. With his right, he grasped the shaft of the spear and pulled it free. A gush of blood. He threw the sectioned spear to the ground, covered the wound with his hand, staunching the flow. He advanced on Mimkɨtawo'qu'sk. Mimkɨtawo'qu'sk slipped his flensing knife at his calf from its sheath. He crouched low, ready to spring. Unseen by either, Eugainia retrieved what remained of the spear. In a tight, two-fisted grip she pressed the bloodied tip of the halved spear to her belly.

"Stop it! Now! Stop it or God and Goddess help you both, I will bury this stone blade in the Holy Child."

Mimkɨtawo'qu'sk sheathed his knife. The broadsword fell from Henry's hand. He collapsed into darkness.

Prince Henry Sinclair found himself back in the jaws of Jipijka'maq, Horned Serpent Person, thundering hell-bound through earth and solid rock.

PART FOUR

....

THE WORLD ABOVE THE SKY

Summer, 1399

CHAPTER SIXTEEN

The Singing Stone of The People jutted from the centre of the green, circular meadow. The black obelisk appeared to pierce the surface of the earth at an angle, suggesting an arrow shot from the sky or, according to The People, a spear hurled from the Sky World by the Creator Himself, a sign of His dominion. Its height exceeded that of a tall man. At its widest, near the base, its girth doubled. More flat than round, the stone tapered to shoulder width near the apex, where it curved in on itself from two sides, not unlike a tongue. Its lingual shape supported both its name and prophetic capability.

The meadow lay subdued beneath a low, grey sky. Mimkitawo'qu'sk stood alone, his back to the great stone. Both rock and man glistened, wet with moisture condensed from the sodden air. Tooth of Wolverine, its handle restored with a stout shaft of ash, stood inverted against the rock, its head indistinguishable from the star-stone, and the sister stone in Scotland from which the spearhead had been cut two thousand years ago.

Mimkitawo'qu'sk cut and removed four small rectangles from each of the corners of a square of birchbark. Spruce-root filaments, stripped and oiled, lay in a tight coil beside him. He scored and folded the bark into a box large enough to contain a

clenched fist or, he thought, an enemy's beating heart. He regret-
ted injuring Henry. He had no choice. Henry had shamed him
and humiliated him. He had assaulted his wife. He had betrayed
them both and would happily have murdered Mimkitawo'qu'sk.
"Then he would steal Moon Woman and my child. I did what
any man must do when those he loves are threatened," he said
aloud to the stone, his only witness, his voice muffled by the
thick air.

He pierced adjacent edges of the box's four corners with a thin
bone awl, and threaded the spruce roots. He examined the box
from every angle and found it pleased him. He set the box aside,
near a small white-onyx bowl, traded for sturgeon roe far to the
south some seasons past. Still warm from the fire, the bowl contained tar, tar from the pool at the base of the Smoking Mountain.
Tar, he recalled, from the same pool that covered Moon Woman
the day she shape-shifted, struggling to free her heart of its double
grief, the loss of Morgase and her ill-made child.

He retrieved and examined the box more closely. Whatever
could have prompted him to make such a thing as this, he wondered. Not since boyhood had such a childish notion overtaken
him. He cut a length of willow, feathered one end with his knife,
dipped the brush into tar. He dabbed the box seams inside and
out, then set the finished box aside to dry.

Across Claw of Spirit Bird Bay, the Smoking Mountain
belched a sulphurous cloud of vapour and black smoke.
Mimkitawo'qu'sk watched the cloud rise. It dispersed quickly,
absorbed by the dense overcast. He offered his dilemma up to
the Creator, hoping the smoke would carry his question swiftly
to the Power he trusted would bring comfort and guidance.

"Great Spirit, why did you make me? All my life Keswalqw
says it is I the tribe awaited, since the days of the Great River

wars. 'The People awaited you, Mimkitawo'qu'sk,' she said, 'the shaman/warrior/chief who will lead and heal The People.' Then the white-as-a-ghost-persons came. I see Eugainia and I know...she is for me. She says I was sent down to the earth, one of their three Gods made flesh, to walk beside her. How can this be? I'm a man like any other. I walk by myself. Did You, Great Spirit, in Your wisdom direct Kluscap to fill those sails, cause Henry's wind-catching blankets to puff out, to push his great canoes across the ocean sea? Did Kluscap bring me She Who Is My Love and Sorrow for a reason? I wish to be a simple man again. A man of The People who loves an ordinary woman. I know this can't be. When we join, Great Power fires our coupling. I feel that we are great and pure and good alone. Not ordinary, either of us. But together? We are eternal. How can I be of The People and not of The People at the same time? Mysterious are Your ways, Great Spirit. Your heart and my heart, are they not one and the same? Why is your purpose kept from us? Must I subdue my own sorrow to know the greater sorrow of the whole world? Can he who knows no illness, only vigour, hope to heal? Can he who walks alone give comfort only to the lonely? You direct us to tell a new story, the story of all women and all men, a tale beyond telling or remembering, to tell the old stories in a new way, in a white-as-a-ghost-person way and, at the same time, in the way of The People, so that all the people may understand, may find harmony in Your words, in the hearts and minds of the animals, in the voice of winds and mountains, in the minds of the earth and the sea, in the words and deeds of each other, so all may find new ways to love the Earth World and all who tread upon it. It is said at every turn of the great sky wheel a new voice sings the story-songs of the God. Were we— was I—sent by You to reveal a new world? To tell this new tale?

This old tale in a new way? Almighty Voice...is it time for Two to sing the song together? Not his song. Not her song. The human song, the earth and sea and sky song; the song of perfect kindness in the time of the Two Made One?"

The ground below Mimkitawo'qu'sk's feet trembled. He placed his hand on the obelisk. A slight vibration then a gentle tone, ineffable, sweet, stirred the hair on his arm. He lifted his hand from the surface. The vibration ceased. The tone faded. He lay his hand on the stone again. The vibration resumed, increased in volume, holding precise pitch. Tooth of Wolverine rattled against the stone, its movement slight, too gentle to account for the sparks that flashed from rock to the spearhead and back. The tooth of ravenous Wolverine, the point of the Spear of Destiny, began to glow. Mimkitawo'qu'sk took the spear in both hands. He touched the spearhead to the obelisk. A fissure opened in the rock. He set Wolverine aside. The black-as-night Singing Stone of The People bled bright red blood. He held the birchbark box to the flow.

So this is why this childish box compelled me to make it, thought Mimkitawo'qu'sk. "Enough," he said when the box filled to overflowing. The bleeding stopped. The fissure healed. The star-stone stood unmarked and silent.

Mimkitawo'qu'sk held the box of blood above his head. The blood dissolved, ascended as vapour, indistinguishable from the grey, distillate air.

"Great Spirit, I asked a question. You answered. With Your blood, from the bones of the earth You answered."

Mimkitawo'qu'sk lowered the box, examined the interior. All that remained was a faint rose glow. He sat cross-legged at the base of the stone. He took up the last square of birchbark. He began to fashion a lid.

A day's journey distant, on the ocean side of the peninsula, Athol Gunn dismissed the slight tremor below his feet, confident the fruit of this fortnight's labours stood unthreatened; the recent Grail Chapel repairs would, he was certain, hold. Under direct orders from Eugainia, Sir Athol had halted reparations to the Grail Castle and relocated the expedition's artisans from the castle and the shipyard in Spirit Bird Bay to the Well of Baphomet, their task the immediate penetration of the well and retrieval of the Holy Grail. The timing of her orders, he reflected as he walked, seemed divinely ordained; the construction of the two longboats was all but complete. Both lay at anchor in a tidal estuary of Spirit Bay where the ship's timbers—seams and joints caulked—had swollen tight in the tidal estuary. Cured masts, ready to be footed and raised, lay on rafts alongside. All had been on schedule for a late-June, early-July departure. Sooner would have been better: the summer seas of the North Atlantic, though less prone to violent outbursts than those of a fall or winter crossing were known to be capricious. A small matter, Sir Athol believed, considering the opening of the well and retrieval of its treasure would save three lives; those of Eugainia St. Clair Delacroix, her unborn child, and his cousin, Prince Henry Sinclair.

The moccasined feet of generations of The People had moulded the path along The Gold River as it became known to the visitors, so named by Antonio who, before his banishment, scoured its bed clean of even the most minute nugget and flake. Athol walked at a brisk pace beside the pillaged river of the yellow stones. A clear purpose always put a spring in the sturdy man's step. He glanced back at the castle, its outline softened by the green tracery of unfolding leaves. All things considered, Athol was relieved the Chapel and Lady's quarters were finally inhab-ited. Eugainia had installed herself voluntarily in the unfinished castle fortress, the better to tend Prince Henry's wound. Still, there was much to do. The main concern throughout—the repaired chapel and bedchambers aside—were roofs and windows. Though the Great Hall's stone and rubble walls suffered least in its hundred years of neglect, its slate roof had collapsed as rafters decayed. Door and window casements had deteriorated. Leaded glass windows sagged over time and slumped to the ground. The kitchens—the two great hearths at least—were still viable. For this Sir Athol offered up a second prayer of thanks.

Eugainia remained convinced the healing power of the Grail was the only source of hope. It became clear in the minds of The People—less than a week since his side was pierced—that Henry's life depended on Keswalqw's ministrations. Eugainia felt the truth of this but still could not untangle her drive for survival and that of the child from the recovery of the sacred relic. She had no inkling that Henry's imprudence and her fury at the Well of Baphomet had reduced the Stone Grail to unholy rubble.

Nor had Athol Gunn. She's right, of course, he thought, the smell of the ocean sharp in his nostrils. As always. First, the Holy Grail.

The Grail's remains lay wrapped in cloth inside Baphomet some seventy metres and three treacherous floodtraps below the rock-hard surface, at the centre of the grove of oaks outlining the Templar cross pattée. An elaborate system of tunnels and traps had long ago been engineered to flood the well with tonnes of sea water if safeguards were rashly breached. None but Templars, or those privy to their singular skills as engineers, could hope to open the Well of Baphomet and survive. Templars had dug the Oak Island well a hundred years ago, and were in possession of the same techniques employed by the Crusaders who penetrated the stone walls of Jerusalem. Under the noses of the Saracens, Henry and Athol's forbears, the proto-Templars of the first crusade, breached the foundations of the Second Temple and, below it, constructed the tunnels that gave access to the great hall of the First Temple built by King Solomon himself.

Sir Athol roused himself from these reflections, crossed the wooden bridge to the island where, finally, good news awaited him; his men were in reach of the sacred prize.

The cold stone walls of Eugainia's bedchamber were smothered in tapestries, their bright threads worked to illuminate the grim miseries of big-eyed, flat-faced saints. If poor Henry woke to these dismal visions, Eugainia feared he'd wish he himself had drowned with the poor souls who'd met their fates in the Great Gulf, since named for the too lightly grilled St. Lawrence. Eugainia directed Henry be moved from her heavily draped bedchamber to the soft rose light and open air of the graceful chapel.

The chapel's vaulted ceilings commanded the eye to rise. The high, rounded rose window above the alter invited souls to soar, not shrink in despair. In the apse, Henry lay white and silent upon a bier before the alter, draped in quilted linen, his breathing light and irregular. The flag of the Knights Templar stood furled upon a standard at his head. At Henry's feet, a sweetgrass smudge pot issued fragrant smoke.

Keswalqw folded back the linen coverlet. Eugainia rolled up Henry's shirt, exposing the broad swath of cloth that circled his waist. The bandage, folded back, revealed a second linen pad. Beneath it, Keswalqw's spent poultice of moss infused with shaved willow bark and tar from the Smoking Mountain, packed with tidal mud from Turned Up Whale Belly Bay, lay in direct contact with the wound.

Eugainia cupped a fresh poultice, warmed by her hands. "I know the healing powers of tar. And the power of moss to dry and absorb. But mud on an open wound?"

"For every Earth World sickness, the Great Spirit provides a remedy—in the trees, the plants, the earth under your feet. From the World Above the Sky, Grandfather Sun sends great healing power to the weak in spirit. Grandmother Moon with her sky children, the stars, send strong medicine from the Sky World to her earth children who feel they've lost their way, who live fearful and alone. Earth medicine has the greatest healing power of all," Keswalqw said as she moulded the poultice, its final shape that of a thick ash leaf. "The Power that causes a seed to sprout is heightened by the ocean's salt. Nothing has more Power than a sea-mud pack of willow and moss when wounded flesh turns putrid. Earth, sea and sky medicine. Together. Very strong."

"And the tar?"

"Healing power from the World Below the Earth. Something in it helps bind the wound and keep it sweet. "

"Tar is a great balm for the stomach."

"Yes. And most diseases of the skin. Henry's flesh, once healed, won't decay again."

"Still something taints his blood."

"Only Henry himself, with the help of the sun and moon can find and kill that poison. All we can do is treat the wound and keep it clean."

"And pray for him," Eugainia said.

Keswalqw gently peeled the spent pack from Henry's side. His was an angry red-lipped mouth of a wound, its scabbed edges crusted yellow, seeping liquid flecked with blood.

Eugainia reeled at the sight. "Lord Help Me! The stench of his wound....I can barely breathe."

Keswalqw withdrew the white-tipped feather from her braid. She wafted sweetgrass from Henry's feet upward. The spirit bird's wing feather traced two half-circles, the smoke broke and swirled above the wound. She placed the new poultice, redressed the wound. Eugainia replaced the coverlet, folded Henry's arms upon his chest. Keswalqw sat by the bier, keeping silent watch.

Eugainia had reverted to European court dress. At her neck, layer upon choking layer of cloth constricted her throat. She paced the centre aisle. God help me, she thought, as she tugged at the high brocade collar. There are times a rage boils up in me and I wish poor Henry dead. Her fair skin, more used to woodland trails and open air than stones and mortar, chaffed. The doeskin dress was gone, displaced by five layers of floor-to-shoulder clothing. A dress of thick green wool, its cuffs laced tight to her wrists, covered three layers of linen and silk undergarments, the white silk shift she'd treasured once again lay closest to her skin. A floor-length tunic covered the heavy wool dress, its tight weave dense with thick embroidery. The sleeveless tunic was cinched at the waist, close-laced at the back, drawn as tight as her blooming pregnancy would allow.

Her hair was hidden—hair that had flowed free through three seasons, enthralling Mimkitawo'qu'sk with its lustre, thick, honey-coloured hair curling down to her broad white hips. The same hair lay flat today in braids, the braids knotted once again in tightly coiled ropes at the nape of her neck beneath a translucent veil. The veil softened the ridges of a squat, ungainly wire-framed headdress stuffed with horsehair, upholstered in gold-embroidered silk. From the front, the headdress recalled the gables of a hipped roof.

"Heaven help me," she said to Keswalqw that morning as they hoisted the bizarre structure upon her head, securing it with hairpins and a chinstrap. "I look as though I was assaulted by a small house or conquered by a cottage."

"Why do your wear these things," Keswalqw asked, "if they give such discomfort?"

"If I wear the costume, perhaps I'll better play the role."

She stopped, mid-way down the centre aisle, transfixed by motes of dust raised by her skirts swirling in a shaft of light from the rose window. It came to her that guilt advanced no cause but regret. Dressing the part was a useless gesture at best, counter-productive at worst. The trappings of the past confounded the present and circumscribed the future. Henry's was the sin of betrayal: his healing would arise from forgiveness, not retreat into empty ritual.

"These grotesque garments!" she railed, as the train of the underskirt tangled in the upturned toe of her satin slipper. "After what I have been in the Six Worlds, how can I live behind castle walls again?" She sat, her back to Keswalqw. "Please. In the name of all that is holy. Remove this monstrosity."

Keswalqw unpinned and untied the headdress, set it aside.

Eugainia stood, presented her back to Keswalqw. Keswalqw unlaced the bodice. The tunic was soon in a jumbled pile on the floor beneath the green wool dress. She kicked both aside.

She stared at the tasselled toes. "Ridiculous," she muttered. She yanked both off, threw them on the pile of rejected courtly gear. She removed all but the bottom of the three layers of under-garments. The thin, white silk shift hung with simple elegance, refracting light where it clung to her belly, breasts and thighs.

Eugainia unpinned the veil and loosed her braids. They fell the length of her back. She pulled one forward and began unplaiting. Keswalqw freed the others.

"This pile of rock and mortar," Eugainia said. "All our mir-acles are cast in stone. What rank have they in your land where rocks still sing? We should gather our possessions and our poor battered faith and quietly go."

"Go where, Woman with the Moon?"

Eugainia drew a thick-toothed comb through her braid-crimped hair. "I don't know. I do not know! Poor fools. Trapped by their own trickery. Twice these infernal traps have sprung and nearly drowned my workers. The closer they get to the Grail, the more swiftly she recedes."

Keswalqw returned to Henry's side at the bier. His breathing remained shallow but regular.

"While you slept I walked to the pine forest in search of Mimkitawo'qu'sk," Keswalqw said quietly.

"Did you find him?"

"No. But he was there. I found this. "

Keswalqw handed Eugainia the small birchbark box, tightly fitted with its closely worked lid. Inside, Eugainia found her clamshell, three blue feathers and the small polished stone.

"Sea, sky and earth. Your totem gifts to me last summer, when I was healed. I lost them at the well, the day Henry assaulted us."

"Yes."

"Where did you find this?"

"On the ground. By my spirit tree."

"The old pine on the hill."

"Yes. Where he knew I'd find it."

"He made this birchbark box, didn't he."

"He did. I know because it is perfect. Though why a warrior of his prowess occupies himself with the work of children and elder women, I cannot tell."

"It's sealed with tar, stitched tight, corners folded back. A replica in miniature of the maple syrup buckets we used on the day of the *sismo'qonapu*. A happy day in memory, that. *Printemps et l'eau de vie.*"

"This box isn't for *sismo'qonapu*. Mimkitawo'qu'sk isn't a man to waste his time on trinkets. It has some greater purpose."

"There was nothing else? No other sign?"

"What I saw I will tell you. I entered the trunk and sent my spirit down through the roots to the World Below the Earth. No sooner had I settled myself then *Jipijka'maq*, Horned Serpent Person, thundered past with poor Henry clenched in his jaws, the serpent's fang still piercing his side. Henry spoke, though I knew it was agony for him to do so. 'Tell Eugainia she is in great danger,' he told me. 'Tell Mimkitawo'qu'sk I beg his forgiveness. Tell him I was wrong. I tell you, Keswalqw, The People are in danger.'"

"What danger?"

"His words died in the tumble of rock that sealed the serpent's wake. Up through root, trunk and branches, to the top of the tree I rose; Raven, Owl and Hawk said, 'We know what awaits The People. We know what you must do but cannot tell you.' My spirit flew to the World Above the Sky. Grandfather Sun and Grandmother Moon said, 'Only that which lies within can heal them.' Inside what? I asked. Heal who? Sun and Moon kept silent. I thought, they mean Eugainia's star bowl. Lying deep within the well. I dove to the World Below the Sea. I was caught in a rush of sea water, pulled down a stone-lined tunnel. I know. The well has been opened. I saw this Head of Baphomet, Woman with the Moon. Your star-stone has been found."

"God and Goddess be praised."

"It can't help you. Not anymore."

"Why not?"

"You will not drink from it, this Grail you seek."

"Of course I will. Why should I not? It's why I'm here."

"You will not drink from it because no one can."

"Then I am lost."

"No. You have only just been found. Mimkitawo'qu'sk will return. I've seen it. Together you and he will change the world forever."

"I thought so too, once. He deserted me when I needed him most."

"He prepares himself for the great works you and he must perform together."

"He left me."

"He did not leave you. He needed solitude. As we all do when plagued with doubt and fear. When his beloved wife Muini'skw went to the Ghost World, Mimkitawo'qu'sk wandered the woods for weeks on end. His wails of grief were loud as thunder. Rocks split, trees were torn from the earth like grass. For three full moons the Sky World wept, such was the power of Mimkitawo'qu'sk's sorrow. In his grieving, Mimkitawo'qu'sk gained great Power. Great power to protect and nurture The People. Wait and see. He'll return strong. He will heal himself and strengthen you. Together you and Mimkitawo'qu'sk will raise Henry Orkney from the dead."

The chapel doors opened. Sunlight flooded in. Outlined in stolid silhouette stood Athol Gunn. He knelt before Eugainia. He presented a cracked leather sack, streaked with mud.

"Our brother knights secured Baphomet too well."

Eugainia extracted the life-sized bronze bust, cast the leather sack aside.

"Baphomet," she said. "Finally. All the tales are true."

"He is a wondrous God. A wondrous God indeed."

"The drawings represent him precisely."

"They do indeed."

"The Grail?"

"Not yet."

"Still inside Baphomet?"

"I fear so. Yes. Try as we might, I say, we tried our best and we still can't get the blessed thing open."

Eugainia held Baphomet at arm's-length, its weight causing winter-strengthened muscles in her lower back to flex.

"'Tis a grim object," she observed, "for all its beauty. "

She passed the bronze bust on to Keswalqw.

"The face says two things at the same time. A mix of joy and agony." Keswalqw handed Baphomet back to Gunn. "And these blue stones. For the eyes..."

"Lapis," Athol told her. "Note the gilded lips. Hair reddened with oxidized iron, like your red ochre..."

Eugainia observed the head more closely.

"The brow is circled with blunted thorns."

"The blunted thorns of St. John the Baptist," Athol offered. "Not the sharp thorns that pierced the brow of the Christ."

Keswalqw drew their attention to the top of the head. "It looks as though it's been struck by lightning."

"I noted that," Athol confirmed. "Some purposeful flaw, I wondered, intended by the artisan to render it imperfect, I say, imperfect so as not to challenge the unflawed work of God."

"No." The familiar voice rippled from a dark corner. "It's no flaw. It's the mark of one man's cruelty."

All eyes were fixed on Mimkitawo'qu'sk; none noted that, for the first time in several days, Henry stirred.

"Mimkitawo'qu'sk," Eugainia cried. She ran to meet him. Neither found comfort in their brief embrace.

"Are you all right?"

"I am."

"Where have you been?"

"Nearby."

"Look, beloved. Athol recovered Baphomet."

"It is grotesque."

"It's my salvation."

"I'm your salvation."

Eugainia turned from her lover back to Baphomet.

"Have you opened it?" Mimkɨtawo'qu'sk asked Athol Gunn.

"No. There's no clasp. No hook. Just this frontal seam, barely discernable, running vertically, bisecting chin, nose and forehead. Nothing, nothing seems to budge—"

Mimkɨtawo'qu'sk handed Keswalqw Tooth of Wolverine. She lay it alongside Henry on the bier. Mimkɨtawo'qu'sk indicated Baphomet.

"Give the ugly thing to me."

Mimkɨtawo'qu'sk examined Baphomet closely.

"There is a tale from the World Below the Earth," he said. "The head of a brave and noble warrior was struck from his body by The People's enemies. So loved was he, and so wise his counsel, the head was kept and filled with stones that spoke."

Keswalqw picked up the thread of the tale. "It possessed great Power, this talking head. Saw many things. Knew many things. Felt many things. Heard evil when evil was spoken. Tasted selfishness. Smelled jealousy. Heard truth when truth was told."

"The noble head was stolen by a selfish man who lived alone, but very near his tribe. Always lurking. Well enough fed, but always hungry. A thin man, pale and jealous. Envious of others, wanting what he didn't have. Too lazy, too consumed with desire to feed himself, he fed off others." Mimkɨtawo'qu'sk walked to the bier. "His pride and misery poisoned the air."

"The People began to suffer." Keswalqw stood beside Mimkɨtawo'qu'sk. "The People knew why. The thin man's misery tainted the food, soured The People's stomachs."

Mimkɨtawo'qu'sk glanced at Henry. "He loathed and envied the happiness of The People. He—this selfish man—thought, 'If I possess the warrior's spirit—his spirit lodged in the stones inside his severed head—I too will become worthy of the love The People withhold from me.' He tried all kinds of ways to open the head, this selfish man. Determined to find and steal its spirit. He exposed it to sun and wind, hoping it would shrink and crack. He bludgeoned it with his stone axe. He dropped it from *Kluscap's* Cliffs to the rocks on the beach below. But still it remained closed to him. He tired of the head. Determined to throw it into the sea."

Mimkitawo'qu'sk tucked Baphomet under his arm, walked toward the chapel doors.

"As he walked away," Keswalqw continued, "back to his old ways—selfish, cruel, unhappy, and alone—the battered but still noble head rolled its eyes and spoke. It called out to him. 'I am dead,' he said. 'Yet loved by The People.'"

Mimkitawo'qu'sk turned, his voice the thin high whine of the selfish man. "'You are dead but still you walk among men, walk without a body. You speak to men, though your head is full of stones. They honour you in memory. They despise me in life. How can this be.'"

A wash of sunlight flooded through the open doors behind Mimkitawo'qu'sk. He held Baphomet before his face. He spoke his noble warrior voice. "'You are a coward. Vain. Unworthy. Weak,' the noble head filled with speaking stones said to the selfish man. "'You think only of yourself. You take what is not your own. You are not a warrior. Not a provider. Not L'nuk. Not one of The People. You will not be loved until you learn to give.'"

Henry stirred.

"My Lady!" Athol drew Eugainia's attention from Mimkitawo'qu'sk to Henry. Henry moaned, the balm of healing sleep dissolving. Eugainia was torn between her desire to serve and her desire to love.

'You think the gifts of the Great Spirit are gifts to you alone.'" Mimkitawo'qu'sk continued.

Henry uttered a sharp cry of pain. Keswalqw placed a calming hand on his shoulder.

"Mimkitawo'qu'sk, please," Eugainia pleaded. "If you know how to open—"

"In his rage the selfish man gripped the head." Mimkitawo'qu'sk held Baphomet against his chest, hooked his index fingers in the statue's blue eyes. He pressed the lapis stones.

"He ripped it open. Ripped it open with the strength of his own hands."

The lapis eyes sunk back into the heat beneath his steady pressure. The Head of Baphomet cracked with a sharp click along a vertical seam and swung open.

Eugainia rushed forward. "God be praised!"

"But inside were no stones," Mimkitawo'qu'sk continued. "No stones that spoke. Just an old grey sack." Mimkitawo'qu'sk extracted the misshapen bundle from the split head. He set it on the altar, and began to unknot the leather cord.

"No!" Eugainia warned. "If you touch her you will die."

"What?"

"A fiery arrow will be loosed by God, Mimkitawo'qu'sk. It will pierce your heart. I tell you. If you touch her, you will die. You are not of the Royal and Holy Blood."

Mimkitawo'qu'sk unknotted the frail cord. "If I touch it, I will die. If you touch it, you will leave me. I would rather die then lose you and my child. This is how the tale ends. The warrior's head was opened. There were no speaking stones. Instead, a host of tiny birds flew forth, as many birds as there are stars in the sky. They seized the unworthy man, carried him begging for mercy beyond the farthest edge of the sea. He was never seen again."

Mimkitawo'qu'sk opened the bundle. Motes of dust rose and hung inert in the air. Nothing remained of the Holy Grail but rubble.

"Look, Woman with the Moon. My blood's royal and holy, and yours is ancient and honourable. No fiery arrow. No flock of tiny birds. Nothing but the wind and sun of a beautiful spring day."

Eugainia returned to the bier. She stroked Henry's forehead.

"Perhaps a flock of birds, as many as the stars, will come and take your men away from the world of L'nuk," said Mimkitawo'qu'sk. "A great sleep will overcome them. They will forget the Six Worlds, and never return again. All except you, Woman Who Fell in Love with the Moon; my beloved wife and mother of my child."

Henry gasped. His eyes opened, round with pain and terror. He struggled to speak. Athol bent close to listen.

"He says the Grail must be infused."

"Tell him it's too late," Eugainia answered. "There is no Holy Grail." Sunlight flooded through the high arched window. "Tell my Lord Henry Goodbye." Light around Eugainia lost coherence in its struggle to define her. There was nothing to reflect. Her mortal frame became insubstantial. Eugainia vanished.

Mimkitawo'qu'sk grasped Wolverine. He drew the spear point through the sweetgrass smoke and floating motes of dust. The veil between the Earth World and the Ghost World parted. Mimkitawo'qu'sk reached into the rift and caught Eugainia's arm. He strained, determined to pull Eugainia back, all his force centred in his legs and thighs. He could not budge her. Hers was the greater power, the power of a mother drawn to her lost child. Mimkitawo'qu'sk took the fateful step. The young God's head and torso, then his legs, dissolved. Willingly, he entered the Ghost World, not certain either he or Eugainia would ever return.

Sir Athol stood amazed. First Eugainia, and then Mimkitawo'qu'sk, vanished before his waking eyes. A deep, ago-nized moan escaped the pale and dying Henry. Athol and Keswalqw moved to his side.

In the luminous world of the dead, Eugainia lay on the ground, her head thrown back and turned to the right. Mimkitawo'qu'sk helped her to her feet.

"Morgase," she whispered.

Mimkitawo'qu'sk followed her line of vision.

On the red beach of Apekwit, in perpetual high summer, Morgase chased a toddler, a year-old boy struggling to remain vertical, wobbling forward as fast as he could, his fat, distorted little legs pumping, his face radiant, his twisted little mouth, its upper lip cruelly cleft, squealing with delight. Morgase caught the child, raised him above her head and swung him in great circles. She carried him to the water and bathed him. The child emerged from the water, not crippled, not deformed but whole, spurting water through perfect lips, his strong legs straight and striding. He scampered beyond Morgase who, herself reborn, Eugainia recognized as the young woman who had tended her in her own infancy.

Eugainia reached to touch the child running past. She recoiled when her hand passed through him. Anger clutched at her swollen heart. She looked to Morgase for comfort but found none: the young girl Morgase had become ran off laughing in pursuit of Eugainia's remade stillborn child.

"We can be with them if we let go our mortal selves." Mimkitawo'qu'sk lay his hand on Eugainia's belly. "If we do, we can't return to the Earth World again. Come. I've something to show you."

At the edge of the beach on a deerhide robe sat a young woman of The People. A girl-child, in age six moons or younger, sat propped before the young mother.

"This is Muini'skw," Mimkitawo'qu'sk told Eugainia. "This is my wife. The little girl is our daughter."

Muini'skw wrapped coloured string around a short stick. At

its head, a dry gourd filled with pebbles ratted. Threaded through a notch at the top, spruce root filaments held flat nuggets of crimped copper. They flashed and clattered against the rattle's skin. The little girl gurgled and chirped, slapping pudgy hands together, her black eyes bright, her brown cheeks round with fat.

"She's beautiful. What's her name?"

"She has none. She died before she could tell us."

"And Muini'skw died with her, in childbirth. I remember. But now...my boy was a poor lifeless thing. Morgase dead. Yet they heal and grow."

"Time has no meaning in the Ghost World. Look again. "

Down the beach, a strong misshapen young man helped Morgase, an old woman now, negotiate the ragged stretch of rock where, ten moons of Earth World time before, Mimkitawo'qu'sk had sent flat stones skipping far beyond sight in the trail of moonlight on the calm breast of the sea.

When Eugainia turned back to the deerhide rug, Mimkitawo'qu'sk's daughter, the unnamed girl-child, was a newborn infant, cradled in Muini'skw's arms, nursing at her mother's breast.

Mimkitawo'qu'sk took Eugainia's arm. "Come, Moon Woman."

"But Morgase...my baby..."

"Will be here when you next wish to see them. I think I'll not return, though. The dead are best left in peace."

Mimkitawo'qu'sk and Eugainia walked along the beach. Night descended quickly, as in a dream. A full moon rose. A figure traced in silhouette against a trail of moonlight emerged from the rippling sea. Water bright with phosphorescent plankton ran in rivulets down Henry's back and shoulders. Mimkitawo'qu'sk stood quietly behind Eugainia with his hands on her shoulders. Flocks of night birds wheeled before the moon.

Henry stood lost, afraid, uncertain.

"No, Henry," Mimkitawo'qu'sk said. "Not yet."

Henry turned and walked back into the sea.

Water welled in Eugainia's sky-coloured eyes.

At the head of Henry's bier, water ran like tears on the still face of the air. Eugainia stepped back from the Ghost World, Mimkitawo'qu'sk behind her. They stood whole, complete, radiant, benevolent, at peace. The walls of the Grail Chapel, stone piled upon stone, became blocks of crystal lightly set one upon the other. The vaulted roof of oak became the thinnest of glass, bright with light as a linnet's wings. The rose windows shone with rainbow hues, their lead work light and airy. The greening world folded in upon the chapel, washed the sacred couple with pristine vernal light.

Sir Athol fell to his knees. Keswalqw wafted sweetgrass around the Two Made One.

"*Akai*," she chanted softly. "*Akai!*"

Henry's torso flexed violently upright. He fell back, hard. A long low rattle signalled the end.

Mimkitawo'qu'sk incised his wrist on the tip of Wolverine. Eugainia held the birchbark box to the flow of Mimkitawo'qu'sk's blood. "Enough," he said. The blood flow stopped. Mimkitawo'qu'sk touched his wrist to Wolverine again. The wound healed instantly, leaving neither blood nor evidence of torn tissue on his arm. The coiled tail of the serpent tattoo, the serpent tattoo circling his arm, rising up to his shoulder, showed a new ring of scales. Eugainia incised her wrist in the same manner. "Enough," she said. The bleeding stopped. The wound closed over. No scar remained.

Mimkitawo'qu'sk elevated the birchbark grail. "This is the blood of transgression forgiven. This blood is the love of the Two Made One." He offered the box to Eugainia.

"This is my blood, the Royal and Holy Blood of my ancestors which I freely mix with the Ancient and Honourable Blood of The People." Eugainia elevated the birchbark vessel. "This is the love of the Two Made One."

Keswalqw spoke softly. "Of all the Powers of all the Worlds none is as worthy as love." She wafted sweetgrass smoke over the surface of the vessel. "This is the blood of hope and forgiveness. This is the blood of all reconciled."

Athol and Keswalqw pricked the tips of their fingers. Blood dropped from each, rippling the surface.

"This is the blood of Keswalqw, great mother of the clan, and Athol Gunn, warrior protector." Eugainia dipped her finger in the sanctified fluid. "Their blood and the blood of the Two Made One will heal and feed and protect the people."

Keswalqw placed a drop of blood on Henry's lips. "Drink Henry. I have seen it. The Holy Child will be born. The Two Made One will need their Lord Protector."

Athol stood at his cousin's head. He withdrew a small leatherbound book. He thumbed through gently, his rough hands liable, he knew, to tear its delicate onion-skin pages. He stared at the words, which swam distorted before his eyes. Athol cleared his throat. He shifted his stance first to one foot and then the other. "This is Templar lore with which, in Henry's stead... " He wiped his eyes. "This was always Henry's job." Athol lost his voice. Keswalqw slipped her arm through his. "With which..." Athol continued, "with which in Henry's stead I do command him."

Henry's pallor deepened.

Sir Athol inhaled deeply. He straightened, read with dignity and purpose. "Henry's bruise is the mark of his transgression. His agony arises from love and friendship betrayed. If the lance once charged with anger touches the wound with forgiveness, it is herein written, and I do in faith believe, the dead will rise again like Lazarus."

Athol held the New Grail low, the Birchbark Grail of tar and spruce, the New Grail washed with the Royal and Holy Blood of the Christ, with the Ancient and Honourable blood of L'nuk, The People.

"Touch the spear to the blood."

Eugainia and Mimkitawo'qu'sk anointed the tip of the spear.

Keswalqw lifted the poultice, exposed the putrid gash. A faint blue tinge fought the angry red streaks that flared from the wound like the rays of a malevolent sun.

"Great Chief Warrior," Athol directed, "and She Who Sits at the Centre. Touch the wound with Wolverine, the Spear of Destiny."

"Do so," Keswalqw urged. "I tell you. This man will live. I have seen it."

The anointed spear touched Henry's wound. The wound closed. The stench of death dispersed. A ruddy flush radiated outward, erasing death's pallor.

Mimkitawo'qu'sk set Tooth of Wolverine/The Spear of Destiny aside. Eugainia placed her hand over Henry's heart. Mimkitawo'qu'sk leaned low. He spoke softly. "Come Henry Orkney," he urged, "the Ghost World's fat with too much pride and sorrow."

Henry stirred.

"Only the strong and brave return from the Ghost World. Come back, Henry Orkney. Come back and set my beloved's heart at ease, that I may walk the earth in peace and friendship with you."

"Rise faithful servant from death's bed," Eugainia commanded. "The evil that befell has been forgiven. Rise and be fed."

"We ask it in Our Name," Mimkitawo'qu'sk said. "The name of the Two Made One."

Henry opened his eyes. By his own strength, he sat upright. He touched his side and found no wound. Athol offered his arm. Henry accepted. He stood, steady, firm, to all appearances unaffected by his long dark sleep. He took Athol's hand. He kissed Keswalqw's face.

Henry looked about. He expressed no surprise that the chapel walls had turned to glass; that the green world arced high above; that clouds trailed through the luminous blue of the vaulted ceiling, uncovering not cherubim and seraphim and saints in celestial glory, but the eternal faces of Grandfather Sun and Grandmother Moon.

"The great wheel turned until it came full circle," he said. "I dreamed a dream of wind and fire. My Lord. My Lady. I dreamed I saw the blessed face of God: it is the face of man and man, of woman and woman, of woman and man, of you and he together." Henry knelt before Eugainia and Mimkitawo'qu'sk. "Living for and with each other; living for and with all, in harmony. In the time of the Two Made One."

CHAPTER SEVENTEEN

It was knowledge common to both cultures: twigs graft best to the common branch when tides are high and the moon full.

The first wedding between L'nuk, The People, and the visitors honoured traditions sacred to both. In the end, though dual-branched, the nuptials were rooted in the same good soil; the couple would rise together, spread strength and happiness under the benevolent eye of the Creator who, they knew, loved them. Why would it be otherwise, all great shamans and spiritual healers of good heart before and since have asked? Would the Great Spirit create creatures as magnificent as human beings and then permit them neither peace nor happiness? Such cruelty, such caprice made no sense to the reborn Scottish Prince. In the same way, who among The People would hesitate to ease the toil and sorrow of their kin-friends? Nor would a clansman or clanswoman of clear conscience withhold the means to another's contentment, no matter race, creed or colour.

The People and the visitors gathered to celebrate the greatest of the Great Spirit's gifts, freely offered to each and to all. At the root of human joy, both cultures agreed, stirs the scared urge of the Two Made One. The greatest sorrow? The loneliness of the One Alone, the solitary soul an unsprouted seed fallen on a bed of stone.

The betrothed couple were subjected to intense scrutiny by their kinfolk. Were they of appropriate age? Was he a canny, agile hunter? What was his history in relation to his family and friends, his reputation in the tribe? Was the woman likewise of good character? Were the accomplishments of his youth and young adulthood impressive or ordinary? What reputation had she carried forward from her girlhood? Could she protect and advance the lives within her care? Was he considerate of the feelings of others, his actions rooted in compassion and self-respect? Did she command and give respect when and where respect was due? Would he work in partnership with his betrothed, fulfilling separate responsibilities equally valued? Were her contributions to the welfare of the community likely to be substantial and abiding? Would both put the welfare of the tribe before that of themselves and members of their own families?

Once the suitor demonstrated his ability to provide and protect, he was invited to display tributes worthy of the virtues of his chosen, and her family's standing in the tribe. Dogs, beaver pelts, weaponry and axes, all signs and symbols of the man's proficiency were acceptable. When the tributes were received and approved (the community assessment of his efforts was a time of great stress for the hopeful man who was obliged to watch and wait in silence) the principals were invited to repair to the *wikuom* inhabited by the woman and her extended family.

Solemn vows of fealty—the second to the last step in the three-day nuptials—were spoken shielded from public view in Keswalqw's cream-skinned wigwam. Its red and yellow ochre loon totem was recently refreshed for the event. The water bird's stark outline and spirit marks (wavering lines flowing back from the head suggesting its sweet, plaintive call) were defined by charcoal-blackened seal oil. The loon's red eye was focused precisely on the petitioners by the artfully placed dot of ground clamshell and seal-oil white.

The dedication and exchange of totems, the one act of intimacy the public was invited to witness and the final ritual of the nuptials, drew the wedding party and the villagers up the path to the Meadow of the Singing Stone. After long days of feasting, lavish exchanges of gifts, great high-blown orations thick with drama and suspense, afternoon games of strength and fortune flowing into nights of dance and song, a long nap in the warming sun held more appeal to the principal celebrants than further festivity.

Henry was relieved the grief and strife of the last six weeks had such a happy outcome. The New Order of the Two Made One was well established. The Grail Castle restorations were all but abandoned. It was decided the chapel, which had reverted from crystal to mortar and stone after the miracle of Henry's healing, would be maintained. Its cool high silence invited spirits skyward. Peace bloomed in the womb-warmth of its rose-coloured light.

Thoughts of time slipping past and tides rolling high still weighed heavily on Henry. He paused on the up-winding path. He glanced back and down to Claw of Spirit Bird Bay where his two seaworthy ships, *Verum* and *Reconcilio*, provisioned and disposed, strained at their moorings. Both seemed eager to taste the great salt sea on their maiden voyages. The late-spring outflow would carry Athol and his freshly trained *Verum* crew on a voyage of trade and exploration down the eastern coast as far, they hoped, as the much-storied Great Southern Gulf. Prince Henry Sinclair and his Scots adventurers would embark for the outer Orkney Islands and then Edinburgh abroad *Reconcilio*.

Henry's longing to be at one with his wife again, and to see his daughters, had been intensified beyond bearing in the presence of the lovers. God and Goddess had blessed him, he appreciated now more than ever, with the love of a woman of great intelligence, a woman strong-minded and generous of spirit. He offered a prayer of thanks and yearning. And sorrow. He knew, to his shame, he would not have acted as he had toward Eugainia and Mimkitawo'qu'sk with Igidia at his side.

His attention returned to the happy task at hand. Joyous whoops and ululations, Henry's among them, washed the meadow as Keswalqw and Athol entered the sacred circle smiling nervously, their little fingers linked. Henry, their chief witness and groomsman (the groom's "helper"... an imported tradition The People approved for its display of fraternal cohesion), fell in step behind the couple whose love for each other had, he reflected, grown with discreet inevitability.

A rare and lovely thing, a perfect union. Henry could think of no better match for Athol than Keswalqw. He fell back in step behind the betrothed couple. He quietly praised God and Goddess, hoping this wedding might be the beginning of many fertile unions of their Old and Older worlds.

Mimkitawo'qu'sk and Eugainia sat waiting in the shadow of the Singing Stone, ready to officiate the final binding rite. Their own nuptials had been forged privately in the snow-filled woods and frozen streams of winter, their witnesses the Great Spirit and the stars of the northern heavens, circling flocks of geese, the miracles of cold-running sap and hot maple syrup, and long, cold nights warmed by fire and fur.

From this point onward, like the Sacred Couple seated cross-legged before them, Keswalqw and Athol would walk the Six Worlds together, taking their greatest pleasure in each other and the well-being of The People.

Mimkitawo'qu'sk noted with mild alarm Athol's bagpipes

slung over his shoulder. He recalled the day on Apekwit when the big man's goose with many necks made its first squawk and Athol began his peculiar dance. Mimkitawo'qu'sk admitted growing fondness for the keening of the pipes. Daily at dawn Sir Athol, now known to The People as *Gelusit ta'pu*, welcomed the sun with the bittersweet hope of a slow air played gentle and low. Neither skreel of war nor call to battle, the piped morning meditation brought order and calm to the long stretch of peaceful days that unfurled as Henry's wounded side healed.

Mimkitawo'qu'sk set the New Grail on the ground before them. Tooth of Wolverine/Spear of Destiny, its star-stone head glistening black, stood behind propped against the Singing Stone.

At Mimkitawo'qu'sk's nod, Henry rose to speak.

"My cousin, Sir Athol Lochland Gunn, known to The People as *Gelusit ta'pu*, He Who Speaks Twice, is a good and honest man," Henry began, his command of The People's language approaching fluidity, having evolved over the winter, he admitted with some pride, to a level well-past functional. "He has proven himself a loyal friend and consistent provider." Henry paused, "I say, a loyal and a consistent provider."

Athol flushed red at the laughter, kind though it was, that rippled across the meadow. He cast a sharpish glance over his shoulder at his cousin and in a loud voice replied, "Most things bear repeating, I say, bear repeating, laddie, especially praise!"

"Keswalqw, your wisdom has tempered a good man's fiery steel," Henry continued when the laughter subsided. "One of Athol's much admired traits is his pragmatism. He is a strong man among willful humans, neither expecting more nor deserving less than any other. From our earliest boyhood days together, our Athol was never one to countenance injustice. That will never change. Thanks to you, Keswalqw, and the kindness of The

People, Athol no longer acts swiftly or thoughtlessly when injustice is perceived. Your new husband is diligent, loyal and, above all, he is kind. I commend him to your love—You Who Sit at the Centre, Great Shaman Healer of The People, Great Mother of the Clan. And I commend him to the love and service of The People."

Mimkitawo'qu'sk stood to speak for Keswalqw.

"We like this tradition of yours, this standing and speaking of the suitability of your kin-friend at the time of union. We thank you, Henry Orkney, for your trust, for leaving this precious gift—your most beloved Athol Gunn among us."

To Athol he said, "A great honour has befallen you, *Gelusit ta'pu*. She Who Sits at the Centre But Does Not Rule—the sister of my long-departed father, the kin-friend of my mother who went too soon to the Ghost World—cared for me as her own since I was a little child. Keswalqw is a woman great in spirit, wise in council, kind in kinship. Henry Orkney spoke the truth: Keswalqw is a shaman of great power and a gentle healer of The People. The Great Spirit has sent another bear-man to warm her sleeping robes. This brings selfish comfort to us all. When the great mother is happy, so are her children."

A ripple of amused agreement circled the meadow.

"We thank you *Gelusit ta'pu* for your high good spirits," Mimkitawo'qu'sk concluded. "For your strength and courage. For your kindness, not only to the great, but to the frail among us. We even give thanks for your goose-strangling music and your dog-kicking dance. We are happy Keswalqw. You have chosen well."

Mimkitawo'qu'sk elevated the sacred pipe and then lit the *nespipagn*, exhaled a cloud, passed the pipe on to Eugainia. It travelled from her to Athol, from Athol to Keswalqw, from Keswalqw to Henry, then on to The People, whose communal blessing was carried to the Sky World and the Great Spirit beyond.

Eugainia ignited a braided cord of slow-smouldering sweet-grass. With the wing feather of the Spirit Bird given her by Keswalqw, she wafted smoke between and around the solemn couple.

As the pipe was passed from hand to hand, so followed the sweetgrass and the fanning feather. A translucent haze of sweetgrass smoke so faint as to be barely discernable hung low on the windless meadow, merging with the grass, brushing past the moccasins and leggings of the seated throng, the sacred smoke binding all in holy union before dispersing and ascending to the Great Spirit, lightening hearts, carrying the joy and hope of The People skyward.

Mimkitawo'qu'sk leaned toward Athol, removed the big man's stone-and-copper necklace. Eugainia lifted its lighter twin from Keswalqw's neck. Eugainia and Mimkitawo'qu'sk examined the symbolic stones, the polished thong-threaded globes signifying the Earth World, the burnished copper beads reflecting and representing Grandfather Sun. Like Grandmother Moon, the necklaces changed their size and shape according to the forces acting upon them. When worn they inclined toward the circle, the moon in its plangent state. On the warm flesh of the neck, the stone-and-copper neckpiece traced luna's cold journey around the sun-heated earth.

Mimkitawo'qu'sk and Eugainia elevated the circlets mindful, as were The People, of the leather thongs unifying round stones and copper disks. The binding strands of skin spoke of the Ways of the Animal Powers. Animals and The People bound together in a cycle of life and death grew strong, gathered Power for themselves and each other, as they walked through and lived in the Six Worlds.

"Thanks be to the Great Spirit for the circle of life," Mimkitawo'qu'sk said to the couple.

"Amen, I say amen to that," *Gelusit ta'pu* testified. "May the great wheel ever turn."

Eugainia lifted the lid from the Birchbark Grail, the New Grail lately infused with the Royal and Holy Blood of the east, the blood of King Solomon and the Goddess Isis, and the Ancient and Honourable Blood of the West, the blood of L'nuk, The People, the New Grail made by her Warrior God husband in the shadow of the Singing Stone, made from the skin and roots of a tree and the coal black blood of the Smoking Mountain. Inside lay Athol and Keswalqw's totem gifts to each other, their most intimate personal symbols, their spiritual essences given shape and substance. Once exchanged, the totems signalled their commitment to permanent union, and mutual expectations of fidelity.

Keswalqw withdrew her totem from the Grail. "The venerable loon," she said as she elevated the stone-carved pendant, "lives in three worlds and carries her young upon her back."

She attached mother loon, with three loon feathers affixed, to Athol's necklace.

Athol attached his thumb-sized black bear totem to Keswalqw's neckpiece, like the loon carved from soapstone traded with The People's cousins, who had prized it from the fierce Ice Hunter Thules far to the north. A tuft of bear fur had been artfully attached, the white fur of the ice bear Keswalqw so admired, whose fur she coveted.

Each accepted the other's spirit gift in silence. Keswalqw's loon nested in the fur of Athol's chest: Athol's bear slipped down to slumber in the warm cleft between Keswalqw's breasts.

The People gave voice to their approval. Eugainia felt a surge of warmth deep in her belly, and the beginnings of a steady pulse from the stone at her back. She exchanged a glance with

Mimkitawo'qu'sk. His smile confirmed her suspicion: the Singing Stone vibrated in sympathy with the rising voices of the visitors and The People. The Great Spirit approved this union of two ancient worlds. The vibration became a steady unwavering vocal tone. Harmonic variations emerged, twisting and circling, blending with human voices, rising skyward as dense and taut as a plaited thong.

Keswalqw placed Athol's fingertips on her throat. He felt the Sacred Song of the Marriage Circle. Keswalqw slipped her hand in the side-slit of Athol's wedding vest (partly obscured by the shoulder swath of his sky blue, sea green great kilt), the vest she'd quilled and beaded while he sat with the men, carving his totem gift for her. With the flat of her palm she felt the sacred tone pulse within her loon totem, on the chest of the bear man from across the sea, who came to warm her sleeping robes and bring her joy.

For the first time in his life, Sir Athol Gunn felt peace. He turned his face, eyes closed, to the rising breeze. Under the touch of the hand he loved above all others, he felt the Great Wheel revolve. He opened his ears to the resonant harmonies of the spheres. He opened his mouth, released a deep and vibrant tone. Sir Athol Gunn became a Man of The People.

Mimkitawo'qu'sk, his heart a well of joy, turned to Eugainia. The People's song enfolded her. Her eyes were closed. Her face gently set. Her light soprano voice rose water-clear in the early summer air. The People's tone-song stirred the tiny heart beating in Eugainia's womb. The twitches and flutters of the past few weeks had lately become the toss and turn, the bunts and kicks of He Who Yearns to Walk Free.

"Not yet, little stranger," Eugainia whispered. "Not yet."

Mimkitawo'qu'sk directed Eugainia's attention to Henry

whose eyes were fixed in horror upon the ground. No sound emerged from his lips, moving in supplication then pressed tight together—tight, thought Eugainia, as the jaws of *Jipijka'maq*.

Henry couldn't breathe. Panic clenched his chest. He heard his Lady's voice:

Henry?

He knew without looking she spoke no words. Her thoughts were his.

What troubles My Lord Protector?

Henry's doubt—a shard of glass cold and sharp—hung in the air between them.

I would know my fate, My Lady. And that of my wife and daughters. If they no longer...if they have been...I see no point in returning to Scotland. I'd be better here, would I not, with you and with The People?

Wrap your dilemma in prayer, Henry, and cast it up to the Creator. We'll make a spirit quest together, you and me. All will be revealed. I promise. You'll have your answer before the turning of the tides.

Still, his heart was troubled. My Lady...leave or stay I cannot live a good and happy life until I confess my shame. Though I know you bear me no ill will, I can't forgive myself for the shame I brought You and My Lord your husband that awful day at the well, where I acted with no thought for your feelings, or for those of your husband, whose honour I was determined to destroy.

Mimkitawo'qu'sk opened his eyes and smiled. He sent a silent prayer of forgiveness across the short distance between them, echoed by Eugainia. His Lord and Lady's Benediction washed over Henry. He raised his head and opened his eyes.

Could the sun have moved so far in the brief instant Henry's eyes had been closed? Was it a trick of the light, playing off the jet black surface of the rock? Eugainia and Mimkitawo'qu'sk's heads were ringed with glory. Their gaze sat kindly upon his face. Guilt fell from Henry like the shed skin of a serpent. Remorse rose and vanished on the wings of the flock of tiny spirit birds Mimkitawo'qu'sk caused to flutter past. In a far distant chamber of Henry's strengthening heart, a cold breath, the final memory of a White Wolf, of a night of a soul turned to ice, hard with sorrow, dissolved.

Henry nodded his gratitude. Eugainia smiled her pleasure.

Mimkitawo'qu'sk sent Henry these thought-words...

Be at peace, kin-friend. Be at peace.

All three closed their eyes. Henry's throat opened. The thin man wanting, the frozen man waiting, the starving man dying, the man of the fallen temple overwhelmed by time and a sense of duty he must soon abandon became kin-friend to The People—Geleiwatl—Lord Protector of the Two Made One and He Who Sings When His Heart Is Full.

Time distorted, the stone-song became a band of colour, a pathway leading outward and up. Eugainia felt the earth slip away. She leaned forward, arms raised, her torso that of a diver prepared to leap forward and up with no expectation of descent, her eyes fixed on the far edge of the universe, her heart doubling and redoubling in size and Power with every sacred beat.

A sharp jab to her stomach killed the illusion. The infant kick wasn't born of simple restlessness: it was sharp with purpose. Eugainia rubbed her belly, prodding gently. The first kick was followed in quick succession by two sharp jabs, each harder than the last. Two strong kicks, she thought, the first to get her attention, the second more subtle. The child delivered a third kick, a strong kick. A warning.

Eugainia looked to her husband. Mimkitawo'qu'sk's profile

was set, hard, his eyes fixed on the horizon. Eugainia looked to the east. The turmoil in Eugainia's belly ceased. The unborn child lay still, a fawn in the forest, silent, barely breathing in the presence of fang and jaw.

The Singing Stone went silent. One by one The People's voices stilled. Moments passed before Henry realized he sang alone. He opened his eyes, surprised to find The People on their feet. All looked to the east. Henry rose to stand among them. What he saw chilled the marrow of his bones with a cold unmatched since his White-Wolf agony in the frozen grove of the starving time.

Sails. Ships. A great fleet of ships.

God have mercy on The People of the Six Worlds, Henry thought.

The Red Lion of Venice flapped at the mast of *Reclamation*, surmounted by the long tapered pennant of the Holy See, a whip cracking the trailing wind, pious and aloof, snapping orders above the helmeted head of Antonio Zeno.

Mimkïtawo'qu'sk retrieved Tooth of Wolverine. Eugainia handed the Birchbark Grail to Sir Athol. "Keep this safe." Athol secured the New Grail in the chest folds of his great kilt.

Athol and Keswalqw walked among The People. Athol placed a calming hand on a shoulder here, a back there. "Go quietly back to the village. No harm will come to you." Keswalqw lightly brushed a bare arm. "They're not here for you. Go about your business." Big-eyed children, sensing their parents' unease were comforted by hands laid softly on their heads. "All will be well," Athol assured.

Mimkïtawo'qu'sk spoke with quiet urgency. "My wife and child need time."

Athol looked to the horizon. "The easterlies favour Zeno,

Henry," he warned. "They're not a quarter-hour from shore. They'll be on us before we can lift anchor."

"If you truly love us, Henry," Eugainia said, "you'll take this fight far from this place, back to Europe where it belongs."

"How, My Lady?" Athol asked. "Twelve ships. A thousand men."

Keswalqw touched Wolverine to the Singing Stone. A portal opened, bisecting the stone vertically. Sir Athol moved to follow when Keswalqw stepped inside. "Stay with The People, Husband," she told him. "Tell them not to fear, though the ground will tremble and the waters churn. The Sky World will darken, and a great wind from the World Above the Sky will confound our enemy. Henry. Eugainia. Mimkitawo'qu'sk. Our task is simple: we must reverse the tide and stop the world from turning. Follow me." Eugainia stood ready to step through. Henry trembled before the gaping stone.

"Henry? We need our Lord Protector."

"I'm only mortal. My poor body can't travel through rock. Except in dreams."

"Your time of suffering has passed, Henry. Your spirit quest begins." Eugainia passed into the stone. "Come." Henry followed. The stone's surface closed, leaving no mark.

Athol scanned the horizon. The Red Lion of Venice was clearly visible against a darkening sky. He knew the hated symbol well: the King of Beasts, four feet planted on a white field, its humanized face wearing the scowl of an angry prophet. Athol adjusted the folds of tartan across his chest, assured the Birchbark Grail was safe. He inflated his pipes, tuned the drones and ran a scale on the chanter. He considered a stirring call to battle but thought better of it. He took the path down to the village, piping a hearty four-square reel.

Mimkitawo'qu'sk touched the spear to the wall of the Cave of the Seven Sleepers. A faint glow illuminated the high dome. The rumbling snores of the Seven Sleepers echoed. Their great limbs twitched. Their bear dreams were troubled.

"*Tugwa'latl!*" Mimkitawo'qu'sk commanded. "*Tugwiet!*" One by one, at their master's call, the bears awoke. Mimkitawo'qu'sk, Bear Master, raised Wolverine and traced a circle in the air. Groggy from a century of sleep, their minds still dense with The People's prayers, the bears rose on their hind legs to their full height, thrice that of their human kin, and roared. "*Gesigawwet!*" Mimkitawo'qu'sk ordered. "*Gesigawwet!*" The bear-roar increased in volume, surpassing the sounds of the greatest thunders. Mimkitawo'qu'sk touched the spear point to the floor. As one the great creatures dropped. Their massed weight drove down through shoulder bone and tree-stump legs, cracking the earth surface and waking the core of the world.

From the shores of Claw of Spirit Bird Bay, a great wave rose and rolled out to sea. Aboard *Reclamation*—her bowsprit no longer Eugainia but an oaken Mary, Virgin Queen—Antonio Zeno watched the massive wave roll toward him. How can this be, he wondered. How can a wave roll out from the land to the sea? The dozen ships were lifted twice their mast height, then set gently back on the surface as the wave dispersed. "Nothing to fear," Antonio told his wide-eyed crew. "Only a curious rise and fall of the New World sea."

Inside the cavern, the seven standing bears swung their great heads from side to side.

"Mimkitawo'qu'sk and the spirit bears have sent your countryman a warning," Keswalqw told Henry and Eugainia.

"And summoned Tutji' Jipijka'maq," Mimkitawo'qu'sk added.

Henry blanched. "Jipijka'maq! The serpent pierced my side.

Then slowed my heart and all but killed my spirit. Why should I not fear him?"

"Not the Jipijka'maq you remember, Henry," Keswalqw said. "He calls Tutji' Jipijka'maq…Jipijka'maq's little sister."

Hair-thin cracks criss-crossed the centre of the cavern floor. A slight mound of crumbled stone rose from the surface. A small snake emerged. The little serpent stood upright on its tail and spoke. "Who called me?"

The great bears swung their heads and sighed…

"Us."

Mimkɨtawo'qu'sk lowered the spear. "Come, little sister. Show us the way." As Tutji'j Jipijka'maq wound her way up the shaft of Wolverine, the shaft writhed and twisted, became a living thing of muscle, bone and shining scales. The little serpent, now in length and girth the size of Wolverine, awaited her master's command. Mimkɨtawo'qu'sk plucked the star-stone from the serpent's mouth. He passed the glowing stone to Eugainia. He held the snake in his hand, now stiff as a rod. The snake staff, Tutji'j Jipijka'maq, spoke to Mimkɨtawo'qu'sk, her sweet voice that of a human child clothed in innocence. "Are you ready, Great Shaman?" serpent-child asked.

"I am," Mimkɨtawo'qu'sk answered.

And a little child shall lead them, Henry thought. But where? Eugainia slipped a comforting hand in Henry's. Keswalqw took his free right hand in hers.

Mimkɨtawo'qu'sk said a word he knew. Tutji'j Jipijka'maq lost rigidity, curved and twisted back upon herself, coiled and uncoiled. Tutji'j Jipijka'maq's jaws unhinged, prepared to receive the arm of Mimkɨtawo'qu'sk, Bear Master and Serpent King. Mimkɨtawo'qu'sk slipped his hand beyond her backward-sloping fangs, deep into the expanding throat of the snake, inserting his arm by slow degrees as one would fit a soft leather gauntlet. When

Tutji'j Jipijka'maq's head reached his shoulder, her serpent flesh dissolved. Only the outline of her serpent skin, scales in slight relief, remained. The blue and red serpent tattoo Eugainia traced with her finger on his skin the night on Apekwit when she and Mimkitawo'qu'sk first made love, this same tattoo came to life before her eyes and rippled beneath the surface of the young Man-God's skin. Tutji'j Jipijka'maq's serpent eyes, alive in Mimkitawo'qu'sk's left shoulder, were drawn to a flash of light. Eugainia returned the star-stone to her lover. Back in Mimkitawo'qu'sk's possession, the spearhead—cutting tooth of Wolverine, the piercing tooth of Destiny—pulsed a brighter blue.

The Seven Sleepers, alert and watchful, their deep chests rumbling—dropped to the ground and stamped their great front feet. Mimkitawo'qu'sk raised his hand and pointed the star-stone toward the apex of the dome. The young Shaman God, the warrior husband of Woman Who Fell in Love with the Moon, father of their immortal child, felt the cavern floor slip away as he ascended. He reached down and clasped Eugainia's wrist. Henry held tight to Eugainia's free hand. With the other he clung like a child to Keswalqw.

Four spirit shapes—the souls of Henry, Eugainia, Keswalqw and Mimkitawo'qu'sk— rose from their bodies, hovered near the apex of the dome, waiting. Henry looked down at his living, empty shell. His shoulders were high and tight. His face had flushed a deeper red than usual before he left his body, ashamed perhaps, to feel like a small boy holding tight his mother and older sister's hands for the comfort he might find.

The bears unleashed a final roar. The floor opened.

Mimkitawo'qu'sk tightened his grip on the star-stone. The eyes of the serpent-child floating free in the air glanced down to the depths of the chasm. Mimkitawo'qu'sk aligned the star-stone and plunged from sight. Eugainia and Keswalqw—Henry secured between them—the twisting tail of a kite caught in a radiant spiral twisted down through the outer crust of the earth.

Henry glanced behind. His fear echoed in a flash of shared consciousness.

"It's all right, Henry. We've no need of muscle, blood and bone here."

"Just these...?"

"These golden cords. Tethers of light tying soul to body."

"And if they snap?"

"They rarely do. Hang on, dear Henry. The best is yet to come!"

Mimkitawo'qu'sk directed the spearhead star-stone toward the geometric centre of the earth. The travellers hurtled down, and further down, drawn by the force of a magnet pulled to the source from which it had arisen, from which it drew all its strength, to which it was compelled to return. They broke the barrier between the earth's crust and mantle. Henry became aware of indescribable heat. The matter through which they dove became less solid than rock, though its density was not decreased. Fluid. Rock. At once one and the other. In the way of ice, the magma captured light and held it. Yet light streaked through.

Eugainia looked about in wonder. She imagined the workings of a fevered brain. Flashing webs ferried bolts of light from one churning plane down to the next. Scarlet whorls, fiery plumes, sheets of colour rose, flickered, swirled, blended, fragmented; great spars and pinnacles branched and then dissolved in all directions, before, behind, above and below the questing spirits; lucent spirals arcing up to the lower surface of the reflective crust cast wave upon cascading wave to cycle back down to the earth's core, from which the radiant fires had arisen.

Eugainia recalled her conversation twelve months ago with her earth mother, the spirit woman Garathia, as they sped together in the body of a seal through curtains of fish to the depths of the cold northern sea. "One day," Garathia had told her daughter, "I shall penetrate the core of the earth itself."

In the distance, below, a star. Around it, a luminous sphere. Around both, a radiant globe. The core of the earth and its outer shell awaited. Through the snap and crack of the vast rhythmic swirl—rock not rock, liquid not liquid, heat not born of flame—the travellers plummeted, arrow-straight shafts of light splitting the viscous mantle, storming down to their destiny in the iron-hard heart of the world.

CHAPTER EIGHTEEN

Fiery curtains and radiant spires collapsed in waves of magnetic heat. Expanding vortices stalled, contracted, spiralled down to surround the perfect sphere at the centre of the earth. Polished by heat and time, in shape and size a match for the moon, it revealed its progenitor—the sun—in its star-stone brilliance. Yet after uncountable millenia, the earth's core remained more luminous than Grandmother Moon, and as radiant as Grandfather Sun.

The travellers paused in their descent. Henry felt the workings of this inner world, an electric, fiery template for the minds of all men and beasts. He knew the spirit-traveller's ecstasy. Henry's thoughts travelled the radiant mantle like the sound of words travel through air. There is no dichotomy. We're wrong to think of the centre of the earth as hell. All creation is a set of variations on a single theme.

Eugainia agreed. A great engine of life, not a place of retribution…a fiery seed planted in the womb of mother earth.

Why did they bring us here, Eugainia?

A familiar female voice, not Eugainia's or Keswalqw's, seemed to emanate from all directions at once. To strengthen you both, cousin and daughter. For the trials that await you.

Visions of the bodies, men living and dead, piled high against familiar oaken doors assaulted Henry.

Who spoke? he asked.

Not I. Eugainia scanned the curtain of light swirling past. I think it was Garathia.

Your Mother.

Daughter…cousin I said we'd meet again.

The voice trailed off and was gone.

Henry's anguish flashed like fire. Amid images of blood and slaughter at the doors of Rosslyn Castle, Henry could summon no vision of the fate of his wife Igidia. Or his daughters.

Wait! What trials await me?

The star-stone rose from Mimkitawo'qu'sk's hand. It moved swiftly, of its own accord, etched the face of a woman in the fiery depths of the cloud. As Garathia appeared, her thoughts sped through a tunnel of light toward Henry.

You stand amazed, Henry Sinclair. You don't remember me?

Yes, Garathia. I do. Daughter of the Royal and Holy Blood. Kinswoman by way of the French St. Clairs. Earthly mother to Eugainia. And so my cousin.

Just so.

Please. What of Igidia? My daughters?

Eugainia rose from her place beside Henry. She hovered at Mimkitawo'qu'sk's side. Mimkitawo'qu'sk made a gesture he knew. The star-stone etched a second face upon the first. Garathia's features dissolved. The shift was barely perceptible. A perfect likeness of Keswalqw was overlaid.

They make a handsome pair, do they not, Sister?

Garathia's features, line, plane and shadow, overlaid Keswalqw's.

They do indeed.

The fiery cloud shape-shifted. Two faces became one.

Henry rose in wonder. You are one person? One entity?

Two voices mingled in response. Keswalqw and Garathia revolved though a tight cycle of transformation, the features dissolving one into the other, individual and distinct, two manifestations of the single being.

We were. We are. We will be. We're one. And we are the other.

You know the future as well as the past?

We do.

Then tell me if you can. What shall become of me?

Choose to stay among The People, Henry…Garathia's image faltered with her fading voice. You'll live a long and happy life…

Return to Scotland and die…Keswalqw's image wavered… protecting what you love the most.

My wife and daughters. What will become of them if I stay?

The women's voices fused. Go or stay, it makes no difference. Your daughters will marry well and flourish. Igidia will live a long and peaceful life in a place we will make for her.

The fire faces vanished. The cloud disappeared.

Wait. Wait! Will I see them again? Before—

The star-stone shot toward the silver core. The haze of light Mimkitawo'qu'sk became traced a rising arc and then plunged from sight to the heart of the maelstrom. Henry and Eugainia marvelled at the magnificent turbulence below. Flashes of lightning, white with heat, struck the core and emanated from it. Molten metal thundered against its polished surface. Nacreous gyres eddied up and away. Whip-snap flares of radiant energy lashed outward, curled and, like their counterparts on the surface of the sun, fell back to the surface where they dissipated.

Mimkitawo'qu'sk, an impatient shadow, reclined on the skin of the core. He tossed the star-stone from hand to fiery hand.

When they arrived, Henry and Eugainia felt Mimkitawo'qu'sk's presence but not those of either Keswalqw or Garathia.

They wait inside, Mimkitawo'qu'sk informed them, then hurled the star-stone toward the core's far horizon. The instant it fell from view it reappeared on the near horizon, shot past the spirit travellers and disappeared again. On its second pass, Henry, Eugainia and Mimkitawo'qu'sk, each now a packet of pure energy compelled by a greater binding force, followed. The star-stone's velocity decreased as its orbit declined. Its three tails of light slowed with it. The star-stone struck the skin of the core where it skipped like a stone on the sea. It came to rest, pulsed twice and sank from sight. The three spirit travellers, slaves to the spearhead/star-stone's slightest impulse followed, wafting like thistledown through the star-hard iron-and-nickel core.

Keswalqw and Garathia waited at the centre of the core, the very centre of the earth, each robed in silver radiance. Invisible vectors aligned all five travellers along parallel axes controlled by the unseen force. Each felt a surge of energy speed trough them, a wavering flow of *Kji-knap* that arced up and out. The star-stone serpent head floated above and behind Garathia and Keswalqw. Of its own accord, it edged with a snap into the notch at the centre of all geometry from which it had been carved and given to humankind in the time before memory or meaning.

Garathia and Keswalqw sped away, the others followed. Five points of light, the spirit fire of the five travellers, spun with increasing velocity through individual trajectories, electrons circling the star-stone nucleus. Each left a trail of fire, replicating in miniature the circumference of the core.

At each orbit the star-stone, around which the spirit-questing travellers flew, pulsed with increased intensity. Power accumulated, shared Power. Henry felt *Kji-knap* from the World Below the Earth fuel Mimkitawo'qu'sk and Keswalqw, the two Great Shamans of The People, and the White Goddess Eugainia with Her Mother, The Lady Garathia. In the World Below the Earth, the celestial Ghost World quartet gathered the Power required to work their miracles in the Sea World, the Earth World, the Sky World and the World Above the Sky.

The star-stone commenced a slow revolve, countering that of the core. The magnetic fire fell still. Radiant pillars in the mantle above them collapsed. Molten curtains of liquid rock congealed. Not since the morning of the day of the great cataclysm, in the time before time found its meaning, had the universe known such peace. The earth hung without motion in an infinite field of star-studded black.

The spirit travellers spun to a starry blur. The star-stone shot upward, broke through the core's skin. In their race to follow, the travellers abandoned their ordered elliptical flights, traced collapsing orbits until they collided. Five white-hot Star Persons—Prince Henry Sinclair and Eugainia St. Clair Delacroix among them—fused in the centre of the earth.

Great *Kji-knap* was born.

Athol Gunn, piping his way down the path to the village, felt the Earth World tremble. Lightning shot from an open seam on the side of the Smoking Mountain. The bright bolt forked. Five fiery arrows, led by a brighter sixth, shot high into the northwest quadrant of the mid-day sky.

One of the fiery arrows circled the moon. The traces of light it described dissolved in a boreal bloom. Keswalqw, Goddess of the Earth, parted the wavering curtain. She walked the lunar surface. She danced a circle dance she knew, nudging Grandmother Moon from her solitary walk toward the face of Grandfather Sun.

Another bolt, glowing white with Sky World heat, pierced

earth's atmosphere, dove down and struck the surface of the sea. A plume of water and steam shot high into the air above *Reclamation* when Garathia with her great earth-core heat plunged below the surface. Antonio Zeno found shelter in the fore-castle from a fathom of fish which fell from the sky and smashed to the deck. Blood and sperm, guts and roe washed overboard when tonnes of sea water fell in a black squall of rain.

Below *Reclamation*, a pair of white-beaked dolphins circled Garathia. One rolled to her back, inviting the Goddess of the Ocean Seas to enter. When settled inside the warm sea mammal's body, Garathia found her dolphin voice. She called to the whale fish of the northern seas in her high, thin song. The great ocean-going mammals answered. Garathia, in her dolphin form, broke the surface, her hind flukes sculling lightly to keep her vertical. She called to her sister in the World Above the Sky. On the surface of the moon, Keswalqw slowed her dance.

The weakest bolt of light fell from the Sky to the Earth World. It struck the ground behind Athol Gunn. He recoiled at the hiss, snap and bone-rattling crack. He found himself airborne. He looked back to where he'd stood a split second before his muscles' instinctive twitch. Henry, unsteady, stared at the ground below his feet. He regarded his cousin sprawled in bracken bordering the path.

"Where've you been, laddie," Athol asked, extracting himself from the vegetation. "You look completely flummoxed!"

"Where no living human being, with the possible exception of Orpheus seeking Euridice, has ever gone before."

"You disappeared into that rock not five minutes past, the time it took me to walk down this path."

"Then we've no time to waste. We must weigh anchor before it gets dark."

"It's high noon, laddie, on a sunny day!"

"Not for long."

"Eh?"

"Hadn't you noticed the stars?"

Athol looked up to the sky.

"Stars. In a brilliant blue sky. Bright as night in the middle of the day? What next?"

Henry nodded toward a young pine beside the path. On a low branch, a mated pair of goldfinches, black-capped heads tucked underwing, slept.

"Birds fast asleep and it not noon! Keswalqw! Where's Keswalqw?"

"Look. Up."

In the World Above the Sky, Grandmother Moon, with deep apology to Grandfather Sun, smudged a crescent wedge of shadow on his shining face.

Night fell swiftly upon the face of the earth. Keswalqw looked across the sky from the moon to the indigo globe, dark and still, starlight ghosting its swaths of blanketing cloud. Satisfied, she looked above and behind her, up into infinite black. The star-stone, closely pursued by two lesser stars, sped across the zenith toward the constellation of the Great Bear.

Antonio Zeno paced the slippery deck of *Reclamation*. First there was light. Too much light. Now no light at all. No eclipse had been predicted. According to *Reclamation's* garrulous astrologer (the man was given to great declarations pronounced in a loud, academic voice), a total eclipse was not possible when the moon was full—an eclipse being, by definition, a new moon phenomenon. Nor did a solar eclipse, total and unmoving, occur within seconds. As had this. And, the astrologer reminded him in a voice uncharacteristically low, fish did not normally fall from the sky in clouds of steam.

Antonio brushed him aside. A greater discord troubled him.

No stars rose in the east or fell from view in the west. "God in heaven help us," he said aloud, suspecting the magnitude of the forces aligning against him. "Is it possible the earth has stopped turning?" His eye was directed by the astounded astrologer to sudden motion among the fixed, unmoving stars.

In the World Above the Sky, the constellation known to The People as the Canoe of the Two Hunters broke free from its eternal mooring. In the opposite quadrant, the constellation Bear-Child cowered. In-between shone the constellation of the Great Bear, Bear-Child's mother who, since the earth was made, stood between him and those who would do him harm. The Canoe constellation crossed the sky. Never before in the static chase in the slow revolve of the infinite sky had such a thing occurred. Yet here it was. And that star, that new star—not only brighter but bigger by half than any star Bear-Child or his mother had ever seen—was leading the hunters, their canoe moving toward them with terrible speed.

On the spit of sand on the Earth World below where Claw of Spirit Bird Bay opened to the gulf, Henry dragged his canoe through small lapping waves out into rising surf. Athol was well ahead, paddling from the mid-section of his canoe, bagpipes and Birchbark Grail stowed safely in the stern beneath a square of canvas. Athol gained momentum with every stroke, veering off under starlight toward *Verum*, anchored slightly north of Henry's *Reconcilio*. Both ships lay quiet close to the central channel where the force of the outflowing tide, when it turned, would be greatest. Henry couldn't tell why Athol stopped rowing until his cousin raised his paddle, barely seen in the gathering dark as the eclipse approached apogee. Henry looked back and up.

The Canoe of the Two Hunters had been commandeered by Eugainia and Mimkitawo'qu'sk, their eyes bright, their features clearly outlined by a host of lesser stars. Secure in the upturned point of the bow, the spearhead star of destiny, brightest star in the heavens, showed the way.

Mimkitawo'qu'sk directed their passage across the sky. Eugainia bent her back, dug deep, pulling her paddle through stardust. At every pull, new galaxies rose from the gyres they raised and spun off into infinity. Eugainia watched glittering swirls of stars stream away from the bow. She remembered phosphorescent plankton flowing down her lover's chest as he swam upturned beneath her in the warm salt waters of the summer island, Apekwit. Mimkitawo'qu'sk watched the same star-spirals spin away from the stern. He remembered points of blue green light swirling through his beloved's honey-coloured hair, caressing her breasts, flowing down the long slope of her strong belly, down along her wide white hips, trailing between her legs, dissolving in the familiar sweetness of her own salt sea.

The sky-paddlers approached Great Bear and her fat cub Bear-Child. Assured they meant no harm, the great she-bear rose on her haunches, her twelve defining stars posed not in threat but in greeting. She grunted her permission, and let Mimkitawo'qu'sk and Eugainia pass. Bear-Child raised his head and bawled, then watched them speed away. As they approached Aquarius, Mimktawo'qu'sk's words the day of Henry's healing came back to Eugainia:

> "Perhaps a flock of birds, as many as the stars, will come and take your men away from the world of L'nuk," he had said. "A great sleep will overcome them. They will forget the Six Worlds, leave and never return again. All except you, Woman Who Fell in Love with the Moon—my beloved wife and mother of my child."

Eugainia raised her paddle and nudged Aquaria the Water Bearer's vessel. Stars poured forth from Aquaria's jar in a torrent. The milky way traversed the World Above the Sky, flowed down past Keswalqw on the surface of the moon. Keswalqw laughed with delight as Aquaria's stars tumbled down past her, bound for the Earth World and their role in the drama unfolding below. Keswalqw loved the impulsive woman-child Henry Sinclair had brought The People, loved Eugainia from the day the battered ship appeared in the strait off Claw of Spirit Bird Bay. The day the lives of The People—and those of the visitors —changed forever.

From the stern of the star canoe in the World Above the Sky, Mimkitawo'qu'sk echoed Keswalqw's prayer of thanksgiving. Eugainia turned. She glowed with a radiance her husband thought, until this moment, existed only in the realm of dreams.

Aquaria's stars poured down through the Sky World to the Earth World in their hundreds and hundreds and thousands and thousands. As each star hit the earth's atmosphere, its shape began to shift. Rays of light transformed themselves to miniature beating wings. Each star sprouted a head and feathery tail. The flock of little birds from the Sky World formed a cloud so vast it covered the emerging face of Grandfather Sun. The great avian host wheeled as one, angled sharply, and spiralled down through the sky. Like smoke in a gust of wind, or a school of silvery fish bedazzling a predator, their myriad wings beat in unison, their little bodies twisting simultaneously, their iridescent underbellies flashing starlight, evoking the ethereal beauty of the star-beings from which they had come.

Keswalqw plucked three small stones from the moon's dusty surface. She rolled them in her hands. She spoke three words she knew. She opened her palms. The stones became a rattle. She sang a song she knew. She raised the rattle stones above her head. She danced the circle dance.

At the centre of the earth, the core recommenced its slow revolve. Magnetic heat recharged the outer core. The molten mantle which had lain inert until all the players of the great celestial drama were in place churned up toward the earth's crust, where it fell back down to the outer core again, its dynamic rise and fall the perpetual engine of quake and drift. The Earth World bulged from pole to pole and began to revolve again.

The Celestial Canoe bearing the God and Goddess of the Time of the Two Made One began its descent from the World Above the Sky to the Sky World. The star-stone pulsed in the bow.

In the Sky World, the cloud of star birds assumed the shape of a great white-headed eagle. A skree of anger escaped the splayed beak. The left wing of the spirit bird broke free. Its thousand tiny birds assumed an arrow shape and shot toward Henry's new ship *Reconcilio.* The right wing detached from the star-cloud eagle's amorphous body, then formed an arrow that sped toward *Verum.* In their tens of thousands, the bulk of the flock of tiny star birds which had amassed to form the spirit eagle's body, reshaped themselves into a great fiery spear. The bird/spear plunged seaward toward Antonio Zeno's mesmerized fleet.

Their final strokes brought Henry and Athol to within reach of their vessel's side ladders. Agitated little star birds, the size of bumblebees, their chatter urgent, had reached *Verum* first. They grasped every millimetre of sail, every scrap of rope, every banner and fringed flag, every uneven, upraised joint or carved detail upon which their sharp, three-toed little feet could establish a claw-hold. Any handhold hastily grasped would annihilate dozens. When Athol and Henry shook the rope ladders free of the little creatures, the little birds fluttered in place until the men had boarded and then settled back immediately.

Athol snatched a straggler from the air and peered at it. It peered back. The bird's miniature face was more human than avian. Its eyes—one blue, one brown—were pitched forward, set above round, fat, featherless cheeks; its fleshy little nose with wide nostrils replaced the upper half of the beak; the lower half formed a soft-lipped pout of a mouth.

It opened its mouth to speak. It said, "Flee!"

Every graspable surface aboard *Reconcilio* had been claimed, the air gently fanned. Their scent, Henry noted as several little birds settled kindly in his hair and on his shoulders, was a mix of rose and hyacinth. Silent and still, they waited.

Antonio Zeno watched the shore disappear as the chattering cloud of little birds, dense as smoke, swooped down upon him. Latecomers, outraged they found no purchase, fought to dislodge others. The air was thick with protest, their cries shrill. Zeno's men swatted the feathered hordes, afraid for their eyes as the birds swirled about in chaos, clutching at clothes and hair. Their intent, Antonio feared, was to lift him bodily, drop him overboard where a monstrous great whale fish would crush and then drown him or, as with the intractable Jonah, swallow him whole. One persistent creature dove repeatedly for Antonio's eyes. He snatched it from the air. No soft-lipped mouths or nostrils in this flock; hard-edged beaks separated red eyes, bold and piercing. Antonio crushed the angry little bird. It stank of human waste and sulphur. He threw it overboard where it floated, bait to no predator.

Keswalqw rose from the surface of the moon. She sought a vision. None came. Only questions. What would become of them all, The People and visitors alike? Henry's fate was sealed, his conscience clear, his history written. What of Eugainia? Had she been right to encourage Eugainia's bond with Mimkitawo'qu'sk? What of Athol? Her marriage to Athol Gunn was no mystery to her or anyone who knew her; she loved the man with all her heart. And he loved her. It was long established in the realms of glory, celestial and temporal, that the immortal great must from time to time take a mortal mate, that god and goddess and woman and man, woman and woman and man and man, must refresh each other, gather and share Power as they walk the universe in search of peace and harmony, on earth, and in heaven. All would be well, Keswalqw hoped. Who better to walk her side than Gelusit tapu. He Who Speaks Twice. Athol Gunn. Her earthy bear man had strength enough to love her and the endurance to abide.

Mimkitawo'qu'sk and Eugainia searched the sky for Keswalqw. Eugainia spotted an unfamiliar star floating above the moon. Mimkitawo'qu'sk redirected their course. They bent their backs, redoubling their efforts.

Keswalqw's circle dance devolved into a minimal foot shuffle, head held lightly on the shoulders, tilted slightly to the right. Her arms hung loose, close to her sides. She danced the resting shaman's slow dance in place. What of these puzzling others, she wondered. So unlike Henry and Athol. Antonio Zeno seemed incapable of guilt or shame. Protected by his narrow faith and cold self-interest. Unwavering fealty to the Time of the One Alone blinded even good men, brought pain and sorrow down upon others distant and nearby, all at a terrible cost to their own fearful souls. Yet they are blind to the harm they do. First time I saw him, she recalled, I thought a thought and I was right. Nothing has changed. Antonio *is* Jipijka'maq, the Horned Serpent who conceals himself, uses his Power to frighten and destroy. Like many, Antonio's *Kji-knap* is split: half alive on the earth he seems to fear and deplore, half alive in the hope of heaven. He is two men, this Antonio. Both are weak. How can he speak truth, this serpent man, when he does not seek it? His heart is cold and his tongue is split.

Keswalqw and Garathia, with help from Eugainia and Mimkitawo'qu'sk, had it in their power to hurl Zeno and his ilk out past the farther edges of deep oblivion. They also knew it was not to be. Antonio embodied a vast surge of misguided Power, a dark force twisting back upon itself, a profoundly misguided quest for the immortal glory thought to lie beyond human reach. His dark desires drove him to attain life immortal by obliterating paradise apparent, the world in which both he and L'nuk, The People, were born to live. Antonio and his kind existed at the first pulse and would always walk among them. They would shout self in a loud voice and, in a quiet steady tone, they must be answered. Keswalqw knew in her heart of hearts that neither she nor her sister, both sworn enemies of inequity, would hesitate when the lives of those they loved, the weak, the dependant, the poor of spirit—or, for that matter, the powerful good, those rich in mercy, kind of heart, men, women and children honourable in deed and conscience—were threatened. It was their dual nature to nurture and protect. Without a second thought, they would loose fiery arrows and hurl spears of death straight to the murderous hearts of all enemies of the common good. It was their right and duty. It was right they should so do.

Garathia broke the surface off *Reclamation*'s stern. She sculled vertically, marking time, awaiting Keswalqw's signal from the World Above the Sky. The second dolphin, waiting to host Keswalqw, circled nearby. No one, Garathia reflected, knew the mind of the Creator as well as she and Keswalqw. Even so, Garathia suspected the supreme power, to which all answered, revealed little. The Great Spirit had little inclination to reveal powers that history showed were more likely to be abused than honoured. Garathia and her sister were its first guardians when *Kji-knap* burst forth at the beginning of time. *Kji-knap*, born in chaos, constantly bloomed anew in the eternal tension between the unity, and dichotomy, of God and man. It was the task of the Great Mothers, with the help of the Two Made One, to balance the forces of creation and destruction, knowledge and doubt, faith and fear. In the mist of a universe forever fading and becoming, mooring posts fall quickly astern. It is the task of all to sail with faith and courage into the grey unknown, setting course toward the random shafts of light which, from time to longed-for time, penetrate the gloom and show the way.

Keswalqw climbed aboard the star canoe, settled herself cross-legged in the mid-section. She tucked the star blanket handed her by Eugainia beneath her chin, tossed its corners back to cover her shoulders. She was happy to have it. She found space to be miserably cold compared with the warmth generated on earth in the eternal dance between the air and Grandfather Sun, whose face Grandmother Moon had at last wiped clean, except for a smudge of crescent shadow trailing off his cheek and chin as the eclipse passed.

Mimkitawo'qu'sk aligned their final trajectory. Eugainia shipped her oar. At the bow Eugainia was first to reinhabit flesh and bone. The cold rush of air drew tears from the corners of her eyes. She opened her mouth, threw back her head and inhaled. The thong securing her single braid flew free. Her hair streamed back, a wild tangle of earthly joy and human desire. Keswalqw's hand materialized. She reached, quick as a cat, and caught the flying thong. "Ha!" she cried. She raised both arms in triumph. The star blanket flew from her shoulders and wrapped itself around Mimkitawo'qu'sk's face. It slipped free, taking all but the two stars that burned from that day forward in his bright and shining eyes. He saw as if for the first time the beauty of the women seated before him, women he loved above all things including his own life, women shrieking with joy, their shoulders taut with terror and delight, knuckles white, their hair streaming back, their voices wild and high.

The canoe disappeared into the uppermost peak of a cumulus cloud that welled high in the air above Claw of Spirit Bird Bay. "*E'ee!*" all three cried at the shock of cold, waterlogged air. Their cry reached the Earth World. High in Reconcilio's main mast, a single bird repeated the star-travellers call. Forty thousand times forty thousand miniature wings beat in unison. *Reconcilio* and *Verum* started away at speed unmatched by the strongest wind.

Athol watched his canoe, which he'd left untethered, fall away in Verum's wake.

"My pipes!" he called.

"Never mind your blessed pipes, Athol," Henry yelled across the growing distance. "Where's the New Holy Grail!"

In the dense grey cloud surrounding the star travellers, the curtains of light from the Great Spirit's eye that had formed the canoe gave way to earthly ribs of ash, panels of bark stitched with spruce root, sealed with pitch. Its passengers' matted human hair dripped icy water. Their exposed skin summoned warm blood up to its shivering surface. Mimkitawo'qu'sk and Eugainia bent their backs, hefted their paddles, steadied the fragile craft. Keswalqw stood upright mid-canoe, arms stretched wide. She raised her arms above her head, flexed her knees and dove from the canoe into the heart of the cloud. As she plunged earthward, she called to her sister in the World Below the Sea. "*E'ee!*" she called, hurtling arrow-straight down through whorls of snow, up-welling vapour and patches of freezing rain. "*E'eee-e-e-e!*"

Mimkɨtawo'qu'sk and Eugainia steadied the craft, dug deep into the fog, making their way home.

Garathia repeated the call from the Sky World. She ordered the great families *Phocedea* and *Catecea*—the multitudes of seals, dolphins and whales awaiting her command—to circle Antonio Zeno's fleet and, in their manner of driving prey, force a tight, contained circle.

Athol knew the ray of light that shot from the base of the cloud was not born of the sun but of the moon. "Glory be. It's Keswalqw. She's back!" he called to Henry. "I say, glory be!"

The canoe paused in the calm heart of the cloud. Eugainia plucked the star-stone from the bow, handed it to Mimkɨtawo'qu'sk. He raised the stone above his head. Tutji'j Jipijka'maq, the little serpent sleeping between the layers of his skin, asleep in the green and blue tattoo, opened her eyes. Tutji'j Jipijka'maq crawled down his arm, unhinged her jaws, received the star-stone from her master, Mimkɨtawo'qu'sk the Serpent King. As she slipped off his flexed wrist, her serpent form became rigid. The shaft of the Spear of Destiny, Tooth of Wolverine, re-emerged, the star-stone head secure in place. The weapon of the Gods had, like those who bore it, been revitalized; it would fly of its own accord to the heart of those who would harm Mimkɨtawo'qu'sk, Eugainia or the Child of the Two Made One.

Keswalqw plunged into the sea. Beneath the surface, the white-beaked dolphin shadowing Garathia, the second of the matched pair, rolled to her belly. Grateful for the dolphin's body warmth, Keswalqw slipped inside, thanked her hostess who, like her gracious Delphinidae sister, remained present but subdued and unharmed.

Antonio heard the splash and scanned the water at *Reclamation*'s bow. Flippers and flukes rose in the air and beat the surface in a clamorous two-world tattoo. At the sisters' command, creatures of the sea and air began their work in tandem. Antonio looked to the sails and rigging, their edges a blur of beating wings. Below the water pooled and curled forward, instead of slipping past on either side. *Reclamation* and the eleven ships of his fleet were being drawn stern first into the heart of a rising vortex.

Henry looked astern, expecting an unruffled wake. Athol looked up and then aft to *Reconcilio*. Neither *Verum* nor *Reconcilio* was being dragged to safety by the outflow; the tide had not yet turned. The sails of both were bowed back where they should be puffed, full-bellied, forward. The waters foamed in turmoil. Both ships were being dragged—not blown, not carried on the falling tide—by innumerable beating wings.

The canoe broke the cloud and hovered north and a little east of the summer island, Apekwit. Mimkitawo'qu'sk stood in the stern of the canoe, Eugainia knelt in the bow.

Garathia and Keswalqw urged dolphins, seals and whales to circle the fleet at peak velocity. In the centre of the vortex, Antonio's vessels drew together as if magnetized, adhering without benefit of ropes or lines. The birds in their thousands on sails and rigging remained still, awaiting their signal.

The Sky Canoe descended slowly. Eugainia raised her arms to shoulder height. She looked past her right arm to the north. Beating wings aligned *Reconcilio*'s bow to nor'ward. Eugainia sighted past her left thumb. *Verum*'s bow swung due south. Mimkitawo'qu'sk sighted along the shaft of Destiny/Wolverine. He traced a line along the shore of Claw of Spirit Bird Bay.

Water poured from marshes and tidal rivers at Mimkitawo'qu'sk's command. Their exposed beds flapped with fish. The People, wicker baskets at hand, rushed to the harvest. Mimkitawo'qu'sk directed the spear to the centre of the gyre. He raised the spearhead skyward. Silence blanketed the Earth World. All was still in the World Below the Sea. The wind ceased to blow in the Sky World. The spirit birds took their ease, folded their wings. The People, baskets filled with fish, made their way back to high ground. The canoe bearing their Shaman Chief, Star King, and the White Goddess, Queen of Heaven, descended to the surface where it rested at the landward edge of the gyre. It held its place, though the waters beneath circled away with increasing velocity.

The matched pair of white-beaked dolphins broke the surface, arced up and over in opposite directions, easily clearing the mid-section of the canoe. Keswalqw positioned herself off the bow. Her powerful tail sculled the waves, keeping her perfectly upright. Garathia mirrored her sister's position at the stern. Henry unfurled His Lady's Standard on *Reconcilio*'s mast. It hung limp in the dearth of wind until industrious spirit birds grasped its edges in their beaks where it rippled horizontal beneath their wings. On *Verum*, Athol unfurled the Standard of the Holy Grail, and wondered not at the fate of the New Grail, The Birchbark Grail itself, but at the fate of his pipes.

Eugainia pursed her lips; a gentle flow of breath escaped. Forty thousand times forty thousand wings fluttered back to life. Keswalqw and Garathia slipped below the surface. Mimk̇itawo'qu'sk raised his spear. Antonio's fleet rose higher, four times the height of the tallest masts, then higher still. The waters bubbled and roiled beneath. Eugainia blew a stream of breath toward the base of the cloud. It tuned to ashen grey then charcoal black. Mimk̇itawo'qu'sk pointed Destiny/Wolverine toward the Smoking Mountain. Smoke poured forth with a fiery hail of stones, all rattling down to the deck of *Reclamation*, stones no bigger than quail eggs meant to warn but not destroy.

The People raised a chant when Eugainia caused the cloud, now black and oily as pitch, to swirl above Antonio's head, Antonio who had ravaged the burial grounds of their sacred dead, Antonio who had stripped the rivers of its yellow stones without revealing their value, Antonio who had cursed their friends. Antonio who had stolen their children. Antonio who would break their spirits, burn their bones, and make them slaves to the scarlet-robed wolves of Rome.

The dolphin sisters broke the surface. At the apex of mirrored arcs, they cried their final orders. A hundred times a hundred whales beat the surface. The dome at the centre of the vortex lost coherence. The waters below Antonio's fleet poured seaward. Seals and dolphins rode the great cascade. Wings in the sails and rigging beat with clockwork fury. Antonio's fleet sped down the collapsing cataract.

Reclamation was bound due east, back across the sea.

Henry had never seen a wake as wide or deep as that trailing *Reconcilio*. He felt the rush of wind perfumed with the scents of hyacinths and roses. He looked to the stern. His ship sped east nor'east, then veered toward the north. Henry stood at the rail looking back toward the shore. "Farewell," he said, knowing his words were lost in the sea-feathered wind. "May the Great Spirit bless and keep you."

Athol felt *Verum* veer southward. Chatter in the rigging pulled his attention to the sails. The little spirit birds, flapping and squawking, their job done, lifted off and wheeled to the west. Their bellies shone like that of a single creature, flashed once in the sun and disappeared.

Apekwit soon slipped from sight as Mimkitawo'qu'sk and Eugainia took their bearings, bound for the mouth of the Great River. They found a common rhythm, their strokes set by the beating heart in Eugainia's belly. The canoe sped north and west with Power, grace and purpose. A pair of bounding dolphins led the way.

On the south shore of Apekwit, the Summer Island, Athol Gunn's rogue canoe nudged the red sand beach. A small brown hand, a girl-child's hand, lifted the square of canvas concealing the Bear Man's bagpipes.

Beside them unmolested sat the Birchbark Holy Grail.

The End

PRONUNCIATION GUIDE
AND MI'KMAQ DICTIONARY

EUROPEAN NAMES

Eugainia: Eu gain ia (hard g, as in good)
Morgase: More gaze
Igidia: Ee gide (soft g) ee ah

MI'KMAQ NAMES

Mimkitawo'qu'sk: This is a very beautiful word, from
Ruth Whitehead's book *Stories from the Six Worlds*.
Say it at a moderate pace with fairly even emphasis
on each syllable and you've got it!

Mim	like *sim* in *sim*ilar
kit	the barred *i* gives it a sound like the *e* in rosé, and shortens, almost halves, the value of the length of the vowel
a	*ah*
wo'	long *o*, lengthened slightly in duration by the '
qu'	almost like *keh*, the soft *u* sound is extended slightly
sk	is as you'd expect

Keswalqw: Another lovely word. Say it as you'd imagine,
but with a little puff of wind at the end instead of
a hard w.

Kes wall qw
as though you'd begun to say *awww* but changed
your mind—again, very little difference in stress
per syllable

For other Mi'kmaq words in the text, there are great resources
online. It's a beautiful, gentle language to my eye and ear. I
hope you'll enjoy it too.

- See a Mi'kmaq pronunciation and spelling guide at
  www.native-languages.org/mikmaq_guide.htm
- Hear Mi'kmaq spoken at
  www.mikmaqonline.org
- Find an extensive English/Mi'kmaq dictionary at
  www.mikmaqonline.org

ACKNOWLEDGEMENTS

Before we both left Nova Scotia in the eighties, my friend Donna Anthony, historical sociologist, counsellor and feminist adventurer, handed me a book—Michael Bradley's provocative, speculative history *The Holy Grail Across the Atlantic*. I met with Michael and his partner in Toronto in the late nineties. The ideas, remarkable for their well-grounded, exhaustively researched vision of what might have been, set me on the much-forked path that has led to *The World Above the Sky*. At about the same time, Frederick Pohl's *Prince Henry Sinclair: His Expedition to the New World in 1398* came to my attention. These books, and those of Dr. Ruth Whitehead (see below), fuelled a slow-burning fire that erupted when Michael Fuller, artistic director of The Ship's Company Theatre in Parrsboro, Nova Scotia, commissioned a play exploring the Sinclair voyage.

Kim McArthur liked the resulting play in two acts, *New Arcadia: A New World Grail Romance*, and asked me to reconsider the material as a piece of prose fiction. I thought it would take about eighteen months. Four years later, I'd completed my first novel: *The World Above the Sky*. I can't say which I appreciate more: Kim's vision or her patience. Or her great heart and keen eye.

The Writers' Trust of Canada helped with the writing of *The World Above the Sky*. I am indebted to their kindness and thank them for their financial assistance when assistance was badly needed. The Canada Council for the Arts supported research for this project with a generous project grant.

Candace Burley read the manuscript and had concise, thoughtful things to say. Her work for the Ontario Government with First Nations communities and her years at Canadian Stage Company in Toronto as dramaturge helped clarify my intent as I strove to honour the heart and soul of our country.

Wolfram von Eschenbach's twelfth-century Grail epic *Parzival* continues to beguile the Western imagination more than eight hundred years after its composition. Von Eschenbach's themes of decline and renewal, and the power of good to heal the wounded body and spirit, retain their acuity and their relevance.

Dr. Ruth Holmes Whitehead has given Canada's First, and subsequent and varied Nations, an enormous gift. Ruth is a world-renowned authority on pre-Columbian Mi'kmaq culture. She shares her life's work, conducted privately and as staff ethnologist and associate curator in history at the Nova Scotia Museum, with wit, charm and great respect for all people. Among her extensive publications, her wonderful collection *Stories from the Six Worlds* continues to delight, enlighten and defeat misconception. I'm profoundly grateful for Ruth's advice, friendship and encouragement.

"We don't have to control the Spirit," John Joe Sark tells us, "we just have to let it work." Born of the Lennox Island Mi'kmaq band, John Joe and I have enjoyed long discussions over several decades, many of a Saturday morning at the Farmer's Market in Charlottetown, Prince Edward Island. We met almost four decades ago. I represented the Opportunities for Youth program, he was recently returned from the United States. John Joe challenged my inherited suppositions and encouraged me to look not only backward and forward, but up. John Joe's work as an educator, social activist and keeper of the old ways continues to enlighten and inspire. John Joe is the recipient of the National Aboriginal Achievement Foundation's Award in Heritage and Spirituality, and I thank him for his vision, his patience and his fortitude.

I also want to thank Her Excellency, The Right Honourable Michaëlle Jean, Governor General of Canada. Madame Jean's impassioned, considered, gracefully articulated response to my question regarding the relationship between indigenous peoples and dominant cultures, 'After insult and apology, what comes next?' caused me, as did John Joe Sark's wise counsel, to look forward and up. Where cosmologies blend, comprehension and compassion arise.

Kent Stetson
Montreal, March 2010